# THE LEG~~ACY OF~~
# THE TEMPLARS

## Volume 2 of the Languedoc Trilogy

## AMR (Adventure, Mystery, Romance)
## Series No 5

# Michael Hillier

*To my late wife Sue.*

*Inspiration, researcher, critic, editor and best friend*

# Author's Introductory Note

Most people have heard of the Templars. However, for those who know little about the subject, I provide a few of the known facts about the Order, which may provide a background to the novel.

The Order of the Knights Templar was founded in about 1119 by a French knight, Hugh de Payns, to provide protection to pilgrims travelling to the Holy Land which, at that time, was a Christian kingdom. A grateful King Baldwin II provided them with accommodation beneath the former Temple of Solomon in Jerusalem and this led to the establishment of their name.

They were formally set up as an Order at the Catholic Council of Troyes in 1129 and Saint Bernard of Clairvaux, the highest spiritual authority in Western Europe after the Pope at that time, drew up the Rules of the Knights Templar. They were the only holy order permitted to carry weapons and to fight against the infidels. As a result, they quickly became the disciplined front-line troops in the Crusades despatched against the Muslims.

Meanwhile the Templars had also become international bankers, receiving deposits from nobles and other individuals before they set out on their travels, and providing them with letters of credit which the travellers could draw on when they reached their destinations. The funds built up by the Order became huge over a period of time and were often loaned to the rulers of the various states in Europe to finance their Crusades and other wars. As a result, the Templars soon became the most financially powerful organisation in Europe.

However, during the thirteenth century, the Muslims gradually regained complete control over the Holy Land and the remainder of the Middle East. In 1291 the Templars were finally driven out and retreated with their possessions to the island of Cyprus. It is presumed this included their archives. These would have been most of the very few written records of legal and financial transactions kept at the time. It has been assumed that these were destroyed by the Turks when they overran the island in 1571 and this is regarded as a great loss to historians.

Now that their original purpose had come to an end, the Templars found themselves becoming increasingly unpopular. They were thought of as wealthy, arrogant and uncaring. Furthermore, worse accusations of heresy and blasphemy were being levelled at them.

The King of France, Philip IV, was deeply in debt to the Order. He decided that the number of accusations his hirelings had fabricated were sufficient for him to act. On Friday 13th October 1307, Philip, with the acquiescence of the weak Pope Clement V, suddenly arrested the leaders of the Templars, including the Grand Master, Jacques de Molay, who had been ordered back to Paris. Confessions were extracted from them under torture and the Order was formally dissolved four years later. The leaders were burned at the stake as heretics. When he died, Jacques de Molay, is said to have summoned the King and the Pope to meet him before God to answer his charges. Both men were dead within the year.

If King Philip was hoping to seize the Templars´ wealth, he was frustrated. It is believed that the enormous treasure was spirited away from their headquarters in Paris the day before the arrests. The theories about where it disappeared are many, but it was apparently never discovered. The Templars are known to have had a strong presence in the Languedoc and the prominent Cathar, Bertrand de Blanchefort, was the fourth Grand Master of the Knights Templar and was credited with reforming their administration. De Blanchefort had extensive estates in the Languedoc before the Albigensian crusade and these included the chateau at Rennes-le-Chateau. It is believed that he gave his property to the Templars to prevent their annexation by the French king.

**The Legacy of the Templars** is the sequel to **The Secret of the Cathars**, the main action of which has taken place a couple of weeks before the start of this story. Most of the main characters appear in both novels:-

**Philip Sinclair** discovers he is the descendant of Phillipe de Saint Claire, one of the four *parfaits* who escaped from the mountain-top eyrie of Montségur in the Pyrenees when the Cathars were wiped out in AD 1244. His ancestor was carrying the 'Treasure of the Cathars' on his back.

**Jacqueline Blontard (Jackie)** is the beautiful archaeologist, a darling of the French television screens, who is conducting excavations at the remote Pyrenean castle of le Bézu, south of Carcassonne, when Philip turns up to try to find his heritage. They discover a common purpose and fall in love.

**César Renoir** is the daughter of the recently-murdered godfather of a criminal organisation known as *La Force Marseillaise,* who was sent to keep an eye on the activities at le Bézu where *La Force* intends to take possession of the treasure of the Templars which they have been told is hidden there.

**Armand Séjour** is an agent employed by a mysterious organisation based in Paris to safeguard their interests at le Bézu during the excavations. He is accompanied by a voluptuous Paris *poule* called **Jeanette Picard**.

**Jean-Luc Lerenard** is an enforcer employed by Cardinal Gambaccino on behalf of the Vatican to protect their interests.

**Gustav Amboisard** is the local Mayor and the lawyer appointed to investigate the death of Jackie's manager/assistant, André Jolyon

**Gaston Lesmoines** is a man who was recruited by Jackie's manager to help with the excavations at le Bézu.

# 1

It was a late spring evening when Philip Sinclair arrived back in Quillan. The setting sun was lighting up the fresh greenery of the forests that climbed the mountainsides above the rushing river Aude, which was still carrying the last of the melt-waters from the high Pyrenees. The warm stone of the castle was glowing gold in the sunlight. It was a lovely time to be alive.

The young Englishman parked his little red sports car outside the Castle Hotel in the corner of the square and unwound his tall frame from the driver's seat. He stretched his back, feeling stiff after the long drive, and looked up at the rather faded grandeur of the four-storey building that stood above the gorge through which the river ran. Then he bent to retrieve his bag from the boot.

"I'll have to think about getting a bigger car," he told himself. "This little vehicle isn't suitable for a man who's about to get married and - who knows - may possibly become a father in the not-too-distant future."

He crossed the front terrace, where an aged couple were sitting on one of the public benches enjoying the last of the setting sun. He went up the steps and through the slightly pretentious portico into reception.

"Ah, Monsieur," the concierge welcomed him, "how is Mademoiselle?"

"Hello Henri. Are you asking about Miss Blontard?"

The man nodded, the action shaking his drooping frame. He could have been a tall man if he stood upright. His grey hair was brushed back from his sloping forehead. But he had a cadaverous look about him, with his unpressed suit and his unbuttoned shirt collar. He also seemed to have a permanent sniffle.

"I don't know how Jackie is," said Philip. "I've only just got back from England." Then, with a sudden anxiety, "Why? Isn't she here?"

"But no, Monsieur. We haven't seen her for two days. We assumed she had gone to meet you."

A sudden cold hand clamped round his heart. "Are you telling me she has booked out?"

"Well, Monsieur, it *was* a little strange. Two days ago she was at breakfast as usual. She said nothing to me. Then she went out. That, too, was usual. She had done that every day since you left, only returning in the evening."

Philip nodded. "That's right. She has been meeting the experts who are preparing for her to inspect the treasure we found at le Bézu."

"So I understand, but on Monday she did not return in the evening." Henri coughed weakly. "When I rose from my siesta, I found a note on my desk." He indicated the broad shelf beneath the reception counter. "It was in an envelope addressed to me, and it informed me that she was leaving – nothing more – except that it enclosed five hundred euros to settle the account."

"What did it say? Did she say she was coming to meet me?"

He shook his head. "The note didn't mention you, Monsieur. Do you wish to see it? I have kept it in case you did."

"Yes please."

The concierge opened a drawer and selected an envelope which he handed over. As Philip opened it, he caught the characteristic scent of Jacqueline, which took him straight back to those evenings only two weeks ago by the riverside, when they had discovered they were falling in love. It made him realise how desperately he had missed her during the few days he had been in London.

From the envelope he extracted the single piece of paper and unfolded it. The note consisted of two stark sentences written in her clear hand :-

*Henri - I am leaving today and enclose the money to settle my account.*
*Thank you for your service. - Mlle J. Blontard*

There was nothing else – no mention even, of Philip's existence; no reason given for her departure; no proposed destination; no hint of future plans.

Henri coughed discreetly. "I have banked the money, monsieur."

"Of course." But Philip wasn't interested in that. "What about the room? Has she taken her things?"

"I have briefly looked into the room, monsieur." He raised his eyebrows. "As far as I can tell, all her clothes and her other belongings have gone."

"What about *my* things. There were some clothes and other things in there which belonged to me."

"I believe they are still there, Monsieur. I have touched nothing."

Philip looked round the reception area in bewilderment. His mind was in a whirl. What had happened to make her leave? He had telephoned and spoken to her some time during the morning of the very day that she had departed. Because of travelling and the need for him to call in to Paris to sort out some paperwork connected with the large payment he had received from the Church, she knew she wouldn't be talking to him again until he arrived in Quillan two days later. There had been no suggestion that anything was wrong.

Their conversation had been just as personal and as loving as it had been before he left, and on the occasions when they had been in touch with each other while he was away. She had told him again how infuriated she was with the time-wasting paperwork, and the bureaucracy she had to comply with, before she could be permitted to start inspecting and dating the contents of the chests and cupboards they had found in the underground room in the remains of the castle of le Bézu. She said she was certain that a secret, influential group in Paris were trying to frustrate her attempts to catalogue and publicise the wonderful objects which she believed the world was entitled to know about.

There had been no suggestion that any problems had arisen in their personal relationship, no hint of second thoughts about their planned marriage. Now, suddenly, she had left the room in the hotel that they had been sharing, and disappeared without a word of explanation. It was most uncharacteristic.

He looked up at Henri. "Was there was no other note? She left nothing for *me*? Was there nothing in the bedroom – no envelope by the bedside or on the dressing table?"

"Not as far as I am aware, Monsieur."

9

Did he detect a slight expression of satisfaction on the concierge's closed face? Philip guessed that the local people might have viewed with suspicion, the young Englishman who had suddenly turned up and stolen the heart of their beautiful and famous star archaeologist in a whirlwind romance. He could imagine Henri discussing it with his friends in the town bar and, observing with glee, that the woman had at last come to her senses and ditched the interloper.

"Can I see the room?"

"Of course, Monsieur. I have not moved anything which you left behind. You may continue to stay there if you wish. The money which mademoiselle left will cover the rental for at least a further week."

"But I won't find anything up there which has been left by Mademoiselle Blontard?"

"I do not think so, monsieur."

"What about the experts from Paris, Henri? Do you know where she was meeting them?"

The man shook his head. "She did not confide in me, Monsieur, and I did not ask. Perhaps, if you enquire at the town hall, they would be able to tell you about what happened to them."

"Ah, yes. Good idea. Maitre Amboisard would probably know what is going on. I'm sure she must have told him what her plans were." Philip shook his head. "Of course, he won't be there now."

"The Mayor will be in his office at 9.30 in the morning."

"OK. I'll go and see him then. Well," he sighed, "I suppose I'd better go and have a shower."

The concierge took down the room-key and handed it to him. "Will Monsieur be having dinner in the hotel tonight?"

"Yes, I might as well."

"Would you mind coming down in half an hour, Monsieur? There is only one other couple booked in for tonight."

"Certainly." Philip picked up his bag and climbed the stairs to his room on the second floor, more confused than alarmed at this stage.

# 2

At about the time that Philip was looking round the hotel bedroom he had shared with Jackie, for any clue as to what might have happened to her, César Renoir received a surprise visit from Gustav Amboisard in her single room at the prison hospital at Toulouse. She was a woman who was now well into her thirties and nobody would call her beautiful, but she had strong facial features and a presence about her that commanded attention, even in her present condition.

The old lawyer was the Mayor of Quillan. He was of medium stature and a little stout as a result of the good food Madame Amboisard plied him with. However, he was immaculately dressed as usual, and his nearly white beard was trimmed close to his face. His deep-set, dark brown eyes seemed to take in everything about the lady he was visiting.

Amboisard had been appointed examining magistrate into the death of André Jolyon, who had been Jackie's assistant at the start of the excavations at le Bézu. Subsequently the investigation had expanded, when Alain Hébert and Henri Montluçon had been shot in the treasure room at the castle, the latter by César herself. Subsequently, she had been knifed in the stomach by one of the criminals, after shooting their leader.

Fortunately her father's friend, Pierre, had gone to help her, and had possessed the sense not to try to remove the stiletto, which the surgeon later said would have certainly resulted in her bleeding to death within a few minutes. Luckily also, the paramedics in the helicopter had understood the importance of stemming the blood-flow above all else, until they could get her to hospital to receive a transfusion.

Notwithstanding the fact that Mademoiselle Renoir had been described to him as the daughter of a recently-deceased Marseilles godfather, the surgeon had fought most of the night to save her life. He found the knife had miraculously missed all the vital organs and they were still functioning satisfactorily. Even the artery which had been punctured, was still intact enough to continue passing blood to the lower part of her body, although it was haemorrhaging badly.

There followed a slow and extremely messy series of operations to repair the damage, during which she was given three litres of blood. By dawn it appeared likely that she would survive, and ten days later she was sitting up and eating normal food, benefitting from a strong constitution and a fit and healthy lifestyle.

Amboisard had previously interviewed César in Toulouse general hospital, when the woman was judged well enough to be questioned. Her life was no longer in danger after a week or so, and two days earlier she had been judged to have recovered sufficiently to be transferred to a bedroom in the hospital wing of the prison, where he was paying her a second visit.

He looked round the room, somewhat bleak and bare of ornamentation, but otherwise comfortable. As well as the bed there was a low chest surmounted by a mirror, and an upright chair. In the corner was a second door which presumably gave access to a bathroom. The lawyer was politeness itself as he picked up the chair and placed it close to the bed.

"May I sit down?"

"Of course." She looked at him suspiciously. She had been told that she was being held in prison awaiting a probable charge of homicide for shooting the Marseilles gangster, Montluçon, who had killed her father, Camille Renoir. He had been the boss of the infamous *Force Marseillaise*. She had also just witnessed the man shooting her lover.

"I believe you are aware that I am the examining magistrate, looking into the deaths of the three men at le Bézu," he explained.

She nodded and waited.

"I have spoken to a number of people who were present in the underground room where you shot the man Montluçon," he continued. "and in particular to the Englishman. Monsieur Sinclair told me, that if you hadn't fired when you did, Montluçon intended to shoot him several times in a most painful way and to end by killing him completely." He paused while he assembled the correct words to tell her of his decision. "In the circumstances, I have therefore come to the conclusion that your shooting of Montluçon was justified and probably prevented even worse bloodshed."

"Oh." César couldn't think of anything else to say.

"That is what I shall say in my report, which I am confident will be accepted by the Justice Department. Therefore, once you are judged to be sufficiently recovered to be released from hospital, you will be free to return to your friends in the outside world."

"What friends?" she asked bitterly.

"I believe there is one of them outside, waiting for my departure." The old lawyer smiled. "Now that you are no longer technically under arrest, he is permitted to visit you."

"Who is that?"

Amboisard shook his head. "I do not know his name." He raised a finger. "However, there is also one thing I must warn you about before I leave. I shall retain your passport in my possession until the Justice Department confirms they will not be taking any action against you. That means you will not be permitted to leave France, and you should also let me know the place where I can contact you at all times. Do you understand?"

"Yes. I will tell you where I go when I leave hospital."

"That's right." The Maitre rose, his hand burrowed into an inside pocket in his jacket and emerged with a card. "This is how to contact me." He smiled again. "The Justice Department is not known for its rapid response to reports, so it will be in your interest not to lose contact with me in the next few weeks."

Amboisard gave a little bow, turned and departed, leaving the door open. A few seconds later, a welcome face appeared in the opening.

"Pierre!"

Her friend was a burly, bearded man with a cheerful expression on his scarred face. He hurried across the room and took the chair recently vacated by the lawyer. His big hand rested gently on the counterpane. "How are you, Mademoiselle?"

"I am well and recovering fast." She patted the muscled forearm. "I understand I have you to thank for the fact that I am still alive."

His hang-dog expression deepened. "I let your father down when they killed him." He shook his head. "I couldn't abandon his daughter as well."

"Hush, Pierre. You were not there when papa died. How could you help him?"

"But I *should* have been with him,"

"If you had been, then they would probably have killed you too." She stroked his hand. "Then you would have been no help to me in solving the problem I now have."

He looked at her suspiciously."What do you mean?"

"Have you been back to Marseilles since Montluçon died?"

"Yes. When they told me you would live, I took the news back to the Force,"

*La Force Marseillaise* was the criminal organisation of which her father had been the undisputed leader, until an attack on him that had resulted in him receiving severe injuries. This had given Montluçon the opportunity to take over the leadership.

"And how did they receive it?"

"I will be honest with you, Mademoiselle. I could not say they were pleased."

César struggled into a sitting position. "*Who* is not pleased, Pierre? Who is 'they', now that my father and that Judas, Montluçon, are no longer in power?"

"I am not sure, Mademoiselle. I am nothing now in the Force, so I have to ask others. When I do that, they tell me there is a man known as '*Le comte*'. He is the one who now gives the orders. I am told he is displeased that the Force has spent a lot of money on the Bézu operation, and it was a failure. I heard it said that you are the only important one connected with the disaster who has survived." A brief smile crossed his face. "But I think you are safe as long you are here. Surely they would not dare to attack you while you are in the prison hospital."

"I will not be here much longer, Pierre. That gentleman who was leaving when you came in, is the lawyer who has been investigating what happened at Bézu. He tells me I am free to go when I am well enough."

"You will be leaving here in the next few days?"

She nodded.

"That is dangerous." He shook his head. "Nobody must know that you are soon going to be free."

"At present only *you* know that is going to happen, Pierre."

"I will tell no-one. You must be certain to disappear when you leave this prison. I will not tell them I have been back to see you. If they ask me, I will tell them that the authorities would not let me into the prison hospital."

"I see." She looked at him quizzically. "So, you were sent by this man, *Le comte*?"

"They know I was close to your father, and that I care for you. But they have only sent me to collect information about you. They have not told me what they intend to do with that information."

César took a breath. "Very well. You must go, Pierre. Since you have not seen me, I will not say goodbye."

"I wish you good luck, Mademoiselle." He bent forward and kissed her hand. "You know how you can contact me if you wish. But it may be dangerous if you do it soon."

He rose to his feet, took one last look at her, and left without further comment.

César lay back on the bed and thought about what her plans should be. The assassination arm of *La Force* was a long one, and she knew too much about their organisation to be left free in the world. She would be in danger the minute she left the protection of Toulouse prison – perhaps even before then. She would need to be alert. There was a lot of planning to do.

# 3

Philip was awake very early next morning. His previous confusion about Jackie's whereabouts had now turned to serious worry. He had slept little, tossing in the wide, empty bed as he turned over all the possibilities of what might have happened to her, or what she might have chosen to do.

A very thorough search the previous evening of the bedroom and the en-suite bathroom they had shared, had revealed only that she seemed to have comprehensively cleared everything of hers out of the place. Nothing remained even to suggest that she had occupied the room for a lot of the previous two months. Every single item of clothing, make-up and other personal effects had been removed. All the papers and equipment connected with her professional work as an archaeologist had gone. Even the rubbish bins had been emptied. Nothing that was linked to her had been left.

He had to admit there was no sign that she had been suddenly snatched and carried off by force. And surely no kidnapper would risk so much time clearing away every single item of her personal effects. It seemed clear that she had chosen to move out of her own accord. But why had she left no message, even if it was only one to say goodbye?

Somehow he couldn't believe that she had so suddenly decided that she wanted to abandon the future they had planned together during the last two weeks, before he had returned to England to sort out his affairs there. Despite the fact that they had only known each other for such a short time, they had found their characters fitted so well together that they believed the whole of their lives, up until then, had been building up to the moment when they met in Quillan. Now it was obvious to Philip that Henri, the concierge, had at least come to the view that she had tired of him, and had taken the opportunity of his absence to get away from him and continue her previous, independent life.

Of course, he acknowledged that Jacqueline Blontard was a star in her field. Hundreds of people over the last few years had been happy to trail in her shadow. She was used to having men fall in love with her, believing they could build a future with her, hoping she would choose them above the others in the crowd. But surely she had never committed herself to any other man in the way she had to Philip.

He shook his head. This was all nonsense. He must find her and discuss it with her. Then he would know for sure what the future held for them both.

Now that he was wide awake, he couldn't remain in bed any longer. He checked his watch. It was only a quarter past six, but they were well into May and there was already a lightness in the sky outside. He got up, dressed quietly and washed his face. The shower and shave could wait until he got back. He shuffled through his unpacked bag and found the torch he'd still kept at the bottom. He pulled on a dark jacket against the fresh morning air. Then he let himself out of his room and went quietly downstairs.

The reception was closed of course. That was to be expected at this hour. There was no night porter in this small hotel. The front door was locked and bolted, but it was easy to pull back the bolts and slip the latch aside. He closed the door carefully behind him, making sure he heard the click of the latch re-engaging. By the time he got back, he didn't doubt the place would have opened up and be preparing for breakfast.

His car was parked across the square. There was nobody around to see him start up and pull away, taking the Limoux road to the north. After a few kilometres, he turned off into the narrow country lanes which led to the ruined chateau at le Bézu. It was half an hour before he reached the turning bay below the castle, where they usually parked. During the drive through the wooded countryside beneath the towering peaks, he had only seen a couple of farmers in the distance, collecting their livestock. There hadn't been a single other vehicle.

He got out of the car and locked it. Then he looked round. The sun hadn't yet risen high enough to shine into this deep valley and the black forest looked down on him in a glowering silence. The remains of the castle were hidden from him where he was standing. Nobody was about. Checking that the torch was in his pocket, he first set off up the new track which the Marseilles criminals had cut up the slope through the woods to the underground treasure store. He stumbled over projecting roots and pushed aside overhanging branches.

It was no surprise to him, when he got to the opening in the ancient stone wall, to find the heavy oak door was locked shut. There were new steel straps across it linked by three high-strength padlocks with tungsten steel loops. Nobody was going to break in through that door without a substantial charge of explosive. The only surprise was that the police guard had been withdrawn. The authorities obviously thought their precautions against the theft of the treasure were adequate, without needing the presence of their scarce gendarmes.

Philip smiled grimly to himself. Had they protected the rear entry to the underground room? In fact, had they even known about it? He decided he must check. So he retraced his steps to the road. Then he made his way up the steep, rough path through the woods to the old castle entrance.

Ten minutes later he arrived at the archaeological site, breathing heavily from the ascent. Nothing seemed to have changed from when it was closed down nearly a fortnight ago. The ruined castle walls were ranged round the site. The hut, the protective railings round the excavations, and the scaffolding were still in the same places. TV France had said they were sending contractors to clear the area. Those people obviously hadn't turned up yet. Was that important? Perhaps they had been delayed by the authorities until the treasure had been moved to safety. Philip was suddenly struck by the sadness of the abandoned site which had been so full of activity just a couple of weeks ago.

At least it appeared that nobody had been snooping round since the excavation was closed down. He hoped the equipment and finds would still be safe, and they wouldn't have been stolen as souvenirs by inquisitive callers. Of course, not many individuals knew what had been happening here recently, and the remoteness of the place meant it usually received very few visitors. In addition, there had been a police presence in the few days after the discovery which would have deterred the casual observer.

He took a look round. The air was cold and very still. The dark forest surrounding much of the site was silent. In the sky above, the wisps of cloud which filtered the rays of the rising sun seemed to be thinning. Philip thought it was going to be a fine day. It was as though le Bézu had returned to being an isolated backwater in the foothills of the Pyrenees.

The entrance to the path, which led to the lower site that he and Armand had excavated, was quite well hidden. So there was a good chance nobody had explored thoroughly enough to find it. As he made his way down the path's irregular, rough surface, he noticed the brambles had already started to grow across it, reclaiming it for nature. It was now fully daylight and Philip had little difficulty in negotiating the path despite its steepness.

In another five minutes he was standing on the large stone slabs they had cleared, and which had turned out to be the roof to the treasure room. He couldn't help smiling when he saw that, not only had the wall to the shallow cave not been rebuilt to block his way in, but the rope which he had climbed down into the underground room was still dangling down the hole. Nobody seemed to have realised that this back way in to the treasure even existed.

Philip bent down and checked that the rope was still securely tied to the trunk of the small tree on the slope above the wall. Then he caught hold of it and shinned down into the void. Landing on the heap of rubble he had caused when he inadvertently demolished the wall across the face of the shallow cave ten days before, he displaced a number of stones before he gained a stable footing and picked his way on to the floor of the narrow passageway behind the treasure cupboards that were scarcely discernible in the feeble light.

He let go the rope and reached in his pocket for the torch. When he switched it on, the light fell first onto the heap of stones and he noticed an object that hadn't been visible before. He bent down and picked it up. It seemed to be a roll of waxed material tied by a thin strip of leather which was tightly knotted. After a brief, unsuccessful attempt to untie it, Philip gave up and stuck it in his pocket. Before he bothered with that, he was anxious to look at the treasure that he hadn't had a chance to inspect previously. He promised himself he would be careful, as Jackie would have urged. He plucked a clean handkerchief from his pocket so as not to contaminate any of the objects when he touched them.

Following the beam of the torch, he forced his body through the narrow gap between the two large cupboards that he had negotiated on several previous occasions and emerged into the centre of the room. There he received a nasty shock. Sweeping the torch beam round the room, he could see that all the cupboards and chests which had contained the treasure were still there, but their contents had gone. Some of the fine carved doors to the cupboards stood open, revealing that they were completely empty. The lids of various chests were thrown back, and Philip could see there was nothing left in them but the remains of the protective packaging.

For the next ten minutes he searched the room thoroughly, opening every cupboard and chest and shining the torch into all the corners. He went through the short corridor which led to the heavily barred exit door. This was also empty. Absolutely no vestige remained of the magnificent treasure which he and Jackie had discovered. It had all disappeared, as completely as his fiancée and her belongings had vanished from the hotel bedroom. Were the two disappearances connected?

Philip didn't know what to make of the mysteries. His investigations so far had got him nowhere. Pensively he left the empty room by the way he had entered it, went back to his car and returned to Quillan. Now he had to hope that Maitre Amboisard could give him some useful information.

# 4

Armand Séjour took the lift up to the third floor of the unimposing but luxurious building owned by the Order in the Rue Cambriet. It was the first time he had been contacted by the Council of the Order since his return to Paris from the Languedoc. That caused him no concern. The payment for his few weeks in Quillan was nestling in his bank account and, after paying off his helper, Jeanette Picard, it left him enough to live in considerable comfort for the next year and a half. He had no idea why they should want to talk to him now. Perhaps they had a new task for him. Normally the jobs he carried out for the Council were arranged through his father, who was one of its members. The le Bézu project had been different because it was so important. And that was why he had been paid so well.

The worrying thought was that perhaps something had gone wrong with that last project. The negotiations to clear up the business of the treasure were being handled by much more senior members of the Order. He was only a fairly junior fixer by comparison. Had they discovered some problem which had been caused by his intervention when he had prevented the Marseilles criminals from taking the treasure?

Deep in thought, he crossed the thickly carpeted lobby and knocked on the padded pink baize door. After a brief wait, a young secretary with an arm-full of papers opened it to admit him. She gave him an embarrassed smile as he bowed to her, then slipped past on her way to her own office. Armand entered one of the major centres of power in France before closing the door behind her.

The room was of modest size. Three of the walls were panelled two metres high in rich mahogany. The other wall had four full-height narrow windows. The open shutters matched the panelling. The only other person present was Marcus Heilberg. He was sitting at the head of the conference table that occupied the majority of the room, surrounded by its ten high-backed chairs. The table seemed to be half-covered by a sea of papers which spilled over the white tablecloth with its wine-red cross in the centre.

"Come and sit down." The Grand Treasurer indicated the chair to his right facing the tall windows. "The President cannot be here this morning. He is temporarily indisposed."

Armand knew that the President of the Order, who was one of the most powerful and well-connected men in France, was over ninety. How long he could continue his high-pressure role was an open question.

"In his absence I have had to assume some of his functions, with the consent of the Council, of course." Heilberg was reminding the young man of his importance. "As you know, the question of the property at le Bézu has been passed to others." The Grand Treasurer looked over the top of his pince-nez. "However, there is another connected matter which is causing us concern."

The young man kept silent, but felt the sweat begin to prickle his forehead.

"Apparently," said Heilberg, "the archaeologist lady – Jacqueline Blontard – has disappeared. That is an unwelcome development."

"Why?" Armand had thought that Mademoiselle Blontard was regarded as a thorn in the side of the Order.

"For the simple reason, Monsieur Séjour, that we want her to be somewhere where we can keep an eye on her and know what she is doing and saying. If she has gone underground, we don't want her to surface suddenly in a place where she might cause us embarrassment. If she chooses to tell the story of what happened at le Bézu, it might result in the Order receiving unwelcome publicity." He smiled bleakly. "We consider it of prime importance that she should be located."

"And you wish me to find her?"

"Of course." The Grand Treasurer leaned forward. "I may tell you that your behaviour at le Bézu a week or two ago reflected well on the Order and naturally you are regarded as one of our most satisfactory operatives. I have confidence that, in carrying out this latest task, you will not fail to increase further your stature in the Order's eyes."

Armand did not allow the glow which such a compliment engendered in his breast, to deflect him from the practical problems of this new task. "Do you have any clues about the direction she has gone? Are there any starting points?"

"Naturally, her employers are suspect. Alain Gisours at TV France was not happy when higher authorities instructed him to cancel the series about the Cathars."

"Can I approach him directly?"

"You will have to use a round-about approach. If the man is involved in some way in his star's disappearance, he will not admit it just like that. I have here a list of his contacts who may be willing to let you know about his activities." Heilberg pushed a sheet of paper across the table. "There are notes against the ones most likely to have been aware of a covert operation such as this."

Armand picked up the list and scanned it briefly. There were seven names. Three of them were underlined, as possibly being involved in the disappearance of Jacqueline Blontard. He only recognised one name. It gave him little confidence.

"Is TV France the most likely body to arrange for her to disappear? Are there no other possibilities?"

"Hmm. There is of course the Bishopric of Narbonne. It is known that they were showing a close interest in the discoveries that Blontard and her associate – the Englishman, Sinclair – were making at le Bézu." Heilberg coughed self-consciously. "We do not have information at present on how that matter was resolved, or if it is still on-going."

"But what about Philip Sinclair? Wouldn't it be natural for him to be involved in hiding his lover for some reason we don't yet know?"

"That is certainly a possibility." The Grand Treasurer peered over the top of his glasses. "You are sure they are lovers?"

"That is what it looked like. I have never before seen two people so wrapped up in each other."

"Then you should certainly get close to the Englishman."

Armand's thoughts immediately turned to Jeanette. "I don't think that will be difficult."

"There is one other possibility." Heilberg wrinkled his nose in distaste. "You are aware of the criminal organisation called *La Force Marseillaise*?"

"Yes, I am. It was they who caused the bloodshed at le Bézu. I thought they had been eliminated from this one."

"I am told that, with the old leadership liquidated, a new shadowy figure has taken control of that organisation. We only know at this stage that he is called *Le comte*. You should keep an eye open for them."

"I will." Armand's mind however was already working on how he should get close to Philip Sinclair without making it obvious that he was doing it.

Marcus Heilberg cleared his throat. "As to payment, if you can discover Mademoiselle Blontard's location and keep your eye on her for the next month and report her activities to me during that time, we will double the money you received for your last duty. Are you happy with that?"

"Thank you, Grand Treasurer. That is most generous."

"Then you can start straight away. If you need any further information or assistance from the Order, you can go through the usual channels." Heilberg clearly had no wish to prolong the interview. "Goodbye. I look forward to receiving your first report as soon as possible."

Armand rose and departed. He already had in mind the way in which he was going to start his search.

# 5

After breakfast in the hotel, Philip telephoned the town hall to arrange a meeting with Maitre Amboisard. He was told the mayor's arrival was delayed by an early morning appointment and he would be in later. He had no other meetings arranged. So he crossed the square at just after eleven, climbed the steps to the upper floor of the splendidly decorated old building which housed the Mairie, and asked to see the venerable lawyer. He was admitted to Amboisard's plush office remarkably quickly. The mayor rose from behind his large desk to shake Philip's hand.

"How nice it is to see you again," said the courteous old man in his excellent English. "Will you join me with a cup of coffee?"

Philip assented, and the mayor's secretary was called in and asked to provide the drinks.

"Will you take a chair?" When his guest was seated Amboisard asked, "Now, how can I help you?"

"I got back from England yesterday and found that Jackie – er, Mademoiselle Blontard - seems to have disappeared. I wondered if you could tell me where she has gone."

"Disappeared? Dear, oh dear." The mayor seemed genuinely distressed. "Now that the question of the murder of her assistant, André Jolyon, has been resolved and she had finished her negotiations with the men from Paris, I assumed she had gone to meet you."

Philip shook his head. "Well, *I* thought she was still here, having meetings with those officials, and waiting for me to return. Can you confirm she *was* actually meeting them?"

"Oh yes, but the two men from the Ministry of Culture returned to Paris three days ago."

"Would Jackie have gone to Paris with them?"

"She was not with them when I saw them off." Amboisard paused while their coffee was poured out, then he continued. "Of course, she may have arranged to travel independently to meet them when they reached Paris."

"That's a possibility," agreed Philip. "As far as I can check, her car doesn't seem to be here. It's not parked in the square or anywhere I can think of locally. Perhaps I need to go to Paris to look for her."

There was a pause. Amboisard seemed to be struggling to decide what he ought to say next, while he sipped his coffee. After a moment he said, "Young man – er, may I call you Philip?"

"Please do."

"Well, Philip, I think perhaps that you should pause a while before you go rushing across France on some new quest of discovery. Do you not think you should allow Jacqueline a little time to sort out her thoughts?"

"What do you mean?"

"She has had a lot of difficult experiences in the last few days. As I understand it, she had arrived at a new pinnacle in her meteoric career with the series she is doing about the Cathars, and that has suddenly been snatched from her. She has seen men killed in front of her and has been close to death herself. She has also found a new man – you – who has then departed to London for a week, leaving her to argue with the professionals from Paris on her own. Her mind must be in a whirl. Do you not think she might wish to escape all this activity, and go away and try to think calmly about the direction her life should take in the near future?"

After a moment's thought, Philip agreed. "Yes, I can see that would be reasonable. But why, if she wanted to do that, didn't she simply leave me a note saying what she was doing? She could have told me not to follow her, and she would contact me again when she was ready. Then I wouldn't have any reason to worry about what has happened to her."

"Ah, I cannot answer that question. I agree that it would have been better for her to let you know what she was doing." He shook his head. "It does however suggest that her mental turmoil was perhaps even more serious than I previously thought. Of course she had been closeted with these officials for several days, arguing over the legal details which had to be cleared up, before she could be permitted to remove the seals from the door to the treasure room and enter to start inspecting and cataloguing the contents. That must have been most frustrating for her."

"You talk as though the treasures we discovered were still in that underground room at le Bézu."

Amboisard stared at him. "Of course. As far as I am aware, they have not been removed."

"I went out there early this morning. I noticed the police guard was no longer there."

"Ah, yes. Paris told me they were not needed any longer."

"Not needed?"

"You must understand, Philip, that we are a small town. Sergeant Leblanc has only three men in addition to himself to cover a large area. On his behalf I requested some additional men to relieve the pressure. The reply from Paris was that I could withdraw the gendarmes from guard duty at le Bézu." He smiled. "It was a great relief, I can tell you."

"I wonder what Paris are playing at."

"What do you mean?"

"I told you I went up to the castle this morning, Monsieur Amboisard. I found the door to the treasure room was still triple padlocked, but I knew a back way into the room, which I discovered when we were excavating at le Bézu, so I went in that way."

The mayor's eyebrows raised. "I have never been told about an alternative way in."

"I don't think anybody knows about it except Jackie and me. But the important thing, is that I searched the room a few hours ago, and discovered that the treasure is no longer there. The cupboards and chests are still in place, but they are completely empty. Do you know what has happened to it?"

The mayor's mouth fell open. "The treasure is not there? How exactly did you get into the room?"

Philip gave the mayor all the details about the way he had gained entry to the treasure room and what he had discovered there. "You can go and check if you wish," he ended. "Do you have a set of keys?"

"They are in my safe." The lawyer jumped to his feet, crossed the room and moved a tall chair aside to expose a wall safe. He reached into his pocket, brought out a bunch of keys and searched through them for the correct one. Then he opened the safe and rummaged around inside. After a minute he emerged with another small bunch of new keys.

"There you are. They are still there."

"Did anyone else have any keys?" asked Philip.

"Not as far as I am aware. There are two sets on this ring."

"Forgive me. Do any other people have a key to your safe?"

"This is the only one." He paused. "Unless the safe company has one. There was an occasion quite recently when I lost the key to the safe for a couple of days and they had to send a man to open it for me."

"But you found it again?"

"Oh, yes."

"Where did you find it?"

"Here in my desk drawer." The old man smiled weakly. "Would you believe it? I had never put it in there before, but it must have been there all the time. After that I put it on this key-ring with my house and car keys."

"You said that was recently?"

"Only a week or so ago. Aah!"

He looked at Philip with the light dawning in his eyes. "You think somebody may have borrowed it to make copies." He shook his head. "My office is not usually locked. I will have to ask some questions around the Mairie, to see what anybody can remember about any strangers being here." He grinned. "You, for example."

"I didn't need keys to get into the treasure room."

Amboisard reached out and patted his hand. "I know that. I was just being droll."

"Did the men from Paris have a set?"

"They may have had one, but if so, they presumably took their set back with them. But if somebody has access to my safe, that is terrible. I will have to replace it." He lapsed into silence.

"Did Mademoiselle Blontard know the treasure had been removed?"

"I'm sure she did not. At least she said nothing to me."

Philip said, "I am certain she would have made a big fuss if somebody had told her that it was going to be taken away. I remember her saying that the surroundings in which it had been found were almost as important as the treasure itself. That would tell her a lot about who had hidden it." He stopped suddenly. "I wonder if that is what those faceless men in Paris were worried about."

Amboisard shook his head. "I think you may be seeing conspiracies where none exist, young man."

"Well, Jackie was certain something was going on in Paris. Why was the excavation at le Bézu suddenly halted? Why was it so difficult for her to gain access to start cataloguing the treasure? Why were you told you could remove your men from guarding one of the most valuable finds of the century? Why has the treasure disappeared?" Philip took a breath. "How can you explain it except to wonder whether someone with huge influence in Paris is trying to prevent news about the treasure from becoming public knowledge?"

The old lawyer raised his eyebrows but didn't respond.

"One thing I can assure you about - the treasure *has* disappeared. Do you want me to take you to le Bézu to show you that I am telling the truth."

Amboisard nodded. "Yes. I must go there before I report this disaster to Paris." He locked the safe and pocketed both bunches of keys. "We will get Sergeant Leblanc to drive us."

He returned to his desk and gulped down the rest of his coffee. "Come. I will tell Celine that we are going out."

Philip followed the anxious lawyer down to the ground floor of the town hall where the gendarmerie was located at the rear of the building.

# 6

The penthouse apartment took up the whole of the top floor of the luxury block of flats which overlooked Marseilles to the north. The city was deep in the evening shade but up here, high above the teeming, dirty *faubourgs*, the large room was still bathed in light as the sun sank towards the mountains of the Massif Central far to the northwest.

Pierre had been told it was most unusual to be invited to enter the personal space of *le comte*. The self-styled count kept himself well away from the everyday criminals who made up most of *La Force Marseillaise,* which he now commanded. He kept control of the violent organisation through a few favoured lieutenants. Most of La Force's nefarious rank and file members did not even know where he lived.

A limousine had collected Pierre from the Vieux Port and, although no attempt had been made to blindfold him or prevent his eyes from straying, the route taken by the car with its darkened windows had made it almost impossible for him, a Marseillais all his life, to know precisely how to reach this tallest building on the upper-class hill to the south of the city.

The car had nosed down a ramp into the basement and pulled up by the entrance to the elevators. The chauffeur got out at the same time as he did and wordlessly indicated the doors to one of the lifts which already stood open. Pierre entered and looked round. There were no buttons to press. The doors whispered shut behind him and the elevator suddenly accelerated upwards. Seconds later it came to a silent halt and they opened to admit the sunshine.

A nubile attendant was waiting. Her expression was neutral as she silently turned and gestured to him to follow her. She led him across the lobby and through a pair of glass doors to the right, which slid open as she approached. Pierre found himself immediately in the presence of *le comte*. The man was seated in a deep leather swivel chair with the sun directly behind him. It was difficult to make out any of the man's features, except that he was nearly bald and sported a thick black beard. His expression was impossible to discern. By his right hand was a small table on which lay a large automatic pistol. Behind him, an air conditioning unit filled the space with a rush of wind and caused the long, thin veil of curtains to billow half-way across the room. Pierre came to a halt just inside the doors and waited. The attendant had disappeared.

After a brief pause, the count spoke in a deep cultured voice. "You are Pierre Schmidt?"

"Yes, Monsieur."

"You are a friend of the daughter of Camille Renoir." It was a statement.

"Yes, Monsieur."

"She has been seriously injured."

"The man called Mickey threw a knife at her which penetrated twenty centimetres into her stomach after she had shot and killed Henri Montluçon."

"Will she survive?"

Pierre paused. He knew it was unwise to lie to *le comte*. "I believe she will, Monsieur."

"Hmm." The leader considered. "I understand she is in the prison hospital in Toulouse at the moment. I also understand she is not expected to be charged with the murder of Montluçon."

Pierre gulped. How had *le comte* found out about that?

"So - she will be released when she has recovered." The man licked his lips. "Montluçon killed her lover. She will not be a friend of *La Force*."

Pierre found he was breathing rather quickly. "I do not know about that, Monsieur."

"There is a possibility that she would try to be revenged on us if she could find a way."

Pierre swallowed. "I assume she only wishes to be left alone to regain her health, Monsieur."

"Hmm. She will have to convince me of that. Until then, she will need my protection." The count almost appeared to be talking to himself, so Pierre remained silent. "You are well-known to the lady, Schmidt. I wish you to go and talk to her."

"I may not be permitted to see her, Monsieur."

"Nonsense. If she is going to be released from prison, people she knows will be allowed to visit her while she is recovering."

Pierre´s only response was a doubtful expression.

"You must ensure you are the first one to see her," continued *le comte*, "and, when she has recovered enough to travel, you will bring her to me. I will arrange for her care while she – er – regains her health."

Pierre took a breath. "Very well, Monsieur."

"You must understand, Schmidt, that this is necessary for her own good. Impress upon her that she will come to no harm, as long as she behaves correctly. You must explain that to her."

"I will do my best, Monsieur."

*Le comte* nodded. "I will give you a car and a driver. It will be Candice Ambré. The two of you can stay in a hotel in Toulouse until César's release. It will only be few days – no?"

"I hope you are right. Monsieur." Pierre realised he was being given a minder.

"Candice will pay the bills. I will expect you to bring the Renoir woman to me as soon as she can travel."

"Very well, Monsieur."

*Le comte* suddenly sat upright. His head jutted forward, and he spat out, "It is important that there will be no slip-ups, Schmidt. *La Force* already looks foolish as a result of the mess that was made over the attempted recovery of the Templar treasure. I will not allow things like that to occur now that I am in control. There must be no *more* slip-ups. Do you understand?"

Pierre gulped. "I understand, Monsieur. I will do my best."

"Just make sure you succeed." The big man relaxed and leaned back in his seat again. "Very well, Schmidt. Candice is waiting for you in the lobby."

Observing that he was dismissed, Pierre turned in some confusion and made his way out of the room. The door whispered shut behind him.

In the entrance hall outside, an attractive young woman was waiting. The chauffeur's uniform had been well tailored to flatter her shapely figure. Her long blonde hair trailed over her shoulders. Her full lips were slightly parted, giving the impression that she was waiting for him to give her instructions. But the eyes were as hard as steel, warning him not to mess with her.

"You are Candice?" he asked unnecessarily.

She inclined her head towards the lift. "We will go to Toulouse this afternoon. The car is waiting in the basement."

"First of all, I need to go to my flat to collect some things?"

"I will take you there."

He nodded and followed her into the elevator.

As they sank rapidly towards the basement he said, "You can't wear that chauffeur's uniform while you are with me."

"Why not?"

"Everyone will notice you."

She tossed her head. "Everybody *always* notices me."

"People will ask why a scar-faced ex-convict is being driven by a posh woman in a chauffeur's uniform. We should not draw unnecessary attention to ourselves."

The lift came to a halt. A big, but standard Citroen was parked just outside the opened doors with the engine ticking over quietly. Candice went and opened the boot. Without hesitation or any apparent embarrassment she stripped off her uniform and carefully folded it. She bent over in her bra and pants, undid the large bag inside and extracted a light sweater and short skirt which she proceeded to put on.

She turned to him. "Is this better?"

He nodded. "That'll do. But you need lighter shoes."

"I like to drive in these shoes."

"You will not be driving. I shall drive."

Candice tossed her head. "I *must* drive. *Le comte* will expect me to drive."

"A Frenchman does not get driven by his wife."

"I am not your wife."

"You are for the next few days." He paused. "Do as I say, or we will go back up to *le comte* and arrange for another, more suitable minder."

"He would not like that."

"He will understand that we do not wish to raise unnecessary interest in our activities."

"What activities?"

"The abduction of César Renoir back to Marseilles."

She was silent for a while. Then she said, "OK. You will drive." She looked straight into his eyes. "But do not expect me to behave as your wife." She opened the passenger door.

Pierre grinned to himself as he walked round to the driver's side of the car. "You only have to look the part to a casual observer," he said.

He climbed in behind the wheel and put the car into gear.

# 7

Philip arrived in Paris in the afternoon of the following day. Once he had shown Maitre Amboisard and Sergeant Leblanc that the treasure had indeed been removed from the underground room, they had rushed back to Quillan and the mayor had made a string of frantic phone calls to everyone he could think of, without getting a satisfactory response from anybody.

Amboisard had then begun a long report to the authorities in Paris. To accompany this, he had required a detailed statement from Philip. As far as he was concerned, the disappearance of the treasure was now his new priority.

Philip was still only interested in trying to find Jackie. It appeared to him that all the roads led to Paris, and therefore he decided that he must go there next. The old lawyer advised him against this course of action but, when he realised Philip was adamant, agreed to give him a letter of introduction to the Ministry of Culture officials who had been dealing with the le Bézu discoveries the previous week. He also telephoned them, and they agreed that they also wanted to speak to *him,* because he had first-hand information about the treasure which they had not actually seen themselves.

When he reached the capital, Philip went at once to the grand building in the Rue Antoine to which he had been directed. This housed the headquarters of the Ministry of Culture. Armed with his letter of introduction he was admitted, after a frustratingly long wait, to one of the persons who had met Jackie. This Monsieur Frison was very courteous, but he had no English and his secretary acted as a somewhat hesitant interpreter. The interview took place in the man's small office on the fifth floor, and it was a slow and, for Philip, a frustrating one.

"I understand," said Philip, "that you were one of the two men who negotiated with Mademoiselle Blontard about her obtaining access to the treasure, which we found at le Bézu."

"That is correct."

"Did you give her permission to start looking at the articles we found in the underground room?"

"No. It was not for us to give permission."

"Who was able to give permission?"

"I do not know." A Gallic shrug. "It was someone above my head."

"But you don't know exactly who that is?"

"I do not. Perhaps it was the minister. Perhaps not."

"Is it possible to find out?"

A shake of the head. "I'm afraid not. Not at this time."

"Was Mademoiselle Blontard unhappy about the delay in getting permission?"

"Naturally - as were we."

"Was that the reason why you were recalled to Paris?"

Another shrug. "There was nothing more we could do in Quillan."

"Did Mademoiselle Blontard say what she was going to do next?"

"I do not understand your question."

"When she was told that you were returning to Paris, did she say whether she was going to try and contact somebody else to try to get permission?"

"No – not to me."

"What did she actually say?"

"She said nothing much to me." He shrugged again. "I would say – how do you tell it in English – that she had nothing more to talk to me about."

"And she didn't indicate what her plans were, once you had left?"

"No. She closed her face to me."

"You see, Monsieur Frison, she seems to have disappeared and I am trying to find her."

"Yes. I understand." His smile was genuinely sympathetic. "However, I regret I can tell you nothing which I think might help you in your search."

Philip did his best to explain how they had found the treasure and how he had discovered that it was now missing. The secretary took down the details as well as she could. It appeared that Frison was expected to report to his superior about the disappearance, but he was unwilling to allow Philip to speak directly to the senior man.

"What are you doing, now that the treasure has disappeared?" he asked.

"Ah, that is out of my hands," said Frison spreading them wide to show how empty they were.

"Can I meet the man who is making the decisions about this?"

"I am afraid there is no-one available at this time."

"If I leave my phone number with you, can you ask him to ring me when he is available?"

"Of course." He put his head on one side. "However, I cannot tell you when that will be, or even if it will be at any time."

That was the most he could get out of Monsieur Frison. Philip left the Ministry of Culture confused and frustrated. He guessed he wouldn't get any more help there.


Next he went to the offices of TV France which were housed in one of the modern tower blocks in Montparnasse. By now it was already early evening and, somewhat to his surprise, he was admitted to the lofty presence of Alain Gisours after a wait of only ten minutes.

The Executive Director of Documentary Programmes proved to be a small, slim man in his forties with jet black hair and eyes which were nearly as dark. In contrast to Monsieur Frison, he was full of energy and seldom stayed still for more than a few seconds. He waved Philip to a chair across his massive, empty desk.

"So you wish to talk to me about Jackie Blontard," he began in passable English. "First of all, can you tell me where she is?"

Philip grunted. "I came here to ask you the same question."

"You mean she is not with you?" Gisours smiled briefly. "Forgive me. My information was that she had – how do you say in England - gone overboard for you."

"Well. We are planning to get married. Before we could do that, I had to go back to London for a few days to make various arrangements. When I returned, I found that she seemed to have disappeared without leaving a message."

He proceeded to tell the director the whole story of what had happened in the last two days and concluded, "I was hoping that she would have got in touch with you and told you what she was doing." Philip leaned forward, trying to convince the other man of his sincerity. "If you wish to protect her privacy, I would only ask you to give her a message from me? I assure you that all I want, is to hear from her that she is all right, and will give me some sort of decision at some time in the future. I can wait. I will not harass her."

Gisours shook his head sadly. "I am sorry, Monsieur Sinclair, but I cannot help you. I have heard nothing from her since I was forced to close down the excavations at le Bézu. I can understand that she was furious with me." He smiled again briefly. "Not without some reason. But I must talk to her soon about the future. We cannot allow this minor problem to derail the arrangements to produce a new series of her discoveries this autumn. The programme time has been allocated and a large part of the French public is waiting to see what she will serve up to them in October."

"I understand that *you* need to talk to her as well." Philip sighed. "All I can tell you is that she was most unhappy about the cancellation of the series about the Cathars."

"No more than I was."

"She called you a number of unrepeatable names."

"I'm sure she did." Gisours grinned more broadly this time. "Nevertheless, she accepted the generous compensation, just as I did." He straightened his shoulders. "However, we have to put that behind us and get on with the replacement series. October is only a few months away and we have to plan the series, select the locations, research the background and get the whole thing in the can. That's going to cause everyone a lot of overtime."

"Do you know about the treasure we found?"

The director nodded.

"The uncovering and classifying of that would make a good series."

"Indeed it would."

"She was trying to get permission from the Ministry of Culture to work on that. After all, it was she and I who found it. I believe her disappearance may have something to do with the fact that she wasn't getting anywhere with the Ministry. Meanwhile, the treasure has been spirited away somewhere."

"Ah!" Alain Gisours was suddenly alert. "You think I can find out something about that?"

"You have much better contacts than I have."

"All right. That's a good idea. I will see what I can find out. How can I contact you?"

"I need to get a French mobile. Meanwhile, I'll give you the phone number of the hotel in Quillan. If I'm not there, you can leave a message for me. Do you have a contact number or address for Jackie?"

"All our contacts with her are through her agent."

"Bernard Cambray is away for another two days."

"Of course." The director smiled wryly. "Spending some of his ill-gotten gains no doubt. Well, I will give you his contact details so that you can ring him when he returns. I will also contact him myself and let you know what I can find out."

They exchanged information. Before he parted from Alain Gisours, he had one further question. "We were told that you were arranging for contractors to go to le Bézu to clear the site, but nobody seems to have arrived yet. Do you know what has happened to them?"

Gisours shook his head. "That will have been dealt with by my assistant and she has gone home for the night. She will be able to find out tomorrow what is going on there."

"So you don't know the name or phone number of those contractors?"

"I'm afraid not."

"Do you think your assistant could give me that information? I was wondering if they would have sent a man down to check what labour force and equipment was needed and he might have met Jackie and know something about what was in her mind."

"My goodness." The little man's eyes sparkled. "You don't believe in leaving any stone unturned, do you?"

"It's just a chance."

Gisours reached across the desk and patted his hand. "Of course it is. I will ask my assistant to check up on that first thing on Monday morning."

"Thank you."

39

The director concluded by promising that he would telephone Philip as soon as he had anything to report to him.

# 8

When Philip left the TV France building, it was already well into the evening and the sky was darkening. He hadn't booked himself into a hotel and he didn't know the area of Paris well enough to immediately select one. But he was hungry, and he decided his first priority was to choose somewhere to have a meal. He had eaten nothing since breakfast in Quillan. To satisfy his hunger, he stopped at the first pavement café he passed and ordered something from the menu together with a bottle of red wine.

Philip sat watching the evening crowds passing by and felt deflated. It seemed to him that he had been rushing around now for the best part of three days. He'd driven more than a thousand miles in his noisy little sports car. He was worried about his vanished fiancée, and he seemed to have had no luck in even finding any clues as to where she might have gone. He had slept very little for the past two nights, and he felt lonely and sorry for himself.

Almost before he had realised it, he found he had finished his meal and the first bottle of wine. It was a nice wine, so he ordered another bottle. As he drank and worried, he was hardly aware that he was gradually becoming intoxicated. He sat back in his chair, his hand resting on the table and clasping the glass which he raised frequently to his lips. To an observer his face was a picture of misery, but he paid little attention to the increasingly fuzzy shapes which moved around him as he turned over the insoluble problems which he was facing.

"It's Philip, isn't it? Philip Sinclair?"

He blinked, trying to clear his vision so that he could concentrate on the woman leaning over him.

"Philip, are you all right?"

Now he managed to see enough to work out that he was gazing down the front of a splendid cleavage.

"Sorry," he slurred. "Drunk too much."

"Don't you recognise me? It's Jeanette. You know – I was with Armand in Quillan."

41

"Oh, Jeanette." He tried to lift his head to focus on her face – anything to stop peering down the front of her rather loose dress. "How are *you*, Jeanette?"

"I've never seen you like this before, Philip. What are you doing here?"

"Doing here?" That was a good question. He transferred his attention to his glass, trying not to look at those wonderful boobs. "I'm drinking some wine. Would you like a glass of wine? It's a very good wine."

"Yes please." She sat down opposite him and picked up an empty glass. She leaned forward and offered her glass to him to be filled. The front of her dress seemed to fall partly open, and he had to concentrate very hard on the glass as he lifted the bottle and began pouring. He used two hands to hold it steady as he reached out. He had to turn the bottle completely upside down and still only a little trickle came out. Some of that seemed to splash down the outside of the glass. He didn't know how it did that.

"Oh, dear. I'm sorry, Jeanette. This bottle seems to be empty." He pulled himself upright. "I'll order another bottle."

"No. That's all right, Philip. This is plenty for me."

She raised her glass to her full smiling lips and tipped her head back to swallow the miniscule portion of wine. The sight was magnificent. Philip remembered that Jeanette was a very attractive girl. There was a drip trickling down the stem. Was it going to fall off on to her swelling breasts? Would it trickle down her cleavage? He was almost disappointed when she replaced the glass before the dark wine stained her white skin.

"You still haven't told me why you're here, Philip."

He tried to concentrate on her face. It was a very pretty face. The eyes seemed to be full of sympathy.

"I'm trying to find Jackie," he said.

"What – in Paris? Do you think you'll find her in Paris?"

"I don't think I will," he admitted. "In fact I don't think she's here. The man from the Ministry of Culture doesn't know where she is. Alain Gisours doesn't know either." He shook his head. "I don't know what's happened to her."

"I don't think you'll find her in Paris if you don't know where to look. Paris is a very big place."

"Yes, I've found that out." He took another drink from his glass and discovered it was empty. "We need another bottle of wine," he concluded.

"No, we don't, Philip. I think you've had enough."

"They won't let us sit here if we're not drinking."

"Philip," she said, and her voice was surprisingly gentle, "I think you should pay the bill and then I'll see you back to your hotel."

"Oh." He was managing to concentrate on her face more now. "I haven't got a hotel at the moment."

"Where are you staying?"

"I don't know. I haven't got anywhere yet."

"It won't be easy to get into a hotel at this time of night, particularly in your condition." She leaned forward again, and her boobs threatened to fall out of the front of her low-cut neckline. "Where are your things?"

"What things?"

"You know – your pyjamas, your washing kit – things like that."

"Oh! Well, my bag is in the boot of the car."

"Where's your car?"

"In an underground car park near the Opéra."

"But that's a long way away."

He nodded vaguely. "I suppose it is."

She studied him closely for a minute. "I think you'd better come back to my place. It's only just round the corner."

"Oh. Is Armand there?"

"Armand?" She shook her head. "I haven't seen Armand for a week."

"Oh, I thought -."

"Well, you thought wrong. Now, where's your wallet?"

"Wallet?"

"You need to pay the account."

"Oh – yes."

A few minutes later she had settled the bill for him and had him standing by the roadside, none too steadily. She put an arm round his waist, and he leaned on her a little and enjoyed gazing down the front of her dress. She didn't seem to mind.

"Come on. It's only a short walk."

Ten minutes later they had reached her flat. It was on the top floor of a building in a traditional six-storey terrace reached by a small, old, clanking lift and through a short, dark corridor. She led him in and shut the door behind him.

"I think we'd better get you undressed and into bed. You're going to feel terrible in the morning."

She started to strip his clothes from him as he stood statue-like in front of her. Then she sat him on a chair while she folded them up and laid them carefully on the table.

"Do you want to go to the loo?"

"Oh." It suddenly struck him that, after all that wine, he was absolutely desperate for a pee. "Oh, yes please."

As she shepherded him to the bathroom, he could feel the softness of her through her cotton dress. She felt good. She was really a very pretty girl.

"You can use my tooth-brush. Will you be all right if I leave you for few minutes?"

"I suppose so."

He felt quite disappointed that she was going. He managed to urinate, then washed his hands and face and cleaned his teeth. He dried himself on a towel by the bath. He was able to find his way back to the bathroom door where he came face to face with Jeanette. All she was wearing now was a thin negligee, which left little even to *his* befuddled imagination.

"The bedroom's through there." She pointed. "I will join you in a minute."

Obediently, he went into the room she indicated and sat on the edge of the bed. It was a big bed – a double bed. He supposed she shared it with Armand.

She joined him a couple of minutes later. "Don't just sit there, Philip. You need to get into bed and sleep off all that wine."

"Are we going to sleep together?"

"Certainly. Did you think you were going to kick me out of my own bed?"

"No, but . . ."

"Oh, don't be an English prude, Philip. You're in Paris now."

She pushed him into the bed, threw off her flimsy covering, turned off the light and climbed in beside him.

"How do you manage to be so warm?" she asked as she snuggled up to him. "I think it must be the alcohol in the wine."

He could feel all the shape of her beautiful body rubbing up against him and her cold hands were exploring in places where they really shouldn't be exploring.

"Jeanette, do you think we ought to be doing this?"

"Don't be silly, Philip. I can tell from the size of you that you really want it. Lie on your back and let a Parisian *poule* make you forget all your worries."

So his intoxicated brain allowed him to be made love to, and afterwards to be comforted by her enveloping softness.

# 9

Philip's alcohol-sodden brain struggled to the surface. He detected a thin shaft of bright light cutting through the gloom. It was making his head ache. He pulled the sheet over his face and closed his eyes again. He decided he would wake up later. However, there was something that wouldn't let him sink back into sleep. Maybe it was the sharp, delicious scent of coffee drifting into the room. Then suddenly he realised he was desperate to visit the toilet. With a sigh, he dragged himself into an upright position on the edge of the bed and groaned as his head threatened to split into two pieces.

Yet he *had* to go to the loo. He stood up unsteadily, trying to ignore the pain that the movement brought. He hung his head as he waited for the world to stop spinning. Then he became aware that he was completely naked. What had happened to his clothes? Where was he? But far more important – where was the bloody toilet?

He staggered to the open door and leaned against the jamb. Everywhere seemed so damned bright. It must be morning. He groaned again. Jeanette appeared at the kitchen door, dressed only in that thin negligee thing which gave a clear view of her breasts. They looked magnificent, even to a man near to death and seriously needing to urinate.

"Ah, there you are." Why did she have to sound so bloody cheerful? "Did you have a good night?"

"I need the loo."

"Over there, my darling." She pointed to the bathroom door with a smile. "Do you want me to help you?"

"No thanks."

He staggered to the toilet and stood gazing down into the pink bowl. What an awful colour! It took an age before he could manage to go. After he had finished, he rinsed his face and hands and dried them off on a towel draped over the side of the bath. As he emerged from the bathroom, Jeanette appeared from the bedroom carrying something that looked like a coat.

"Here, you'd better put this on. It's my winter dressing-gown. Armand will be here in a few minutes, and we don't want you to show off your splendid body to him, do we?"

"Armand? Oh, my God. What will he say when he finds me here?"

"He already knows you are here. That's why he's coming round. He wants to talk to you."

Philip shook his head and it hurt. "Will he realise we've spent the night together? What will he say?"

"What will he say? Nothing. Why else would you be in my flat?"

"Aren't you his – er -?"

"No, I am *not* his woman. I am nobody's woman. I choose for myself which men I have in my bed." She wrinkled her nose. "I may say that most of them pay me very well for the privilege."

"Oh." As he thought about that, he noticed for the first time that she had now pulled on a sweater and jeans, although it was clear she had no bra on under the tight top, and her feet were still bare.

"I think I'd better get dressed," he said.

"OK. Your clothes are on the chair by the window. Hurry up! I've got some coffee ready."

She disappeared into the kitchen, and he went to look for his clothes. He found the curtains had now been drawn back in the bedroom and the sun was streaming into the room and hurting his eyes. But he ignored that and dressed hurriedly. There was a woman's hair- brush on the fancy dressing table in the corner and he used that to tidy his hair. By the time he got to the kitchen he had more or less pulled himself together, although there was still a dull ache behind his temples.

Jeanette turned from the stove to face him. "Ah, that's better. That's more like the Philip who makes the ladies go soft in the centre. Sit down there."

He took the chair by the small table which she indicated. She placed a steaming mug of black coffee in front of him and a large plate of lightly buttered toast in the middle of the table. Then she returned with her own mug of coffee and sat opposite him.

She leaned forward, her loose breasts resting on the edge of the table. "So how do you feel after your night's exertions?"

"What?" Philip spluttered in the middle of a gulp of hot coffee. "What do you mean?"

She smiled. "It was the best night I've had for quite some time." She wagged a finger at him. "You are some performer, Philip Sinclair."

He shook his head but stopped when it hurt. "I don't remember anything about it."

"What a pity, Philip. All that fun and you can't remember what happened." She looked smug. "Well, I remember everything, and I enjoyed it a lot."

He took a deep breath. "Jeanette, I'm sorry. I don't normally behave like that. I was drunk. I'd had too much wine. I wasn't in control of my actions."

"Really?" She raised her eyebrows. "Well, if you weren't in control last night, I can't wait until I have you in full control. I'm looking forward to *that* experience."

"No! No, Jeanette. This must never happen again. I'm sorry." An effort of mental will summoned up the current main purpose in his life. "You know that I am – er – looking for Jackie. Last night was a – an aberration."

"Oh. What is this aberration? I do not know that English word."

"I mean it was a mistake. I was depressed, because I couldn't get any news about Jackie. I had drunk too much. I promise you it won't happen again."

She gave him a calculating look but, before she could respond, the door-bell rang. She jumped to her feet.

"That will be Armand. Perhaps he will have something to tell you."

She hurried out of the kitchen and returned a few moments later, followed by Armand. He had a broad grin on his face as he shook Philip warmly by the hand. He burst into a torrent of French.

"Ah," Jeanette translated, "he – um – asks if you had a good night last night."

It sounded to Philip's unpractised ears that he'd said a lot more than that, and the grin on Armand's face made him squirm with embarrassment.

"I was not quite myself," he mumbled.

Jeanette pulled up a third chair. "Café, Armand?"

"*Oui, bien sûr.*"

She poured out a third mug and came back to sit with them. Armand made another amused comment.

Jeanette smiled at Philip. "He says I also make good coffee."

Philip felt he was the centre of a big joke between them. He decided to change the subject.

"How did Armand know I was here?"

She answered. "He telephoned me this morning. He wanted me to help him find you. I told him you had spent the night here."

Philip hadn't heard the phone ring, but maybe he had been deep in his alcohol and sex-induced slumber.

"You are looking for Mademoiselle Blontard?" Armand asked.

"That's right. Do you have any idea . . .?"

"She is not in Paris."

The simple comment startled Philip. "How do you know? How can you be so sure?"

Jeanette translated and Armand tapped his nose. "I know everything that goes on in Paris."

"Everything?"

"Well, everything that happens in the centre of Paris. French society is much more compact than in England. If the famous Jacqueline Blontard had come to Paris, somebody I know would have heard about it."

"OK. But if she's not in Paris, where is she?"

Armand shrugged. "Ah, that I don't know. But I think she is perhaps still in the Languedoc."

"But where in the Languedoc? It's a big area and nobody even seems to have her home address."

When Jeanette translated for him, Armand pulled a face. "That is strange, is it not? Did she not tell you where she lived?"

"I never thought to ask her. We just seemed to be together in Quillan, and that was all that mattered. I believe her agent, Bernard Cambray, should know how to get hold of her, but he doesn't get back from the Seychelles until tomorrow."

"Which airport?"

"I presume Charles de Gaulle."

Armand shook his head. "It will not be easy to find him there, unless he knows you are waiting for him."

"So what do I do? How am I going to get her address from him?"

"Oh. Is no problem," said Armand when Jeanette passed on the question. "I know where his office is, but he probably won't be there until Monday morning."

"And today is Saturday," added Jeanette.

Philip sighed. "What am I going to do for two days?"

"You can stay here."

Philip thought she sounded a trifle too enthusiastic.

"I think you should go back to Languedoc," said Armand. "That is where I think you will find her."

"But what about Cambray?"

"I will meet him for you," volunteered Armand. "He knows me from Quillan. You can give me a note. He will tell me if he knows where she is, and he will let me have her address. You must write your phone number for me, and I will telephone you on Monday to tell you what I have found out from him."

"Well." Philip was in a quandary. "I suppose I'll at least be closer to her when you phone. That's if she still *is* somewhere in the Languedoc."

"Jeanette will go with you. She will be able to help you."

Philip wasn't sure that was a good idea. He shook his head. "No. That won't be necessary."

"She can speak to people who wouldn't talk to you. Many people do not speak to a foreigner, but they will speak to a French woman. She will get much more information from them."

Philip opened his mouth to argue but Jeanette stepped in. "Your French isn't very good. You will need someone to translate for you."

"And," said Armand, "Jeanette will know how to get in touch with me whenever you need information from Paris."

"Also, I can drive if you are tired. You should not drive today in the state you are in. I will be like a second pair of hands and a second pair of eyes for you." She stuck out her chin. "You will get nowhere without me."

50

Philip felt a certain suspicion that he was being manoeuvred by a combination of Jeanette and Armand. Why were they doing this? Was it really a coincidence that Jeanette had happened by the pavement cafe where he was drinking the previous night? Was it merely by chance that Armand had rung up and decided to come round to talk to him this morning? However, despite his suspicions, he felt there was a chance they might lead him to Jackie. So he allowed himself to be persuaded.

An hour later he and Jeanette were on the Metro, going to pick up his car from the underground car park near the Opéra. Then she took the wheel while they drove out of Paris, and he was able to rest his aching head. He decided it wasn't really such a bad idea after all, to have the shapely lady with him to do most of the driving.

# 10

The big man walked purposefully across St Peter's Square. At first sight one might be forgiven for dismissing him as a tall, somewhat overweight, fifty year-old. But more careful inspection revealed the substantial muscling of the shoulders, chest and upper arms. And a close look into his eyes would reveal the man's steely determination. He knocked at the small insignificant door at one corner of the Vatican Palace. It was promptly opened by a Swiss Guard out of uniform, and Jean-Luc Lerenard was permitted to enter a small lobby where he presented his letter from Cardinal Galbaccino. While the guard frisked him to check for weapons, his colleague at the reception desk telephoned ahead for permission to admit the new arrival.

A few minutes later the inner door opened, and a third guard appeared to escort him up to the cardinal's office. They turned right along a broad corridor leading away from the public areas. After about fifty metres they came into a circular lobby, where elevators were waiting to whisk them up to the top floor. Twenty metres down a side corridor from the lift brought them to a door in the corner, where the guard knocked briefly before swinging it open. Lerenard found he was in a small, sparsely-furnished, sunlit office.

The cardinal rose from a desk which was placed side-on to the open window, giving views on to the square below. He advanced towards Lerenard with a broad smile and with his arm held out for a firm hand-shake. What a change, Jean-Luc thought, from the occasion only a few weeks ago, when he had first met the great man in the bishop's palace at Narbonne.

"Thank you for coming so promptly, my friend."

"It was my pleasure to receive your invitation, Your Eminence," responded Jean Luc.

No doubt it would also be to his profit, if past experience was any guide.

Galbaccino's expression became serious. "I apologise for calling you back from your well-earned – er – retirement." He flashed a brief smile of understanding at Lerenard. "However,

I'm afraid that this business at le Bézu refuses to die, and you are the most knowledgeable of my contacts about the matter."

"What is the problem now, Eminence?"

"Well, firstly, the treasure in the underground room, which some are calling the Templars' treasure, has disappeared." He made a gesture of disdain. "Of course, that means nothing to us." He paused and looked piercingly at Lerenard. "What is more important is that the French archaeologist, Jacqueline Blontard, has apparently also disappeared at about the same time."

"Do you think she has taken it?"

The cardinal shook his head. "I believe there is no possibility of that. For a start, additional wealth is of no importance to her. Then, the logistics of moving it would be far beyond the abilities of a single individual – even one as well connected as Mademoiselle Blontard. I am told that four large vans were required to transport the stuff. That means a large organisation was involved. Besides which, she was going to gain great publicity from investigating and dating all the objects in front of the television cameras. It could turn out to be one of the greatest collections of treasures in the world to have been discovered in this century. The publicity would be far more important to her."

Lerenard nodded and waited. No doubt the cardinal would get to the point in due course.

"My colleague in Narbonne has obtained a report from the local priest in Quillan. The man has been able to find out very little. Apparently, the Englishman we met at Prouille – Philip Sinclair – has been asking questions round the town. In fact, it was Sinclair who exposed that the treasure had disappeared."

"Hmm." Jean-Luc wrinkled his nose. "Sinclair has very little French and, being a foreigner, will not get very far with the local people."

"I don't know about that. He already seems to have the ear of the mayor." Galbaccino smiled briefly. "I expect you remember Maitre Amboisard."

Lerenard did indeed remember an embarrassing interview he had been put through by the wily old lawyer when he first arrived in Quillan. In fact, he suspected it was only the cardinal's explanatory letter which had prevented him from being arrested and incarcerated on suspicion of André Jolyon's murder. He guessed it was that damned archaeologist who had cast suspicion upon him. The irony did not escape him that it was likely he was now going to be asked to find, and possibly rescue the woman.

He looked up to see that Galbaccino had been watching the play of emotions across his face.

The cardinal smiled again. "You cannot blame Mademoiselle Blontard for your problems after her assistant's death. Perhaps I am to blame for that. The way in which we introduced you to their activities was less than subtle." He shook his head. "Unfortunately, events hurried us into action."

Jean-Luc nodded his acceptance. "Presumably, Eminence, you wish me to return to the Languedoc to find this lady – and, perhaps, the location of the treasure at the same time."

"As I said, you are the only one I can turn to. We wish to avoid any chance of a tragedy occurring. It would not reflect well on the Church if it was made public that we had been involved in the preceding events." He raised a hand. "I promise that you will be well remunerated. Shall we say a further fifty percent of your previous payment?"

Lerenard raised his eyebrows. That was very generous. "Thank you, Eminence. However, there are a few questions I must ask before I accept."

"Please do."

"Firstly, what attitude will the authorities take to my re-appearance after I left them on such an unsatisfactory footing only a couple of weeks ago?"

"I have here," the cardinal indicated an envelope lying on his desk, "a further explanatory letter for you to hand personally to Maitre Amboisard. That will explain that you are there to co-operate with the Mairie and I will expect you to keep them informed of your actions as far as possible." The cardinal cleared his throat. "Also the local priest, an Albert Puissant, will be told to pass the word of your coming to a few important individuals."

The big man nodded. "There are also a few other questions. Do I approach the young Englishman?"

"If you consider it appropriate. I have another general letter you can show to other people if you consider it absolutely necessary. This tells them that you are acting with my authority." Galbaccino eyed him quizzically. "It shows the trust I am prepared to place in you. Therefore you must only make others aware of it if you are put in a position where it becomes essential."

Lerenard was warmed by the compliment as he continued. "Also, is the agent, Séjour, likely to be involved? He is a man with hidden depths. On the surface he seems to be an innocent young lad, but underneath he can handle himself very well. It was he who prevented the Marseillaises from making off with the treasure."

The cardinal shrugged. "I confess we do not know. The Council of the Order hold their cards very close to their chests, as do we. They are not likely to tell us if we ask. However, you would be wise to be prepared for his intervention or possibly that of another of their agents."

"And *La Force Marseillaise* – are they still around?"

Galbaccino smiled. "We know very little about what has happened to them. There is a rumour that a new man has taken over. His name is given as *Le comte* but the name is all that is known about him. It may not mean much."

Lerenard knew there was no point in asking for more information. His suspicious nature, which had saved him from getting into very deep trouble in the past, was nevertheless roused by this news. He realised he would have to tread very carefully on this new mission.

"Very well, your Eminence," he said. "I presume you would like me to be in Quillan as soon as possible."

"I was hoping," admitted the cardinal, "that you would be able to present my letter to the mayor on Monday."

"You can be assured of that."

In fact Lerenard intended to be in position at least twenty-four hours before he met the mayor, but there was no need to tell Galbaccino that. The cardinal might be startled to find out about his agent's intention to stay well ahead of the game.

Galbaccino turned away and walked to his desk. He returned with three envelopes which he handed over. Jean-Luc inspected them and saw they were entitled "Maitre Amboisard", "Letter of Introduction" and "Expenses". On investigation, the third envelope contained a debit card drawn on the Vatican Bank with a number paper-clipped to it. He memorised it instantly and gave back the small piece of paper to Galbaccino, whose hand was held out.

"Thank you Jean-Luc and good fortune."

"Thank *you*, Eminence."

He turned and left without a further word. The Swiss guard was waiting outside the door to escort him to the exit. Lerenard checked his watch. He had a little under three hours to get to Leonardo da Vinci Airport and board the flight to Marseilles, there to change to the local flight to Toulouse. Even with Rome's traffic, he should manage that.

Unfortunately, the pneumatic Gloria in the Trastevere would have to wait until his next visit.

# 11

Philip and Jeanette arrived in Quillan in the early evening. She had driven most of the way from Paris in her aggressive, slightly irregular fashion. At first he was amused by the way she swore at the other drivers on the road, particularly the truck drivers. The intention had been that Philip should spend plenty of his time asleep, so as to get rid of his sore head which resulted from the excess of wine he had consumed the previous night. However, Jeanette had dressed in a tight sweater with a low neckline that displayed a lot of cleavage whenever she leaned towards him, and a short skirt which tended to ride up to the top of her shapely legs, and he found these distracting. Even more, her fury at the other road users and her frequent and often violent changes of direction had made any sort of rest more or less impossible. Finally, he decided he had had enough of her driving. He took over the wheel and consigned his helper to the passenger seat, where she pouted and grumbled about his arrogant assumption that he was a better driver than her. So Philip was exhausted when they finally pulled in to the square and stopped in front of the hotel. Jeanette hastily got out of the car, still complaining about him. She grabbed her two large suitcases from the back seat and flounced up the steps into the main entrance. After retrieving his own bag and locking the car, Philip arrived in Reception to find the concierge eyeing her askance.

"Have you got a room available for mademoiselle?" he asked.

Henri sniffed. "It will have to be on the third floor."

Philip suppressed a smile. He knew that, unless there had been a big change in the last two days, the hotel was virtually empty. Yet the man had decided to put Jeanette up under the roof where the least-welcome guests were placed. He had himself previously been consigned to one of those rooms, until his developing love affair with Jacqueline had promoted him to share her superior suite on the first floor overlooking the river. Of course the present arrangement didn't worry him. In fact, he thought it would be a good idea for Jeanette to be a couple of floors away from him.

"I will pay for her for a week in advance." He handed over his credit card.

Henri raised his eyebrows but said nothing more. He pushed the registration slip across the counter for Jeanette to sign, which she did with an annoyed flourish.

The man recovered the card, inspected it, sniffed and turned back to Philip. "There is a letter for monsieur."

"A letter?" Philip's hopes soared. Perhaps it was going to explain Jackie's strange departure.

Henri retreated to the back of the office and hunted round for a minute. He returned with it held triumphantly in his right hand. Philip grabbed it and ripped it open. But it wasn't from Jackie. He couldn't immediately decide who had written to him. The language was French, and he realised he needed his dictionary to decipher it.

"Where's the porter?" Jeanette demanded. She had stayed at the place before when she was playing the role of Armand's wife, so she knew full well that there was no such person.

"*I'm* the porter." Philip pocketed the unread letter to cover his disappointment and started to go through the ridiculous charade of trying to carry three heavy bags at once.

Jeanette took pity on him and decided to carry one case herself. Nevertheless, it was a struggle to carry his own and her remaining heavy case up to the first floor. The Hotel du Chateau didn't boast a lift. He left his own bag on the landing outside his room and continued to the top floor with her puffing behind him.

When they got to her room, she inserted the key in the lock and led the way in. He deposited her case by the bed and turned back to the door.

"Are you going to just leave me here alone, after all I have done for you?" she asked.

"Of course. You will want a rest to recover from the long drive and to take a shower to freshen up. I will meet you in Reception at seven o'clock and we'll find somewhere to eat."

She sighed and pouted, but he turned his back on her and went down to his own room. He unpacked his bag and stretched out on the bed to relax. At last his headache was starting to fade. Then he remembered the letter that Henri had given him. He wondered who it was from.

He got to his feet and recovered it from his jacket pocket. It was quite short, and he soon discovered it was signed by César Renoir. After reading it through twice, he worked out, with the help of his pocket dictionary, that she wanted some sort of help from him. At first he discarded the letter. However, he soon started to feel guilty about being disappointed to be asked for help by this woman. After all, she had saved his life by shooting the criminal Montluçon. So he picked it up again and went through it for a third time, rather more carefully.

The letter told him that she was still in the prison hospital in Toulouse, and she wanted him to visit her there. Once he had got the full sense of the letter, he thought it sounded quite urgent. Losing a brief struggle with his conscience, he decided to go and see her next morning, despite the place being nearly a hundred and fifty kilometres away. After all, tomorrow was Sunday, and there would be no chance of seeing Maitre Amboisard to get an update on the man's progress in searching for the treasure, or receiving any new information from Paris. So, in a way, he wouldn't be wasting time that he could put to other uses. Who knew, perhaps César would be able to tell him something useful.

His mind made up, he stripped off and took a shower to refresh himself. The sharp needles of lukewarm water brightened him up as he soaped and rinsed his body. He gyrated in the exhilarating freshness, his eyes closed, his headache now completely disappeared. When he opened them, Jeanette was standing just outside the shower in her negligee, clearly with nothing on underneath. She slid the garment off, tossed it onto the stool in the corner and stepped naked into the shower to join him.

For a minute, Philip was speechless. When he had recovered, he said, "What on earth are you doing, Jeanette?"

"What do you think?" She giggled and rubbed her heavy breasts against his chest.

"How did you get in here?"

"You didn't lock your door."

"Did anybody see you walking through the hotel in that thin – er – that dressing gown?"

She shrugged. "I don't think so. I don't think there is anyone else in the hotel but you and me. But if so, what? The concierge will expect you to be coming to my room to have sex with me. Why else would you turn up with a Paris *poule* and book a room for her for a whole week?"

"Why should he think that? He knows I am looking for Jackie."

"Never mind." She shook her head. "This is France, Philip. He would expect you to find someone like me to take your mind off what you have lost. I have known many men like the concierge. By now the whole of Quillan will have been told that you have turned up with your replacement woman."

Philip was rendered temporarily speechless. "But we've got to stop that. How can we make them realise that this is a purely business arrangement."

"Look down at yourself." She giggled again. "Your body is telling you that our relationship has nothing to do with business. I can see that you are very pleased for me to be here."

He realised, without looking down that he had a large erection. It was a dreadfully embarrassing and, at the same time, a quite exciting sensation. What on earth was he going to do about it? He tried for one last time to stop her.

"Jeanette, it is wrong for us to have sex together."

"We did last night. You enjoyed it then."

"You know that I was drunk. I agree it was my fault, but I wasn't responsible for my behaviour, and I'm sorry that I lost control of myself."

"Well, I'm *not*." The pout was back. "I don't turn myself on and off like you do."

"I'm sorry, Jeanette. You're a lovely and a very sexy lady, but I have already committed myself to Jackie. I feel it would be wrong of me to get into the habit of making love to you."

Philip extricated himself from her close contact and got out of the shower. He picked up his towel and wrapped it round his middle.

"Hah," she accused. "You're afraid you might like it too much. You're afraid I might – how do you say – get my claws into you."

"Perhaps you're right." Philip started towelling himself down briskly to reduce his erection. "Anyway, now you're wet you might as well have a proper shower. There's my soap and face-cloth, and you can use the other towel."

He turned his back on her and returned to the bedroom, ignoring the screech that followed him out of the bathroom. He dressed hastily and a few minutes later she joined him. She was pink and damp with wet, tousled hair. The towel was clasped round her breasts with one hand and in the other she carried the scrap of her negligee. Philip thought she looked absolutely delightful.

"Are you going to send me back to my room?" she asked.

"Of course I am. Now look, Jeanette, from what you say, Henri, the concierge, will take great pleasure in telling Jackie, when she returns, that you and I have been having sex together. I intend to be able to tell her that it is quite incorrect, and we have been sleeping in separate rooms two floors apart."

She threw her head back. "When she returns? Hah. It is *if* she returns."

"Well, I believe she will. In fact, I believe she would have been waiting for me here last Wednesday if she could. That is why I am so worried about her."

She shrugged. "OK. So I have lost. I will go back to my room and dry my hair." She dropped the towel and pulled on her negligee, not tying the belt and leaving it to hang open to display her naked front.

"Make sure nobody sees you looking like that."

"Huh!" She pulled a face. "There will be nobody to see me even if I have nothing on." Then she was gone with a bang of the door.

At seven o'clock they met in Reception. Jeanette was wearing baggy trousers and a jacket which was buttoned up to the neck. Philip was pleased to see her looking so prim. They walked across the square to a bistro which was serving food. They entered and she led the way to a quiet alcove near the back. He was slightly surprised to find the usually irrepressible young woman was so muted. He guessed she had decided to make him pay for his earlier rejection.

They made their selections from the menu and, while they were waiting for the food to be prepared, he told her about his intention to visit César Renoir in Toulouse the following day. He said he wanted to go alone.

"She is too old for you. And she is too plain."

Philip shook his head. "I am going because she has asked me to – not because I want to have sex with her. In any case, since she had a knife stuck deep in her stomach less than two weeks ago, I should think sex is the last thing she would be able to manage."

"I will not come with you," she said.

"I've told you, I don't want you to."

"I will stay here and ask questions of some of the people who might know something." She smiled sweetly. "They will tell me things which they would never tell you."

"What do you mean? What people? What questions?"

She sniffed. "I will tell you when you return. I will come to your room tomorrow night and we will make our plans."

Philip wasn't sure exactly what that meant, but he decided he would have to wait and see.

# 12

The hospital at Toulouse prison occupied a separate two-storey wing with its own entrance and reception. Philip had got Jeanette to telephone ahead to confirm his visit would be permitted, and he found he had no trouble in gaining entrance. He merely had to show his passport and sign a form to be allowed in.

César had been moved to a separate room near reception. There were bars on the window and a locked door which was opened by an attendant to admit him. Otherwise, the room seemed to him to be like a single bedroom in a private hospital. She was sitting, fully dressed, in a comfortable chair near the window and looked quite healthy, but she made no attempt to rise when he entered.

"How are you feeling?" Philip asked her.

"I am a lot better, thank you. As long as I make no sudden movements, I am quite comfortable. I can walk slowly but I feel it is necessary to support my stomach with my hands when I do so."

"It is remarkable to see you looking so well," he said. "The last time I saw you, I was doubtful whether you would even survive."

She smiled gently. "As you can see, it takes more than a knife thrown into my stomach to get rid of me."

Philip thought about his debt to César. "I want to thank you again for shooting Montluçon when you did. If you hadn't been so quick, I don't know what might have happened."

He remembered the sick feeling in his stomach as the ginger-haired criminal moved the muzzle of the gun, pointing it through his cheek towards his ear, so as to cause him as much pain as possible before he killed him. He thought the memory of the evil look on Montluçon's face as he took aim would stay with him forever.

"Have you been told," she asked, "that I will not be charged with homicide for killing Montluçon? It is because it was judged that I had saved your life by doing it."

"What a relief." Philip sighed. "That seems like true justice. It is one of the benefits of the French system that so much power is in the hands of the examining magistrate."

"As long as it is used correctly."

"Yes."

Philip thought of the experienced honesty of Maitre Amboisard. It was fortunate that so just a man was supervising the investigations into the criminal acts which had occurred in the last two weeks.

"However," said César, "I have reason to think that my own life may be in danger when I leave this hospital."

"In danger? How?"

"A new man has taken charge of *La Force Marseillaise*. He is known as *Le comte*."

"How do you know that?"

"Do you remember there was also a man called Pierre in the treasure room at le Bézu. He helped me when I was injured?"

"That's right. He was a big, tough-looking guy."

"Well, he was my father's personal driver. He has known me since I was a little girl. He has told me *Le comte* is sending him to get information about me. I am afraid this new man will want to have me taken back to him in Marseilles and that would not be good for my chances of surviving. So I thought carefully about what I should do, and I realised you are the only person I know who can help me." She looked at him searchingly. "Will you do that for me, please?"

"Of course I will if I can. What do you want me to do?"

"I know a place near Rennes-les-Bains where I can hide. I want you to take me there."

"OK." Philip looked round. "But what about the prison authorities? Will they let you go?"

"Oh, I have my release papers - there." She pointed to an envelope on the small cupboard beside her chair. "The governor signed them yesterday. I can leave any time I wish."

"What, just walk out?"

"If necessary. But what I want *you* to do, is hire a car to get me away from Toulouse. I have found out there is a company in the Boulevard Victor Hugo which stays open on Sundays. I have here a street map which shows you how to find them."

She pulled a brochure from the book on the small table, which she had presumably been reading.

Philip took it from her and studied it. "I think this company is right down in the centre of the city. It will take me some time to arrange it. Why don't I take you to Rennes-les-Bains in my car?"

"La Force will know your car. There will be somebody posted out there to watch. They will have seen you arrive. So they will follow your car and see where you are taking me. I don't want that to happen."

"Do you really think there is someone from the Force watching this prison to make sure they see you when you leave?"

"I am certain of it. They will not risk me getting out when they are not quite ready."

"Blimey." Philip thought rapidly. "If what you say is correct, they will have seen my car arrive and will be keeping an eye on it. Won't they follow me when I leave?"

She shook her head. "I don't think they will be so bothered about you if you leave on your own without me. They will assume you have just been visiting to see how I am. And I don't expect they have enough spare men for one to follow you, when you leave the prison on your own. So, what I want you to do is this." She stood up slowly and carefully. "Come over to the window."

He followed her as instructed.

"Keep back. I don't want us to be seen by any watchers outside. Now," she pointed. "Do you see that little side street over there just outside the prison wall?"

"Yes."

"I want you to drive the hire car along the main road at the far end of that street at five minutes before ten o'clock this evening. It will be dark. I will be waiting for you to stop to pick me up. Here - I have marked the place on the street map."

"Are you able to walk that far?"

She nodded. "I have been practising walking round my room for the last week. I will not be carrying a bag. I will get there all right."

"What about returning the hire car? Won't the company be closed at that time of night?"

"I'm sure they will." She turned and looked into his eyes. "I want you to drive me to Rennes-les-Bains in the hire car if you will. That means you will have to come back tomorrow to return the hire car and collect your own. Are you willing to do this? It is very important for me."

Philip hesitated only for a second before he decided that he owed it to César to do just as she asked. "Of course I will. But what if you're delayed by something unexpected? Do you want me to keep going round the town centre and then come back again?"

"Yes please, but I do not think I will be delayed."

"OK, I will see you at five to ten." He helped her back to her chair and left.

In fact, everything went well. Philip hired the car soon after lunch. He did several practice runs to check that he knew exactly where he had to stop – the last one was as it was getting dark - so that he was ready for the pick-up.

A little before ten, he pulled in to the side of the road just past the junction and a darkly-clad figure detached itself from the shadows of the side street and hurried to the car. Philip leaned across and opened the door for César, who was breathing rather heavily, but otherwise seemed all right.

He let off the hand brake and pulled away from the kerb. "Did it all go OK?"

"Yes."

"You don't think you were seen?"

"No."

Nevertheless, he kept an eye on the mirror as he made his way out of Toulouse. The traffic seemed quite light and there was no sign of any vehicles following them. When he reached the *autoroute* leading to Carcassonne, he relaxed and only occasionally checked the rear view. The drive was uneventful and, two hours later, he was driving through the little town of Rennes-les-Bains. At César's direction, he took a side road just beyond where the houses ended.

After a few hundred yards she pointed to a modest cottage set atop a grassy bank just off the road. He drove up a gravelled track and stopped beside the cottage.

"How did you know about this place?"

"It was rented for the summer by Alain Hébert – the man who was killed in front of you in the treasure room at le Bézu."

"Oh." Philip had to be careful about what he said next. "Did you live here with him?"

"Part of the time. We were just planning to make a life together." She shrugged. "That seems to have been my destiny." She opened her car door.

He followed her. "Is the house locked?"

"I have the key." She removed it from a jacket pocket and displayed it to him. "Come on."

They went round to the front of the cottage. Philip noticed a small circular wooden table and two chairs on the terrace outside. He could see, even in the dark, that there was a good view from here down the valley looking east.

César unlocked the front door. "Will you come in for a drink?"

"I think I should get back to my hotel in Quillan. I don't want to be locked out for the night."

She smiled. "Very well, but will you do one more thing more for me, please?"

"What is that?"

"I think it is important for me to stay inside the house here for a few days. Will you give me your mobile number in case I need to contact you?"

"Of course."

He followed her into the living room which occupied the left side of the front of the cottage. She produced a pen and paper, and he wrote down his number.

"This is mine." She scribbled it at the bottom, folded the paper, tore the strip off and handed it to him. "There is one other thing."

"What's that?"

"The mayor told me I must leave a note of where he can contact me in case the Justice Ministry in Paris wants to get hold of me. Will you tell him that you know where I am, but I am afraid of *La Force* finding me. Therefore, he should see you first if he wants to talk to me and you will collect me and take me to see him. Will you do that for me?"

"Certainly I will. I am going to see Maitre Amboisard tomorrow morning." Philip suddenly had another idea. "What are you doing about food?"

"I have some here."

"Will it be enough if you're going to stay out of sight for some days?"

"Hmm." She pondered. "I suppose I should think about that."

"If I come back early tomorrow morning, you could give me a list."

"Thank you, Philip. That is a good idea. But will you please use the hire car and come alone and check you are not being followed?"

"Of course I will. I can get whatever you want from Limoux before I go back to collect my car. And I will see the mayor at the same time."

She accompanied him to the door and thanked him for his help. But, as he drove away, he couldn't help feeling worried about her being alone in that isolated location.

# 13

Philip got back to his hotel just before one in the morning. He had telephoned to warn the concierge he would be late and found Henri had waited up for him before he closed the place. The man sniffed superciliously and gave him his room key.

"The woman has been complaining about you being late."

"Where is she?"

He shrugged expressively. "I do not know, Monsieur."

"Well, I'm tired. She'll have to wait until the morning." He nodded as he handed the concierge a substantial tip for waiting up. "Good night, Henri."

"Good night, Monsieur."

Philip plodded up the stairs to the first floor. His room was the second on the right. When he put his key in the lock he found the door was already unlocked. Suspiciously, he opened it and stepped inside.

Jeanette sat up, leaped out of bed and hurried across to him. She was wearing a skimpy, see-through night-dress that just about covered the private parts of her body.

"I was worried about you." She hugged her warm body against him. "I must have phoned you at least a dozen times."

"My mobile was turned off. How did you get into my bedroom, Jeanette? I am absolutely sure I locked the door when I went out this morning."

"Oh, I borrowed the key from reception."

"What did Henri say when you did that?"

She shook her head. "He did not know. The reception is often unmanned when he goes to the kitchen for a drink. He stays there for a long time. I think he is having an affair with the cook."

"Now look here, Jeanette, haven't I made it clear to you that I want us to keep to our separate rooms?"

"But this is very important, Philip. I have found out lots of important things for you."

"Nevertheless you could have pushed a note under the door, asking me to come to your room to tell me these important things. But you chose to climb into my bed covered by nothing

69

but a slip of silk. It's not the way you should be trying to get my attention."

"But I've got it, haven't I?" She exulted. "If you were a real man you would have taken advantage of what I'm offering, and would be in bed with me by now." She pointed at him. "I don't think you are a *real* man, except when you are drunk, of course. Then you are very real."

He tried to ignore her words, aware at the same time of a degree of hypocrisy in his response.

"So what is this important information you have found out?"

"I am getting cold." She hugged herself. "I will get back into the bed. You can take your clothes off and join me and I will tell you."

"Jeanette -."

"Or," she shrugged, "you can sit on the edge of the bed and get cold."

She climbed back between the sheets. Philip decided he would have to play her game until she had confided the information she had gathered. Then he intended to kick her out.

He took off his jacket and hung it over the back of the chair by the dressing table. He removed his shoes which were starting to feel uncomfortable. Then he sat down on the edge of the bed.

"OK. I'm ready for this important information."

She snuggled against his back. "Well, when I realised you had gone and would be away all day, and that you had left me all alone with not enough money to go out and enjoy myself, I decided the only thing I could do was go to the police station. It is in the basement of the Mairie."

"I know. I've been there."

"Because it was a Sunday, there was only one gendarme on duty. He was a young man called Georges. He was quite good looking and he was very pleased to see *me*."

"I bet he was."

She looked at him sharply. "He was very young – much too young." She sniffed. "Yes. Well, after chatting for a while, I got round to talking to him about the treasure that had disappeared from the castle at le Bézu. He was very surprised that I knew about that. He said that it was supposed to be a secret."

70

"But *he* knew about it."

"Oh, yes. He said the police knew all about it. He had stood guard up at the castle himself several times."

"Did he realise it had disappeared?"

"This is the interesting thing." She poked him in the ribs. "It took me a long time to get the whole story out of him. I had to let him take certain advantages."

"I see," said Philip, feeling oddly jealous about her admission that she had allowed the young gendarme to make love to her. "Where did he have you? – on the bed in one of the cells?"

"It did not quite get to that," she said, sounding affronted. "He thought I was going to let him, but I had to tell him that you would be very annoyed if somebody else had sex with your woman."

"You said *what*?"

"Well, I had to protect myself." She shook her head. "But, in any case, I had got the information I wanted by then. This is the interesting bit. Last Tuesday night, he and three other policemen, including Sergeant Leblanc, escorted four large vans from le Bézu to an industrial estate in Carcassonne. He didn't know what was in the vans, but we can guess, can't we."

"Blimey." Philip thought about what it meant for the authorities to arrange a police escort to accompany those vehicles. And why hadn´t the mayor been told? It surely meant that some secret official organisation must have been involved. He wondered whether Jackie might have been with them in one of the vans.

"Did your friend see any of the people who were in the vans?"

She shook her head again. "Sorry, he didn't. He said he was told to stay in the car all the time. The gendarmes were only there in case any unexpected problems occurred. It was already dark when they got to le Bézu. They drove to Carcassonne through the night without stopping, and the warehouse doors were open when they got there. The vans drove straight in and the doors were closed. The police stayed outside. Sergeant Leblanc got out to check that the doors were locked, and nobody came out to talk to him. Then they drove back to

Quillan. It was late and they were all sent straight home and told not to talk to anybody."

"Did he tell you where this warehouse was?"

"He scribbled me a rough plan." She burrowed under the pillow and produced a rather crumpled piece of paper. "It should be quite easy to find the place."

Philip inspected the plan. As she had said, it was only a rough sketch, but it seemed to have quite a lot of notes scrawled on it. He wasn't sure he could decipher the directions, but presumably Jeanette understood what it all meant.

"I think I will get you to translate all this for me in the morning, and I will go and have a look at the place tomorrow. I've got to go back to Toulouse to collect my car."

He explained what had happened during the day, without giving any details of where he had left César.

"I will have to come with you," she insisted. "You will never find the warehouse without me. I will probably also remember some extra things which Georges told me, but which won't be on the plan."

"OK." He gave in, realising it made sense that she should accompany him. "Well, thank you, Jeanette. It does look as though this could be important information."

"Are you pleased with me?"

"I certainly am. You obviously have a talent for information gathering which I hadn't previously fully appreciated."

She smiled provocatively at him. "I put myself in some danger as well. I thought for a moment that he was going to rape me, when I told him I wasn't willing to have sex with him. He was so angry. But I told him you were friends with the mayor, and you would ruin his career if there was any trouble. That made him see sense."

"I don't know that I want to have the sordid details."

"I also told him that you were very jealous if anybody put their hands on your mistress, and you would stop at nothing to be avenged." She warmed to her theme. "I promised him that he could have me for free, just once, if you left me here on my own for a few days."

Philip couldn't help laughing at her. He shook his head. "What *have* I done, letting myself get involved with you?"

"Well." She sat up. "Now that you agree we're involved, you can get undressed and come into bed with me."

"Jeanette, how many times have I told you that we are not going to get involved in the way that you are suggesting?" He had become aware that one of her substantial breasts had escaped from the inadequate covering of her night-dress and hung invitingly less than a foot away. He thrust the temptation from him and stood up.

"Come on now. Thank you for the information. Now it's time for you to get back to your own bed."

"But it's cold and spooky up there."

"Well, I'm sure you'll soon warm it up."

He noticed her negligee hanging over the foot of the bed and he picked it up. Some fluffy concoctions which she would probably describe as slippers were lying nearby. He held out the dressing-gown.

"Come on please, Jeanette."

She reluctantly climbed out of bed, put her arms in the sleeves of her negligee and her feet in the slippers.

"A gentleman would see me safely up to my room."

Philip sighed. "OK. But I want you to do up your dressing gown. If we should meet anybody, with your boobs virtually falling out of your night-dress like that, you'd probably give them a heart attack."

"All right, if you insist." She giggled and wrapped her gown tight around her as she led the way up to her room. Outside the door, she stopped and turned to face him.

"Will you kiss me to show you're pleased with me?"

When he bent forward, she presented him with an open mouth full of tongue and teeth and he hastily disengaged, pushed her through her unlocked door, and quickly returned to his own room. He thought it would be so easy to submit to her suggestion that they share the night together.

# 14

Lerenard presented himself at the town hall at 8.30 on the Monday morning. Maitre Amboisard was already there, having arrived early in response to the note posted through the door of his private residence the previous evening. He met Lerenard himself in Reception and invited him up to his office.

The big man handed over the introductory letter from the cardinal and settled himself in a chair facing the mayor. The lawyer's eyebrows rose as he read the letter and, when he had finished, he read it through again a second time. At last he put the piece of paper down on his clean, uncluttered blotter. He took off his spectacles, wiped them with a clean white handkerchief which he extracted from his top pocket, put them on again and gazed across the desk at Galbaccino's agent.

"So you are Jean-Luc Lerenard."

"Yes."

"You are one of the people who I, as examining magistrate, wished to interview about the death of André Jolyon, assistant to the eminent archaeologist, Jacqueline Blontard. Jolyon, as you know, was thrown or pushed from the cliffs of le Bézu chateau on thirtieth April. However, you then absented yourself from Quillan, without my consent, without first offering to be questioned."

Lerenard squirmed slightly in his seat. Even though he knew the cardinal's letter explained the reasons for his absence, the big man, perturbed by very few other men, felt a frisson of alarm.

Amboisard took a deep breath. "Well, the letter from the cardinal goes a long way towards explaining your behaviour. Nevertheless, your actions have been in direct defiance of the laws of this country. I cannot completely disregard that." He paused and his steady eyes bored into the other man. "I do not wish to make an unnecessary fuss about the matter. However, I do need to see that all the requirements of the law are upheld. Therefore, there are some questions which you must answer before we go any further. Do you understand?"

"Yes, sir."

The mayor took out a file from the deep right-hand drawer of his desk, opened it and looked inside. He pulled out an official-looking sheet of paper and spread it on the blotter in front of him. Then he extracted a fountain pen from the inside pocket of his jacket and unscrewed the top. He marked the numeral 1 at the top left corner of the sheet of paper and returned his gaze to Lerenard.

"You are aware of the death of André Jolyon on the night of Wednesday, 30th April?"

"Yes, sir."

"Where were you on the night in question?"

"I was lodged in a house in the small town of Fanjeaux."

"Which is only about fifty kilometres from here."

"Yes."

"What were you doing in Fanjeaux?"

"I was being trained by the Abbé Dugard in some of the techniques of archaeology."

The magistrate's eyebrows rose again. "What was the purpose of this – er – training?"

"I was being trained to make me suitable to offer myself as an archaeological assistant to Jacqueline Blontard."

"Indeed?" The mayor shook his head. "So the good Abbé can confirm this?"

"He can."

"And when did you come to Quillan?"

"Two days after the death of Jolyon."

"The cardinal says you were offered to Mademoiselle Blontard as the replacement for Jolyon. That means you had a direct interest in – er – removing him from the scene."

Lerenard hesitated. "I can see how you might reach that conclusion. However, I assure you that I had no part in his death."

"No," admitted Amboisard. "The other evidence which I have gathered suggests that there were different persons who caused the death of André Jolyon. However, I require you to state on oath that, firstly, you were not present in the Quillan or le Bézu areas on the night he died and, secondly, that you took no part in the planning or the carrying out of his murder. Are you prepared to do that?"

75

"I am."

The lawyer nodded. "Very well, I will have a statement prepared later today which will include the information you have given me and the undertakings we have just discussed. I will require you to read the statement, swear before me on the Holy Bible that it is the full truth, and sign each page. You should do that in the next few days and certainly before you leave the Quillan area again. Will you assure me that you will do that?"

"I certainly will," said Lerenard, relieved to be let off the hook so lightly.

Amboisard wagged a finger at him. "If you do not, I will personally make sure that it causes considerable embarrassment to Cardinal Galbaccino."

"I understand. I will not let you down."

"Good." the lawyer put down his pen and leaned back in his chair. "Now – what do you intend to do while you are here?"

Jean-Luc took a deep breath. "The cardinal has sent me to render what help I can to young Philip Sinclair in his attempts to discover the whereabouts of Jacqueline Blontard."

"Why should the Catholic Church wish to do that?"

Lerenard hesitated. "His Eminence did not give me any reasons. However, I believe he feels some sympathy and – er – perhaps some responsibility for the sequence of events which led up to her disappearance."

"How interesting. Do you mean to say that it has nothing to do with the coincidental disappearance of what may turn out to have been one of the most valuable treasures to have been discovered in the Western World?"

"Ah – that I do not know."

"No matter." Amboisard smiled bleakly. "Of course, if you do find out anything which might be useful to the police or to me in my investigations concerning the disappearance of the treasure, you will immediately give full details to Sergeant Leblanc."

"I certainly will."

"Very well. I think that concludes our interview for now. If you wish to make contact with Mr Sinclair, you will find he is staying at the Castle Hotel."

"As I shall be."

The mayor wrinkled his nose in distaste. "He is apparently accompanied by a young woman from Paris called Jeanette Picard."

"What is she doing here?"

"I don't know. The concierge at the hotel is suspicious of their relationship." Amboisard sighed. "But perhaps the man is just being mischievous."

"That is a very interesting idea. Previously a woman called Jeanette Picard was one of the helpers of Jacqueline Blontard. At that time this woman was in a relationship with a young man, also from Paris, called Armand Séjour. Is he here as well?"

"Armand Séjour?" The lawyer checked back through his file. "Indeed I hope he is. He is another of the witnesses who, like yourself, suddenly disappeared before I could interview him." He leaned forward. "If you discover his whereabouts, it is important that you tell me where he is immediately."

Lerenard was silent, apparently lost in thought.

Amboisard leaned forward. "Did you hear what I said?"

The agent came alert again. "I certainly did." Then almost to himself, "This situation seems to be getting more complicated."

"It is already complicated enough for me, thank you very much," said the mayor. "But, as I said, please keep me informed about anything you find out."

The big man stood up. "I shall certainly do that."

Neither offered a hand to shake so Lerenard turned and left the office without further comment.

# 15

Candice Ambré got back to Marseilles in the late afternoon. She left the car in the basement car park of the seven-storey block on the hill high above the old city, and walked across to the lift. To the casual observer she would appear to be a beautiful, self-confident woman in control of her life. She was smartly dressed, her shoulders were back, her chest thrust out in front of her and she walked with a measured, elegant step. However, underneath the exterior poise, she was acutely apprehensive. She was not looking forward to her interview with the head of *La Force Marseillaise*.

As usual, the doors to the private lift whispered open without the need to press a button, and she entered. After a few seconds, they closed and the lift accelerated up towards the top floor. She noticed there were no selector buttons on the panel for the lower floors. *Le comte's* penthouse was on the seventh floor. How did he choose who he would allow to invade his private space? She presumed there must be hidden cameras, including one behind the full-length mirror at the back of the lift.

It came to a halt and the doors slid back. Candice blinked as she saw the bulky shadow of the boss standing in the middle of the lobby, surrounded by the glare of the low evening sun. She heard the doors glide shut behind her and she was trapped. Squinting at him in his position of superiority did nothing to reduce her acute sense of apprehension.

"Where is the woman?" The voice was calm, almost quiet, but that didn't lessen the menace in his tone.

"I'm sorry. I haven't been able to find out yet."

"And Pierre Schmidt – where is he?"

She shook her head. "I cannot tell you with certainty. I presume he is still in Toulouse. He refused to come back with me."

"Tell me exactly what has happened since last Friday. I want every detail."

She swallowed. "We went first to Schmidt's flat for him to pick up some clothes and things."

"Did you go into the flat with him?"

"No. I stayed in the car."

"So you do not know whether he made any phone calls or left any messages for others."

"No." She gulped. "He didn't invite me in and I would have been suspicious of his intentions if he had." Did this man trust no-one?

Le comte sneered, but only said, "Very well. Continue."

"Schmidt then drove us to Toulouse. He said he should drive because we were supposed to appear as if we were a married couple. He booked us in to a double room at the Ibis Hotel." She saw him take a quick breath and hurriedly added, "Although we shared a room, he didn't touch me. I took the bed and he slept in a chair by the window. He didn't mind. He told me he had spent many nights like that."

"Go on."

"We stayed there for three nights. Schmidt said it was too late to find out about Mademoiselle Renoir on Friday night. So we went to the prison on Saturday morning."

Le comte only nodded.

"When we got to the square outside the prison, we spoke first to a man called Josef who was keeping watch from an old car which was parked opposite the hospital block. Schmidt questioned him carefully in front of me about what he had seen. It amounted to nothing of importance."

She paused, but le comte didn't speak so she continued. "Then Schmidt went in to see if he could meet Renoir and arrange about collecting her. I stayed in the car." She turned frightened eyes on him. "He said the woman would be suspicious if I went in with him, and I thought that might be correct."

"I see."

"When he came out, he told me that she hadn't yet received her release papers which were necessary before the guards would let her out of the hospital. He said they wouldn't be given to her until Monday."

"Did Schmidt see the woman and talk to her?"

"I – er – I assume he did. All he said was that we would have to go back again first thing on Monday morning – er – that is today."

She looked at the boss quickly. Did he agree they had done the right thing, or did he think they should have pushed harder?

"I had to do what Schmidt said," she explained defensively. "I couldn't do anything on my own."

There was a long pause. At last he said, "So what did you do for the rest of the weekend?"

"On Saturday afternoon Schmidt stayed in the room and I went shopping."

"Shopping?" he suddenly shouted. "What kind of shopping?"

The shout made Candice jump but she attempted a shrug. "Oh – just a few things."

"And what did Schmidt do while you were shopping for your few things?"

"I told you – he stayed in the room."

"You mean he was in the room when you returned from your shopping?"

She swallowed hard and nodded. She realised the boss was suggesting that Pierre may well have gone out without her knowing anything about it.

"Did you take your meals together?" he asked.

"Yes, but Schmidt said we should not be seen together outside the hotel in case we were recognised."

"Who was likely to recognise you?"

She shook her head. "I don't know. That was what Schmidt said."

"So, what did you do on the Sunday?"

"We waited until late morning and then we went back to the prison to check, just in case the release papers would be issued on a Sunday. But we were told we had to wait until Monday – until this morning."

"You were told this by the prison authorities?"

"Er – not exactly. Schmidt was told this. Again I stayed in the car."

*Le comte* continued to stare at her. She felt like a rabbit dazzled in the headlights of an advancing car, unable to escape from the piercing glare.

"So you went back again this morning?"

"Er – yes."

"And what happened this morning?" Although his voice was remarkably quiet, it seemed to have an edge as sharp as a scalpel.

"Once again I – er – I stayed in the car. Schmidt went into the hospital reception on his own." She took a deep breath and stammered. "He - he came out again quite quickly and – er - he seemed very annoyed. He came over to the car and he told me Renoir had already gone. He said she must have been given the release papers earlier, but she - she hadn't told him. Now she had disappeared. Schmidt said she must have been suspicious of him before he arrived, because he agreed the woman couldn't possibly have seen me in the car."

"She could not have escaped on her own in her condition," roared *le comte*. "She must have been helped by someone."

"Yes. Yes, that is what Schmidt said. He was angry. He went straight across to talk to Josef. I - I got out of the car and followed him. He asked Josef if anyone might have come to visit Renoir since we were there yesterday morning. He told him to think very carefully. After a minute, Josef admitted that a young man had been the only visitor to the hospital wing late yesterday morning. That was Sunday. As he had been instructed, he had made a note of anybody visiting the hospital. He had taken the car's number plate. It was a British registration number. However, when the man had left again after about an hour, Josef said he was certain the young man was on his own."

"Did Schmidt know who that young man was?"

"Well, he told Josef to describe the car and the driver as best he could. Josef remembered the car quite well because it was a British sports car. After that Schmidt seemed to know who the man was."

"So – who was it?"

"Er - Schmidt didn't tell me. That was when he said he would go after the man straight away and see if he would lead him to Renoir. He told me I should come back to report to you and he said he will contact you as soon as there is more information."

"Hah!" It was the first loud ejaculation *le comte* had released for some time, and it made her jump. "So why didn't you ask Schmidt the name of this Englishman? How will we find him? I suppose you don't even have the registration number of the car."

She shook her head wordlessly.

Suddenly his hand shot out and grasped her by the throat. His grip was strong and began to cut off her breathing. She opened her mouth to scream but no sound came out.

"I am very displeased with you, Candice," his voice grated. "You and Schmidt have made a mess of this operation. Do you understand how annoyed I am?"

She tried to nod but she couldn't move her head. She felt as though her eyes were starting to pop out of their sockets. Her hands had come up to grab at his wrist, but they were completely ineffectual against his vice-like grip on her throat.

"You must understand, Candice, that your presence in my bed means nothing if you are useless in the field. I will not tolerate assistants who cannot serve me properly."

The world was starting to turn black before her eyes. Her legs could no longer carry her weight and her body sagged. She was convinced at that moment that she was going to die. Then, just as suddenly, he released her and she collapsed in a heap on the floor.

"You have only one way to prove to me that you are of any value to this organisation, Candice." He spoke the words slowly and with emphasis. "You are to go straight back to Toulouse. First, you will contact this man Josef, and get all the information he has and write it down – IN FULL DETAIL. Then you must find Schmidt and obtain all the information he has discovered. Then you are to telephone me and tell me everything. Finally, you will collect Schmidt and the woman and bring them back here to me. When you have done that, you will have partly redeemed yourself. Do you understand me?"

Candice dragged herself to her feet and faced him.

"I said – do you understand me?"

"Yes, monsieur."

He nodded. "Very well. Be on your way. Expenses are unimportant. Success is essential."

She turned and made her way back to the lift where the doors were standing open again. She would not allow herself to cry while he could see her through the hidden cameras, and it was only when she got back into the car that she broke down in tears.

But that was only for a few minutes. She didn't want anyone to be sent to check why she hadn't already left the underground car park, so she straightened her hair, wiped her eyes and drove back to her flat.

Candice knew now that she hated this violent man who was her boss as well as her lover.

# 16

Philip and Jeanette finally reached the warehouse in Carcassonne, after spending more than an hour trying to find it from the somewhat inaccurate directions she had been given by the young gendarme. Once they were confident they had found the right place, they stayed in the car and watched the building for some time. It was the last unit on the left side of a road near the edge of an industrial estate in the western suburbs of the city. Immediately past the warehouse, there was a fence with a gate leading into a field of growing wheat. None of the other units in the road appeared to be occupied. There were no vehicles in sight. Philip noticed a couple of street lights as they approached, but there were no other lights or security cameras on the front of any of the buildings or on the forecourts. It didn't look to him, to be the kind of place where one would hide a priceless collection of treasures.

He asked, "Are you sure that this is the right place at last?"

"I'm absolutely certain. Look at the front door. It has dark green and white diagonal stripes on it, just as young Robert said."

"There are several units with roller-shutter doors like that."

"But this is the only one on this road painted that colour, and it's at the end of the road just as he told me."

Philip noted the place was a modern unit, constructed from block walls about eight feet high. It was topped with another ten feet or so of corrugated metal sheeting. The roof looked as though it was made from the same material laid to a shallow slope. There didn't seem to be any windows in the walls. He guessed any daylight was let into the unit through translucent plastic panels in the roof, which couldn't be seen from the road. The only break he could see in the walls was the large roller-shutter door, which was big enough to admit trucks and vans to the unit. The warehouse wasn't very large, but it would certainly be able to accommodate the four treasure vans which Jeanette had been told about.

"There doesn't seem to be anybody around," he said. "In fact, the whole area seems absolutely deserted."

She shrugged. "Well, they probably chose this place for that reason. They wouldn't want anybody watching while they were sorting through the treasure."

"I suppose I'd better take a look at the place." Philip opened the car door.

"I'll come with you."

"No. You stay here and keep watch. Give a couple of toots on the horn if anyone turns up."

He got out and walked towards the building. He noted this was different from the adjacent plots. There were no weeds around the area at the front, which suggested somebody might have been here recently to clean the place up. Otherwise, the whole area seemed deserted. He agreed that whoever had removed the treasure from le Bézu, had certainly chosen somewhere out of the way to hide it – if it really *was* here.

With a quick glance to check that he was unobserved, Philip went up the narrow path beside the warehouse. To his right was a six-foot-high fence, partly overgrown on the other side with climbing weeds, beyond which was a field of young wheat. A large tree stood in the field just outside the fence near the back of the unit, its lower branches brushing the corner of the roof.

Round the back of the warehouse there was the concrete path and a ten-foot-wide strip of rough grass before the same fence continued. Beyond that was a copse of young trees. This unit was obviously at the far corner of the industrial estate. He saw that the rear wall had a single steel door in the middle. He went to it and tried the handle, but it was clearly locked into its rigid frame. There was no easy way in through that door without the key.

Philip continued to the far corner from where he could see back to the road. This side of the warehouse was just another blank wall, with a narrow strip of ground and a fence about four feet high between this and the next property. He went back to look at the tree.

He decided he would need a short ladder to start him off but, once he was ten feet up, it was eminently climbable. From there it should be possible to get on to the roof. The question was whether he would be able to cut a hole in the corner to gain access into the warehouse and then to climb down inside to investigate the contents. He could see no sign that the place had an alarm system.

He pondered for only a moment whether he should commit the clear offence of breaking in and entering a building in order to see what was inside. However, he had already come a long way in his search for Jackie. He didn't really expect to find her imprisoned against her will in this isolated spot. Nevertheless, he hoped he might get some clues as to what had happened to her. Philip decided he couldn't turn back now. He had to find out what was in the warehouse. Full of thought, he returned to the car.

"Did you find anything?" asked Jeanette as he got in.

"There's nothing obvious from outside," he said. "But I want to take a look inside the place. Can you find your way to a do-it-yourself store?"

She grinned. "Are you thinking of breaking in?"

"I don't want to go away without at least checking the place is empty."

"That's my man of action." She patted his arm. "I saw a *bricolage* in the commercial estate the other side of the main road. I'll direct you."

He started the car, turned round and drove back to the spine road through the estate. They followed the signs to the *Centre Commercial* and found the place he wanted in only a few minutes. Jeanette insisted on accompanying him as he walked round the huge store selecting the items he needed. He ended up with a folding ladder, the most powerful cordless drill he could find and a good range of drill bits to fit it. There was also a large pair of tin snips, a coil of duct tape, a torch, leather gloves and a bag to put it all in (except the ladder). They took their equipment back to the car to check it out. It was then they discovered that the battery in the drill hadn't been charged.

After some thought, Philip decided the only solution was to book a room at the cheap hotel on the commercial estate, and stay there for four hours while the battery was charged up. He found it slightly embarrassing, with Jeanette by his side, to book the room for one night carrying only a small bag containing the tools. By the time they got to the room she was giggling.

"You know what the receptionist was thinking," she said.

"I know. The usual purpose of two young people booking into a hotel in the middle of the afternoon without luggage is to have sex." He busied himself with plugging in the charger and starting it going.

"How long does it take to charge the battery?"

"Four hours."

"That is good," said Jeanette. "We can find lots to do for the next four hours?"

He waved a brochure at her. "I want to study the map of Carcassonne so that I can find my way round the place on my own."

"That will not take four hours."

"So – perhaps I will have a rest as well.

She grinned cheekily. "I will rest on the bed with you."

"We'll have one side each."

"Very well. I will take the side near the window." She kicked off her boots, stripped off her outer clothes and stretched out on the bed, clad in nothing but her bra and panties.

It took Philip a long time to concentrate on the street map of Carcassonne.

# 17

Philip and Jeanette returned to the warehouse unit on the outskirts of the industrial estate at ten minutes after midnight. They were both dressed in dark clothes. Jeanette had her jacket buttoned up to the neck and her jeans were tucked into short high-heeled boots. Philip's clothing was more relaxed but ready for the expected action ahead. The whole industrial estate was dark and deserted when they parked the car in the forecourt of the empty warehouse unit opposite their target and switched off the car lights. There was a single street light half-way back to the junction which gave only a small amount of light to the scene. Jeanette was again left in the car to keep watch while Philip extracted his bag of tools and the folding ladder from the boot.

He walked over to the field and found the gate was chained up and padlocked. However, after a quick look round to confirm that he was unobserved, he had no trouble in climbing over it and making his way along the edge of the field towards the corner of the warehouse. When he reached the tree, there was just enough light to unfold the ladder and set it against the trunk. He put on the gloves, hooked the bag over his shoulder and started to climb. From the top of the ladder, he worked his way carefully up through the branches until he was suspended directly above the corner of the building. He leaned down and dropped the bag the three feet or so on to the roof, then lowered himself on to the corrugated metal sheeting which easily took his weight. He paused for a second before he started his next undertaking. What he was about to do was definitely illegal, but he was nevertheless determined to continue.

He removed the drill from the bag and checked again that it was fully powered up. Then he took out one of the two drill bits, which he had selected as being the best for his purpose, from an inside pocket of his anorak and fitted it into the chuck and tightened it. Next, he started to drill a pattern of holes in the aluminium sheet in order to form an opening large enough to get his body through. Although the drill was very quiet, it still seemed to make a lot of noise in the silence of the night, particularly the screech as the bit was withdrawn from each hole.

When he had drilled half a dozen holes, he was able to insert the tin-snips, and cutting through the thin metal with these was a lot quieter. After half an hour he had cut three sides of a flap of metal which he was able to fold back to gain access. He took his torch from his pocket and shone it through the hole.

Philip discovered that by cutting the hole near the corner of the roof, he had only just missed the end of the last roof truss. That was constructed of much heavier structural steel and was painted a dark red. However, he thought he could still lower himself through the restricted hole he had made. But, before he did that, he shone the torch round the interior of the warehouse to see what it contained.

The answer was absolutely nothing. There was no sign of any large vans or, indeed, any vehicle at all in the place. There were no storage chests or containers that might have held the treasure. In fact it was quite clear that, whether or not it had been deposited here last Tuesday night as the young gendarme claimed, the treasure had certainly not remained here.

He looked round to see if he could detect any sign, from up on the roof, that it might have been lodged in the place temporarily. He thought he could see tyre marks on the smooth concrete floor which could have been made by the treasure vans, but there was no other sign that the place had been occupied recently. It was then that Philip noticed for the first time that there was a single-storey room in the corner of the unit, possibly intended to be used as an office. Perhaps there would be a clue in there. The problem was how to reach it.

He turned the torch on the metal walling below his corner. He saw the roof was supported by steel columns which extended the whole height of the building. Above the block walls, there were four horizontal rows of heavy angles about five feet apart to which the aluminium cladding was fixed with galvanised hook-clips. Heavy-duty diagonal rods between the columns braced the structure to prevent distortion under wind pressure. The steel angles would easily support his weight and the rods would give him something to hang on to, while he was working his way along to the single-storey room.

Putting the torch in an inside pocket and leaving the bag of tools behind on the roof, Philip lowered himself gingerly through the hole. He had a nasty moment while he scrabbled around with his feet to find an angle to rest his weight on, but he soon found a suitable support. He started to descend carefully towards the top of the block wall, and then edged along to the flat slab which roofed the single-storey room. From there it was easy to jump down to the warehouse floor.

First, he walked all around the main area, using his torch to look for any clues about what had been there and when. However, there seemed to be nothing, except the few tyre marks he had already observed, and it was impossible to tell if they had been made recently. The only clue was that they had been made by cars or medium-sized vans – not large lorries. The other interesting thing was that the floor seemed to have recently been swept clean. There was no litter of any sort in the place.

Finding nothing to help him out here, he tried the single-storey room. The door wasn't locked. He pressed the light switch just inside the door and discovered the electricity was still connected. At the same time as the light came on, an extractor fan high on the outside wall started to hum. He realised he was in what was probably a personnel room. Beside the steel door to the outside was a sink and drainer unit, fed by a single cold tap which emitted water when he turned it on experimentally. He found an internal door on the other side of the sink unit that led into a toilet with a wash basin in the corner.

Philip looked round. Except for the fixed plumbing facilities, there seemed to be absolutely nothing in the place. Then suddenly he noticed something hanging on a hook on the back of the door. He crossed the room to inspect it.

When he took it off the hook, he discovered it was a rather smart jacket. The first thing that struck him was a splendid badge on the outside of the breast pocket. It represented a grey double-headed eagle above a shield and a coat of arms. He slipped his hand into one of the inside pockets and felt something smooth and square. When he pulled it out, he found he was holding a slim leather wallet. With mounting excitement, he started to open it.

At that precise moment the light went out, and Philip was suddenly completely blind. For a second he was disorientated. Then he remembered he'd left his torch on the sink. As he turned towards the steel door, a light came on which shone straight into his face. He raised his hand to shield his eyes and turned away. The next moment he felt a violent pain on the back of his head and he collapsed, unconscious.

# 18

Philip didn't know exactly when it was that he regained consciousness. He found he was lying on his side on the concrete floor. He was still in the same room, the light was on, and the steel door leading to the outside was standing open. A man whom he vaguely recognised, dressed in jeans and a loose jacket, was standing in the doorway leading to the warehouse.

Jean-Luc Lerenard came in and bent over him. He gently patted the back of his head with a handkerchief which he held in his hand. The pain exploded inside Philip's throbbing skull and made him groan.

"Do not worry," said the big man. "It is not serious."

"Did you do this?" demanded Philip.

"I certainly did not. I was following you, but I had difficulty getting through the small hole you had cut in the roof. Look where I have torn my jacket." He straightened up. "By the time I had caught up with you, your assailant had already left."

With some difficulty Philip sat up. Now he recognised the other man. He tried to ignore the throbbing in his head as he pointed to the outside door.

"That door was locked when I tried it earlier."

Lerenard said, "It was open, just as it is now, when I came into the room. I have not touched it."

Another thought occurred to Philip. "There was a blazer hanging on that hook behind the door. It had a magnificent badge on the breast pocket. There was a wallet in the inside pocket."

"Well, it's not here now." The big man went to look in the main warehouse. Then he came back, looked in the toilet and outside the open steel door. "There is no blazer or wallet in this place."

"And you didn't see who attacked me? Did they have a car?"

Lerenard shook his head. "They had already gone when I reached you. I didn't hear a car drive away."

Philip said, "Jeanette must have seen them as they left. Perhaps she was clever enough to take the number."

"Who is Jeanette?"

"Surely you remember Jeanette Picard. She was Armand Séjour's girlfriend. She – er – she was with me because she had been given the directions to find this place, and her French was better than mine," he ended lamely.

"You mean she is waiting outside now?"

"She should be. She was in my car keeping watch to warn me if anybody turned up." Philip scrambled to his feet, his face screwed up with the pain. "She didn't do her job properly. Why didn't she let me know when this character who attacked me arrived?"

"Stay there," said Lerenard. "Run some cold water over your wrists and rinse your face while I go and check."

The fellow returned a couple of minutes later as Philip was clinging to the sink and waiting for the dizziness to pass. "Your woman is not there."

"What?"

"There is no car there. She must have driven away without you hearing."

Philip was astounded. "You mean there's no car parked in the forecourt of the unit across the road?"

"Correct."

"Was it there when you arrived?"

"Yes, but I decided I should park in the next road so that nobody should see that I was following you."

"How did you know what I was going to do?"

Lerenard grinned. "I saw you surveying the place this afternoon and it was obvious you were interested in using the tree to get on to the roof. Then I saw the tools you bought in the *bricolage*. It was not difficult to work out what you were planning."

"I didn't know it was so obvious." Philip shook his head gingerly, but stopped when he discovered it hurt too much. "I wonder what on earth has happened to Jeanette? Perhaps she followed my attacker to find out where he was going."

"That's a possibility. Do you have a way of contacting her?"

"Not at the moment. She doesn't have a mobile phone."

"So you must wait for her to contact you. How will she do that?"

"I suppose, when she finds out where they have gone, she will come back here to pick me up."

"OK. I'll get my car and we will wait for her to turn up." He put an arm round the young man's shoulders. "Come. I will take you outside and you can sit on the low wall at the front while I get it."

Philip allowed himself to be shepherded outside while Lerenard extinguished the light and closed the door. He noticed the mystery assailant had taken possession of his torch. Then he was helped round to the front where he subsided in a heap on the wall.

Lerenard was back in a few minutes in his car, and helped Philip into the front passenger seat. "It will be a good idea if you try to sleep while we are waiting." He showed him how to recline the seat and offered a folded rug as a pillow.

"Meanwhile, I will go and repair the hole in the roof. I see you have brought tape to seal the cuts in the metal from the weather."

"That duct tape won't last for long in heavy rain," warned Philip. "You will need to use a lot to make a good seal."

"Don't worry. I will make sure it will be a long time before they discover they have a hole in their roof."

Philip lay back in the seat and was soon asleep. He was awakened by Lerenard opening the rear door and putting the bag of tools and the folding ladder into the back.

"What's the time?" he asked.

"It's one-thirty." The big man got into the driving seat. "I don't think you can wait any longer for your woman to come back. You need to go to bed. It will take an hour to reach Quillan. When she finds you are not here, she will guess you have gone back to your hotel. You can let her give you her information in the morning."

"We do not have to go back to Quillan. I, have taken a room in a hotel just up the road from here." He reached in his pocket. "This is the key." He managed a brief grin. "We will have to share a double bed but somehow I think I will be safer with you than I would have been with Jeanette."

# 19

Philip woke at seven the next morning, conscious only of a mild headache and a sensation of slight nausea. His colleague had disappeared. However, by the time he had showered and dressed and gone down to the dining room, he found the big man was there drinking coffee.

"Well," said Lerenard, "your girl-friend hasn't turned up here and there's no sign of your car. I've also been back to look at the warehouse. That whole area is deserted. So I think she must have gone back to Quillan."

Philip was starting to feel worried. "I'm surprised she didn't think of coming here first." He shrugged. "Although - perhaps she did. Of course, she wouldn't have had a key to get in and I presume reception wasn't manned."

He grinned to himself. He guessed Jeanette wouldn't enjoy facing a night's discomfort, trying to sleep on her own in his little car. She would probably prefer the idea of driving back to Quillan where she might at least be able to wake somebody up to let her back into her room.

"I'll ring Henri to find out if she is there."

However, the call to the concierge at the Hotel du Chateau elicited the reply, "She did not sleep here last night, Monsieur. Nobody slept here. *You* were not here and even the new – er – gentleman who booked in yesterday morning did not occupy his room."

"Don't worry about him," said Philip. "He is with me. We're in Carcassonne, but we'll be back in an hour or so."

"Very well, Monsieur." Philip could almost hear the contemptuous sniff. "I will await your return."

When he went back to the dining room, he told Lerenard, "Well, she hasn't gone back to Quillan. I'm a bit worried about her. She seems to be the second woman I've lost in a week."

The big man grinned broadly. "Aren't you worried about your car? It ought to be somewhere around the area."

"But where? We can't just drive round the streets looking for it."

"We will go to the police station and see what they have to say."

First of all, they went back to the warehouse unit once again to check whether anyone had called in to the place since last night, but there was still no sign of any activity. When they tried it, they found the steel door remained unlocked. The well-repaired hole in the corner of the roof was virtually invisible.

So it was that, twenty minutes later, Philip found himself sitting outside the central Carcassonne police station while Lerenard went in to check whether there was any news about Jeanette or the car, but he came out again a few minutes later to report that they knew nothing about either.

"I think we can only go back to Quillan," he said. "She won't expect you to spend a second night in Carcassonne. So I expect she will return your car to you at the Hotel du Chateau and explain what she has been doing."

"And if she isn't there?"

The big man shrugged expressively. "Then you will have to think of something else."

"What will I say to Armand if she has disappeared?"

That started Philip thinking laterally. Had Jeanette been planted on him? Perhaps she had reported back to Armand Séjour or to the organisation he represented. He decided he would need to contact the young Parisian to find out. In fact, he needed to speak to Armand in any case, because he should have met Bernard Cambray yesterday on his return from his holiday in the Seychelles. However, he preferred to phone him from the security of his hotel room, so he agreed to return to Quillan.

On the way, he quizzed Lerenard about the man´s reasons for turning up at the warehouse unit.

"It was easy. I had been following you all day."

"How come I never saw you?"

"That sort of thing is my business, and you weren't expecting to be followed. The strange thing is that I never noticed anybody else following you, so I think they must have just come back to collect the blazer and run into you by chance."

Philip rubbed his head gingerly. "They didn't take long to put me out of action."

"Well, once again, you weren't expecting them to turn up."

"So why were *you* following me?"

"I was supposed to be checking that you were all right. Unfortunately I failed in my job. I will have to be more careful in future."

"What's the reason for checking up on me?"

"Mr Sinclair, you obviously don't realise your investigations into the disappearance of Mademoiselle Blontard may be leading you into danger. I am here to try to minimise that danger."

"Why should I be in any danger?"

"That I don't yet know, but your experience last night must have made it clear to you that you are coming into contact with violent people."

"Goodness knows why. All I want to do is contact my fiancée. Why should anybody object to that?"

Lerenard smiled slightly. "It is not as simple as that. I am sure you are also aware that a priceless treasure is involved. That is what interests the people of violence."

"That still doesn't explain why *you* are involved. Who has asked you to look after me?"

"That I cannot tell you, although you may easily guess."

Philip thought about it. He was aware of Lerenard's previous contact with the Roman Catholic Church, who had paid him a substantial sum of money for the Cathar documents he had discovered, but he didn't know why they should be interested in what happened to him now.

"So why has Cardinal Galbaccino sent you?"

"I will say no more." The big man turned and looked straight into his eyes for a second. "All I *will* say, is that I intend to keep close to you for the next few days, whether you wish me to or not."

And Philip had to be content with that.

# 20

They arrived back at the hotel in Quillan just before lunch.

Henri greeted Philip with, "I have two messages for you, Monsieur. One is from a man called Séjour and the other from a woman who said she was phoning from TV France."

Philip took the proffered envelopes from the concierge and opened them. The message from Armand was brief: "Have met Cambray. Ring (and a Paris number)" The other message was similarly short and to the point. It said, "The contractors employed to clear the site at le Bézu are Granviers Frères from Toulouse." The name meant nothing to Philip, so he tucked it in a side pocket and forgot about it.

"I'm going to my room to rest," he announced. "I will be down for dinner at seven." To Lerenard he said. "Thank you for the lift. You are welcome to join me this evening."

He went up to his room and immediately rang the Paris number. It was answered after only a brief interval.

"Hello Armand. It's Philip."

"Philip, good you call me back." He was obviously struggling with his English. "I see Bernard Cambray. He not know where is Mademoiselle Blontard. But I have address. Do you have pen?"

"Just a minute." Philip got out his pen and prepared to scribble on the back of the envelope containing Armand's message. "OK."

"It is Béziers. You know where is that?"

"I think so. It's on the coast about a hundred kilometres from Quillan."

"That is so. Address is Flat 6, 76 Rue de Quercy. He say it used belong her uncle but now she share with aunt. She look after it when she away."

"Do you know the phone number?"

He took it down as Séjour read it out.

"Thank you. Do you know the name of the aunt?"

"Sorry - no."

"I wonder whether it's Tante Charlotte? Jackie mentioned her to me several times."

"You ring her. I sorry, but Cambray say no more."

"I'll go and see her."

There was a brief pause, then Armand asked, "How is Jeanette?"

"Has she been in touch with you?"

"No."

"She hasn't rung you?"

"No."

"Because, Armand, she seems to have disappeared and taken my car with her."

"I not understand?"

Philip made sure he spoke slowly and clearly. "Last night Jeanette and I went to look at a warehouse unit in Carcassonne where she was told the treasure had been taken from le Bézu. I went into the warehouse and found it was empty. However, somebody must have been waiting for me. They banged me on the head and knocked me out. When I recovered consciousness, I found both Jeanette and the car had gone. She hasn't been in touch since."

"*Mon Dieu!*"

"That's why I wondered if she might have rung you, because she didn't know how to contact me. Now I'm back in Quillan, but she still hasn't turned up. She may have seen the people who attacked me. She may have followed them. But that was twelve hours ago. I don't understand why she hasn't been in touch with either of us."

There was a silence at the other end. Then Armand said, "This serious. You cannot look for two on your own. I come help you."

"You're coming to Quillan?" Philip wondered how Armand and Lerenard would get on.

"I not do that. Problem with mayor in Quillan. I stay in Carcassonne where Jeanette has disappeared. This my mobile number. Please write down."

Philip did so.

"You get French mobile. Then you ring and give me the number and we are in touch if we need."

"All right. I'll get one this afternoon."

"This is problem," said Armand seriously. "We both work on this. You ring me tomorrow? We meet – but not in Quillan."

After he had disconnected, Philip realised that he hadn't mentioned Lerenard to Armand. On reflection, he thought that was perhaps a good thing.

After talking to Armand, Philip lay on his bed, tired out. His mind began to turn over the mystery of Jeanette's disappearance, but he was soon asleep. He was surprised at how deeply he slept, forgetting he had only had a short rest the previous night, in addition to the damage he had suffered to his head. He awoke at about five o'clock and felt almost instantly alert. He noted it was a couple of hours before dinner, so he decided to have a shower and a change of clothes.

Refreshed from his shower, he dived into his bag searching for a clean set of clothes. At the bottom of the bag he came across the roll of waxed fabric that he had picked up on his last visit to the treasure room at le Bézu, and which he realised he must have casually tossed into the bag before he went to see Maitre Amboisard. Since then, the pressure of events had caused him to forget about it.

Now he took it out and looked at it carefully. It both smelled and felt very old. The fact that it was tied with a strip of leather gave it an antique feel. He fiddled with the knot for a while, trying to untie it, but time seemed to have cemented the ends together. After a couple of minutes, he tossed it on the bed and left it, while he got dressed. Then he went down to the kitchen to get a sharp knife. Henri was there with the plump cook, Marie.

"What do you want it for?" he asked.

"The laces in my shoes have become knotted and I need to cut out the old ones before I put in the new pair," Philip lied. He had become so suspicious of all the different characters around him, each with their own agenda, that he didn't feel inclined to tell anybody the truth at present.

The cook loaned him one of her special knives with the warning that it was very sharp and he was not to cut towards any part of his body. Philip promised to comply with her instructions.

Back in his bedroom, he found that the knife easily cut through the thin strip of leather and the roll of fabric sprang open. Mindful of the care Jackie had taken when she was opening the Cathar scrolls, Philip was careful in his handling of the roll. He didn't have any cotton gloves, but he took care only to touch the edges of the fabric. He contrived a way of weighting down the top edge of the coil. Then, using a clean handkerchief to prevent his hands from contaminating the document, he carefully unrolled it.

He was slightly disappointed to discover it was only a piece of ragged-edged material about the size of an A4 sheet of paper. He guessed it was parchment. Philip inspected the fabric carefully. It was very smooth. He suspected it was vellum or calf-skin. It was largely covered by handwriting in a beautiful flowing script and had what he assumed was a signature alongside a wax seal at the bottom. He didn't recognise the language in which it was written, but he guessed it might be old Occitan – the same as the journal of his Cathar ancestor, Phillipe de Saint Claire.

He decided, as he still had more than an hour before dinner time, to make as accurate a copy as he could of the document to avoid the need to open it a second time. It was a slow, painstaking business transferring all the details to a sheet of paper. Philip had particular difficulty in exactly copying the signature at the bottom of the sheet and made several attempts before he was satisfied. Similarly, the seal was almost indecipherable, consisting of a misshapen dollop of wax with half of an imprint of a shield that seemed to have slid off the dark red lump. Finally, when he had completed the task, he carefully rolled up the document again, wrapped it round with a couple of his clean socks and returned it to the bottom of his bag. Then it was time to go down to dinner.

He shared a table with Jean-Luc Lerenard. Philip still wasn't sure how much he could trust him, so at first he said nothing about the document he had just copied. However, he was reliant on the big man for transport at the moment, which he seemed willing to provide, so he thought he should tell the fellow something of his plans.

"There is still no news of Jeanette," said Philip.

"And you have no idea where to look for her."

"No. However I have spoken to Armand Séjour who is obviously close to her, and he is coming down to Carcassonne to see if he can find any clues to her whereabouts. I think he will make a much better job of it than I can, so I will leave that search to him."

The big man nodded. "That is wise."

"However, it leaves me without a car."

"You may use my car. That is what I am here for."

Philip eyed him carefully. "Would you be willing to take me to see Abbé Dugard?"

"Dugard? Why do you want to see him?"

Philip was aware that Lerenard had received a short training course with the good Abbé before the Roman Catholic Church had introduced the man to Jacqueline Blontard as a replacement for her murdered senior assistant, André Jolyon. Dugard had been persuaded, against his wishes, to do this, because he already had a high regard for Jackie. The result had been a suspicion of the big man which was partly unjustified.

"I want Bertrand Dugard to translate another document for me."

"What document is that?"

"I won't know until he has translated it."

Lerenard looked at him carefully. He probably understood that the young man was demonstrating his distrust, resulting from what had taken place a couple of weeks earlier. However, he kept silent and Philip continued with a second request.

"Then I would also like to visit Jackie's aunt in Béziers."

"Béziers – in the same day? That will be about three hundred kilometres."

"Or you can take me to Limoux where I expect I will be able to hire a car."

The big man smiled faintly. "No – I will take you to both places. That way I will be able to keep an eye on you."

"The other thing I would like your help on is this. Do you know how to contact the good Abbé to warn him we are coming, and to check that he will be able to meet us?"

The smile broadened. "Yes. I can do that after dinner."

Philip thought how convenient it was to have a fixer to arrange things for him. Since Lerenard said he had been sent to look after him, he might as well be used to the full.

# 21

The next morning they left at about eight-thirty, so that Philip was able to buy his promised French mobile phone in Limoux en-route. They reached the monastery at Prouille a little before ten. They parked in the shade of the beautiful trees which lined the avenue leading to the abbey buildings. Philip led the way through a small side-gate and along a path that took them to the ancient cemetery where the Abbé Dugard was carrying out his archaeological excavations.

Jean-Luc had telephoned ahead as promised and Bertrand Dugard welcomed them outside his modest site hut. His face bore a beaming smile. "How are you, Monsieur Sinclair, and how is Jacqueline?"

"Er – we're not sure," said Philip. "At the moment she has disappeared."

"Disappeared?" The smile vanished. "What has happened to her?"

"I don't know." Philip explained the events since his return to Quillan. "I'm trying to follow every clue I can turn up until I find her. That's why I would be grateful if you could translate this for me." He handed over the piece of paper onto which he had copied the contents of the scroll. "This is a copy I made of an ancient document I found."

"So this is one of your clues, eh?"

The old man took the sheet of paper into his office and spread it out in front of him. He belatedly motioned to his guests to take a couple of seats which stood along the wall of the shed. Philip did so, but Lerenard chose instead to walk outside and look down into the progress of the Abbé's excavations.

Dugard worked his way down the piece of paper, then returned to the top and read it for a second time. Philip watched him carefully until at last the old man looked up.

"Well, this is a copy of a very old document," he said carefully. "I would say, by the style of the writing and the peculiarities of the language, that the original is maybe more than seven hundred years old."

"I found the original. I made the copy as carefully as I could."

The old man's eyebrows went up. "Did you indeed? It seems to me, young man, that you have a remarkable talent for discovering old documents. I was absolutely astonished by the ones which you and Jackie showed me two weeks ago. I would say this one isn't as old, but it is still quite ancient. I hope you are caring for it properly."

"I am doing my best."

"Yes, I am sure you are." Dugard paused. "Well now, this one is written in old Occitan. That language is not a speciality of mine, but I understand quite a lot of it." He looked at Philip over the top of his glasses. "I presume you are aware that Occitan used to be the common language of this area and it is a little surprising to see an important document like this written in Occitan rather than the more official Latin."

Philip sat forward. "You say it is important?"

"Well, it certainly would be to the recipient. It seems to be a receipt for the depositing of goods with the person who has signed the foot of the document here. The signature is rather difficult to decipher, and I notice you have copied it several times together with the adjacent seal. However, from the various clues I can pick up, it could be the signature of a certain Thiebault de Blanchefort. Do you know anything about him?"

"No."

"Well, if it *is* his signature, he was the grandson of the famous Bertrand de Blanchefort who was an interesting person. He was both a Cathar and also the fourth Grand Master of the Order of Templars. You know all about the Cathars and will certainly have heard of the Templars."

"Goodness."

"Yes," said the Abbé. "As far as I can make out, this document says that Thiebault de Blanchefort received seventeen chests of goods and coin from a man called Raymonde de Perella and that he will account for them to the said Raymonde when called upon to do so. It says they will be held securely in the Chateau de Blanchefort until required by the Order. It is not quite clear to me which Order this is referring to."

"That *is* strange wording," agreed Philip.

"The other thing I can tell you is the date. It is the 12th November 1243."

"Isn't that a few months before the Cathars surrendered at Montségur?"

"Indeed it is."

There was a long pregnant pause as the two men looked at each other.

At last Philip said, "That means there's a possibility that this could be the treasure of the Cathars, which was supposed to have disappeared some time before they surrendered. It was rumoured that they had hidden it somewhere, but it was never found. It certainly wasn't in the citadel when they capitulated to the French at Montségur in March 1244."

Lerenard chose this moment to return to the shed.

"Well," he asked, "have you found out what your sheet of paper is?"

"Yes." Philip grinned at him. "It is a copy of a receipt for goods issued by a man called Thiebault de Blanchefort in 1243."

"Ah. Is that important?"

"It may be. This Thiebault de Blanchefort who took the goods into his care may have been a prominent Templar. I understand that storing goods for others was one of the services provided by the Templars."

"I believe that is correct," said Dugard.

"When I was looking at the map of the area the other day, I noticed that the Chateau de Blanchefort is marked." Philip felt the excitement begin to rise in his chest. "I must check where it is. If possible I would like to pay the place a visit tomorrow."

"You should be careful," warned the Abbé. "You may not be the only person to be interested in that chateau if it is a possible repository of the Cathar treasure."

"But nobody else will have seen this receipt."

"That is true, but I have often noticed how difficult it is to keep these things secret."

"I *will* be careful," said Philip, "but I *must* see the place." He turned to Lerenard. "Will you come with me?"

"Try to keep me away." But the big man seemed less than enthusiastic as he turned and stumped out of the shed.

Soon after that Philip offered his grateful thanks to the Abbé and they departed for Béziers.

# 22

Candice Ambré reached Quillan about half-way through the morning. She found a convenient gap to park just round the corner from the Place de Ville, got out of the little car she had hired and carefully locked the door. Then she walked round the corner to the square.

Her appearance had completely changed from the stylish young woman who had left le comte's penthouse in Marseilles twenty-four hours earlier. Now she was dressed in patched jeans and a loose T-shirt. Over this was a floppy brown cardigan which hung open and revealed to anybody who inspected her carefully that she hadn't bothered to wear a bra. On her feet was a pair of well-worn trainers. She had no make-up. Her hair was uncombed and was almost totally covered by a wide-brimmed, tatty straw hat with a large, half-dead daisy stuck in the hat-band. On her right shoulder she carried a small rucksack.

She called into a *chambre d'hôte* almost opposite Quillan's only hotel and hired a room. Candice told the owner who booked her in that she was following the Cathar trail but wished to rest for a couple of nights. She specified that she wanted a room overlooking the square. The woman gave her a hard look but found nothing to object to as long as she paid her fifty euros in advance. Candice went up to her room to plan the next step in her pursuit of Pierre Schmidt and César Renoir.

She already knew a lot about the Renoir woman and the experiences she had been through during the last two weeks. The daughter of a previous leader of *La Force Marseillaise* had been living with a person by the name of Alain Hébert, who had made arrangements with *La Force* to take possession of the treasure, which he had discovered was hidden at the chateau of le Bézu. Candice also knew that Hébert had been killed by a previous senior man in *La Force* called Montluçon and that Mademoiselle Renoir had herself shot the killer in retaliation, before being knifed by another crook in the gang who was now imprisoned at Toulouse. The woman had subsequently spent two weeks recovering in the prison hospital before being released. The question was – where was Renoir now?

The previous day Candice had travelled to Toulouse. She was unable to find any trace there of Pierre Schmidt, but she had unearthed the man known as Josef. He was a local petty criminal who had been paid by *La Force* to watch the prison while César was there. It had been easy to pump the information out of him, using a mixture of sexual allure and *le comte's* money.

"You are sure," she had asked him, "that this young Englishman was the only person to visit Mademoiselle Renoir over the weekend?"

"That place does not have many visitors," Josef replied. "The only occupants are criminals who have been injured during arrest, or fools who have tried to commit suicide. He was easy to finger."

"And you are sure he was English?"

"Of course. He had an English car."

"What sort of car?"

Josef turned out to be an enthusiast when it came to cars. He knew the make and the model and even had a good idea of the year of manufacture. He had recorded the colour and the registration number. Candice had no doubt he could have told her the car's top speed and the fuel consumption if she had asked for it.

"Can you describe the Englishman for me?"

Here Josef was a little less precise. He said the man was young and fair-haired and obviously English. He was quite tall and fairly slim, but Josef was unable to be accurate about these attributes. His clothing was ordinary English – a white shirt beneath a dark jacket with grey trousers and black shoes. He was quite tidy and his hair was brushed to the right. Josef wasn't sure about the colour of his eyes. One thing the thief was certain about was that he carried his wallet deep in an inside top pocket in his jacket, where it would be difficult to pick. Candice had to be content with that summary.

She gave the man his promised fifty euros and thanked him. He offered to buy her a drink but, to his disappointment, she turned him down. He had to be satisfied with the sight of her undulating buttocks in the tight skirt as she returned to her car,

He wasn't to know that she was putting some extra hip movement into the action in order to accentuate her superiority over him.

It seemed most likely to Candice that César had been helped to get away from the Toulouse prison hospital by the young Englishman, even though Josef had only seen him call there once on Sunday morning and was adamant that the man had left the building on his own. However, if he was the person who had spirited César away, where had he taken her? The most likely place would be the house where she had been living with Hébert. There was a good chance she would find Schmidt there as well.

The problem, was that *La Force's* records did not indicate where Hébert's house was located. César had been sent to find the man and to be his link with them, but she had not passed that information back to Marseilles. The culture of secrecy in La Force was working against them on this occasion.

Candice could only hope that the Englishman knew where the woman was and that he would go to see her from time to time. She decided, if that was the case, that she had only to follow him, to be led to her quarry in due course. First of all, however, she had to find the Englishman. He was known to have been staying in Quillan, so that was where she went for a start, making sure she was suitably disguised.

Hitching her rucksack over her shoulder, Candice went out into Quillan's square by the river and took in the scene. It was early in the season and there were only a couple of sight-seeing visitors and a few locals about. The weather was fine but cold, and the two cafés had put out several tables, some of which were occupied by people well-wrapped up against the keen breeze. Ignoring the vacant tables, she crossed the square to the hotel where she entered and ordered a *café Americain*.

The concierge told her that the bar was closed at this time, but he was happy to go downstairs to the kitchen to get one specially made. Candice thanked him and sat in one of the chairs in reception, apparently to wait patiently for her coffee.

However as soon as the concierge had disappeared downstairs, she got up and slipped behind the desk to inspect the register.

Working through the recent pages, she noted that one of the large rooms on the first floor had been occupied by a J. Blontard, whose name had been crossed out and a P. Sinclair had been written over the top. The room was apparently reserved for the next ten days. Another room on the first floor was occupied by a person signed in as J-L Lerenard, who had arrived yesterday and was booked in for a week. A room on the top floor was occupied by J. Picard, who had booked in on Saturday, also for a week. That person did not appear to have taken dinner last night or breakfast this morning. There were no other residents.

Candice returned to her seat to wait for the drink. She presumed that P. Sinclair was the Englishman. The other two were French names. So now she had to find out where Sinclair was at present.

When the concierge came back with her coffee she said, "I am looking for an Englishman called Sinclair. Can you tell me if he is staying here?"

"He is." The man looked at her with interest. "Why do you want to know?"

"I have a message for him."

"Alas," said the concierge. "He is not here at the moment. You can leave the message with me, and I will see he gets it when he returns."

"It is a verbal message." She smiled demurely. "And it is for Mr Sinclair's ears only. When do you expect him to return?"

"Ah! I'm afraid he did not tell me that."

"Do you know where he has gone?"

The man shook his head. "He did not take me into his confidence. All I can tell you is that he went out after breakfast with the man Lerenard. I do not know where they went."

Candice stored away the information that Sinclair and Lerenard were connected in some way.

"When do you expect them to return?"

"That I do not know. As far as I am aware, they will be here for dinner." He raised his head with a trace of insolence. "Do you wish to book in for the meal?"

"That won't be necessary."

"I'm sure he will want to talk to you, if you have a message for him. I believe he is expecting to hear from his – er – his lady-friend."

She recorded the additional little nugget of information. "I will make my own contact with him," she said.

The man sniffed. "Very well, Mademoiselle." He buried his head in a book below the reception desk and pointedly ignored her after that.

Meanwhile, Candice concentrated on finishing her coffee. She would have to keep a long vigil in her room overlooking the square. At least she had a detailed description of Sinclair's car, so there was a good chance of spotting him when he turned up. She also had a tracking device, which she could attach to his rear bumper, to make it easier to follow him while keeping out of sight, when he next left the hotel.

First of all, she would carry out a careful survey of the little town so that she would be ready to decide the best route to take when the Englishman started driving. She hoped he would lead her to César Renoir without being aware of it.

# 23

Béziers is a beautiful city set on a hill above the river. Jackie's large second floor flat was in a post-war block built along one of the streets which circled the city centre. It was only a short walk from the cathedral.

Philip knew the flat had originally belonged to her uncle who had been a professor at the university in the city and who seemed to have been something of a replacement father to her. So far, she hadn't told him about her parents – only about this particular uncle.

Apparently, the old boy had been a specialist in the history of the Languedoc region of Southern France. Although she had seldom talked about him, Philip had gathered, from her occasional comments, that Uncle Albert had proposed certain novel theories about the Cathars and the Templars and their even earlier links to the Visigoths and the sacking of Rome and the theft of the treasures of Jerusalem. It seemed that his academic colleagues had poured scorn on these ideas when he published them, and Jackie had partly blamed this humiliation for her uncle's professional isolation and early death. Philip suspected that she still hoped she would be able to uncover real evidence to support his beliefs.

He had earlier telephoned Jackie's Aunt Charlotte, who shared the flat with her niece, to arrange the visit. So he approached the block of flats in the early afternoon, having abandoned Lerenard in a bistro near the city centre, where he was having a late and rather liquid lunch. Philip was gradually getting to like his enigmatic companion, after spending the best part of the day with him. It was certainly good to feel he had a man like Jean-Luc on his side.

The big man had been happy to let Philip call at the flats on his own, once he had been shown where they were. "I do not expect you to have any trouble here during the daylight hours," he agreed.

So Philip ascended the steps into the entrance hall alone, and rang the bell to flat six. After a short interval a woman's voice came over the speaker.

"*Oui?*"

"*Est-ce que vous êtes Tante Charlotte?* This is Philip Sinclair. Jackie's friend."

"I know who you are." She seemed pleased to greet him. "Take the *ascenseur* to the second floor, Philip, and I will meet you in the lobby."

As he came out of the lift, he found a smartly-dressed, middle-aged lady was waiting for him. She opened her arms and gave him a big hug.

"You are welcome. Jackie has told me all about you."

"Is there any chance that she has been here recently?"

"No. I haven't seen her since she met you." Aunt Charlotte's English proved to be nearly as good as her niece's. "But she spoke to me at some length on the telephone last week. I am so pleased that she has found herself a man who isn't interested in her only because she is wealthy and famous."

"Tante Charlotte – do you have any idea where Jackie might be?"

The lady shook her head. "I thought she was with you until you telephoned earlier."

"Well, she *was* until a week ago."

Philip launched into an explanation of his trip to London, ending with the fact that his fiancée had disappeared by the time he returned.

"I just don't know how to contact her," he ended lamely.

She patted his shoulder. "What a strange tale. It is most unlike Jackie to just disappear like that. She has always been most considerate of any other people who might be involved."

"I'm really worried about her."

"I'm sure you must be. I'm a bit anxious myself, now that you've explained about it to me."

"I was hoping that you might have some idea of where she may be staying. Do you know of any secret hideaway where she might have gone, if she wanted to be alone?"

"There is nowhere that I can think of immediately." Charlotte turned away. "Please come in and sit down. I will get you a cup of coffee."

She settled Philip in a comfortable armchair and bustled off to the kitchen. He looked round the room. It was his first sight of Jackie's home – her escape from the hectic life of the TV star and highly-regarded academic. He noticed there were two large bookcases on opposite walls, a couple of original scenic watercolours by an unknown but talented local artist, a set of comfortable armchairs and a sofa, an unlit gas fire and a large window with a splendid view of the river and the countryside to the south of the city.

Aunt Charlotte came back in with a tray on which were the *cafetière* and cups. There was also a small jug of the evaporated milk which the French seemed to love in their coffee, but which Philip detested. He said he would take his black.

The old lady sat down opposite him. "I've been trying to think of anywhere that she might have gone, but I honestly haven't a clue as to where she may be now. She has always come back here to rest in her quiet periods."

"What about when she was researching a new series?"

"Oh, that is usually done at the company's studios in Paris. I understand there is a hotel almost next door to the company headquarters, and she is allocated a suite there whenever she needs it. You would have to ask TV France about that."

"I have already been to see Alain Gisours, the director of the company who is responsible for producing her next series. He says he doesn't know where she is either. In fact, he's worried that she hasn't yet started work on the new series."

"And when she's working on location," continued Aunt Charlotte, "the whole team is booked into a local hotel so that they can all be together. There is always a lot of pressure to finish the site work as quickly as possible."

"I understand that. Of course, I met her when she working on site near Quillan – at le Bézu castle." Philip scratched his head. "What about her other work – her academic duties?"

"Oh, I don't think she is doing much teaching at present. She still has a professorship at the Sorbonne, but I think it is virtually an honorary position now. I don't think she goes there very often, except for the occasional lecture about the results of her site work."

"Does she have a flat near the university? Presumably she had one when she was working there full-time."

"Oh, yes. But I know that she gave that up a couple of years ago, because she moved a van-load of her papers and other things back here when she started doing her first series for TV France." Charlotte had a sudden thought. "All her papers are in her uncle's study. Would you like to see them?"

"Yes, please."

"The old lady stood up. "Bring your coffee with you. You can drink it while you are looking through her stuff."

Philip followed her back into the hallway by the front door. Charlotte turned to the left through another door. Following her, Philip found himself in a large room which also had a window with a panoramic view to the south. He thought it was the most splendid study he had ever been in.

"This extra room behind the staircase was the reason why Albert chose this flat," she explained. "My brother used to spend nearly all his time in here."

"It is a super place," agreed Philip. "I'm surprised Jackie can drag herself away from it."

"Well, she does spend some time in here when she's at home, but I suppose the room holds sad memories for both of us. I seldom come in here."

"I'm sorry. Would you rather we left?"

Charlotte turned to face him. "I will go, but you are welcome to stay here as long as you wish." She swept an arm round, indicating the bookshelves and filing cabinets. "Have a good look at anything you want to. See if you can find anything which might help you in your search for her. But please don't damage anything or throw anything away and, if you want to take anything with you, please let me know what it is before you go."

"Of course I will."

She left the room, closing the door behind her and leaving Philip free to search the place. First of all, he had a general look round. In front of the window was a large leather-topped desk with a widescreen lap-top computer and a swivelling chair in front of it. To the right of the desk was an armchair and a comfortable-looking sofa with a low coffee table between them. That area was no doubt intended for relaxing and reading.

Against the wall to the left of the desk was a row of filing cabinets and a large photo-copier. The other three walls were mainly covered with floor-to-ceiling bookshelves almost completely filled with a wide variety of books from popular novels to academic tomes. The shelving was only interrupted by the doorway and three spaces where more of the water-colour scenes were hung. The furnishings were completed by a couple of strong upright chairs which Philip guessed were often used as steps to reach the higher shelves. There was also a comfortable, though not luxurious, patterned carpet on the floor. She could doubtless have held a decent party in the large clear area in the middle of the room.

The sheer size of the study was almost overwhelming. Philip was uncertain where he should start his search. The desk seemed the most obvious place, so he walked across and sat in the leather-upholstered executive chair. The top of the desk was clear, except for the computer which was switched off and probably would need a password to start. So he tried the drawers. The centre one contained a variety of pens and other office equipment. The shallow drawer on the right seemed to contain various publications and a number of maps and street plans. He opened these to check if any locations were marked which might indicate addresses of interest to her, but he had no luck there.

The drawer on the left was filled with mainly blank sheets of paper although some had addresses printed on them. There were papers with Jackie's personal Béziers address, and that of the now defunct Sorbonne flat, TV France and her agent, Bernard Cambray, whom Philip had met. He took two of each and laid them on the desk-top.

He turned his attention to the deep drawer on the left side. This contained filed and annotated records of her various archaeological digs and TV series. He observed that Jackie was obviously a very well-organised person in her professional life. A quick check through the files revealed, that in addition to the Louvre, Egypt and the one planned for the Cathars, she had also spent some time investigating the Normandy war graves (which he already knew about) and evidence of the Templars and the Visigoths in Languedoc.

Most of the stuff in this drawer appeared to be records of the actual work she had done and did not include research papers, so he transferred his attention to the deep drawer on the right. This seemed to be totally filled with summaries of research into her uncle's theories. Philip had a hunch that Jackie's disappearance might have had something to do with the old man's beliefs. He noted there was a lot of cross-referencing to cabinets and drawer letters and numbers. That led him to get up and start looking into the filing cabinets which were conveniently unlocked.

Sure enough, five of the cabinets were filled with documents, annotated publications and other papers where the writing and the added notes were in a different hand from Jackie's. He could only presume they were written by her uncle. Once again, they were neatly filed and tabulated, and no doubt she had been able to find her way through them without difficulty. However, with his limited knowledge of French, they meant little to Philip.

The next three filing cabinets were filled with her researches into her three TV series. He opened the top drawer, the one labelled Cathar, with a degree of increased anticipation. Maybe this would provide him with some useful clues. However, a fairly quick leaf through the papers failed to reveal anything which might give him an idea of where she might be now. As a result of his struggles to understand what the various files were about, he promised himself that he would start a course to improve his French as soon as this business was over.

Much of the paperwork consisted of computer print-outs of her research, and photocopies of documents and extracts from journals. There were also sheets of references to relevant points in books which she must have trawled through, and which were probably located on various shelves in the bookcases around the room. Once again, it was all neatly filed and cross-referenced and he was beginning to understand the amount of detail Jackie went into before she started a series.

The only thing he did find on his second check through the drawers was a list of contact names with their phone numbers, which she obviously thought were important. This sheet was right at the front of the top drawer and Philip had missed it when he first started looking through the cabinet. He ran his finger down the list of names, trying to decide whether any of them would be able to help him. It would be a big job to try and contact everyone. Most were located in France, but two were in the Lebanon, one in Israel and one in Egypt. In the end he decided to take a copy. When he switched it on, the photocopier started up easily enough, but its noise brought Aunt Charlotte back into the room.

Philip explained what he was doing. He gave her the copy to look at while he put the original back in the cabinet.

"Do any of the names mean anything to you?" he asked.

She carefully checked through the list before shaking her head. "No, I don't think so."

"Well, if you don't mind, I'll take this copy away with me. Maybe I'll try to contact some of the names at the top of the list to see if they are able to help me with anything they remember about her."

Philip also explained that he was taking some of the letter-headed paper, "So that I've got the information if I want to get in touch with them."

"Is that all?"

"Yes. To be honest, I'd need a month to search through this lot thoroughly. And I'd also have to improve my French a lot."

She smiled. "As far as I am concerned you can continue looking for as long as you like. I can even put you up overnight if you wish."

"Thank you, but no. Not this time. I left my driver in a bistro in the town square more than an hour ago. He'll be wondering what's happened to me."

She rested a hand on his arm. "But you *will* keep in touch with me, won't you? I'm as anxious as you are to find out what has happened to Jacqueline."

"Of course I will."

"You know where I am and you have the telephone number on that piece of paper. Please come back any time you wish,"

"I will. Thank you."

"Can I get in touch with *you* if I think of anything else or hear of anything that might help."

"Here is my number." He took out his new mobile and gave her the number, which she wrote down. "Well, Tante Charlotte, I hope to speak to you soon."

With that, he left her and set out to find Lerenard.

118

# 24

Jeanette was in a dreadful state. She still didn't quite understand why she had behaved so stupidly. Why on earth had she agreed to go with the bloke? If questioned, she would no doubt excuse herself by saying she didn't have much choice. Also, if she had been honest, she might have admitted there was a desire to prove to Philip that she could do something useful that would impress him. However she wasn't used to practising self-analysis.

On Monday night she had been sitting in the passenger seat of the little sports car opposite the industrial unit in Carcassonne for what seemed like hours, while Philip was trying to find a way into the building. She was struggling to stay awake on her watch. In fact, she was not doing her job very well. That was why she was completely surprised by the driver's door of the car suddenly opening. She hadn't even been aware that there was anybody approaching the car. Her sleepy eyes cleared, and she looked up expecting to see Philip. Instead, it was another man.

"Remember me?"

Startled, she stared at him. "It's Gaston, isn't it – Gaston Lesmoines?"

"Right first time."

From what she could see of him, he was short and swarthy with a dark moustache and a slight lisp. He was dressed all in black, the sweater stretched tight over his muscled upper body. She remembered him as one of the archaeologists who had been working on the excavations at le Bézu. In fact, she seemed to recall that the man had nursed ambitions to become Jacqueline Blontard's personal assistant - a hope which had been destroyed by Philip's arrival in Quillan.

"What are *you* doing here?"

He slipped into the driver's seat without replying and pulled the door quietly shut behind him. "Shush," he whispered.

"Why? Does Philip know you're here?"

"Not yet."

She stretched across to the steering wheel so that she could sound the horn to warn him that he was not alone, but Gaston caught hold of her hand before she could reach it.

"Wait." His grip was like a vice. "Your friend is being followed."

"What do you mean?"

"He has cut a hole in the corner of the roof to get into the warehouse and he has gone down inside the place. But somebody else has just followed him into the building."

"How do you know that?"

"I have been trailing the man. It is Jean-Luc Lerenard. Do you remember him?"

"Lerenard? Of course I do. He was the new man who turned up to take over as Jackie Blontard's number two when André Jolyon was killed." She took a frightened breath. "He's a tough guy. What is *he* doing here?"

"I do not know. I think he is the man employed by the Catholic Church to investigate various things they have taken an interest in. He has been following you all day. He sat outside your hotel for more than four hours while you and Philip were in there."

"Really?" She caught her breath. "Why would he do that?"

"I think he must have a very good reason." Gaston's voice was deep and low. "By now he will have confronted your lover. Philip will have to deal with him from now on. We should go before the man comes out and you are forced to do whatever he wants."

"What does that mean?"

"I think he wants you to lead him to the treasure."

"If it is in the warehouse, he will have found it."

"It isn't."

It didn't occur to Jeanette to ask how Gaston knew that. She said, "I don't think Philip knows where it is either."

"But Lerenard knows you are looking for it. He thinks you must have had a reason to come to this place."

"Shouldn't we go into the warehouse and help Philip?"

Gaston shook his head. "The man has a gun. We can help your lover best by finding the treasure ourselves. Then we will be able to negotiate with Lerenard."

"But how on earth are we going to be able to do that?"

"Ah." He tapped his nose. "I know where it is. I will show you how to find it."

"Why would you do that?"

"I don't want to have anything to do with the treasure. It is much too dangerous for me to be involved. Everybody knows about this treasure. Nobody can get away with it. The police will make sure of that. I just want to pass on the information and then fade into the background. As far as I am concerned, you can be the person who tells the world about it."

The picture of being the centre of public attention swam in front of Jeanette's eyes. Armand would be impressed. Most of all, Philip would be pleased with her. But she was still suspicious.

"How do you know where it is?"

"I was watching when it was moved. I followed the vans at a safe distance."

"Was Mademoiselle Blontard there?"

"I don't know. I didn't get close enough to see who was involved."

"So where is this treasure now?"

"I will take you there. Then you can drive back to your hotel and return Philip's car to him and tell him what you have found."

"What do we do about Philip getting back to Quillan?"

"He will be all right. He will deal with Lerenard. I will not share my information with Lerenard. When they see that Philip's car has gone, they will go back to the Hotel du Chateau. You will meet them there."

"What – both of them?"

"Lerenard has also booked a room at the hotel in Quillan."

He switched on the ignition. The engine started at the first attempt and ticked over quietly. He took off the handbrake, gently let out the clutch and they rolled down the road. It all happened so suddenly that Jeanette felt unable to do anything else but let him lead the way. Once they had turned the corner into the estate's spine road, Gaston accelerated. Ten minutes later they were following the ring road round Carcassonne.

Jeanette realised too late that she should not have fitted in so easily with Lesmoines' plans. But, by the time she had absorbed his promise about taking her to find the treasure, they were already too far down the road. If she made a fuss now, he might agree to drop her by the roadside, but that would mean she was abandoned in the middle of the night many kilometres from anybody who could help her. And, if Gaston really knew where the treasure was, she might be able to help Philip immeasurably in his quest to find Jackie.

So she kept quiet, watched the darkened countryside and made a note in her mind of the road signs they passed and the distances from towns whose names she recognised. However, it soon became clear to her that Gaston was taking the road back through Limoux towards Quillan.

After they'd been driving for about an hour, they reached a little town called Couiza. Here they turned off on a steep road which led up through pine forests. The road was narrow and wound uphill with a number of sharp hairpin bends. Jeanette thought it would have been a demanding road for the treasure vans to follow.

When they had ascended this road for a couple of kilometres, it suddenly levelled out and they found themselves in a little village on top of a hill. There were no street lights or any other signs of occupation. Gaston turned off the road, went through a dusty square and pulled up under a lean-to roof. Jeanette looked round. As far as she could tell, they were among some farm buildings with various items of equipment in them. Across a rough, grassy area behind a fence were the semi-ruined remains of a chateau, perhaps three or four storeys high.

Lesmoines switched off the car lights and blackness descended upon them. There didn't seem to be any other lights or signs of life anywhere. Suddenly Jeanette was afraid.

"Is this the place where the treasure is supposed to be hidden," she asked in a quavering voice.

"It is."

"So what do we do now?"

"We go inside."

"Inside where?"

He indicated the dilapidated building in front of them. He took the ignition keys and put them in his pocket.

"What are we going to do with Philip's car?"

"It will be quite safe here. We can return it to him tomorrow. Quillan is not far away."

"I wonder what has happened to him."

"He will be quite safe as long as he co-operates with Lerenard. I don't think the man has any bad intentions towards him." He turned to her. "Now, we need to go inside."

Jeanette stayed in her seat. "Is there anybody in this place?"

"I don't know. I hope not."

"Where are we?"

"This village is called the Castereau. It is just a few unused buildings and a castle"

"It isn't much of a place, is it? It looks half-ruined."

"It is only partly ruined. The other side of the chateau and the basement are still habitable."

"And the village seems to be deserted."

"It is, at night. The people who own land up here prefer to live down in the valley and only come up during the day. Now, come with me and I will show you the purpose of our visit."

Somewhat unwillingly, Jeanette got out of the car and Lesmoines took her arm.

"This is the way."

He led her to a gate in the fence and opened it for her to enter. Jeanette held back. This seemed to her, in a strange way, to be the moment of decision and she wasn't at all sure that she wanted to continue.

"You go first," she suggested.

"No." He grinned as he pulled a small automatic out of his pocket. "I insist that you go first."

The shock of seeing the gun made Jeanette go cold, but she wasn't going to let him scare her into submission. She summoned as much bravado into her voice as she could.

"You wouldn't dare to use that thing."

"Would I not?"

He aimed the gun to one side of her head, slipped off the safety catch and pulled the trigger. There was a sharp report, and she felt the wind of the bullet passing her face. Her mouth dropped open and her whole body trembled.

"Don't bother to scream," he said. "There is nobody here to listen to you. Now, please go ahead of me and open that door."

It was a severely shaken Jeanette who made for the door in the side wall of the chateau which he indicated. She stumbled slightly on the rough stone path. The threshold was up a single step. When she pressed down on the handle, the door swung silently open on well-oiled hinges. She passed through a short, stone-lined corridor and came out into the central courtyard. This was surrounded by the castle buildings which were three storeys high.

As Lesmoines had said, the part of the castle facing her seemed to be in good repair with glass in the windows. He directed her to a door straight across the courtyard and Jeanette, all sense of resistance now extinguished, followed his instructions. Again, the door opened easily, and she found herself in a substantial hallway with a staircase in front of her. Lesmoines switched on the light, and she heard a generator start up somewhere nearby. The bulb flickered for a moment, then steadied into a bright light.

"Go round to the back of the stairs," he told her.

There were stone steps behind the staircase leading down into the basement. As instructed, she descended to the lower floor, turned right along a corridor and was pushed into what appeared to be an empty storeroom.

"I'll be back in a minute."

The light was switched on, the door was closed, and she heard a key turn in the lock. She looked round the room which seemed quite clean and dry. The stone-vaulted ceiling was high and there was a small window just below it, well out of her reach. Otherwise, the place was featureless – just plain stone walls with the single door behind her through which she had entered. There wasn't even anywhere to sit.

A few minutes later, she heard a dragging sound. There was the noise of the key turning and the door swung open again. Lesmoines heaved in two straw bales and dropped them in front of her. He took a clasp knife from his pocket and cut the binding twine on one of them.

"This will have to do for your sleeping for tonight. I've got something for you to eat and drink. I'll bring it in a minute."

Once again, the door was locked behind him and Jeanette sat down dejectedly on the solid bale. What was she going to do? Could she find a way to escape?

Lesmoines was soon back. He brought a couple of baguettes, which proved to be stale, a mug, a plastic container of water and a bucket.

"This will have to do for now," he said sourly. "I've got to go and sort out some things, but I'll be back again as soon as I can."

"Are you going to leave me here all on my own?"

"You'll be quite safe. I will keep the keys." he paused. "Don't waste your energy shouting for help. Nobody will hear you."

The door closed behind his departing back with a hollow click.

Since then she had remained in her prison for two days and two nights. During the daytime light came in from the castle courtyard, but the small window was too high up for her to see anything other than sky. She couldn't reach the cill and, even if she could, she saw that it was glazed with wire-reinforced glass so there was no chance of escape. She had tried calling but there had been no response, as he had warned her. He brought her fresh food and water every day and he emptied the bucket, but he refused to answer any questions.

"Don't worry," he told her. "You're quite safe. You'll be released as soon as certain arrangements have been made."

Despite her bursts of rage or tears when he came, he would tell her no more, so she had to make do with that.

# 25

Philip and Jean-Luc Lerenard set off after breakfast next morning to go to the Chateau de Blanchefort. Philip had consulted the large-scale map he had of the area. He discovered the castle remains were located on top of a prominent, forested mountain about half a mile from the Arques road. However, no roads went close to the actual castle and, because of the extremely precipitous nature of the mountainside below the chateau, they had to park in Rennes-les-Bains and climb a steeply-rising footpath for at least two miles to reach the chateau.

Philip had a rucksack in which they had packed a couple of litres of water and some chocolate to sustain them on the climb. Lerenard grumbled that they were going to need every bit of sustenance. It was slightly surprising and amusing to discover that the big man, who seemed such a strong individual in other ways, wasn't looking forward to walking a couple of miles up a steep path.

"You don't *have* to come," said Philip. "It's quite isolated up there and I doubt if I'll meet anybody, so I shan't be in any danger."

"I will go with you," replied Jean-Luc humourlessly.

The weather was dull, with lowering clouds in the west and gusty winds when they started out. They followed the road north for about half a mile while Philip kept a lookout for the start of the path. They came upon it suddenly, just before a bend.

The track led up a steady gradient through thick woods, and then bent round the head of a small side valley. On the other side of the gully it started to climb steeply up the edge of a big hill, still in dense woodland. After a further mile or so, the going became less steep and Philip agreed to a break for a drink of water.

"This chateau seems to be a long way off the beaten track," complained Lerenard.

"Yes. I can't imagine they would carry all that treasure up here," agreed Philip. "To do that would take a regiment of fit men."

"Perhaps there's another route that you can drive vans up."

"If there is, it's not shown on the map."

To prove his point, Philip burrowed inside his rucksack and pulled out the folded sheet of paper which he opened. "Look at this." He showed it to the big man. "Can you see any roads? The nearest one indicated is a narrow road from the west, but that only leads to the farm." He pointed at it. "And it's at least two kilometres from there to the castle."

"What date is the map?"

Philip opened it out and searched for that information. He found it near the bottom corner.

"Here it is – it was last up-dated in 2000."

"The road may have been extended since the map was printed."

Philip shrugged. "Possibly. We'll find out when we get there, but the treasure would have been brought here centuries ago." He put away the water and shouldered the rucksack. "Come on. It's only another kilometre or so."

The forest thinned out now they were higher on the mountain and the ground was sloping less steeply. A quarter of an hour later they were approaching their objective, but when they got there, heading into the wind through waist-high scrub, they found it was hardly more than a large heap of stones on a bleak hill-top.

"This is a waste of time," grunted Lerenard.

Philip climbed on to one of the partly tumbled-down walls and looked around. "What a fantastic position. The views all round are tremendous."

"You don't hide treasure where there is a good view of the place from the surrounding countryside."

"No," he admitted. "And there's no sign of any road leading up here and I can't see any underground locations where they might have been able to hide all that stuff."

"We're just wasting our time," the big man repeated. "Are you sure the piece of paper the Abbé translated for you said it was the Chateau de Blanchefort where the treasure was stored."

"Wait a minute. I've got my translation of the receipt here."

Philip took off his rucksack, unzipped it and rummaged inside. Triumphantly, he pulled out a folded piece of paper, which he opened carefully to prevent the wind tearing it. He read through it quickly.

"Yes. Here is the important bit. It says there were seventeen chests of goods and coin which would be held securely in the Chateau de Blanchefort."

He handed it over to Lerenard to read. Jean-Luc did so and snorted. "Of course, that was nearly eight hundred years ago. A lot must have changed since then." He shrugged. "But it certainly isn't here any more."

"Well, I'm going to have a good look round. Perhaps there are more remains of the chateau in among the surrounding woods. Now we've come up here, we might as well at least give the place a proper check-over."

Somewhat reluctantly Lerenard agreed, and they set out to search the area thoroughly, taking half each. Philip had chosen the more level, less wooded area on top of the hill and he returned after half an hour, without any success. It seemed clear to him that, if the treasure had ever been hidden in the Chateau de Blanchefort, it was not here any longer. He sat down and waited for his companion to return.

Suddenly, he heard a sharp squeal which brought him to his feet. Surely that couldn't be Lerenard. He looked uncertainly at the woods from where the noise seemed to have come, and wondered what could have caused it. They had seen no humans since they left Rennes-les-Bains. It didn't sound like the cry of a bird. He wondered for a moment if it might be something like a wild boar. But, as he stood irresolute, Jean-Luc emerged from the forest half-dragging a protesting young girl. He led her over to Philip.

"I caught this one hiding behind a tree. I think she has been following us and watching what we are doing."

The girl, who appeared to be in her early twenties, was dressed in rough walking gear and a straw hat. She burst into a long string of French, from which Philip gathered she was denying Lerenard's accusations.

"In that case," said her capturer, who was keeping a firm grasp of her right arm, "why did you try to hide behind a tree when I first caught sight of you."

"Because you frightened me, you great brute. You're enough to frighten anybody." She wriggled in his grip. "Will you please let me go?"

Philip tended to sympathise with her. He wasn't sure he would have been happy suddenly to bump unexpectedly into Jean-Luc in a remote area like this.

"What are you doing here?" he asked. "Not many people come here, especially in unpleasant weather like this."

She threw back her head and he noticed she had a small mole high on her right cheek. "I am walking the Cathar Trail. Why can't a person walk along a national footpath without being molested by strange men?"

"*Is* this the Cathar Trail?" Philip unfolded his map again to check. After a while he said, "I'm afraid you're a long way from the Cathar Trail. That's about seven kilometres south of here – the other side of le Bézu. In fact, I think you must be lost because none of the national footpaths come through this area."

He proffered the map for her to look at and was slightly amused to see that she didn't have the least idea where to look. He suspected this was the first time she had even seen the map.

"Have you got a copy of this?" he asked.

"No."

"Well, no wonder you're lost. I suggest you get one when you reach the next town on your itinerary. Which way are you going?"

"What do you mean?"

"Are you heading for Quillan or Bugarach?"

"Er." She hesitated, "I'm going to Quillan."

"Well, you've got a very long day's walk ahead of you. We'll be driving back there after lunch. We can give you a lift if you like." He looked at his companion. "Is that all right with you, Jean-Luc?"

The big man eyed the girl suspiciously. "I think we should leave her to get out of the mess on her own."

"That's a bit unfair."

"Don't bother about me." The girl tossed her head. "I can look after myself. Now - will you please leave me alone?"

"On your way then." Lerenard let go of her arm. "Just make sure you don't come snooping around us again."

129

"Huh." With another toss of her head the girl turned her back on them and set off down the path back towards Rennes-les-Bains. Philip watched her go with a troubled expression.

"It seems to me that she hasn't a clue about where she's going, and she doesn't know how to read a map. She'll get thoroughly lost, and this is wild country to be wandering around in after dark."

Lerenard snorted. "That one isn't walking the Cathar Trail. That was just something she invented when I caught her snooping after us. I think she's been sent to spy on us by somebody who's hoping we're going to lead them to the treasure."

"You've just got a strong imagination, Jean-Luc." Philip smiled. "That girl's not clever enough to snoop on us."

"If you don't believe me, we'll follow her now and see where she goes."

"All right, we might as well. I think we've drawn a blank here."

Philip closed the rucksack and shouldered it again and they set off back towards Rennes-les-Bains, with Lerenard leading. He set quite a fast pace for the first mile and Philip had difficulty keeping up with him. Then he suddenly halted.

"There's the girl on the path along the other side of the valley." He pointed. "Duck down behind the bushes. She's just coming to a clear stretch and I don't want her to see us."

They crouched by the side of the path. Sure enough, the girl came into view about two hundred yards away. She kept pausing to look behind her, obviously checking to see if she was being followed. She didn't seem to be concentrating on where she was going. Philip found himself becoming as suspicious of her as his companion.

Further down the path she disappeared again, and the two men followed her. Once again Lerenard took the lead. It wasn't long before they reached the road where he called a halt while they were still screened by the trees. He went ahead to check the girl's progress.

When he returned he told Philip. "She's walking down the road into Rennes-les-Bains. We'll wait a couple of minutes and then we'll follow her."

Ten minutes later, they reached the car park on the outskirts of the little town where they had left their car.

"Don't look round or take any notice of my car." Jean-Luc instructed. "We'll go straight into the town and find somewhere to have lunch."

However, as soon as they were seated in a local bar, Lerenard said, "I will leave you for ten minutes. I am going back to see if I can find the girl." And he left Philip to order his own food.

In fact, it was nearly half an hour later when he returned and slid into the seat opposite.

"Did you find her?"

The waiter arrived at that minute. Jean-Luc gave his order and paused for the man to depart before he replied. "She was sitting in her little Peugeot just across the road and keeping watch on my car. That is bad news. It means she has certainly been following us. She must know a lot about us – where we came from and what we've been doing for the last few days. I think we must go back to Limoux as soon as we can and hire you a new car."

"But won't she just follow us?"

Lerenard allowed himself a brief grin. "She may try, but she won't get far."

"Why not?"

"I have put a screw into the wall of her rear tyre just above the tread and made sure it is loose enough to come out again quite easily. As soon as she starts driving the screw will fall out and the tyre will go flat. She will need a new tyre before she can go far."

Philip absorbed what the big man said. "Did you do that while she was sitting in the car?"

"Yes. She was parked with the rear wheel against the kerb and there was a steep bank sloping down behind the kerb. It was easy but slow work."

"How do you know it will come out as you expect?"

"I learned the trick many years ago from a man who was in the *Résistance*. He was full of all sorts of little tricks. He showed me how to do it properly. I have used that trick several times before and it has always worked." He took a breath.

"Now, eat up and we will be on our way. We need to get to Limoux as soon as possible."

It all worked out just as Lerenard had planned. They made their way back to the car, ignoring the small Peugeot across the road with the girl huddled down low in the driver's seat. They set off, driving as though on a gentle journey back to Quillan. Presumably she started out to follow them at a safe distance, but they didn't see her again.

# 26

When they arrived back in Quillan in the mid-afternoon they were driving in two separate cars. However, Lerenard was taking no chances. He led Philip to a place on a road the other side of the river, where he told him to park the newly-hired vehicle.

"We will leave your car here and both arrive back at the hotel in my car," he instructed. "If the girl has returned, she will think we have been together all the time, although she will not know where we have been."

They parked Jean-Luc's car in the town square as before. When they got to the hotel Philip was feeling weary, and he informed his companion that he was going to take a rest. Lerenard was happy to agree that they should have a break and meet for dinner. The concierge handed Jean-Luc his key and went back to the cabinet to get Philip's. When he returned, the big man had already left and they were alone. With a suspicious sniff and a glance at Lerenard's departing back, Henri reached under the desk and extracted an envelope.

"I took a telephone message for you, Monsieur." He handed it across the counter and tapped his nose. "It is from a lady who says it is to remain private."

Philip slit open the envelope and extracted a note in the concierge's pretentious, flowing hand. He couldn't repress a grin when he saw it was from César. Presumably Henri would now suspect him of conducting affairs with several women at the same time.

The note was brief:-

*It is important that you come to see me as soon as possible. Please make sure you are not followed - César.*

Philip hoped the concierge would respect her wish for secrecy. He put the note in his pocket, picked up the key and said, "Thank you. Henri. I will see you later."

Then he went to his bedroom. He was tired after the long climb to the Chateau de Blanchefort, so he lay on the bed intending to have a short sleep. César would just have to wait.

However, her message nagged at the back of his mind. It sounded quite urgent. What could have suddenly come up that made her risk leaving him a telephone message? Perhaps it was some news about Jackie.

Sleep was denied him, and after ten minutes he gave up trying. He got up, put his shoes back on and went downstairs. Now there was no-one in reception to see him set off up the road to his new hire car. He was confident nobody would follow him in this vehicle.

It took him about half an hour to drive to César's cottage. As he approached it up the narrow road through the woods, he noticed another car was already parked outside. Feeling a sudden stab of suspicion, he turned the car onto the grass verge about a hundred yards from the house and made the rest of the way on foot in the shelter of the trees. However, he needn't have worried. As he approached, she came out of the front door and waved to him.

"Don't worry about the car," she called. "It is used by Pierre. Please come in. He has some interesting things to tell you."

She turned and preceded him into the cottage. In the hallway she indicated the door leading into the front room where she had obviously been when she saw him approach. The bulky form of Pierre pulled himself up out of the chair he was occupying.

"I thought you told me nobody but you knew about this place," said Philip.

"Oh, I forgot to say to you about Pierre. He is my friend and I keep in touch with him. He has things to tell you but he has no English. So I will translate for you."

Philip reached to shake hands with the tough guy who was grinning at him, and nearly got his knuckles crushed. He extracted his hand with some difficulty and shook the fingers loose.

"The first thing," said César, "Pierre came to tell me is that le comte wishes to take me into his protective custody. That is what I feared. We can all guess what that means."

"Has Pierre been sent to collect you?"

She nodded. "That is correct and he will say he cannot find me. But he wasn't sent alone. He was sent with Le comte's girlfriend. He says she is a sexy-looking piece called Candice. Pierre managed to get away from her, but he says she knows you rescued me. Because of that, she will probably follow you. She hopes you will lead her to me. Have you seen anybody like that?"

"Well, there *was* a woman following us this morning." He shook his head. "But I certainly wouldn't call her a sexy piece. In fact she was quite a frump. I mean she was dressed in a loose grey sweater and jeans with an old cardigan over her shoulders and a tatty straw hat with a flower on it."

César turned to Pierre with this description. He replied with a question.

"What height is she?"

"Oh, she's quite tall." He raised his hand, "I suppose she's a bit higher than my shoulder."

Another exchange. "Is her hair blonde?"

"What I could see of it was fair – yes. It was pretty untidy. I don't think she'd brushed it for some time."

The translation of this produced another question. "Did she have a small mole on her right cheek?"

Philip thought carefully, trying to recall the girl's appearance as she argued with Lerenard. He nodded. "Actually, I think perhaps she did."

When César told Pierre that, he nodded furiously and burst into a torrent of French with many expressive hand gestures.

"He is sure that was Candice. He says it must be that she has put on a disguise to make herself look plain and to hide her splendid figure. Usually everyone would notice her as a very pretty girl. She is making sure that nobody notices her. She wishes – how do you say? - to disappear into the crowd." She raised her finger. "But beware. This woman is very dangerous. Please make sure she doesn't follow you when you come here."

"Oh, there's no chance of that today."

Philip told her about the way that Lerenard had put Candice out of action, and she translated it for Pierre, to his amusement.

"I have also hired a new car, so she won't know what sort of vehicle I am driving any longer. But I will of course keep an eye open for her in the future."

"And what is this about the man Lerenard?"

So Philip explained about Jean-Luc's arrival. That also led him to tell them about what had happened to the treasure, how he had been attacked in Carcassonne and the disappearance of Jeanette with his car. He was asked to break off from his tale while César went to collect a bottle of wine and glasses for them to share. Then he continued to the end of his story.

She laughed when he had finished. "You *have* been leading an adventurous life."

"Yes, but it hasn't got me any closer to finding Jackie."

"Ah, I hope Pierre might have some information which will help you. That is why I asked you to come to see me." She addressed a few words to her friend, and he nodded. "This is what he has been able to find out. I believe there was a man called Lesmoines working for Jacqueline Blontard."

"Oh, yes. That's right – Gaston Lesmoines. I'd forgotten about him. I didn't really take to the fellow, and he strongly objected to me. He even accused me at one stage of murdering her helper, André Jolyon."

"Really? That is very interesting. Well, Pierre has come across this fellow Lesmoines before. He tells me the man is a member of the Toulouse – what do you call them? – the Toulouse underworld?"

Philip's mouth dropped open. "You mean he's a criminal?"

"That is correct. Pierre saw Lesmoines once at a meeting with *La Force*. The man had been sent as a link from Toulouse in some scheme they were both involved in. Pierre doesn't think the man recognised him when they met recently, but *he* has a good memory. He is sure it is the same person."

Philip thought about it. "That's very interesting. I presume Jackie checked the man out when she first took him on. I wonder how he managed to fool her advisers."

"Oh, that is easy. People like Lesmoines usually have several other names. I think you call them aliases. One of my jobs for my father used to be to build up aliases like that for members of *La Force*. I used to design new life experiences, new families, new friends, new passports."

"My God!" He was only just beginning to understand the complex structure of the criminal underworld she had been brought up in.

"The point is," continued César, "if Lesmoines managed to get himself planted on Mademoiselle Blontard, there would have been a reason. Toulouse had probably found out something about the treasure. Since Marseilles failed *they* may now be searching for the treasure. He will then be involved in the disappearance of both the treasure and your lover."

Philip was stunned by this new information. He could indeed see how Jackie might have been willing to trust Lesmoines, if he came to her with some sort of proposal. After all, she had employed him as a helper, and he would be somebody in whom she felt she could place trust.

"In that case, I'll have to find some way of catching up with him. He may lead me to Jackie."

César had been watching him, waiting for his response. Now she revealed she was very unhappy with his suggestion.

"I think you should not do that," she strongly advised. "Pierre says Lesmoines is very dangerous. If you were to discover where he is, you might put yourself in danger. You might also endanger Mademoiselle Blontard, if he knows where she is. He would not hesitate to kill somebody if he felt he needed to."

"But this seems to be the first positive lead which has come along."

"One moment." César took Pierre by the arm and there ensued a short conversation in French. She turned back to Philip. "Pierre says he is willing to see what he can find out about Lesmoines in the next few days, and he will report back to me. We can then plan what you should do next."

"Is he really willing to do that? Won't he put *himself* in danger?"

She shook her head. "Because of his previous contacts with the Toulouse group, they will accept him without suspicion. Also he says he wants to help you because you rescued me from le comte."

"Well, thank you." Philip felt a warm glow of camaraderie towards these people who did not know him well.

She put her head on one side. "However, there is one condition."

"What is that?"

"You must not tell anyone about this or about where I am hiding. You must promise not to tell Lerenard or, when you see her again, the girl Jeanette – even if you think they are trying to help you. Please remember you can trust nobody in the world that I come from – not a single person."

He thought about those other people. What about Jean-Luc? He seemed to have appointed himself as Philip's personal guardian. What about Armand and Jeanette? Could he trust none of them? He shook his head. From now on, he would have to be very careful about what he told everyone, and that included César.

"OK. Nobody will hear anything from my lips about you or Pierre or your whereabouts."

"Thank you." César straightened up. "Now we need to arrange a way for me to contact you. I don't want to leave any more messages with your hotel Receptionist. Concierges can be bought cheaply."

"I've now got my own French mobile. It's 'pay-as-as-you-go', so it can't be traced back to me." He took it out of his pocket. "This is the number."

Having given her the details, Philip got up to leave. He shook Pierre firmly by the hand and thanked them both for their help. As he made his way through the hall towards the front door, he suddenly noticed something that caught his attention. Underneath a side table was a bag, and on its side was the same badge with the double-headed eagle that he had seen on the pocket of the jacket in the warehouse, where he had been attacked and knocked out.

"What's that," he asked, pointing to the bag.

César bent down to inspect it. "Oh, it's a bag belonging to Alain Hébert. He was the man who rented this cottage for the summer."

Philip knew of the relationship between César and Hébert and had witnessed its tragic end.

"I was interested in the badge on the side." He pointed at it. "Do you know what it means?"

"I assume it is some family crest." She shrugged. "But I don't know anything about it. Alain was always very secretive about his personal connections. All I knew about him was that he came from Paris."

Philip decided not to ask any more questions. Although César seemed very self-controlled, he didn't want to upset her by prying into her relationship with Hébert. So he thanked her again and departed.

# 27

Armand arrived in the Languedoc on Thursday morning. He had spent Wednesday talking to Marcus Heilberg and then on the telephone to the five contacts which the Grand Treasurer had been able to find for him. He left Paris in the early hours and reached Carcassonne before lunch.

The best of the contacts he had been given was a local police inspector called Félix Martin, who was serving with the Carcassonne police. When he rang the inspector, Félix had warned him that they wouldn't be able to meet until the late evening so, after booking himself into a small hotel in a side street just off the main square, Armand spent the next few hours exploring the so-called new city, which he did not know well. He also made sure that he had found the location of the bistro bar called *L'Homme Vert* where Martin had suggested they meet.

After a late dinner without wine, he went to 'The Green Man', ordered a café solo and took a corner seat some way from the noisy bar. Promptly, at the appointed hour of ten o'clock, the inspector arrived. Armand didn't need to see the copy of *Toulouse Soir* which the man carried tucked under his arm to help him recognise the detective.

Martin was a typical member of the *Police Nationale*, dressed in a shabby, unpressed suit with the top button of his shirt undone and his greasy tie loosened. His thinning hair and care-creased face suggested a fellow well into his fifties, or perhaps a younger man who had not worn well. The glass of absinthe and the iced water he collected from the bar made the latter more likely. Martin didn't hesitate as he brought his drinks to Armand's table.

"*Bon soir*," he grunted and seated himself without offering to shake hands.

Armand watched him for a second before he asked, "Have you brought the video tapes for me to look through?"

"They're at headquarters." The inspector grinned at Armand's doubtful expression. "Don't worry. I'm the only one on duty tonight and I will sign you in. Nobody will ask questions. I down-loaded the tapes earlier this evening on to my second computer. I'm there all night, so you can take as long as you need."

The young man nodded. He didn't feel grateful to Martin because he knew the detective's palm had been well-greased to compensate for his help. He only wished he'd had the foresight to take a siesta this afternoon, since he guessed he had a long night ahead of him.

"I told you I'm looking for an English sports car?"

The inspector only raised his eyebrows.

"It is possibly being driven by a young woman from Paris. I know the woman. There is no problem with *her*. It is whoever is in the car with her that I am really interested in. Have you had any unexpected arrivals in the city recently?"

Martin would know Armand was referring to members of the criminal fraternity. He looked at the young man shrewdly.

"Why do you ask that question?"

"The woman who took the car and disappeared – she is called Jeanette Picard. She would not willingly have deserted the owner. He is an Englishman called Philip Sinclair. Jeanette was trying to help him find his fiancée who is the famous archaeologist Jacqueline Blontard, who has also disappeared."

Armand was aware that he now had the inspector's full attention.

"I have heard of Mademoiselle Blontard. Is there a missing persons alert for her?"

"Not yet. In any case I think the publicity might be counter-productive at this stage. I am here to try to find the two of them. If I don't succeed in a few days, I may have to call on the help of your lot." He squinted at Martin. "So I repeat my question. Have there been any unexpected arrivals in the last few days?"

The detective gazed into the distance, as though assembling his thoughts, before he replied.

"I wonder if there is a connection?" he surmised. "It is possible. My colleagues up the road in Toulouse let it be known that a batch of their miscreants had suddenly disappeared – six of them altogether. Apparently, the word was that they had business down this way. We have been keeping our eyes and ears open but so far we've seen nothing in the city."

Armand leaned forward. "Do you have any information about these men? – names, addresses, details of past crimes?"

"Not yet. The report only came through a couple of days ago." Martin pulled out a small notebook and pen from an inside pocket. "I'll ask for details tomorrow."

He scribbled himself a reminder, put away the pen and notebook and tossed back the remains of his absinthe without coughing. "Well, we'd better go and have a look at these videos."

Ten minutes later, they were in Martin's office on the top floor of a dirty, concrete office block near the city centre. The inspector went straight to a computer on a side desk and booted it up. As soon as the screen lit up, he chose the appropriate program and explained to Armand how to search through the tapes and isolate and enlarge any frames he was interested in.

"What type of car is it?"

"It's an MG – a British-made sports car. It's red with a black hard-top fitted."

"What's the registration number?"

Armand shook his head. "That I don't know."

"Well, there aren't many cars of that description in this area."

"That's right. I'm sure I'll recognise it when I see it."

Martin pointed at the screen. "We've only got four cameras round the city. They're located on the four main roads in and out. This video is from the one on the Toulouse road. There are two more in the Old City, but I don't think you'll be interested in those. There are mainly pedestrians up there – just a few local delivery vehicles. What time do you think this car theft took place?"

"Soon after midnight on Monday."

"That should narrow it down to less than twelve hours' viewing." The inspector smirked, "Unless of course the thieves had some hideaway just round the corner."

Armand shrugged. "Well, I've got to try the videos before I look for alternatives. I'd better get started."

"Best of luck. Let me know when you want a coffee to relieve the boredom."

The young man sat down and started on the video clips from the Toulouse road which were already on the screen. He had been shown how to speed up the film and the light traffic at this time of night made it possible to view the images at several times the actual speed of filming. It took him less than an hour to check through that video up until dawn. There were only a couple of vehicles which looked anything like the sports car he was searching for. When he froze them on the screen, they were clearly not Philip's car.

So Armand switched to the video from the second camera. He found he was now looking at the road going south towards Limoux. By good luck, he'd only been watching it at high speed for ten minutes when he hit the jackpot. He froze the image, moved back a few frames to the point where it was nearest the camera, and blew it up to maximum magnification. The image was grainy, but it was clearly Philip's car with the hard-top on. He could even read the number plate and he made a note of it on a scrap of paper in front of him. Unfortunately, the vehicle was moving away from the camera, so he couldn't get a clear view of the occupants, but he thought there were two people visible through the rear window.

"Success!" he called to the inspector across the room.

Martin came over to look at the image. He showed Armand how to improve the resolution (though not by much), then how to print it out. With the damp A4 photo in his hand, the young man could see the picture more clearly.

"I think the slight figure in the left seat will be Jeanette," he said. "Remember it's an English car so the driver will be on the right. That looks like a bulkier individual, so it's probably a man driving."

"The woman seems to be sitting upright," Martin grunted, "so there's no reason to think she's tied up or anything like that. That would suggest she is complying with whatever the driver is doing."

"I guess so," said Armand, a little reluctantly.

"So it's somebody she knows. You say it's not this guy Sinclair."

"No. He was the one who told me she had disappeared. And I know where he is."

143

"OK. So how many other men would she know in this area?"

"Not very many. She spent several weeks in Quillan last month, helping with an archaeological dig. It could really only be one of those guys." Armand shook his head. "But I thought they'd all left the area, except Sinclair, since the dig's been closed down."

Martin straightened up from the screen. "The next question is – they are clearly leaving Carcassonne. Where do you think they're going?"

"I suppose the obvious answer to that is back to Quillan, or perhaps to the dig site at le Bézu."

"Where is that?"

Armand gave him a brief description of the chateau and the events which had taken place there in the last few weeks.

Martin sighed. "So the next step is to see this lawyer guy, Amboisard."

"I can't very well do that." He explained to the inspector that he was technically in breach of an order from the mayor to keep him informed of his whereabouts.

Martin grinned. "Well, I'll leave you to sort that one out as you think fit. In the meantime, I'll issue this car description and registration number to our patrol cars and the local gendarmeries. They may turn something up. Give me your phone number so that I can keep you informed."

"Thanks, and I'll ring Sinclair in the morning and tell him what I've found out here. He can have a good look for the car round Quillan and maybe he'll have some other ideas."

With that plan, he left the police station and went back to get some sleep in what remained of the night.

# 28

Philip was at breakfast with Jean-Luc when his phone rang. In case it was César, he excused himself, rose, and went through reception into the town square.

When he pressed the answer button he heard, "Is that Philip? This is Armand. I am in Carcassonne."

"Oh, hello Armand." He leaned against the wall, looking down into the now gently flowing river. "How are you getting on?"

"One moment please."

A woman's voice came on the phone. "Hello, Philip. I am Béatrice. I am a friend of Armand. I will translate for him."

"Oh." Philip shrugged. Why not, if that was what Armand wanted.

"Armand says he is doing a lot. Last night he went to police headquarters here in Carcassonne. They have let him see the spy camera films from Monday night. He has seen your car on that night. It was leaving Carcassonne on the Limoux road. That is going towards you in Quillan."

"That's interesting. Does he have a time when that happened?"

There was an exchange in French at the other end. Philip let the rapidly rising sun warm his back as he waited.

"It was after midnight. He says it was timed at twelve fifty-eight."

"That's great. So it seems that Jeanette was on her way back to Quillan. I wonder why she didn't turn up here at the hotel."

"One minute." There was another short discussion. "Armand says there were two people in the car. He couldn't see their faces because the camera was looking at the back of the car, but he thought the one in the passenger seat was probably Jeanette, because she was quite small. However, the person driving the car was a bigger person - probably a man."

"Does that mean Jeanette was a prisoner?"

He had to wait while she asked Armand the question and he replied at some length.

"He says he can't be sure of that. She was sitting upright in the car so she may have been willing to go with the man. It may have been somebody she already knew."

"Goodness." Philip gazed up at the castle on the other side of the river, trying to work out why Jeanette might decide to go off with some other man in his car.

"Armand says you will have to look round to see if you can find the car in Quillan. He says you know he cannot come to you locally. If you are able to find the car, Jeanette and the man may be somewhere near. But he says you must be careful because the man may be dangerous."

"Really?" The Englishman paused, aware of the repetition of the fact that he may be facing danger by continuing his investigations. After a while he said, "OK. We'll start looking round this morning, and we'll be careful."

She repeated this to Armand who asked, "Who is we?"

"I've got Jean-Luc Lerenard with me. Armand knows him."

There was another muttered conversation, then Béatrice came back on the line. "Armand says very good for you and *bonne chance*. Will you please call him when you have some news?"

"Of course I will. So what is Armand doing at the moment?"

Another brief exchange. "He is finding out about some other people."

"OK." Philip shrugged. "Good luck to him as well."

The call was ended, and Philip returned to his cold breakfast in the hotel dining room. A somewhat grumpy Lerenard asked, "What was that all about?"

"It was Armand ringing from Carcassonne. He's come down to help find Jeanette and he's finding out what he can about Jackie at the same time."

He gave his colleague a potted version of his phone conversation and concluded, "So it looks as though my car is back somewhere in this area. Armand can't come to look himself – something to do with problems with the mayor – so it's up to us to try to find it."

Philip was aware that he was assuming that Jean-Luc would help him. The big man grunted, but stayed silent while Philip went to get a fresh cup of coffee.

146

When he came back Lerenard said, "We will start here in the town. You can take the area to the south of the town square off the Axat road, and I will take the area to the north. We can also keep an eye open for the girl we saw yesterday, in case she has come back to follow us again, which would not surprise me."

Philip agreed without enthusiasm. He wasn't psychologically prepared for the dreary foot-slogging which he was discovering was the essence of detective work. However, he didn't see any alternative, therefore he set off after breakfast with as much enthusiasm as he could muster.

"The town is quite small," said Lerenard, "so we will meet back here in two hours to compare notes."

Philip had only a couple of dozen side roads to search, and he made his way steadily along them, occasionally receiving hostile glances from residents in front gardens, but often getting cheerful greetings from other pedestrians. There was no sign of the little red sports car, and he hadn't really expected that there would be. He thought that, no matter whether Jeanette was a prisoner or a willing helper, they would be unlikely to leave the car where it could be easily found and might lead searchers to their hiding place. It was probable that the car would have been hidden out of sight.

In less than an hour he was coming to the end of his search area, and was planning a return to the hotel for a coffee while he waited for his colleague, who had a larger area to cover. Then his phone rang.

"Who is it this time?" he asked himself as he pulled out the mobile and pressed the green button. It turned out to be Aunt Charlotte, for whom he had left a message yesterday about his new phone number.

"Is that Philip?"

"Yes, it is. Hello, Tante Charlotte."

"Thank you for giving me your new telephone number. It was lucky you did that, because I suddenly had a thought the previous night, just as I was dropping off to sleep. It kept me awake for hours, wondering how I could get in touch with you to tell you about it."

"I'm sorry to hear I was the unwitting cause of your losing sleep."

"Oh, that doesn't matter. We old folks have nothing better to do than sleep. We can sleep whenever we want to." She took a breath. "Now, Philip, you remember that list of names you gave me – the ones you found in Jacqueline's filing cabinet?"

"I certainly do."

"Well, I realised I had come across one of the names before. It was Hector Ramise." She hesitated. "And I remembered who he was – who he *is*, in fact."

"Oh, that's interesting." Philip wasn't sure if it really was.

"Yes. He was a tutor at the university here. He was a colleague of Albert – my brother and Jackie's uncle."

"You mean he was an archaeologist?"

"Oh, yes - quite an eminent one." She paused. "He was one of the colleagues who wasn't willing to accept poor Albert's theories about the Cathars. They fell out quite badly about it. Soon after that he left Béziers, because he was offered a better-paid post at the Sorbonne in Paris. In fact, he became Professor of Archaeology there. He was later head of the department where Jacqueline went to study for her doctorate."

"Oh, dear. I expect that caused some problems."

"Well, do you know, I never heard that it did – cause problems I mean. You see, her uncle was already dead, and I didn't think it was a good idea to enlighten Jacqueline about their falling out earlier. After all, she was only a child at the time it happened. I presume that Hector also had the sense not to tell her about their problems either, because she never mentioned it to me. She always had a high regard for the professor and I didn't think it was a good idea to change her views on him." Another brief pause. "Do you think I did wrong?"

"Of course not," he replied. "As you say, it wasn't your place to stir up ill-feeling between them. That wouldn't have been a good idea at all."

"Oh, thank goodness. I was afraid you might think I had betrayed Albert."

"Not at all. Tell me, Tante Charlotte, when did all this trouble with your brother occur?" Philip was now retracing his route to the hotel.

"Oh, it must have been at least twenty years ago. As I said, Jacqueline was just a young girl. She didn't have any parents.

Daphne had died soon after Jackie's birth and I had to stand in for her. We lived with Albert, and the girl absolutely adored him. I think that is why she took his disgrace so badly, but I don't think he ever told her the names of the other people involved."

"And this Hector Ramise – do you know if he's still at the Sorbonne?"

"Oh, yes, as far as I know."

"Well, thank you for telling me all this, Tante Charlotte. I will have to think carefully about whether to approach Professor Ramise."

They said goodbye, and Philip disconnected and wandered back to the hotel, deep in thought. Was Professor Ramise important? He could be, and Philip was adamant that he would leave no stone unturned until he had found Jackie.

He had nearly finished his second coffee before Lerenard turned up. The big man slumped down beside him and ordered an *americano*.

"I take it you had no luck either," said Philip.

"I am sure your car is nowhere in the streets of Quillan," Jean-Luc agreed.

"Of course, it may be hidden in a garage or a large shed or warehouse."

"Would your woman know of any place like that in Quillan?"

"You mean Jeanette?" Philip snorted. "I wouldn't put anything past her. But the question is – who is the man Armand saw *with* her? It is likely to be someone she knew."

"I also asked Sergeant Leblanc at the gendarmerie if he had seen anything about the car or its occupants. It is surprising what these local police pick up every day."

"What did he say?"

Lerenard shook his head. "He says they are not in Quillan. He cannot say they did not turn up in the middle of Monday night, but he is sure he would have received some report if they had stopped in the town."

"So what do we do now?" Philip sighed. "Every path we follow seems to come to a dead end."

"I have found one other thing." Jean-Luc raised a finger. "I have seen the car of that woman who was following us yesterday. It was parked only two places away from my own car."

"Did you see Candice herself?"

"Who?"

Philip realised he had slipped up. "It's the name I've given her. Candid means being honest." He grinned. "Which she isn't."

Lerenard nodded but didn't smile. He didn't seem to possess a sense of humour after his travails. "No. I didn't."

"But she is probably staying somewhere nearby."

"That's right. I think she may follow us again next time we drive somewhere."

"I've been thinking about that," said Philip. "I want to go to the central library for the Languedoc region in Carcassonne. I want to find out if there are any other castles in the area which might be known as Blanchefort. Will you come with me to act as interpreter?"

"Of course."

They agreed to go that afternoon.

# 29

To overcome language difficulties, Lerenard agreed to ring Armand before they left for Carcassonne to tell him what they were doing.

"Tell him we would like to see him to discuss progress," said Philip.

Armand's reply was to suggest a bar near the city centre where they agreed to meet at six o'clock.

As they left Quillan in Jean-Luc´s car, he said, "I think we are being followed by that woman again."

Philip turned to watch the small white Peugeot following them. It looked just like the car Lerenard had disabled the previous day in Rennes-les-Bains, but he wanted to check.

"When we come to a lay-by just round a corner let's make a stop to be sure."

They pulled in to a suitable place a few miles later and parked in the shade of some trees. Sure enough, the girl cruised past, obviously following them. However this was a changed ,Candice. Gone was the straw hat and the sloppy clothing. Now she was a smart, well-groomed beauty. If they hadn't known otherwise, they might have thought it was a different woman.

"Wow," breathed Philip. "What a change."

Lerenard made a note of her number. "You can take over and drive," he said. "I'm going to put a spoke in her wheel."

As Philip started off, his colleague picked up his phone and dialled Armand's number. He told him, "We're being followed by some woman. Can you do anything about it?"

Philip didn't hear what Armand said, but it seemed to be helpful because Jean-Luc then gave him Candice's car type and colour and her registration number. There was another exchange of French before he grunted, "Thank you," and rang off.

When they passed the next lay-by, they were amused to see Candice waiting there. As soon as they passed, she pulled out and continued to follow them, now only a couple of hundred yards behind.

"She knows we've seen her," said Lerenard, "so she's not even bothering to pretend anymore."

Half an hour later, as they approached Carcassonne, they passed a police patrol vehicle pulled in at the side of the road. A gendarme got out of the vehicle. He paid them no attention, but he stepped into the path of the little white Peugeot with his hand held up. As Candice pulled in to the side of the road his appreciative gaze took in the smartly-dressed young driver.

"Can you please switch off your engine and let me see your personal documents?" he asked politely.

With a thunderous expression she did as instructed, ferreted around in her handbag and handed over her identity card. He proceeded to inspect it carefully, noting he was interviewing a Mademoiselle Candice Ambré. The next thing he asked for were the documents for the hire car, which he went through very thoroughly including going round to the front of the car to check the registration number.

"Can you please get out and open the boot for me?"

The young woman was seething as she went round to the back of the car and opened the rear hatch. The policeman then very carefully inspected the whole interior of the completely empty area. He even lifted the floor covering, unscrewed the bolt which held the spare wheel in place, and lifted it out so that he could check the well had nothing hidden in it.

As he was putting everything back, she asked, "Why are you doing this to me?"

"We have received a report that a car of this description is carrying some – er – proscribed materials." He smiled at her warmly. "I am pleased to inform you that the suspect car is not yours."

"So I can go now?"

"Certainly, Mademoiselle." He made a little bow. "Thank you for your co-operation. I hope I haven't made you late for your appointment. I also hope you have a pleasant visit to our beautiful city."

So, after a delay of fifteen minutes during which time Lerenard's car had completely disappeared, a very angry Candice continued into the centre of Carcassonne. She realised she would have completely lost them by now. A couple of hours of pointless searching lay ahead of her.

Meanwhile, Philip had parked in a side street near the city centre from where they could walk just round the corner into the central library. The receptionist directed them to the reference section on the top floor and they were soon seated before a young man in shirt-sleeves with a computer in front of him.

With Lerenard translating, Philip told the man, "We are looking for a castle called the Chateau de Blanchefort. We have been to the one marked on the map near Rennes les Bains but that is now just a few tumble-down walls. Is there another Chateau de Blanchefort?"

The young man consulted his computer at some length. "There is one other listed. It is near Dijon in Eastern France."

Philip pulled a face. "I don't somehow think that's the place we're looking for."

The chap was tapping away and clicking his mouse busily. After a few more moments, he swivelled the screen round for them to see. Philip found himself looking at a fairly grand country house, with a gravel turning circle, in front of which stood a Rolls Royce.

"It looks rather modern," he said.

The man reversed the screen and continued tapping and clicking. After another minute or two he announced. "It was built between 1872 and 1879. The owners are the Soller family." He read the text carefully. "Apparently they are big in mustard."

Philip found it difficult not to snigger. "Was the house built on the site of an ancient castle?" he asked.

The young man continued to tap and click for some time. At last he said, "I do not think so. There is no mention of an older building. It only says that the house is surrounded by many square kilometres of vineyards. It appears that the Sollers are also in the wine trade."

"I don't think that's the place I'm looking for." Then he had a bright idea. "Do chateaux ever change their names over the centuries?"

"But of course. There are many examples of that happening."

"Why might they do that?"

"Well, if the ownership changes, the new owner may not want to keep the old name for all sorts of reasons. For example, he may have inherited the place by marriage. Perhaps his wealth is newly obtained, and he may wish to have the additional prestige, not only of owning an old estate, but which also carries his name. Then again, many big houses were partly destroyed during the Revolution which occurred more than two centuries ago. When they were rebuilt, they were often given new names because the local people did not wish to be reminded of their *seigneur* who had been sent to the guillotine."

"So something like that could have happened to the Blanchefort family, who I believe were big landowners in this area in mediaeval times."

The young man nodded. "Certainly it could."

"Do you have a list of chateau names in the thirteenth century?"

He shook his head. "I'm afraid not."

"OK. Do you have any records of the Blanchefort family estates at that time?" Philip leaned forward. "You see, it occurs to me that they may have owned more than one castle on their estates and that at least one of these may have been known as the Chateau de Blanchefort at that time, but has had its name changed since."

The man looked puzzled as Lerenard struggled with his translation. When it was finished he shook his head again. "I don't think I would know anything about that. I can give you the history of a place for which you give me a present-day name, but I don't know anything about the ownership of properties so long ago, or what previous names they might have had. If that information exists, which I doubt, it hasn't yet been put on my computer data records."

"Is there anywhere I can try to find out that information?"

"Perhaps." But he was doubtful. "I think you would have to go to the national archives at the Ministry of Culture in Paris. They may have information like that among their old documents. But I am not sure."

Philip realised he had gone as far as he could here, so he thanked the helpful young man. There were hand-shakes and bows all round. Then they left to meet Armand.

# 30

Because there was more than an hour before they were due to have their meeting, they used the time to have a meal in a small bistro in a shady side street. As a result, they were a bit late when they reached the rendezvous and they found Armand staring into a small beer.

Philip was pleased to see him again and they shook hands and patted shoulders before they sat down. He noticed Armand's greeting to Lerenard was rather more cautious. He guessed the smart young Parisian and the burly agent of the Catholic Church might well regard each other as opponents,

Ignoring that, Philip launched into his questioning, with Jean-Luc interpreting. "We told you we couldn't find my car in Quillan. Do you have any idea where else Jeanette might have gone?"

"Not yet." Armand straightened up. "But something else has come up. The local police have been told that six men from the Toulouse underworld have come to this area. They are waiting to receive a list of names and aliases from their colleagues in Toulouse."

"Why are you interested in them?"

Armand smiled. "It occurred to me that, for so many criminals to move at the same time to another area, there must be something pretty big at the end of it."

"Ah. You think they may be interested in the treasure?"

"That's right. And furthermore, my friendly police inspector is confident that they have not actually come into the city. So they are probably lying low somewhere in the region. He has instituted additional patrols in rural areas around Carcassonne, but nothing has turned up yet. Of course, he is still waiting for the details of these men to arrive."

"So you're just sitting here waiting for news of these characters to turn up."

Armand looked a bit hurt. "Not only that. I am also making enquiries of some other contacts I have in the area."

"I am asking about that," said Philip, "because I am going to Paris tomorrow. I was hoping you might come with me. You have so many contacts up there."

"Why Paris? I have already told you that Jackie is not in Paris."

"I need to go to the Ministry of Culture." He explained his wish to find out more about the Blanchefort family. "I thought you would be able to get me in there to meet the right people."

Armand shook his head. "I am not the person for that." He suddenly brightened. "The one you need is Bernard Cambray – Jackie's agent. He knows everybody in the cultural world. He represents several of them, and his English is excellent, as you know."

"That's a good idea," agreed Philip. "Do you know how I can get in touch with him?"

"He gave me a card when I met him the other day." Armand burrowed in his inside pocket and brought out a clutch of business cards. He sorted through them and extracted one which he handed to Philip.

"This gives his home number. He may not be there at present, but you can ring him this evening. Of course, you realise you won't be able to go to the Ministry of Culture until Monday."

"Huh. I'd forgotten it's the weekend tomorrow. I'll have to see what Bernard says." He reached out to shake his hand. "Thank you, Armand."

There was little else to discuss, so they left Armand to continue his searches in Carcassonne.

"That was a good idea of Armand's for me to contact Bernard Cambray," said Philip as they were driving back to Quillan. "I think there's a good chance he would know how to get me in to meet someone useful at the Ministry of Culture."

"Do you want me to come to Paris with you?" asked Lerenard a little stiffly.

"I don't think so," said Philip. "I think I should be safe on my own in Paris. It would be more useful if you stayed here and continued to search for my car and tried to find another Chateau de Blanchefort."

The big man bowed his head in acquiescence, but kept his own counsel as he concentrated on his driving.

157

That evening Philip rang Jackie's agent.

"My dear boy," Cambray exclaimed in his usual extravagant manner, "you must be completely devastated by Jackie's disappearance."

Philip replied firmly, "I intend to leave no stone unturned in my search for her."

"Absolutely, dear fellow. I'm with you there, all the way. Jackie is vital to all our futures – both emotional and – er – financial. She must be found."

"I have stumbled upon a document that leads me to think that the whereabouts of a castle called the Chateau de Blanchefort might be important in my search."

"Really? What makes you think that?"

"I think it may be the hiding place of the original treasure of the Cathars. Consequently, I think Jackie might have been taken there."

"Come now – er – Philip, doesn't that sound a bit far-fetched?"

"It's the only possible lead I have at the moment."

"Well, of course it is, but the treasure of the Cathars – really!"

"Well, in the absence of any better leads, I intend to follow this one up. I have already visited one Chateau de Blanchefort, but all that exists there are a few half-ruined walls. So I am trying to find out if any other castles with the same name are in existence."

"And are there?"

"I have found only one so far and I discount that, as being much too modern. As a result, I am trying to find out whether any other chateaux might have had their names changed over the centuries. My enquiries have drawn a blank down here in Carcassonne. However, I am told I may be able to find out some useful information in the archive section of the Ministry of Culture." He paused. "Because I know you will be as anxious as I am to find Jackie, I am ringing to see whether you would be willing to help me get access to them."

There was a short silence at the other end of the line. Obviously, Bernard was thinking furiously about what his response should be. But when he spoke again, it was positive.

"Do you know, I think I might just be able to help you there – not tomorrow, of course – none of these pathetic characters would dream of working at the weekend. But if you give me a tinkle on Monday evening, I hope I'll be able to tell you if I'm getting anywhere."

"Oh, I was hoping I could travel up on Sunday and visit the archive section on Monday morning. You see, I feel that time is important."

There was another pause. Bernard's mind seemed to be working overtime. He responded, "Absolutely, old boy. I can see why you're so anxious. I tell you what – why don't you do *just* that? Come up on Sunday, I mean. I'd be only too happy to put you up at my place overnight. Then, first thing Monday morning, we can attack the jolly old Ministry of Culture together. How's that?"

"That's really splendid of you, Bernard. I accept your kind offer. I'll make sure I get to you some time in the late afternoon."

"Do you know how to find me?"

"I've got a card of yours that Armand Séjour gave me."

"Oh, him. No, I'm afraid that won't be any good to you on Sunday, old boy. That's my business address. The office is closed at weekends. If you've got a pencil and paper, I'll give you my home address."

Philip was ready for that, and he took down the address, which he discovered was on the western outskirts of the capital. Bernard also gave him directions on how to find it.

"Do you think you can understand that?"

"It seems clear enough."

"Good. Well, hopefully I'll see you in time for tea on Sunday. Cheerio!"

He rang off.

# 31

Following a further unproductive trawl round the area on Saturday looking for his car, Philip set out for Paris after breakfast on Sunday. He arrived at Bernard Cambray's house well before the appointed hour. He had allowed plenty of time, in case he had difficulty in finding the place, but Bernard's directions were easy to follow. The villa was a rather splendid building in a tree-lined avenue leading down to the river. Clearly, being Jackie's agent was a rewarding business.

His host came out to meet him as he pulled in to the drive. Bernard was a plump, round-faced fellow, rather given to wearing tweed jackets and brightly-coloured trousers. He always gave Philip the impression of an English country squire. However, today being warm, he only allowed himself a striped shirt with the sleeves rolled up to the elbows and a pair of pink trousers.

As Philip climbed out of the car, the friendly agent grabbed his hand and pumped it up and down, and he couldn't help smiling at the man's enthusiasm, even though he always found it a little over the top.

"No trouble finding me, eh?"

"Your directions were excellent."

"I'm so pleased you could come. An old bachelor like me doesn't have many visitors."

Philip got his bag out of the boot and was ushered into the house, while Bernard prattled on about sundry subjects and particularly his holiday in the Seychelles. He showed Philip into a neat little single bedroom where he deposited his bag.

"Well," said his host, when they were seated and sharing a welcome pot of tea, "I got busy yesterday morning and was able to find out how we should proceed tomorrow. I have discovered that the chap in charge of the archives department is a fellow called Angus McDermid - of Scottish origin, no less."

"How odd."

"Not really. The French and the Scots go back a long way – right back to a guy called Bonnie Prince Charlie." He smiled. "Angus' parents came to Paris in the sixties, and he was brought up here and seems as French as the best of us, despite his name. However, he is still a natural English speaker, the language having been spoken at home by his parents in the main."

"That will make it easier," agreed Philip, "and may save you a lot of trouble translating."

"Indeed it will. The other good thing about Angus is that, like a true Scot, he is at his desk no later than eight-thirty when most other civil servants are likely to turn up getting on for ten. So we can safely phone him before nine and be at the front of the queue for his services."

"OK. I'll make sure I'm up early."

After that the conversation became more general until dinner. Bernard proved to be an enthusiastic cook and was proud of his wine cellar, so Philip staggered up to bed at a late hour. Nevertheless, he made sure he was up early.

After a gastronomic breakfast, they took the metro into Bernard's office in the city centre, arriving soon after eight-thirty. The agent prepared a *cafetière* of coffee and they were seated on opposite sides of his magnificent desk ten minutes later, enjoying a cup. Bernard consulted his notes and was able to ring the direct line to McDermid's office. After a brief conversation in French, the phone was handed over to Philip. Despite Bernard's preparation he was surprised to find the man was able to speak to him in almost accent-less English. He obviously hadn't espoused the Scottish accent of his parents.

"Hello, young Sinclair. That's a good Scottish surname."

"Actually it is the anglicised version of an ancient French name – Saint Claire."

"Never mind. I can forgive you that. Now what did you want to ask me?"

It was clear that McDermid was no man to waste time on small talk, so Philip immediately started to explain as carefully as he could about his wish to discover the history of the Blanchefort family in the thirteenth century, and about their holdings of land and property in the Languedoc.

"This is a most unusual request," said McDermid. "Why should you want this sort of information?"

"My fiancée has disappeared and a document I have discovered leads me to suspect she may be in, or close to, a castle once known as the Chateau de Blanchefort, but perhaps known by a different name nowadays."

"Indeed, and do you think this fiancée wants to be found?"

"I don't know," confessed Philip. "All I want is to hear from her own lips whether she wants our engagement to continue or to be terminated. If it is the latter, I will promise to leave her alone."

McDermid listened carefully. "You are taking a long shot if you are hoping that information you may glean from our records is going to help you find her."

"I accept that, Mr McDermid, but at the moment this course seems to be my only hope."

"OK. OK. You've convinced me that there is no reason to deny you access to our records." He cleared his throat. "However, you will have to appreciate that these records are very complex. You cannot just pick up a document and read off the information you want. There will be much cross-referencing. One small item may result in you having to look through a dozen other relevant papers, some of which may be fragile or sensitive. You would need a specialist with you in those circumstances. How good is your French?"

"Hmm. Not very good at all I am afraid. I am hoping that Bernard will help me with the translation."

"Will he indeed?" Philip could almost see McDermid shaking his head. "Does he realise he might be letting himself in for a great deal of frustrating work?"

"You make it sound like an almost impossible task."

"Oh, it *will* be. Don't be in any doubt about that." The man paused briefly. "However, you may be in for a slice of good luck. At the moment we have a young researcher from Lyons, who is doing a fairly similar thing in connection with the documents we hold about his city. It's a different period, of course. But he's something of a romantic. I think he might be interested in spending a bit of time setting you on the right road. I will ask him when he comes in."

"Thank you very much, Monsieur McDermid. Shall I come along to meet him at about ten?"

"Oh, no. You will have to wait for my phone call. I have your number. I will ring you when I can to let you know what his response is."

"Oh. OK. I'll wait for your call, and thank you very much for listening to me, Monsieur McDermid."

He rang off and Philip had to wait for a frustrating couple of hours for the important phone call. Meanwhile, Bernard was busily engaged in phoning a string of contacts – making appointments, chasing payments and exchanging information. After a quarter of an hour Philip left him to it and took a stroll round the nearby streets, observing the commercial life of the area as it gradually started back to work after the weekend.

In one back-street he came across an old, traditional type of bookshop. He went in and started to read the spines of the books, most of which were not new and some of which were actually in English. Being close to the Ministry of Culture, a lot of the titles were non-fiction. Suddenly his attention was caught by one of the titles. It was called *Une Histoire de la Catharisme*. He took it down from the shelf and started to leaf through it. It was a very wordy book with no photos or illustrations, and of course it was in French.

Nevertheless, he decided to purchase it and carried it back to Bernard's office where he discovered the man was still busy on the phone.

As soon as there was a pause Philip asked, "What happens if McDermid tries to contact me while you are on the phone?"

"Don't worry. I gave him my mobile number." He tapped the phone lying to one side of his desk pad, which was now covered with a mass of scribbles.

Philip nodded and took out his own notebook and pen. For want of something better to do he opened *Une Histoire de la Catharisme* and noted the date of original publication which was in the nineteen seventies – some time ago. He turned to the contents page and started to write down the chapter headings, copying the French carefully. He promised himself he would translate these when he got to his car and could consult his dictionary. Perhaps he would get an idea of exactly what the book was about.

He had hardly started when Bernard's mobile rang. His friend was in the middle of another long call so he waved at it and indicated that Philip should answer it. He picked it up and heard, "*Est-ce Monsieur Cambray?*"

"No – er – this is Philip Sinclair."

"Ah, Monsieur Sinclair, it's McDermid here. This call is to tell you I have spoken to the young researcher, and he would be happy to meet you and see whether he can help you."

"That's great, Thank you, Monsieur McDermid. When would he be able to talk to me?"

"He says he can easily take a break from his other work. His hours are his own so it can be any time you choose. When would you like to come?"

"As soon as possible."

"OK. Lunch-time is approaching, so let's say after lunch – two-thirty. Is that suitable for you? Then you can have a good couple of hours together."

"That's fine with me."

"Very well. His name is Raphael Menton." He spelled it out for Philip to make a note. He has a certain amount of English so you probably won't need Cambray. I will warn Reception you are coming at two-thirty. Just call at the desk and they will direct you."

"I'll be there, and thank you again, Monsieur McDermid."

"No problem." He rang off.

When Bernard next came off the phone, Philip gave him the news.

"I don't even need to trouble you any longer," he said.

"Well, you'll need to stay another night at least, so you can come back here when you are finished. I will be in the office until after seven o'clock."

"I'm very grateful, Bernard."

"Not at all. Pleased to be of help. Well, let's go to lunch and have a beer to celebrate."

*Une Histoire de Catharisme* was forgotten for the time being, in the excitement of this new development.

# 32

Philip made sure he was right on time when he arrived at the Ministry of Culture. He was directed to go to the top floor. There he found that the receptionist had telephoned ahead and Raphael Menton was waiting to greet him. There was no sign of Angus McDermid.

Raphael was a slight young man whose hair had been cut to about a quarter of an inch long all over his scalp. He was good looking, and his only adornment was a small gold ring in his left ear-lobe. He was casually dressed and welcomed Philip with a smile but no handshake.

Philip said, "Thank you for agreeing to see me, Raphael."

"Please call me Rafa. All my friends do." He got straight down to business in a good but accented English. "The manager tells me you are looking for the family name Blanchefort. Where did these people come from?"

"I believe they were big landowners in the Languedoc in the thirteenth century."

"Ah, that is between the years 1200 and 1300, no?"

"That's right. I have found one ruined castle which bears their name, but I am told there may have been others, some of which may have had their names changed since."

"That may be correct. In those times places were often named for their owners, especially if the owners were important people." He beckoned. "Come with me. I am interested in what you say to the manager, so already I have found a document which say about properties which may have belonged to the Blancheforts at some time."

Rafa led Philip across the large open-plan office space to a small desk in the corner near a window.

"This desk is allowed to me when I am working here," he explained. "I have found you a second chair."

They sat side by side at the desk and the Frenchman took a sheet of paper from a bundle on the far corner of the desk. "This is a print-out of part of a property register made in the year 1259 at the time when King Philip III, known as Philip the Bold, was making himself the ruler of the Languedoc.

Philip noted, without saying it, that this was already fifteen years after the fall of the Cathar stronghold of Montségur. He asked, "Are you telling me this includes records of the Blanchefort family?"

"Not actually of the Blancheforts. I will explain. The register includes all the *seigneuries* in the area then known as Razès, which was a large tract of the country south of the town of Limoux."

"And you found all this in one document. That was lucky."

Rafa glanced sideways at him. "It wasn't luck. These registers were made for the purpose of deciding the tax due from each owner of a property. Of course, nobody knew at the time how valuable they would be later to researchers like me."

"And you're saying the Blanchefort family owned part of the land in the Razès area?"

"No, they owned nothing. I can find only one reference to Blanchefort in the register. That is the Chateau de Blanchefort near Couiza, but that was not owned by the Blancheforts. It was held by a man called Pierre de Voisins. When I researched his name, I discovered he was a helper of Simon de Montfort who led the Albigensian Crusade against the Cathars."

"I've heard of Pierre de Voisins. At the time of the fall of Montségur he was living in the castle at le Bézu. That is where I helped Jacqueline Blontard carry out the archaeological exploration which led to the discovery of the room-full of treasure."

"What is this?" Raphael was studying him closely.

Philip told him about what had happened during the last few weeks. "That is why I am here," he concluded. "I am searching for my fiancée."

By the time he had finished, he had young Menton's deepest interest. "This is *fantastique*," he exclaimed. "I have heard nothing about any of this."

"I think everybody involved has been trying to keep the whole thing secret until the treasure could be properly investigated and classified. Unfortunately, the news seems to have got out among the criminal fraternity."

"So this is why you want this information?"

Philip nodded. "That's right. I have come across an old document which says a treasure – probably the treasure of the

Cathars – was held in the Chateau de Blanchefort. I have been to look at the Chateau de Blanchefort which you mention, but I am sure it was never used for storing any treasure. So I believe it may be held in another chateau which now has a different name. That is why I have come here, to see if I can find a list of possible places to look at. I hope, if I can find this chateau, that it will get me closer to finding Jackie."

"And maybe the treasure as well?"

"Maybe, but I'm not bothered about that. It is Jackie who is my priority."

"*Mon dieu! Quelle histoire!* We must see if we can find her for you," Rafa redirected his attention to the sheet of paper in front of him. "From what I found out, I am guessing that de Voisins was awarded at least a part of the land and property previously belonging to the Blanchefort family. I presume they were supporters of the Cathar heresy and probably lost their lands as a consequence. Maybe they even lost their lives."

"You don't have an earlier document listing the properties held by the Blancheforts?"

He shook his head. "Unfortunately, no. Although the people of the Languedoc were theoretically subjects of the French king before the Albigensian crusade, they were in fact almost totally independent. I don't believe they kept records like this, and I wouldn't know where to find them if they did."

"So we're going to assume that anything belonging to de Voisins probably belonged to the Blanchefort family before the Albigensian Crusade."

"That is correct. That is quite likely what happened. During that crusade, the captured lands were often given in big groups to knights fighting with de Montfort, who were to hold them on behalf of the French king. This man de Voisins probably took over the Blanchefort properties. He might even have kept the man Blanchefort as a subordinate. That is because he would hope to have fewer problems with the local people if they could still see their former lord, even if he was no longer in power."

"I understand." Philip took a breath. "So, at any rate, you know the full extent of the de Voisins holdings?"

"That is correct. I have a list of properties and the names they were known by at the time the register was written. We need a suitable map so that we can put a circle round each of the *seigneuries* as we read them from the list. We would then end up with a plan of the lands which de Voisins was given. I hope that one of those might be the Chateau de Blanchefort which you are looking for."

"So I need to get a suitable map?"

Raphael nodded. "I hope I have found out what is the best map for you. I have made a note of it. It is a *Carte de Randonnée* – that is a map of footpaths for walking – which I believe will be most suitable." He handed Philip a slip of paper with the map number and name. "You will see it has a scale of four centimetres to one kilometre which I hope will be big enough to find any of the places listed. There is a big book shop in the Champs Elysées, which also specialises in maps, where you should be able to find it. Then tomorrow morning you can bring it here and we will mark it up."

Philip was full of enthusiasm for the task as he said *au revoir* to Rafa and set off to hunt for the map. The place he'd been directed to was a huge shop with a bewildering variety of maps, atlases and travel guides. However, a helpful assistant, who also possessed a certain amount of English, managed to track down the appropriate sheet.

The following morning Philip was at the Ministry of Culture before ten to meet Raphael as he arrived. They went up to his desk in the Archive Department and Philip spread the map out in front of them. He'd been studying the sheet over-night and immediately pointed out the three places he knew.

"This is the town of Quillan in the Aude valley. That is where I will be staying when I return to the Languedoc." He moved his finger across the map. "This one is called the Chateau des Templiers at le Bézu where we carried out the archaeological exploration and where we found the treasure. According to the journal of my ancestor, it was occupied by Pierre de Voisins at the time of the fall of Montségur."

Then he moved his finger to a point further north. "This is called the Chateau de Blanchefort. But I've walked up there and hardly any remains exist of the castle. Access to it would have been very difficult on anything but horse-back and I don't think it was ever an occupied castle. It certainly has splendid

168

views all round, but I can't imagine it was the actual seat of the Blanchefort family."

"OK. Let's ring those places as our starting points." Rafa drew circles round them with a soft pencil. "Now we will see if we can find any other properties held by de Voisins in 1259."

He reached over and picked up the schedule from the corner of the desk and set it down in front of him. There followed a most frustrating couple of hours while they tried to identify on the map the properties listed in the schedule. Very few of the modern names seemed to fit with the ancient descriptions. Of the total list of about twenty *seigneuries,* they could only locate four, including the Chateaux de Blanchefort and le Bézu. Another five they counted as possibles, and they were unable to identify the remainder. It was nearly lunch-time when Rafa called a halt.

"We haven't found much," said Philip. "All we know is that de Voisins certainly held a strip of land up here." He traced his finger down the map to the west of the Sals river. "But we don't know how far his lands stretched to the Aude river or how far north or south of le Bézu."

"That is correct," agreed Raphael. "I did not expect to find all the properties on the list but this is much worse than I hoped."

Philip looked back at the list. "There are seventeen *seigneuries* which we can't find or which we're not sure about. The fellow must have held quite a lot of properties."

"That is correct. I guess he was in control of most of the land between the Aude and Sals rivers but we cannot prove it. Let us go to lunch. Perhaps we will have a break-through this afternoon."

However, they had no more success when they returned, even though Rafa checked other sections of the register again to try to establish where abutting land holdings might exist.

As evening approached, he said, "I am sorry. I do not think I can help you any more. I think you will have to go to the local *mairies* and ask them if they recognise any of the names on the list. Often local people will be able to say 'Oh, yes. I remember my father using that name,' or something similar. You will have a copy of the schedule and the marked-up map. I hope that will help you find out some more."

"Well, thank you, Rafa. I appreciate all the time and the know-how you have put in to this. I am sorry to have taken you away from your research about Lyons for the best part of two days."

"Do not be sorry. I have liked it very much. I am sorry I cannot help you more. Will you please let me know if you find any of the other places on the list when you ask locally?"

Philip had come to regard Raphael as a friend in the short time they had spent together. They parted with a friendly handshake and he left the details of his hotel in Quillan with the young man, in case he should stumble upon any other information.

That evening, back at Bernard's place, he received a phone call on his mobile from César.

"Pierre has come back from Toulouse," she said. "He may have found out some things which will help you."

"What things?"

"It would be better if you will call round and we can discuss them."

"Well," said Philip, "I am in Paris at the moment, but I think I have more or less finished here. So I will come back to Quillan tomorrow. I will ring you when I get back. Is that OK?"

"That will be very good."

However, he had one further visit he wanted to make, and he discussed that with Bernard after dinner.

"I have got all the information I can from the Ministry of Culture, and I have to go back to Quillan to continue following up the leads locally."

"Of course, I understand that," agreed Bernard. "But please don't think I want to get rid of you. I've enjoyed having you here."

"And I've enjoyed my stay. Thank you very much for your excellent hospitality." He paused. "But I wondered if you could help me with one final visit."

Philip explained about Hector Ramise and his connection with Jackie. "I would like to meet him for a brief chat if that's possible."

"I don't see why not. I don't know the fellow personally, but I can ring the university in the morning and speak to Ramise and see if I can set up a meeting." Bernard smiled benignly. "Will that do for you?"

Profuse with thanks, Philip made for his bed.

# 33

Bernard Cambray rang the Sorbonne from his office at a quarter to ten the next morning. After a short exchange, he paused and turned to Philip.

"Unfortunately, Professor Ramise is not available at the moment. He is on an extended leave of absence."

"Can they tell us where he has gone?"

He returned to his phone conversation. After a while he had to wait while he was put through to another line.

"They're connecting me to his secretary."

A further short conversation ensued before he hung up.

"I have spoken to his secretary," he explained. "She sounds a very pleasant woman. She says she doesn't know exactly where he is, but she has a *poste restante* address for him where she sends mail. You could send a message to him to get in touch with you."

"That's a good idea. What is the address?"

"She started to give it to me, but I thought it would be better for you to meet her and dictate it to her to send direct." He smiled. "Remember, this Professor doesn't have a clue who you are. He might not take any notice of something sent direct from you. I thought it would carry more clout if it went from her with an added explanation. I felt that would be more likely to elicit a response. Do you agree?"

Philip nodded. "Yes, I can see the sense in that."

"So I have agreed we will meet Mademoiselle Palendrin at the university at eleven. It's only three stops on the Metro so I suggest we leave at about twenty minutes to. That means you can spend the next three quarters of an hour working out exactly what you want to say and I can make a few more important phone calls."

They were a few minutes late arriving at the Sorbonne, but it didn't seem to matter. They were directed to the office of the secretary who proved to be a spinster in her forties, with her hair stretched back in a bun and wearing darkened glasses. Philip thought her face and figure could have been attractive if she had taken some trouble with her make-up and clothes, but such considerations were obviously foreign to her nature.

Mademoiselle Palendrin explained she was actually secretary to several senior staff in the department, but she left him with the clear impression that she regarded Professor Ramise as the most important. She seemed to miss his presence at the head of the archaeological department.

Philip asked, "When did the Professor start his leave of absence?"

"About six weeks ago. He didn't return from the Easter vacation. Instead, he had spoken to the Dean during the holiday, and arranged it with him." She peered through her glasses at him. "It caused me a few problems, I can tell you. I had to arrange a number of replacement lectures and tutorials and find other people to take over his duties. It wasn't easy." She smiled tenderly. "But I understood the importance of him having to take time off to deal with the sudden crisis."

"What was this crisis?" asked Bernard.

"I'm afraid I don't know the details. The Dean only told me that he thought he had family problems."

"Does he have a large family?"

"I have no idea. He has never mentioned any of his family to me in the twelve years that he has been here." Her voice took on a peevish tone. "He has never even talked about whether he has a wife or not, although I assume he is unmarried. I am certain he has no close relatives in Paris."

"He doesn't have any family photos in his room?"

"No. The only pictures on his office wall are of official functions he has attended." She brightened. "Would you like to see them?"

"Yes, please."

Philip was aware of Bernard huffing slightly beside him. Obviously, all the agent wanted was for the draft message to be handed over and for them to be on their way. But Philip thought he should find out as much as he could about this man who had been a confidant of Jackie's, but an adversary of her uncle's.

They followed Mademoiselle Palendrin across the corridor and waited while she unlocked the door opposite with a key she had taken from her own top drawer. Professor Ramise's room was only a little larger than her own, but it had the benefit of a large window which looked down on one of the university quadrangles. There they could see a number of students and an occasional gowned academic strolling in discussion or sitting on one of the seats round the perimeter path, reading or simply enjoying the morning sun. However, Philip's interest was immediately taken inside the room by the three framed photographs hanging on the walls.

Two of them showed groups of academics in gowns and mortars, standing, looking seriously towards the cameraman. Presumably, these were taken at some university function. However, the third one interested Philip the most. It was of only two men, dressed as if for a special event. One was handing the other a scroll with a ribbon and seal dangling from it. He went over to look at it more closely.

"Which one is the Professor?"

"Oh - the one on the left. That is him receiving his accolade from the Austrian ambassador in recognition of the valuable research he had done on the dynastic connections of the Habsbourg royal family."

"That sounds a strange thing for a professor of archaeology to do," said Bernard.

Mademoiselle Palendrin was affronted. "Not at all. Archaeology is not only a matter of digging holes in the ground. Research into historical genealogies is closely linked. And the professor was very proud of the fact that he himself had ancient family associations with the Habsbourgs going back to the time of Marie Antoinette."

Philip was studying the photo. The professor looked a typical academic with dark hair and a matching goatee beard. He was shorter than the ambassador, but the most noticeable thing about him were the dark, gimlet eyes set deep into his face below his beetling brows. Philip had first thought he was wearing a suit but, when he got close, he could see the man had on dark slacks and a black jacket over a white shirt and striped tie. Then he felt a sudden shiver run down his spine and the hairs stood up on the back of his neck. The badge on the pocket of the man's blazer was the same double-headed eagle he had seen on the breast pocket of the jacket behind the door in the warehouse in Carcassonne and, later, on the bag in the hall at

174

César's cottage. Was it possible that the two blazers were the same?

For a moment, time seemed to stand still. Then Philip became aware that the room had gone silent. He turned to see the other two gazing at him. Had he gasped or let some other sound escape which warned them of the shock he had received?

"What is this badge on the professor's jacket?" he asked, trying to make his voice sound normal.

Mademoiselle Palendrin hurried forward and peered at it. "Oh, that is his best jacket that he wears to important events. The double-headed eagle on the breast pocket used to be the crest of the Habsbourgs. I believe he wears it to signify his old links with the royal family." She turned to Philip. "They used to be the rulers of the Holy Roman Empire, you know."

The Habsbourgs? Philip wondered how on earth they had become involved in this complex mystery.

"Do you think that's where he may have gone – to Austria, or is it Hungary?"

"Oh no," she said. "He is still in France."

"How do you know that?"

"I told Monsieur Cambray that I have a *poste restante* address to send all personal and important business correspondence to. I am sure he will be somewhere near there."

"And where is that?"

"Come back to my office." Mademoiselle Palendrin led the way out of the professor's room, carefully locking the door behind them, and returned to her desk. She sat down and opened the top right-hand drawer. From it she extracted a sheet of paper which she handed to Philip. He glanced at it and looked up into the dark eyes which were observing him steadfastly.

"This address is in Béziers."

"That's right."

"What a coincidence! Béziers is Jacqueline Blontard's home city. She is the lady I am searching for."

But perhaps it wasn't such a coincidence after all.

"It is also Professor Ramise's home city. He moved from there to Paris when he was awarded the prestigious Professorship of Archaeology at this university."

"You mean he no longer owns a property in Béziers? If he does, why should he need a post box there?"

It was Mademoiselle Palendrin's turn to look surprised. "I understand he does have a place there. I presume he has chosen to have a *poste restante* box because he is moving round, and it is easier for him to pick up mail from the central post office."

"Either that or he doesn't want people to know his address."

"What do you mean?"

"Do *you* know his address?"

"Oh, no." She looked uncomfortable. The secretary was not a good dissembler.

"However," said Philip, "I guess you've been told not to let anybody have it without his specific consent. Is that correct?"

She gave a little nod but stayed silent.

Philip reached out to shake her hand. "Well, thank you very much, Mademoiselle Palendrin. You've been most helpful." He turned to Bernard. "I think we'll go now."

"Don't you want to send him a message?" asked the agent.

"Not just yet."

Outside her office Bernard said, "You spent half an hour this morning drafting a message to send to this professor fellow and now you've dropped the idea."

"That's because I've found out two more things about him."

"What are they?"

"Firstly, that he wants to remain out of contact with everybody except his secretary. That means he's doing something down in the Languedoc that he wants to keep secret. And secondly there's the question of the badge on his jacket."

Philip told Bernard about the two previous occasions on which he'd seen the same badge.

He concluded. "Maybe I'm being unnecessarily suspicious, but I think this Professor Ramise is a bit dodgy. Anyway, I now know what he looks like, and I've got his postal address if I want to use it in the future. I just think I've got to be careful about what I say to the guy when I *do* write to him."

Bernard shook his head as he followed the young man down the corridor. "This business seems to be getting more and more complicated every day," he mumbled, almost to himself.

# 34

Armand had acknowledged that he was getting nowhere in Carcassonne. He was in daily touch with Inspector Martin but, beyond assuring him that all police patrol cars had been instructed to keep an eye open for a red MG sports car, the detective had been unable to provide any further information. In frustration, he decided to call Philip's mobile number on the Wednesday afternoon to see if he had found out anything of use while he was in Paris. When he rang, there was no immediate response, but a few minutes later he got a call back. Fortunately, Béatrice was still with him to do the translation.

A slightly breathless Philip said, "Sorry, I was on the *autoroute* when you rang. I pulled in to the first *aire* I came across, in order to return your call. What did you want to tell me?"

After a short exchange with Séjour, Béatrice took over the conversation, "I am speaking for Armand who is beside me. He says to tell you that he has found out nothing in Carcassonne and thinks he is wasting his time here. He has nothing to do, so he would like to help you as long as it doesn't mean going to Quillan. He asks, what did you find in Paris?"

"Ah." Philip was obviously a bit hesitant in saying too much to a woman he didn't know. "Tell him I spent two days at the Ministry of Culture archive department and I have a list of things that need to be looked at. I will see Jean-Luc tonight when I get back to Quillan and I have to go to see César tomorrow morning. I will try to meet Armand tomorrow afternoon."

Béatrice translated for Armand and his response was. "Ask him if I can look at any of those things for him tomorrow. I am sitting here doing nothing."

When she passed this on to Philip, he was quiet for a while and then he asked, "Would Armand be willing to go to Béziers? I need someone to watch the central post office there."

177

After a brief consultation, she told him, "Armand says anything would be better than sitting around in Carcassonne doing nothing."

"OK," Philip decided, "This man, who I will describe, often goes to the central post office in Béziers to pick up his mail. I want Armand to look out for the man to see if he calls in there." He shook his head. "The trouble is, Armand won't know what he looks like."

"He says does this man have a name?"

"Oh, yes. His name is Hector Ramise."

"Do you have an address for him?"

"I'm afraid not. He lives most of the time at the Sorbonne University in Paris where he is the Professor of Archaeology. I am told he has a place in Béziers, but I don't know the address."

"Wait a minute." There was a consultation between Béatrice and Armand. Then she replied, "Armand says that may not be a problem. He says you have probably given him enough information for him to get a photo from the police computer. He thinks this Hector Ramise will probably be well enough known for them to have him on record."

"My goodness. I'm not sure I like the sound of that. It sounds a bit like the big brother society."

"Well, it may be useful to us. Armand says, if you do not hear any more from him, he will be in Béziers tomorrow."

"Oh! Thank you very much."

"No problem. Goodbye, Monsieur Sinclair."


It was late in the evening when Philip got back to the Castle Hotel in Quillan. He had phoned ahead so Lerenard was waiting for him, drinking black coffee from a nearly cold *cafetière*. Philip surprised himself to find how pleased he was to see his friend.

"Gosh, I'm whacked," he complained as he collapsed into a chair beside Jean-Luc.

"You have been busy. Yes?"

"You can say that again. I've spent the best part of the last two days poring over maps and ancient property registers in the Ministry of Culture. Then, this morning, I was at the Sorbonne, checking up on Jackie's old archaeology professor. That meant I didn't leave Paris until after one o'clock.

Lerenard nodded. "So you have made good time. Did you learn anything useful in Paris?"

"You bet. I've got a lot to tell you. But first – how have *you* got on?"

"I've wasted the last four days and used up hundreds of litres of gasoline looking into every place I could think of for your damn car." He shook his head. "It seems to have disappeared from sight. In fact, I'm beginning to wonder if the vehicle ever came back to this area. Perhaps they were just leaving Carcassonne by the Limoux road to throw us off their trail."

"I don't believe that," said Philip. "They weren't to know we would have access to the police computers, or even if they had been picked up by a camera. No, I believe they are somewhere down this way. After all, they could easily have stuck the car away in a shed in some back street."

"If that is the case, we haven't got a chance of finding it."

"And what about Candice? Has she been trudging round behind you?"

"I haven't seen any sign of her." Lerenard grinned. "I think we did for her in Carcassonne. She's probably still going round in circles in the old city."

"Let's hope so. Now, I've got some ideas to try out on you."

"What are those?" He noticed Jean-Luc was suddenly alert.

"When I was at the Ministry of Culture I was introduced to a young researcher called Raphael Menton. He's something of an expert in searching for information about properties. When I got there, he had already found out that the Blanchefort family had lost all their lands at the time of the Albigensian Crusade which wiped out the Cathars."

"Is that so?"

"That's right, and he thinks it is more than likely that all their property was handed over lock, stock and barrel to a knight called Pierre de Voisins who, as I've probably told you, was the occupant of le Bézu castle at the time when the Cathars surrendered to the French at Montségur."

"What is this lock, stock and barrel?"

"Sorry. It's an English saying meaning the whole lot without exception." Philip hurried on. "Now, I've brought back a list of the lands and other properties that de Voisins held in 1259. That's fifteen years after the fall of Montségur. Unfortunately, we could only find four of his twenty-one properties on the map, and you'll see I've marked them."

He pulled out the sheet and unfolded it so that Lerenard could see what he was talking about.

"Rafa suggests that we should ask round locally to find out if anyone recognises any of the names. Apparently, ancient names often linger on in the speech of the locals without having been picked up by the map-makers. So we need to go to the various small communities, especially those close to castles, to find out if the names mean anything to them. Would you be willing to do that?"

"It sounds a bit better than driving round looking for a hidden car, and I guess *you* can't do it. I don't think your French is good enough."

Philip shook his head. "I don't think it is either. In any case, I've got to go and see someone tomorrow morning who may be able to help me with some more information. We could meet back here at lunch-time to see if there have been any developments and then decide what to do in the afternoon."

"Am I allowed to know who you are meeting?"

"I'm afraid I can't tell you that. I promised to keep the meeting secret."

"Are you sure you will be safe going to meet these people?"

"Oh yes. I'm not worried about *them*," he assured Jean-Luc. "And I will also make sure that I am not followed."

The big man shrugged. "I guess you know what you are doing."

"I promise you, in this case, that I do." Philip paused. "Now something else very interesting came up when I went to the Sorbonne this morning."

Philip told Lerenard the whole story of how he had come to enquire about Hector Ramise and what he had found when he went into the professor's office.

He went on, "You can see that it's almost certain this Ramise guy has been in the Languedoc area for some weeks now. He's probably staying in or somewhere near Béziers, which is less than an hour's drive from Carcassonne. I'm also pretty sure that it was the same jacket that he was wearing in the photograph which I found hanging on the back of the door in the warehouse. That means it was either Ramise or someone employed by him, who came back to collect it and bashed me on the head as a consequence."

Lerenard was smiling slightly as he listened. It was a disturbing sight.

"I agree with you," he said. "This Professor Ramise may come to regret that little mistake he made."

"The only thing I don't understand," said Philip, "is what this whole business has to do with the Habsbourgs." He shook his head. "But I guess that is probably unimportant."

"So this may be what you call in English 'a red fish'. Is that correct?"

Philip grinned. "You mean 'a red herring'. Yes, you're probably right."

He didn't know why he didn't tell Jean-Luc about seeing the same crest on Alain Hébert's bag in the cottage when he last went to see César. It might have changed Lerenard's judgement about the importance of the badge on the blazer.

Instead, he said, "Well, I'm tired. I'll leave you with the list and the map. Best of luck and I'll meet you here at lunch-time tomorrow."

They both made for their beds.

# 35

Next morning, Armand was seated at a pavement café across the central square in Béziers from the Post Office. He was enjoying his second café solo when he suddenly became alert. A middle-aged academic with a dark goatee beard had appeared from a side street and was walking purposefully across the square towards the post office building.

Armand dug in his pocket and pulled out the photo that he had obtained from Inspector Martin and looked at it. He raised his eyes to check it against the man who was now no more than ten metres away from him. One glance confirmed this was certainly Hector Ramise. As the professor mounted the steps and disappeared into the building, Armand called for his bill and got his camera with the telescopic lens ready.

It was only a few minutes later when Ramise came out of the building again and Armand raised his camera to take a picture. Then he stopped, for hanging on to the professor's right elbow was a well-dressed lady of a similar age to the professor. Ramise paused on the top step and looked down at her. Armand couldn't see the man's expression, but from the way she was smiling radiantly up at him, he immediately thought, "They are lovers".

He hastily clicked off three photos of the couple as they started down the steps and began to cross the square almost directly towards him. For a moment he was worried that they might have seen him take the shots and were coming to protest, but it soon became clear they were too wrapped up in each other to even notice they had been photographed.

They passed just a few metres away from him and took a nearby side street out of the square. Once they had disappeared, Armand got to his feet and dug into his trouser pocket for a few euros to pay for the coffee, which he left on the table. He slipped the camera into his jacket pocket and made for the corner where they had just left.

As he entered the street, he could see the couple were fifty metres ahead on the opposite pavement, strolling gently in deep conversation. There were quite a few other pedestrians around, so Armand wandered along his side of the street, pausing to look in the odd shop window from time to time so as to keep his distance from the two he was following.

They turned down the second side street on the right and went first left. A short length of road brought them to another, smaller square. However, they obviously had no intention of stopping there. They crossed the place diagonally and entered another, narrower street.

Pedestrians here were few so Armand lingered near the corner until he saw them exit from the other end of the alleyway, going to the left. Then he hurried after them. As he emerged, he saw he was now in a much wider avenue curving through a residential district of the city and following the contours of the hill on which Béziers stands. It was lined along both sides with low-rise blocks of flats of various architectural merit.

For a moment, he was worried he had lost them because they were not visible on either pavement beneath the shade of the trees. However, he suddenly caught sight of the professor's rather bent back disappearing through the glass door into the entrance lobby of one of the blocks of flats. Without hurrying, Armand crossed straight over the broad street and turned left to pass the block of flats that Ramise and his consort had entered.

By the time he had reached the glazed door where he had last seen them, the lobby was empty, so he went in. The first thing he inspected was the list of occupants. The name Ramise wasn't on the list, nor was any other name he recognised. He therefore had no idea of which flat they had gone to. When he pressed the button to call the lift, he noted that the sound of the doors closing was some distance away and the lift took a while to return to the ground floor. That suggested they had taken it to the top floor. However, when the lift doors opened, there was no clue except a slight flowery scent lingering in the enclosed car.

Armand shrugged. There was very little more that he could glean from his visit to Béziers. He took a photo of the list of flat occupants from close enough to be able to read the individual names. Then he crossed the road and took a couple more shots of the block of flats, so that he could easily identify it if he returned.

With a sigh, he went to collect his car in order to begin his vigil of watching the block until something happened. If necessary, he would remain there for the rest of the day.

# 36

Philip slept in late, so it was mid-morning before he reached César's cottage. As before, he found that her friend, Pierre, was present. The guy seemed to have taken on the role of her protector.

César greeted him warmly and led him into the front room where Pierre was waiting. He rose from the chair he was sitting in and treated Philip again to his bone-crushing handshake. He addressed a brief question to the young man in his coarse Marseillaise, which Philip found particularly difficult to understand.

César smiled sympathetically as she said to him, "Pierre asks if you were followed. Have you seen anything of Candice?"

"No. We think we've finally managed to lose her."

Philip told them about the girl being stopped by the police outside Carcassonne. "We haven't seen a glimpse of her since," he said. "I think she's given up and gone back to Marseilles."

But Pierre didn't agree. "That one will not give up," César translated. "She will not dare to go back to *le comte* and admit she has failed. You must continue to keep your eyes open," she said. Then she changed the subject. "So you have been to Paris?"

"That's right. I'm trying to find out where there is a castle called the Chateau de Blanchefort." He shook his head as she was about to speak. "I mean another one. I have been to the one marked on the map. As I expect you know, there's nothing but a few walls left there. But I believe there was at least one other castle that was owned by the Blanchefort family in the days of the Cathars and that may also have been known as the Chateau de Blanchefort at that time."

She agreed. "I understand what you mean. I will see if I can help you. You know that I had the job of researching the Cathar castles for *l'Observateur*. But first we must tell you what Pierre has found out."

"Yes please."

She nodded to her friend and spoke a few words to him before she said, "I will tell you what he has told me. Pierre went to Toulouse at the weekend. Using his position in *La Force Marseillaise* he was able to talk to some of the criminals there. Toulouse is not as well organised as Marseilles and there is no overall leader like *le comte*. Because of that, the individuals were more willing to talk."

"Was he in any danger?"

She put the question to Pierre and the reply was, "He says not. In fact, there is some jealousy about Gaston Lesmoines and the characters he has chosen to help him. He says the ones who haven't been chosen were more than willing to talk."

Pierre made another comment.

"He says nobody knows exactly what Lesmoines' group is doing. All he was able to find out was that they have gone to a place near Carcassonne. They are in a white Renault Trafic builders' van, and they have been promised a lot of money, even if the operation is only a partial success."

A worm of suspicion led Philip to ask, "Is the van sign-written? Has it got the name of the builders on the side?"

"I don't know."

"Does he have the name of the builders?"

There was another discussion in which he could make out little of what was said.

César translated Pierre's comments. "He says he was told the name of the builders is Granviers Frères."

Philip had a strange feeling he had heard the name before, but he couldn't remember exactly where.

"Well," he said, "Jean-Luc Lerenard and I are hunting round the countryside for my car and, as I told you, for the old names of some chateaux. We may as well keep our eyes open for a big white van with Granviers Frères painted on the side. Does Pierre have any further information?"

A further conversation ensued before César turned back to him.

"He says to be careful. This man Lesmoines has a bad name in Toulouse. He usually carries a gun, so if you find the van it would be good to keep clear of him."

"I agree. We'll call in the gendarmes if we see it. We can have contact with the Carcassonne police through Armand Séjour. They are likely to be looking for the same men."

When César told Pierre this, he looked doubtful and launched into another torrent of words.

"He says even the police in Toulouse will not tackle this group of criminals. They believe they are too dangerous. They are left to the armed response units."

Philip didn't know what to say to that. He commented. "I will pass on Pierre's warning to Jean-Luc . He will know what to do."

"That is wise. I think he is a strong man – no? Now I will talk to you about the chateaux. But first we must say goodbye to Pierre. He has other things to do."

She spoke a few words to her friend and the man got up, gave Philip another of his painful handshakes and made for the door.

"Please thank him for what he has done," said Philip, flexing his hand to restore the blood circulation.

César translated his mumbled reply. "He says he will continue to keep his eyes open."

She accompanied her friend to the front door and returned a few minutes later. Now she was carrying a bundle of papers.

"This is the information I picked up and the notes I made of the Cathar castles in the area. You probably know there are more than a hundred of which the remains can be traced. Some of them are sites which have been almost completely obliterated. There was a time when almost every mountain-top had a castle, or at least a watch-tower on it. I was often unable to find anybody who knew anything about a lot of them."

She spread her papers on the table. "I have notes of about forty of the best known. Here is my list. Do you have the list of properties held by de Voisins?"

"Unfortunately, I've left it and the map with Jean-Luc," Philip confessed. "I can recall a couple of the names, but I can't remember most of them."

"In that case you'd better copy my list and take it away with you to compare. I'll tell you where they are and give you any unusual information as we go through them. If you want to know more, you'll have to come back to me with your own list."

For the next hour Philip was busy noting the various chateaux on César's list, with her additional comments. They agreed there was no need to include the well-known ones. Also, he decided that some of the places were too far away to have been included in de Voisins' land-holdings. However, they ended up with fourteen interesting possible chateaux.

"Thank you, César," said Philip. "This information is most valuable. I'm meeting Jean-Luc for lunch, and we'll go through them and see whether we can find any matches between the two lists."

"If you have any problems, please come back to me. I may be able to add some details which will be useful to you. Also, if you bring the other list with you, it may help me to remember additional information that I picked up on my visits to the chateaux or on my research in the Cathar museum in Carcassonne."

"That's very kind of you. I do appreciate all the help you have given me."

She patted his arm. "I too am grateful for what you have done to help *me*."

Philip judged it was time to leave. As he made his way towards the front door, he again noticed the bag, with the Habsbourg crest on it, that was lying under the table in the hall. He pointed at it.

"Did you know that is the badge of the Austro-Hungarian royal family?"

César stopped and looked where he was pointing. "No. I did not know that."

"I've had a couple of funny experiences in connection with that badge. You know I told you I was banged on the head in a warehouse in Carcassonne?" Philip continued to tell her of his two sightings of the blazer with the crest on the pocket.

"It cannot have been Alain who banged you on the head," said César, "because he had already been shot when that happened."

Philip noted she could talk about her lover's death without getting upset.

"Oh, I'm not suggesting it was," he hastened to assure her.

188

She scratched her head. "Also, I never saw him wear a jacket with that badge on the pocket, so I don't think it was his."

"I'm sure that's right. It's just a strange coincidence that his bag has the same crest on it as Professor Ramise has on his blazer."

"Yes, it is strange," she admitted, then suddenly she said, "Do you want to know what is in the bag?"

"It does intrigue me," he admitted.

"I haven't opened it, so I don´t know what it contains." She picked it up. "But I don't think I should let you look through the contents until I've had a chance to check them myself, in case there is something which Alain would have wished to keep private. When I have seen what is in there, I will show you the contents and let you look at anything that might interest you, but which I don't think would be damaging to Alain's reputation." She smiled bleakly. "Is that reasonable?"

"That's very fair, César. I don't want to nose into Alain's private affairs. I'm only interested in anything which might help me to find Jackie."

So they parted as friends with that understanding between them.

# 37

When Philip arrived at hotel reception, he found that Lerenard was already there. After a brief greeting, he put the list he had brought from César on the low table between them, assuming they would work through the lists to try to find any comparisons. However, Jean-Luc forestalled him.

He was clearly enthusiastic. "At last I have found something useful."

Pulling his list out of an inside pocket he slapped it down on the table and placed a large finger about half-way down. "Do you see this one?"

Philip craned his neck, but Lerenard read it out.

"*Seigneurie de Pointevec.*" He leaned back in his chair. "By chance I went into a bar in Couiza. It was early and there were only two old boys in the place, drinking their cider. It was no problem at all to engage them in conversation. So I started pulling names from the list to see if they meant anything to them. They just shook their heads each time until I got to this one – Pointevec." He grinned. "That obviously stirred a memory and they started talking between themselves. Apparently, the old granny of one of them used to refer to a place nearby which sounded something like Pointevec."

He took a breath. "Then they started arguing about what she meant exactly and, to shut them up, I asked them where it was. At first, they said they didn't know, but gradually they came round to agreeing that it was probably an earlier name of an old ruined village about ten kilometres away, which is now called –." He consulted the note he had scribbled on the side of the list. "- it's called Castereau."

Lerenard sat up, but continued without a pause. "Then they started discussing the village and what was there. Apparently, they used to go up there with their parents when they were kids to collect whortleberries in the autumn. After a bit of chat, they agreed that there had once been a big castle right beside the settlement. That caught my attention, I can tell you. So I asked what the name of the castle was."

By now Philip was hanging on every word the big man was uttering. "Go on," he urged. "So what was the name?"

"Well, at first the only name they could come up with was Castereau – the same name as the village. But when I reminded them of the old name of de Voisins holding – Pointevec – they were confident that wasn't the name of the castle." A grin slowly spread across his face. "So I tried Blanchefort on them and after a further long discussion they decided that was possibly the name it used to be known by."

"That's fantastic."

Jean-Luc raised a cautionary finger. "I didn't want them to have made a mistake. So I asked them, wasn't that the name of the castle marked on the maps at the summit of that mountain nearby that you and I climbed up to the other day? I pointed out that was called Blanchefort. But they dismissed that out of hand as being nothing but a watch-tower that some young mapmaker had labelled incorrectly."

"Yes," agreed Philip, "It's amazing how easy it is to make a mistake about that sort of thing."

"Anyway," said Lerenard, "I got directions from this pair on how to find this ruined village and then I set off to look for it. In fact it's only about five kilometres off the main road but the track to it is difficult. You can't really call it a road because the boundary walls have often collapsed and in places the tarmac surface has broken up. It's more of a farm track and it's probably only used by farmers now to get up to their crops."

"But you managed to reach the village?" asked Philip.

"Oh, yes. The road isn't impassable by any means, so I got there."

Philip could tell Jean-Luc was enjoying making him wait for the punch-line.

"Well, as the old boys had said, nobody lives there anymore, but the buildings aren't ruined. The roofs of the cottages look as if they're in good condition. The doors are locked, and the shutters are closed across the windows and secured from inside, and I think the place could easily be occupied again if anyone wanted to live in such a remote spot."

"Did you say something about a castle?"

"Yes. That *is* partly ruined. It was quite big once – at least three storeys high. But the side that faces the village has partly fallen in and much of the original stone seems to have been used over the years to repair and extend the village buildings. The other side of the castle doesn't look so bad, but it overhangs the valley and is not easily accessible. I must admit I didn't try to explore the place because the next thing I saw changed my outlook and had me hurrying back here to see you." He paused to let the tension build.

Philip couldn't wait. "Go on. What did you find?" he demanded.

"I found your car."

"What?"

"That's right. I stopped my car and got out and took a stroll round the village and just round the corner from the square was a lean-to roof against the back of one of the cottages." He shrugged. "Your car had been parked in it to keep it under cover from the weather. It was locked. It has a thin covering of dust, which suggests it hasn't been used for several days. But otherwise it seems undamaged."

"That's fantastic, Jean-Luc. Well done and thanks a lot."

The big man smiled. "Of course, I couldn't get into it without cutting the hood, so I came back to see if you have a second key for it. If you haven't, I can probably get in through the roof and I can hot-wire the engine to get it started. Once it's running, we can reclaim it."

Philip jumped up. "Actually, I've got the spare key in my bag upstairs. I brought it with me when I left England because I didn't know when I might return. I have it in mind to sell the MG and get something bigger. That was lucky. I'll go up and get it."

"Do you want to have something to eat before we go?"

"I don't think so. How far is this ruined village?"

"Less than twenty kilometres – about half an hour's drive each way, allowing for the state of the track to get up to it."

"So we'll be back here in an hour or so." Philip shook his head. "We can warn Henri to keep lunch for us. We'll be ready to celebrate by then."

He rushed off up to his room to find the key.

# 38

Lerenard drove them to Castereau in his car. As they went, Philip told him about what he had learnt at his meeting with César and Pierre.

"Am I allowed to know who gave you this information?" asked the big man.

On consideration, Philip couldn't see why he shouldn't tell Jean-Luc about César. "I can't tell you where I met her, because I've promised to keep her hiding place secret."

However, he described the help he had given her to make her escape from the Toulouse prison hospital, and the fact that *le comte* was trying to find her to make sure she was taken out of circulation.

When he had finished, Lerenard said, "You've been very kind, I'm sure. Just make certain that you watch your back."

"Pierre told me that is why Candice Ambré is following me."

"I think we have lost her."

"He says she will still be around somewhere. She will not have given up. He says she will be too frightened of *le comte* to go back and tell him she has failed."

Lerenard snorted but didn't reply. Just at that point, they turned off the main road and started the difficult ascent to Castereau. Philip could soon see why very few people now went to visit the place. Even when the road had been properly maintained, it would have been quite a heart-stopping drive. It clung to the side of the mountain, overhung in places by almost vertical cliffs and with deep drops on the other side, frequently without the protection of a low wall alongside the road, lack of maintenance having caused some of those to fall into the valley below.

From time to time they came to sharp hairpin bends that they had to ease round in low gear. On one corner Lerenard even had to reverse a short way to get past, and Philip imagined the rear of the car hanging above a drop of more than three hundred feet for a few moments. Then they came to a section where the tarmac had broken up and had fallen away in places. The car bucked and bounced over the rough surface and stones were thrown up by the spinning tyres to rattle the underside of the vehicle.

"Christ, this *is* rough," muttered Philip at one stage.

Jean-Luc chuckled. "I would not like to drive this route in the wet or when it is dark."

After a while, the road started to level out and they found themselves climbing the last gentle rise with the backs of the village houses rising above them. Then they turned a last sharp bend between two buildings and suddenly burst into the dusty central square. The shuttered buildings stared sightlessly down on them as the car halted in the clear area in the middle.

Lerenard switched off, opened the door and climbed out. Philip did the same, slamming the door behind him. He stared round at the walls of grey stone. As the echoes of their entry died away, an almost tangible silence descended over the place. There was no noise to be heard. Not a cat mewed, not a bird called, even the leaves on the trees hung without a rustle in the still air. Life truly seemed to have abandoned Castereau.

Philip noted that the small square they had entered was surrounded on three sides by single and two-storey cottages, except where the walls were punctuated in two places by tracks between the buildings and in a third place by the road they had just ascended. However, it was dominated on the fourth side by the large half-ruined bulk of the castle, which lay back a little behind a short, overgrown front garden between two high side-walls. There had once been railings along the edge of the square, but these were rusted and broken down in places. He noticed the castle was a bigger building than the rest, more than twice as high as any of the other houses, even where the front wall had been partly destroyed to rob it of its masonry.

Apparently not noticing the sinister atmosphere of the place, Lerenard broke the silence. "Your car is just over here."

He led Philip to a track which went through a gap between the last cottage and the railings along the front of the castle. Just round the end of the building was the lean-to he had described and there stood the little MG, its red colour dimmed by the thin film of dust. He went over to it and tried his key in the lock. It opened without any problem. He brushed off the seat with his hand and climbed in.

Philip had been half expecting to need a tow to start the vehicle if the battery had run down, but it started with only the second turn of the ignition and burst into life, emitting a small cloud of blue smoke, before settling down to a steady tick-over. He climbed out and walked round to where Jean-Luc was standing.

"Well, that seems all right," he said. "What shall we do now – have a look round the castle?"

Lerenard shook his head. "Before we do that, I think I should move my car out of sight down one of the side-tracks, I am a little worried about what would happen if the men who left your car here decide to come back while we are exploring."

"OK. I'll just switch off and relock the MG. There won't be a problem with that car now."

He went over and killed the engine, and the silence settled over them again as he locked the door and returned to Jean-Luc's side. They went back round the corner to the square and there they had a shock. The road into the village was now blocked by a large white Renault Trafic van with the name *Granviers Frères* painted on the side. Gaston Lesmoines was bent down, peering into the unlocked interior of Lerenard's car.

He straightened up as he saw them come round the corner. "How interesting," he said and a strange smile crossed his face. "It is Monsieur Sinclair in the company of the assassin Lerenard."

Philip hadn't previously noticed how stout and muscular Lesmoines was, or how his presence seemed to exude evil. He was aware that Jean-Luc, who was close to the cottage wall, had frozen beside him. Philip took a breath.

"I've come to collect my car, which I presume you took," he said. "At least you seem to have kept it under cover and it started again all right. I'll take it back to Quillan if you'll move your van out of the way."

"You English like your jokes," Lesmoines sneered. "Is that all you've come to collect?"

Philip had a sudden thought. "What have you done with Jeanette?"

"She is quite safe. In fact, I will take you to see her now. But first we must check you for weapons."

Lerenard spoke for the first time. "How will you do that?"

"Quite easily. *Attention*!"

Two men came from behind the van, both carrying guns. Lesmoines, who appeared to be in charge, rapped out an order. One of the men handed his gun to him and approached them. The other kept his weapon trained on Lerenard.

"Don't argue at this moment," said Jean-Luc quietly out of the side of his mouth.

The man patted his hands up and down both their bodies in a professional way before he turned back to Lesmoines, raising his shoulders and opening his hands to show he had found nothing. Philip was surprised he didn't discover a weapon on Lerenard. Somehow he thought his friend would have been better prepared.

"Now I want you to follow me." Lesmoines made for a gate in the railings beside the castle wall.

"Do we have to go?" asked Philip.

Jean-Luc snorted. "Those machine pistols aren't for fun."

So Philip shut up and followed the big man as he trailed Lesmoines down the path and the two gunmen fell in behind. At the bottom of the path, a door in the side wall was unlocked and they entered a short passageway. They emerged into the central courtyard of the castle. From here it was clear that the side of the castle away from the village was still in a reasonable state of repair.

They were ushered none too gently through a doorway and down a dog-leg flight of stone steps. At the bottom, they came into a corridor which ran right and left, apparently towards the extremities of the castle. A short way along this passage Lesmoines stopped in front of a door and took down an old cast iron key from a hook just to the right of the frame.

He unlocked the door. "Please go in."

Philip hesitated for a second, but Lerenard nudged him from behind and said, "Do as he tells you."

As he entered, Philip saw a face peer up at him from a blanket-wrapped bundle huddled on a hay bale in the corner. The next second, she had leapt to her feet and hurled herself at him.

"Oh, Philip. Philip. You have come to rescue me."

It was difficult to realise the person was Jeanette. Her usually splendid figure was wrapped in smelly old clothes with pieces of straw sticking out of them. Her hair was a tangled, uncombed mess. Her dirty, tear-stained face lacked any touch of make-up. She was in a dreadful state.

"What on earth has happened to you, Jeanette?"

"That evil sod," she pointed at Lesmoines, "has kept me imprisoned here for weeks."

"Has he ill-treated you?"

"I haven't touched her," came from the doorway.

"Ill-treated? It's been torture. I've just been left on my own to moulder away."

"But he hasn't hurt you." Philip looked round the room. "Has he fed you?"

"Just cold water and bread and cheese," she sobbed, "and he's never talked to me or answered my questions. Nobody hears me when I cry for help. He must be sent to prison for the way he has treated me."

"I think that may have to wait for a while," said Lerenard.

Then the door banged shut and the three of them were imprisoned in the dungeon. Jeanette again burst into floods of tears and clung to Philip.

# 39

After the door had shut on their prison cell, the two men were left standing, looking at each other. Philip still had the snuffling Jeanette clinging to him.

"Well, we didn't do too well there, did we?"

"No." Jean-Luc shook his head. "We were totally surprised by that lot. I don't know where they came from. I looked behind me several times when we were driving up to the village and I saw no-one. We were only a few minutes with your car and there they were – and I didn't hear any noise."

"It's a mystery," agreed Philip. "The van seemed to have come into the village from outside and the only way was up the same road we used."

Lerenard shrugged. "Well, you can't argue with machine pistols. They have got us now."

"I wonder what they'll do next."

"They will keep you here and just feed you when they have to." Jeanette sniffed. "I don't know how many days I have been kept here with just that bucket in the corner and nowhere to wash."

Philip hugged her dishevelled body. "At least you're not alone anymore."

"They will not want to keep us in here very long," said Jean-Luc. "The police hadn't started a proper hunt for the girl before because we said *we* were doing it but, as soon as Séjour realises we have also disappeared, he will get a full police search under way. They will have our descriptions. It won't be long before they speak to those old guys I met in Couiza."

"That means they'll come straight up to Castereau," Philip agreed. "Even if Lesmoines and his cronies find somewhere to hide our cars, they'll find it difficult to dispose of all the signs that we have been here, so we shouldn't have long to wait."

"It is probably correct that the police will descend on this place in large numbers. They will search everywhere. This place will be too hot for the gang outside to stay here."

"So how long do you reckon?" asked Philip. "Two days – three days?"

Lerenard pulled a face. "Don't be too hopeful, my friend."

"What do you mean?"

"It won't take this guy, Lesmoines, long to reach the same conclusion that we have. He will realise that means his gang can't just sit tight and wait for the search to move on somewhere else. They will have to do something. We should consider what are his options."

Philip suddenly realised their situation was serious. "So what would you say *are* his options?"

"First, they can get out fast and go back to Toulouse. That will mean they abandon any thought of getting hold of the treasure, It will also mean loss of face and power for Lesmoines."

"Right, so he will try to avoid that option. What else?"

"Second, they can abandon this place and move somewhere else, if they have another place in mind." He shook his head. "But are they likely to find another base as good as this one? And in any case, once the police find us, we will be able to give them much more information about names and forms of transport. That will make the whole area much too hot for them to stay."

"So give us the third option," said Philip, his heart sinking as he knew what it was going to be.

"The third option is for them to get rid of us, hide the cars deep in the forest where they won't be found for a long time and bury our bodies in some hidden grave. Then they'll clean up this room and any signs of life in the village and the castle and lie low in the hope that the search will soon move on elsewhere."

"Surely they wouldn't kill us," breathed Jeanette. "What have we done that would make them commit multiple murder?"

"These men are known killers," said Jean-Luc as gently as he could. "If they think it will help them get what they want, they will regard killing us as a necessary chore."

"Oh, God! Why did I get involved in this?" Jeanette subsided into further sobs.

Philip shook his head. This was the second time he had to face death in less than a month. He said, "The Languedoc seems to be a dangerous area."

"You'd better believe it," said Lerenard, "especially when there's a priceless treasure involved."

"So what do we do?"

"We must fight back, of course."

"And how will we do that? We've got no weapons. We're imprisoned in a basement cellar with a thick locked door being the only way out. I'd say the odds are stacked against us."

There was a ghost of a smile on the big man's face as he said, "We do have weapons."

Philip and Jeanette watched in amazement as he bent down and took off his shoe. He pressed in and twisted the sole to one side, reached in with his fingers and extracted what looked to be a flat piece of steel about four inches long and a quarter of an inch thick.

"The man who searched me for weapons was not very good," he said. "Now you must watch me."

He placed the flat piece of steel in the palm of his hand with it extending along his index finger.

"You must hold it like this so that you don't do yourself damage. Then you press the black button just here with your thumb, like this."

As he did so a smaller, very thin piece of steel sprang out of the end.

"This blade is only nine centimetres long but it is very sharp." He pointed to a location on the front of his shoulder. "You see this place just here on the joint of his arm? If you get close enough to your attacker, you release the blade and push it straight into this joint and wriggle it about a bit. That will cause the man a great amount of pain and he will not be able to do anything with his arm. If you are quick enough to do it to the other shoulder, you will completely disable him without killing him."

He pressed the blade back in against the heel of his shoe and handed it to Philip. "Remember the blade is very sharp. It could cut your finger off without applying any pressure."

Philip took hold of the cold, flat piece of steel and put it in the palm of his hand as Jean-Luc had instructed. He gently pressed the black button, which he noticed was slightly recessed. He jumped as the blade shot out, causing Lerenard to snigger. Feeling a little embarrassed, he bent down and pressed the tip of the blade to the floor. He could hear the slight click as the blade was retained in its metal sheath.

"You are right-handed so you should put it in your right jacket pocket with the button on the inside. That way it will not be released by mistake. If you need to use it, lift it out by holding it in the middle and try to do it when you are not being watched, so that you can check it is the right way round in your hand."

"What about you?"

"I have another one." Lerenard changed shoes and extracted a twin strip of steel from the sole of his other shoe, which he then dropped into his pocket.

"So," said Philip, "when the guy with the food comes in we must have the knives ready in our hands and get close enough to stick them in his shoulders."

"No." Lerenard shook his head. "That will not work. There will be at least two men. One will stand near the door with a machine pistol at the ready. The other will be carrying the food."

"OK. What are we going to do?"

"I have another weapon."

He undid the belt on his trousers and slipped it out of the loops. He lifted a small tab behind the buckle and slid out a long length of thin wire.

"This is a garrotte," he said. "The middle twenty centimetres is very sharp. It can cut a man's head off if I use a quick sawing movement."

"My God!" Philip exclaimed. "Thank goodness you're on our side."

"I always carry these things. They are the tools of my trade."

"So what will you do with the garrotte? Surely, to use it, you will have to get behind the man, and he won't want you to do that."

"That is correct. I will stand behind the door. When it opens, I hope the man with the gun will come in first and stand to one side for the other man to bring in the food. I will slam the door and garrotte him. Then I will open the door and turn his machine pistol on the man carrying the food. He will have both his hands full, but I must be very quick."

"How do you know the first man won't look for you behind the door?"

"He will not do that because he will be too interested in the little play which you and Jeanette will be doing for him."

Philip began to suspect something as he asked, "What play do you have in mind?"

Lerenard's smile broadened. "When he opens the door, you will be having sex with the naked Jeanette."

"What!"

"These men have been hidden in this castle for several days without a woman. I expect they have already discussed having sex with her. In fact, I am surprised she has not already been raped several times. It is perhaps because she is not very desirable in her present dirty condition."

Jeanette at last found her voice. "Oh, thank you very much."

"But still," he nodded in apology, "I am sure she will be very interesting to them when she has no clothes on. So she will undress before they come with the food and will be wrapped in some loose clothing which she can throw off quickly when we hear the key in the lock. You, Philip, must be naked from the waist down and it would be good if you can have a – what do you call it – a stiff."

"You mean an erection."

"That's right. You will grab her, and you will start to – er – fuck her – as I think you English call it. I promise you that both men will be so surprised that, for a few vital seconds, they will forget about me."

"I'm not sure I will be able to rape her," said Philip.

"It will not be rape," she said, and smiled at him demurely. "I think Jean-Luc's idea is a very good one. The best way is for you to do it from behind. I will kneel on the straw bale, and you can come up between my buttocks. Even though I have been half-starved for more than a week you can feel my breasts are still big. When you come at me from behind you can put your hands under my breasts to lift them up and show the nipples. I will be facing the door and that will give the men a very fine sight."

"Are you serious?"

"Yes, she is," said Lerenard, "and if you want to live you must be serious too. You must really want to do a fuck on Mademoiselle Jeanette."

The girl actually giggled as she said, "I told you I would have you again, Philip."

"Actually, you will be in great danger," said Jean-Luc. "As I tighten the garrotte the automatic reaction of the man will be to fire the gun. I will try to pull him backwards so that he fires at the ceiling. But I will also shout 'Dive!' and you must both immediately throw yourself on the floor to avoid being shot."

"What about the other man?"

"It will take no more than three seconds with this very sharp wire to sever the wind-pipe and the jugular vein. If the other one is carrying a gun as well as the food, I will try to get him before he can use it."

"So what if this little show doesn't work?"

"I think it will work." Lerenard grinned widely for the first time. "And if it doesn't work you will have had free fuck with Mademoiselle Jeanette."

She giggled again. "Oh, yes. That part will work all right."

Philip found himself chuckling as well, as he said, "What a lovely way to go."

"That is correct. You will be the envy of the six sex-starved men in the gang." He beamed. "In fact, if we don't escape, they may decide that what she so generously shares with you, she can go on and share with all of them."

"*That* is not funny," she pouted.

"Then we must hope our little play works," agreed Lerenard. "Now, there is one other thing. When the door opens, you must tell me how many men are there. Just shout the single word – 'two' for example. That is so I will know what I am dealing with." He took a breath. "Well, we had better get ourselves ready to put our plan into operation as soon as they come for us. We will only have one chance, so I think you two must undress now."

Jeanette started straight away, throwing off her coat, stripping off her sweater and jeans and her rather grubby-looking underclothes. She stood proudly arrayed to the two men, with her full breasts just drooping slightly.

"Come on, Philip," she urged.

203

"Do I need to take everything off?"

"No," said Jean-Luc. "Just take off your trousers and underpants. You can leave your socks on and put your shoes back on after you have removed your trousers. I don't think they will notice that."

"Can't I just push my trousers down to my ankles when we hear the key being turned in the lock?"

"Certainly not." Lerenard shook his head firmly. "You may need to move fast when things start happening. You can't do that if your trousers are round your ankles. I'm afraid you will have to forget your English prudishness for a while."

As he lowered his trousers Jeanette whooped, "I knew why you didn't want to take off your trousers. You didn't want us to see your great big . . . ."

"Will you please be quiet, Jeanette," Philip interrupted her. "No wonder I'm reluctant to do this with you, if you make such a fuss about it."

Crestfallen, she subsided. "I bet you really enjoy it but won't admit it." She turned her back on him. "You must cuddle up to my back to keep me warm. I will drape my coat over my front so that I can throw it off quickly."

So Philip pressed his half-naked front against her soft, warm buttocks and wrapped his arms round her front to hold the coat in place.

"How long do you think we will have to keep this up?" he asked, aware that Jeanette's hands were already starting to explore his nether regions.

"I will go and listen at the door," said Jean-Luc. "Maybe I will be able to hear them when they come down the steps."

But at that very moment there came the sound of the key being pushed into the lock. Lerenard hurried to a position behind the door. After a brief tussle, Jeanette dragged off her coat and threw it aside. She grabbed Philip's hands and pressed them under her breasts and arched her back to make them stick out.

"One," shouted Philip as the door swung open, and then, "No! Don't!"

The dark-haired woman who had entered screamed as the big man pushed the door back, leaped forward and brought the garrotte down over her head.

204

Then everyone froze.

# 40

For a few heartbeats nothing happened. Then Lerenard released one end of the garrotte and pushed the woman towards the centre of the room.

"You were within three millimetres of death," he growled. "Are you alone?"

She gulped. "Yes."

Philip was hastily dressing as he watched the woman. He noticed she was quite small. Her hair was almost black, and a pair of large spectacles partly obscured her face, but there was something vaguely familiar about her features. She was dressed all in black – a quilted bomber jacket with the zip pulled up to the neck and tight trousers tucked into calf-length boots.

The big man moved up behind her and slid a hand into the side pocket of her jacket. It came out holding a small gun.

"How many slugs in this pop-gun?" he asked.

"Five."

"Have you got any spares?"

"One clip in my left pocket."

He extracted it, then swivelled the woman round. "Who are you?"

"My name is Béatrice. I am helping Armand."

"No, you are not." Jeanette, who had been dressing rather more slowly than Philip, faced her, still in her half-dressed state. "I have never seen you with Armand."

Lerenard pointed at her. "You are Candice from Marseilles with your hair dyed black."

In the silence that followed, Philip realised why he had thought there was something familiar about the woman.

Jean-Luc recovered first. "So why are *you* here, Candice?"

"I told you I am helping Armand."

"Armand isn't here."

"No." She turned and pointed. "But Philip is."

"So you are following Philip."

Philip was suspicious of her story. "Why did Armand ask you to follow me?"

206

"I don't know. You will have to ask him. He just asked me to follow you."

"And you did it without asking why?"

"Yes. He just told me that it was important that nothing bad happened to you. He has gone to Béziers as you asked him to. But he will be back in Carcassonne this evening."

"Well," Philip smiled, "it was good luck that you did as he asked. I don't know what would have happened to us if you hadn't turned up. Now, hopefully, you can help us get away from this gang."

"I will do my best."

"We are wasting time," interrupted Lerenard. "Do Granviers Frères know you are here?"

"No. I left my car in a side gulley down the road and walked up. By the time I arrived, they had gone back into their house, so they did not see me."

"Which house is that?"

"The first one on the right as you enter the village."

The big man nodded. "So they are not in the castle."

"How did *you* get in?" asked Philip.

"The same way that you did – through the corridor and down the stairs."

"Is there another way?" demanded Lerenard.

She shook her head. "I did not see them use any other way."

"So," he said, "the men are in the house. How many are there?"

"I saw six."

"Uhuh - the three who caught us and three others." He paused. "Now, where is their van?"

"It is in the same place as it was when they caught you."

"Did you see where it came from?"

"Yes. It was parked round the back. Five men came out and pushed it through the narrow opening with one sitting in the cab, steering. They just pushed it across the yard to block your exit."

"Hmm." Lerenard seemed to think aloud. "I wonder if we could quietly push it back out of the way so that we could get our car past."

"That would be easy. They have left the keys in the ignition."

207

"Have they, by God!"

He paused as he thought out his strategy. "Can you drive enough to start the engine of the van and steer it out of the way?"

Candice looked affronted. "Of course."

He turned to Philip and Jeanette, who were now fully dressed. "Are you two ready to leave?"

"Certainly."

"Philip - I want *you* to go to my car, unlock it, get in the driver's seat and put the key in the ignition ready to start the engine when I give you the signal. But don't start it until I fire the first shot with this pistol. Candice, I want you to do the same with the van. You will only drive it a few metres – enough to stop it blocking the exit from the village square. Then you will switch off, remove the keys from the ignition and go to join Jeanette who will already be lying down in the back of the car."

He paused for a second. "Is that clear? Now Philip, as soon as Candice gets in the car, you must drive it out of the village and stop just round the corner with the passenger door open, ready to set off like hell down the road as soon as I jump in."

Philip pulled a face. "I'm not a rally driver, Jean-Luc. I don't want to crash the car."

"You only have to drive about four hundred metres then, we can stop and change places."

"OK. I'll do my best."

"I have done rally driving," said Candice unexpectedly. "I will drive the car, if you have started the engine running for me and got out of the driver's seat."

Lerenard agreed with that proposal. "That's a good idea. You start the car, Philip. Leave the driver's door open and jump in the back and lie down with Jeanette."

"I will be ready for you," she giggled.

"What about *my* car?" Philip asked.

"For now, that must stay here. I hope we will be able to get it back later."

"Right. That's clear. So when are we going to go?"

"Now! Is everybody ready?"

Lerenard opened the door, the little gun at the ready in his hand. Luckily there was still nobody to be seen outside. They went up the stairs and through the corridor, with the big man leading. Just outside the castle side door, he signalled a halt. He pointed to the house where the crooks were holed up.

"Wait for me to get to that door before you move. I will signal when I'm ready for you to go." He handed Philip the ignition keys. "Remember to hurry but try not to make a noise. Be ready to start both vehicles but wait until you hear my shot before either of you starts your engine. OK?"

They both confirmed that they understood, and Lerenard set off at a low-crouched, scuttling run. Philip noticed the village once again appeared to be deserted. Lesmoines and his cronies must have thought there was no need to keep watch. Presumably, at this moment, they were discussing precisely how they were going to dispose of their prisoners.

Lerenard paused, doubled-up, by the gate and carefully opened it without a creak. Then he hurried over to the door of the cottage. He paused with his hand on the handle, looked back and gesticulated to them to make for the vehicles. He was holding the little gun in his other hand.

Candice led the way, running quietly in her soft-soled shoes. She opened the van door with a gentle creak of the hinges. Philip paused when he reached the car to make sure Jeanette was climbing into the back. Then he got into the driver's seat and pushed the key into the ignition. He gave a thumbs-up sign to the watching Lerenard to indicate he was ready.

The big man pressed down the handle on the cottage door and swung it wide open, keeping to one side so as not to present a target. He fired a shot into the front room of the house, shouted something and fired a second shot. Philip imagined the crooks diving for cover.

Candice started the engine of the van and the big vehicle lurched half-way across the square before coming to a halt. Out of the corner of his eye, Philip saw her jump from the cab and run towards the car as he turned the key in the ignition. The engine started at the second attempt. He had hardly got out before Candice was climbing into the seat. He just had time to get into the back of the car and close the door before she set off.

Jeanette was waiting to hug him close to her recumbent form and plant an open-mouthed kiss on his face. "I'm going to have you when we get back to the hotel," she murmured. "You owe it to me. I've been thinking about it for more than a week."

Philip tried to ignore that. To Candice he said, "It all seems to be going like clockwork – just as Jean-Luc planned."

"No it isn't," she replied. "I couldn't get the van key out of the ignition, There must be some button to press to release it, but I couldn't find it and I didn't want to hold you up. So they will be able to follow us in the van."

"Don't worry. You should be able to outrun them in this car."

"I hope so."

She started forward in a cloud of gravel and dust, drove out of the square and stopped just round the corner. She leaned across and opened the passenger door as instructed. They heard several light shots from the little gun held by Jean-Luc and then there was a burst of machine fire from inside the house. The next moment, the big man came sprinting round the corner and dived into the front seat,

"Move fast," he instructed. "They've recovered quicker than I hoped."

Candice needed no urging. She set off down the narrow, twisting road at what seemed to Philip to be a break-neck speed, four-wheel drifting round the bends just a few feet from the precipitous drop, with stones spurting from under the wheels.

Lerenard had been watching through the rear window. "Keep your heads down," he warned.

The next second there came a burst of firing from one of the machine pistols and a number of bullets slammed into the back of the car.

"Watch out," yelled Candice as the car went into a crazy zig-zagging slide. "I think they've punctured a tyre."

"Can you get round this next bend?" asked Jean-Luc. "If you can, we should be protected by the overhang of the cliff."

Somehow, she got the car round the corner and stayed partly on the road. They came to a halt with one side of the tail of the vehicle hanging over the three-hundred-foot drop. They all got out as hastily as they could. Lerenard bent down to inspect the rear wheels.

"Both rear tyres have been split open," he announced, "and the fuel tank's been hit and is leaking. This car won't go any further." He addressed Candice. "Where did you leave yours?"

"It's about half a kilometre down the road in a short side gulley, but it will take us a while to reach it."

"Well, I'll go back to the corner. I've got this new clip of five rounds to put in the pistol. I should be able to hold them at bay while you get the car and back it up to collect me."

Candice shook her head. "I wasn't able to get the ignition key out of the van so they'll drive down in that. We'll never get there before they're on to us."

As though to accentuate the peril they were in, they heard the roar of the van's engine as it was started up and began to manoeuvre in the square to chase after them.

"We haven't any choice," decided Lerenard. "Do your best to get to the car as quickly as possible. They can't get down the road while my wrecked car is blocking it. So – get moving."

Obediently, they set off at a run down the road. Candice seemed fit and could almost keep up with Philip, but Jeanette was no good at this kind of thing. She lagged behind and complained loudly that they weren't looking after her and that they didn't care what happened to her.

After a short time, he told Candice, "You hurry on and get the car onto the road. I'll go back and help Jeanette."

He turned back. As he returned, he saw the van come out of the village and start down the road towards them. From his vantage point he could see Lerenard crouched in the shelter of the cliff. How was the man going to stop the charging van with his little pop-gun? He saw the vehicle accelerate. It seemed to be going very fast already. It was then he realised the men in the van hadn't been able to see Lerenard's car which obstructed the track just round the corner from them.

He froze as he watched the vehicle gathering ever more pace. Then, when it was no more than about twenty yards from the bend, Lerenard stepped out of cover and discharged his pistol at it. Even from a distance Philip saw the windscreen craze over as the bullets hit it. There came the screaming of brakes as the big van lumbered round the bend, hit the cliff a glancing blow, and ploughed into the wrecked car which instantly burst into flames. The tail end of the van swivelled out and tipped over the edge of the road. The next second it was lumbering backwards down the steep hillside.

Philip watched, fascinated, as the big vehicle gathered speed. It bounced violently a couple of times before it hit a large rock and turned over. Then it began to roll side over side down the steep slope, until it ploughed into a clump of pine trees and finally stopped, resting on its roof. He stood at the side of the road, expecting it to burst into flames at any minute. However, the thing just lay there with its wheels sticking up and a few wisps of steam issuing from the wreck. Nothing moved and nobody climbed out of the vehicle.

"That should have given them a nasty headache." It was Lerenard speaking from just behind him. How had he got past the burning car?

The big man put a hand on his shoulder. "Come on. We'll get Candice to run us into Couiza so that we can report the accident to the police."

Philip followed him down the road, wondering if the wrecking of the *Granviers Frères* van could truly be called an accident.

# 41

It was well into the evening by the time the tired quartet got back to their hotel in Quillan. They had reached Couiza after a hair-raising descent from Castereau in Candice's car at about two o'clock. The one-room *gendarmerie* was manned by a single policeman who took a lot of convincing that a major incident had actually taken place on his patch. It was only when Lerenard produced the gun and showed the man the two bullets left in the little magazine, that he realised he needed to take them seriously.

The first thing he did was to confiscate the gun, for which neither Jean-Luc nor Candice could provide a licence, and proceeded to warn the big man that he was likely to be fined for possession and unlicensed use of an illegal weapon. Lerenard shrugged, no doubt aware that his employers would almost certainly use their influence to have any charges in that connection dismissed.

Only then did the policeman agree to telephone Carcassonne and speak to Inspector Martin. Philip guessed he was anxious to pass responsibility for any decision-making to a higher authority. Unfortunately, the detective was not on duty. However, a call to his home from the Carcassonne headquarters resulted in him ringing back about half an hour later. They were instructed to remain where they were and give their statements to the local man. Martin would reach them as soon as possible.

Meanwhile, they had been able to persuade the gendarme that they were all starving hungry, and Candice was permitted to go out on foot to purchase them some food while the others were kept at the police station under observation. They had barely finished their impromptu meal and making their official statements, when the Inspector arrived. By then it was nearly a quarter to four.

As well as bringing a young colleague in his car, he was followed by a large patrol car with two uniformed officers. After a quick reading of the four statements, he drove Philip and Jean-Luc up to the scene of the "accident". The women were left at the station. A brief inspection of Lerenard's burned-out car was made. They then inspected the marks on the cliff where the van had hit and looked at the place where a chunk of the roadside verge had been carried away by the vehicle as it started its plunge down the hillside.

The young assistant detective and one of the policemen from the patrol car were detailed to scramble down the steep slope to inspect the van, while Martin made his own notes of the damage to Lerenard's car, including the seven bullet holes and the two punctured tyres. Philip and Jean-Luc were instructed to keep away from what was now an official crime scene.

Half an hour later, the two men who had gone down to look at the van, reported back that there were four dead bodies in it, all presumably killed as a result of violent impact with the roof and sides inside the vehicle. Considerable additional resources were going to be required to get the men out and lifted up to the road. Martin got on the phone to headquarters to inform them of the requirements for scene-of-crime officers and ambulance personnel.

The four of them then walked up to the village. First they looked into the cottage, the front door of which was still open. Martin noted there were signs of blood on the floor. Philip said nothing but assumed at least one of Lerenard's shots had hit its target. There were no bodies found anywhere in the area.

After that they went to look round the castle. They went through the corridor and down the stairs. Lerenard opened the unlocked door to the basement room where Jeanette had been imprisoned. Martin made no notes himself, but his assistant was once again busy taking down a description of the place and anything else that occurred to him. Throughout this time, Philip said nothing and left it to Jean-Luc to describe what had happened.

The inspector then decided that the witnesses had provided sufficient information for his initial investigation, and he drove them back down to Couiza, taking great care on the rough road down the hillside. The patrol car with its two police officers was left at the scene until they would be relieved by replacements – probably the following morning.

It was half past six when they reached Couiza. Here they were reunited with Jeanette and Candice and all four were told they could go back to their hotel in Quillan, using Candice's car. However, they were also told they must not leave the area without informing the local police of their future whereabouts. Thus it was a weary, dirty, dishevelled group that wandered into Reception at the Castle Hotel at about seven o'clock.

Philip was surprised to find that the concierge was absent and had been replaced by a young girl. In reply to his question, she told him that Henri was on holiday for two weeks and she was his replacement. Philip shrugged. He presumed the man was entitled to a vacation, but it seemed strange that he should suddenly take it without having previously mentioned it to his guests.

He and Jeanette struggled up the stairs to his room.

"Can I come in and have a bath in your room?" she asked. "I can't face climbing all the way up to my garret."

"Don't be silly, Jeanette. As well as having a long soak in the bath, you'll want to change your clothes and do your hair and make-up. Come down refreshed in an hour's time and we'll go for a nice meal somewhere."

"All right, but make sure you're ready for me." Grumbling gently to herself, she staggered off up the stairs to the top floor.

Philip turned back to his door, fumbled in his pocket until he found the key, and then discovered it was unlocked anyway.

"What the hell? Has someone been ferreting around among my belongings?"

He swung the door wide open and came to an abrupt halt. There, reclining on the bed in her cream silk dressing gown and reading a book, was the famous archaeologist, Jacqueline Blontard.

"Jackie!"

She looked up and smiled, her bright blue eyes sparkling. "Have you missed me?"

"Missed you! I've been worried to death about you. I've been searching everywhere – Paris, Carcassonne, Béziers. Where on earth have you been?"

"There was no need to worry. I told you in my note."

"What note? I haven't received anything from you since I returned from England."

215

She frowned. "I left you a note. I had to make it short. I wasn't allowed to tell you where I was going. But I told you not to worry. I said I would be away for a few days." She shook her head. "I'm sorry. It ended up being nearer two weeks."

"What note? I haven't seen any note. Where did you put it?"

"I left it with Henri. Didn't he give it to you?"

"The bugger!" Philip took a deep breath. "I especially asked whether there was a note for me, and he told me there was nothing. He just showed me the one you left for him with the five hundred euros in it."

Jackie was on her feet now. "I'm going to sort this out with Henri. What on earth does he mean by throwing away the note which was in an envelope distinctly addressed to you?"

"You'd better not go dressed like that." Philip indicated her loosely tied dressing gown which was clearly the only thing she was wearing. "In any case he isn't there. The girl who's replaced him said he has gone on holiday for a fortnight."

"Has he indeed!. *Mon Dieu*! What *is* going on?"

"Besides which," said Philip, "we have our reunion to celebrate."

"Yes. Oh, Philip. . ."

She came into his arms and for the next few minutes all thoughts of notes and misunderstandings were forgotten.

When they separated, she said, "You're a bit grubby and smelly, Mister Sinclair. I think you need a shower before I welcome you into my bed."

"At least it's going to be a welcome."

"You bet! I promise you it will be one hell of a welcome. We can sort out this mystery about the note later."

A quarter of an hour later Philip reappeared, damp but unquestionably cleaner. His naked physique was already showing his anticipation of the next hour or so. Jackie threw off the bed covers to reveal she had removed her dressing gown. He paused for a few seconds to take in the sight of her beautiful body before he advanced on her. At that moment the bedroom door swung open, and Jeanette stood there clothed in nothing but her see-through negligee.

"I'm bathed and I've done my hair and put on my perfume as you asked, Philip. You can't refuse me now." And then she gulped as her gaze moved to take in his fiancée.

"Oh!" She turned and fled.

Jackie had hastily pulled the sheets back over her naked body. "What on earth was that about?"

Philip hesitated for a second. "Er – Jeanette has been imprisoned in a room in the basement of the castle at Castereau for more than a week. We have just got back from rescuing her. Before I knew you were here, I'd told her to get cleaned up and I would take her out for dinner."

"She was hardly dressed to go out for a meal."

"No – er – I think she must have misunderstood my meaning."

"Misunderstood you? I think she understood you only too well. It appears to me, Philip Sinclair, that you have been consoling yourself during my absence with the nubile and very willing Jeanette."

"I certainly have not. In fact, I have been resisting her advances." He didn't include the night he had spent in her bed when he was drunk and unaware of what was happening. "And I have been refusing her offers despite the fact that you had disappeared without trace, and I didn't know if you had decided that our relationship was a bad idea, and that was the reason you had deserted me."

She shook her head. "Let me tell you, Philip, that if I were to decide that you and I were not suited, I would tell you to your face."

"Or perhaps," he said sulkily, "in a note which wasn't given to me."

"No. It would be to your face."

"All right," he grinned, "What was in the note anyway?"

"Er – not very much. I just said I was going to be away for a few days and that you were not to worry. I asked you to wait for me or to leave a message with Henri about where I could contact you when I got back."

"That would have worried me even more, when you were gone for more than a few days."

"Yes, I know, and I've said I'm sorry about that. I wanted to ring you to warn you that I was delayed, but they insisted I

217

hand over my phone and I wasn't allowed to contact anybody while I was there. Their demand for secrecy was absolute."

"Who is they? Where were you, or aren't you allowed even to tell me that?"

"Yes, I *will* tell you, but it's a long story. I'll tell you everything as long as you promise to keep it to yourself." She smiled. "But first I want you to prove to me that you're more interested in me than the sexy Jeanette, and you'd better do it quickly before we both freeze to death."

Philip suddenly became aware that the bedclothes were awry, and they were both naked as they faced each other. He took the necessary action to rectify that straight away.

# 42

It was about an hour later that a well-satisfied Philip murmured in Jackie's ear. "I want to know what you have been doing for the last two weeks?"

"Most of the time," she said, "I've been researching the history of the Cathars in the secret library at the Vatican."

"The Vatican! How did you get in there?"

"It's a long story. Are you lying comfortably?"

He nuzzled up against her. "I certainly am."

"Then I'll begin. As you know, I wasn't very happy with my negotiations with the two men from the Ministry of Culture in Paris. It had become clear to me that they had been told to stonewall my attempts to get permission to inspect the treasure. Every time I put any sort of a proposal to them, their response was that they had to go back to head office to get clearance even to discuss it. And if we actually got to a point where we had something to discuss, the answer was an emphatic no."

"Yes. I could tell you were unhappy with them before I went back to England."

"That's right. In fact I think it was only the risk that I might go public, and show the world the photos you took in the treasure room, that kept them talking to me." She sighed. "Anyway, three days after you left, when I was finally about to blow my top, who should turn up but my old professor from the Sorbonne?"

"Is that Hector Ramise?"

"You know him?" she queried, astonished.

"I know *about* him. I haven't met him. I know that at the moment he is in Béziers, or somewhere near, on an extended leave of absence."

Her questioning led Philip to tell her about his discovery of the man's name and his attempts to meet him.

"My goodness," she said several minutes later, "you *have* been busy."

"You don't know the half of it."

"What else is there to tell?"

"A lot, but I'll fill you in as we talk or after *you* have finished." He took a breath. "So, what about Professor Ramise? Why did he come to see you?"

"It was very interesting. Hector knows anyone who matters in this field. I would describe us as colleagues, when we did excavations as part of my training at the Sorbonne. It was soon obvious to me that he had been chosen as somebody who could come down and, as they thought, talk some sense into me."

"And did he?"

"Well, he obviously had told the authorities that he would have to offer me something to keep me quiet. So, little by little, he unveiled a package that was very interesting. First of all, he told me that the treasure which we stumbled upon was acknowledged to be the property of a large, powerful organisation which is centred in Paris. I believe they are some sort of successors to the Templars, but nobody will admit it. He said the Ministry of Culture had been in secret talks with this body in the last few days and had accepted their right to have the treasure taken into their custody. They were preparing underground vaults in Paris to receive the stuff. I said that they'd better hurry up because I was ready to go public in the next couple of days. I told him about the photos you took and the secret access we had discovered. He told me to hang on while he spoke to Paris. Meanwhile he took me out for a very expensive meal in Carcassonne that night to persuade me to wait for a couple of days."

"You didn't tell me any of this when I phoned you from London."

"I'll explain why it had to be kept secret even from you. Next morning, Hector told me he had received clearance from Paris to fill me in on what was planned for the treasure. The owners had admitted it was time for them to go public about their valuable possessions. They have decided they will give me the freedom of their vaults next winter, so that I can catalogue the treasure items and prepare a television series about these wonderful objects and their history. Then they will loan the most valuable half of the collection to the Louvre, where a new wing will be built by public subscription to house it. The other half will be sold off over the next few years to other museums around the world, so that the whole lot will be

220

available for public viewing. But of course, my series about the treasures will have already whetted the public appetite. It seemed to be a win/win situation for everybody."

"I can see that nobody would blame you for agreeing to that proposal. I take it they won't go back on their offer."

"No. The Ministry of Culture has sent me a written undertaking signed by the minister himself. So I can rely on that. However, I pointed out to Hector that I was still contracted to do a series for TV France this autumn, and the treasure series couldn't possibly be prepared in time for that. I told him all about the work that had been done on the series about the Cathars, which had been knocked on the head only a week or two earlier. He asked me to describe the plans in detail. After he had chewed it over, he said he wanted me to give him another day to see what he could arrange. Meanwhile, I was still meeting the two men from Paris each day and I wasn't allowed to tell anyone – not even them – about the new offer. It was comical really. Both sides were trying to find something to talk about, while we both knew the talks would get nowhere for our different reasons."

"You must have been desperate to get rid of them, so that you could start planning something else."

"It was only one more day. Hector came back to me next morning with a brilliant new idea. He really had been working overtime. Through contacts in Paris, he had been able to persuade the Catholic Church that it was time for them to let all the background facts about the Albigensian Crusade become known, including any mistakes Pope Innocent III might have made. In fact, they now agreed that they would let me look into their own records of the time, provided I would allow them to require omission of any revelations which they believed might harm the Church's mission in the future. I also had to agree to maintain absolute secrecy until I had let them read my draft narrative for the series, which I would prepare while I was in the Vatican."

"So you were mighty pleased with that."

"Of course." She pulled him closer to her. "It meant the original series about Catharism could go ahead again and I would have a lot more authentic background information than I

221

had ever thought possible. The dig could be restarted at le Bézu. Two years´ research wasn't going to be wasted."

"And there was a possibility that you might clear your uncle's name as well."

"Well, yes. I agree there was that possibility as well."

"But what about this shadowy organisation in Paris? Weren't they the ones who got the original dig closed down?"

"That's right. But they lost interest in the site once they'd got their precious treasure out of the room below the castle."

"So off you scuttled to the Vatican without letting anybody know where you had gone." Philip couldn't keep the resentment out of his voice. "It wasn't just me. Alain Gisours hadn't got any idea what had happened to you. And your Aunt Charlotte was worried when I told her you had disappeared."

"I know and I'm, sorry, my darling." She hugged him again. "If you had been here, I might have been able to tell you a little more, provided you agreed to keep it absolutely secret. Or perhaps they might have let you come with me."

"That would have been an interesting experience."

"Mind you, they wouldn't have let us out to explore Rome. They insisted I stayed within the walls of Vatican City, and it's almost as difficult to get out of there, as it is to get in. I stayed at a hotel inside the complex which mainly caters for visiting clerics and high up members of the Catholic Church. But I must admit everyone was very friendly and chatty. The atmosphere was relaxed and I found that there really is a strong movement developing among the younger hierarchy to try and bring the church into line with modern thinking."

"The question though, is this." Philip looked into her eyes. "Was your visit valuable from the research point of view?"

"It was fantastic. That's why I was there for nearly two weeks." She positively glowed with enthusiasm. "The incredible thing was that they didn't seem to mind me asking to look at all kinds of manuscripts from the time of the Cathars."

"They could still locate this ancient stuff after all this time?"

"I tell you what – the French government could learn a lot from the Vatican about filing systems for old documents. Mind you, they have had continuous control of this information for well over a thousand years."

"So they just laid these documents in front of you."

"That's right. Of course, most of them were in Latin so it's a good job I had a working knowledge of the language. But whenever I had a problem – and that was quite often – I only had to ask one of the custodians who make up most of the staff of the library, and they would spend hours of their time, if necessary, trying to find an answer for me. In fact, I think they enjoyed having an informed outsider asking the sort of questions a true Catholic would never dare to ask."

"Did you see Galbaccino? He's probably the guy who organised this for you."

"No. There was no sign of him."

That suddenly started Philip on a new train of thought. He told Jackie about Lerenard turning up to help him in his search for her. "I'm pretty sure Jean-Luc didn't know you were at the Vatican."

"He's really been helpful to you, has he?"

"He gave me the impression he'd sort of been sent to look after me. In fact, I'm not sure I'd have still been here if it hadn't been for him."

Jackie started to question him then about some of the scrapes he'd got into during his search.

"Oh, my God!" she exclaimed when she heard about the adventure in Castereau. "You might have been killed. That would have really served me right if I'd lost the love of my life, because I was concentrating on my research. I'm sorry, Philip. I just didn't realise you'd have got yourself into so much danger as a result of my swanning off to Rome."

"Well, it should make you realise that I was prepared to do a lot to find you. And now I have . . ."

Here talk ended and love-making began again. They finally fell asleep in each other's arms without bothering about dinner.

# 43

Jackie and Philip woke early and indulged in a further love-making session before getting ready and going down for breakfast, ravenously hungry. Jean-Luc Lerenard was already there, tucking into a plate of croissants.

"Candice has disappeared," he announced through a mouthful of pastry.

Philip didn't admit that he had forgotten all about the woman.

"What has happened to her?" asked Jackie.

"I left her booking a room in reception. I told her I would see her bills were paid, so I thought she would stay." He shook his head. "I should have remained with her to see that she booked in."

"Do you know where she has gone?"

"The girl on reception just said that Candice told her that she had decided not to stay here and went out. The girl didn't follow her to see where she went."

"She brought us back here in her car," said Philip. "Is that still outside in the square?"

"No," he grunted. "That was the first thing I checked. She could be anywhere now."

Jackie took a seat beside him. "Does it matter where she is?"

"I don't like the idea of her not being where I can keep an eye on her. We don't know what she might do next. She could be dangerous."

"But," Philip reminded him, "she was the one who rescued us. If she *has* disappeared, I don't think it's because she means to do us any harm."

"Don't you believe it. She is in the pay of *le comte*, and that man is dangerous."

Philip had already explained to Jackie about the new leader of *La Force Marseillaise* and his attempt to get hold of César

"Well," she said, "the girl could be anywhere. There's not much we can do until she turns up."

They were interrupted by the arrival of the waiter with a large jug of coffee and a plateful of food. They were still tucking into it when Jeanette arrived. It was a very subdued young woman who hesitantly took the fourth chair at the table. This morning she was dressed very modestly with her voluptuous figure hidden under jeans and a loose sweater. Philip noticed that Jackie pointedly ignored her.

"I rang Armand just before we came down to let him know you were safe and well," he told her. "We agreed that I should take you to Carcassonne later this morning and hand you over to his care. I think he plans to take you back to Paris, where you'll feel much better among your friends and acquaintances in the city. So, if you get your things ready, we'll leave in about an hour. Is that all right?"

She nodded but made no comment.

He laid a hand on hers. "Thank you very much, Jeanette, for helping me in my search for Jackie."

"*Was* it any help?"

"Of course it was, and I'm sorry you had to go through that ordeal at Castereau, but I'll see you are properly paid for all your time."

She sniffed. "Thank you."

Philip turned to Jackie. "Will you come to Carcassonne? I can fill you in on some the other things that happened as we drive."

"I most certainly will."

"Good," He squeezed her hand under the table.

"But first I must get in touch with Bernard Cambray and with Alain Gisours to tell them my news." She got up. "Can you be ready to leave in an hour, Jeanette?"

"Yes."

"What about me?" demanded Lerenard.

Jackie turned to him. "Are you willing to continue to work for me for a few more weeks?"

He seemed to muse for a few moments before replying, "I don't see why not."

"The reason, Jean-Luc – may I call you Jean-Luc? – is that I want to reopen the site at le Bézu. We won't be doing any serious excavation there, but I want it to look like an archaeological site for the cameras to move in and film a lot of the background shots. I think the atmosphere of the place and its remote location will add drama to the series, which will hook a nationwide audience. Would you be willing to get the place set up to look like a serious dig again?"

"That should be interesting."

"You can hire whatever local labour you want. The two Land Cruisers and quite a bit of equipment – sorting tables, sieves, etcetera – are in a small warehouse in Limoux. I'll give you the keys and directions and we can drop you off there on our way to Carcassonne. You might as well get started straight away. TV France will soon be breathing down my neck to show some results for all their investment."

"OK. I'm willing to do that."

"Thank you. Well, I'll see you all in an hour."

"Wait for me," said Philip. "There are a couple of things I want to say to Alain Gisours."

Up in the bedroom, Jackie first rang Bernard Cambray, and was treated to his extravagant delight on finding that his most valuable client was back in circulation. She promised to contact him later regarding the arrangements to complete the series about the Cathars.

The next call was to the boss at TV France. Philip was impressed to hear that Alain Gisours was already at his desk at 8.30 in the morning. After Jackie had brought him up-to-date, and promised to tell him in the next day or two how soon she would be ready for the cameras to visit le Bézu, she handed the phone to Philip. He told Alain about what had happened the previous day at Castereau.

"Our abductors were a group of six men driving a van with the name *Granviers Frères* painted on the side. Your secretary told me they were the company you employed to clear the site at le Bézu. Where did you get them from?"

"As far as I know they were a company who contacted us, looking for work. As they were a fairly local set-up, Anita decided they could be usefully employed clearing the site, which was hardly a security situation."

"But in fact," said Philip, "they were a group of criminals from Toulouse. Four of them are now dead - killed when their van went off the road and plunged down a steep hillside - but two are still missing and are being sought by police."

"Is that the case?" Gisours didn't seem unduly put out. "Well, no doubt the authorities will be in touch with me in due course, and I will tell them that no formal link existed between our two companies." He sniffed. "In future we'll use one of the big national companies, who may cost a bit more, but at least they can be relied on."

"The leader of the group was a man called Gaston Lesmoines, who we believe is still alive. He was previously taken on as the senior man of a trio of rock climbers to install the safety ropes round the le Bézu site. He then stayed on to work for Mademoiselle Blontard as an archaeologist and seemed to hope to become her senior assistant when André Jolyon was killed. That's a coincidence, don't you think?"

Alain Gisours chuckled. "You can't blame me for that, young Philip. Jolyon arranged the staff on the site himself before his tragic death. In any case, as I understand it, this guy Lesmoines wasn't responsible for Jolyon's death, or for any of the other problems on the site after his death."

"OK." Philip decided to back down. "It's obvious you don't know anything about the bloke. Thanks for the information. Cheerio."

He handed the phone back to Jackie, who rang off after further promises to get back to the producer as soon as she could.

"That was interesting," she said, after she had hung up. "I hadn't thought about those coincidences before."

"Do you know how André got in touch with your friend Gaston?"

"I don't." She shuddered. "And please don't call him my friend. I never did quite trust the man. Thank goodness you turned up and rescued me."

Then she was in his arms again. But this time it was Philip who said, "I don't think we've got the time for this, Jackie. Remember we've promised Jeanette that we would pick her up in an hour."

So they got ready for the trip to Carcassonne.

# 44

When they set off for Carcassonne in Philip's hire car, Jackie was in a conversational mood.

"Bernard was pleased to hear from me." She grinned. "I think he was worried that his best source of income was going to disappear,"

"I must say he was very helpful to me when I was in Paris earlier in the week," volunteered Philip. "He put me up for several nights and got me in to see people at the Ministry of Culture and the Sorbonne, who I'm sure wouldn't have wanted to talk to me if I had approached them direct. He seems to know a lot of important people."

That led him to tell Jackie about his Paris visit, a trip which he hadn't got round to mentioning before.

"Why did you want to find out about the Chateau de Blanchefort?" she wanted to know when he got to that point.

So he told her about finding the scroll signed by Thiebault de Blanchefort, his trip to the Abbé Dugard to have it translated, and his efforts to track down a chateau of that name.

"Where is this scroll?" she demanded.

"It's in my bag at the hotel. I was very careful with it when I unrolled it and copied it for the good Abbé to look at. You would have been proud of me."

"You keep surprising me, Philip Sinclair. You seem to have got a fair bit of French society mobilised in your search for me."

He grinned. "I certainly tried to leave no stone unturned."

"And it was your attempt to find the Chateau de Blanchefort that led you to your disastrous adventure at Castereau."

"Actually, it was Jean-Luc who tracked down that village. We certainly bit off more than we could chew there."

"And you even got into the Sorbonne to try to see my old professor, Hector Ramise. What put you on to him?"

"That was Aunt Charlotte. Armand got your home address in Béziers from Bernard, so I rang up and spoke to her. You must have told her something about me, because she knew who I was when I rang. As a result of my call, I went to see her. Of

228

course, she didn't know where you had gone but she did let me look in your office and, while I was there, I carried out as detailed a search as I could."

"I see," she said sardonically. "Is nowhere of mine private?"

"And what an office it is! I didn't really know where to begin. However, in one drawer I found a list of your contacts and right at the top of it was the name of Hector Ramise. At first Charlotte said the name meant nothing to her, but later she remembered his name rang a bell."

"Rang a bell? What was she talking about? She knows him very well."

"Really? Well, when she rang me a few days later, she said she'd remembered he was a professor at the Sorbonne. So I got Bernard to introduce me."

She chuckled. "I don't think I'd have been able to hide away from you for long if I'd still been in France."

"Jackie! I thought you'd disappeared without leaving a note. I was worried you'd been kidnapped – probably by the people who took the treasure."

"I'm sorry. At least that *has* been explained." She frowned. "Or it had better be, when Henri comes back from his convenient holiday."

Returning to his previous theme, Philip said, "There was a strange coincidence in connection with your Professor Ramise. His secretary took me into his office to see some photos of him. There on the wall was one photo of him receiving a special award. I think it was from the Austrian ambassador or someone similar. But he was wearing a blazer with a badge of the Habsbourg coat of arms on the breast pocket. The point is that it was identical to the blazer I had seen in the warehouse in Carcassonne before I was knocked on the head."

"Knocked on the head?"

"Oh. Didn't I tell you about that?"

So, then he had to tell her how Jeanette had found out from one of the gendarmes about the treasure being moved to Carcassonne and their abortive visit to the warehouse.

"Luckily that was when Jean-Luc turned up and picked me up." He chuckled. "But Jeanette had already been spirited away in my car by your helper Gaston Lesmoines."

It was Jeanette's turn to recount how she had been persuaded to let Gaston drive her to Castereau where he said the treasure was located.

"Oh, my God!" cried Jackie. "This is all so complicated."

"Meanwhile," continued Philip, "Armand had found out about Lesmoines and the company, Granviers Frères, who were taken on by Alain Gisours' secretary to clear the le Bézu site. But arising from this, there are two questions I want answers to. Firstly, I want to know if your professor was at the warehouse and, was he the one who banged me on the head. Secondly, does he have any link with your mate Gaston, and does he know the guy is a crook?"

"Gaston is not my mate."

"No. I'm sorry. It's just my way of speaking. But you can see that the further I get into this business the more questions are raised and the fewer answers I seem to get."

By now they were approaching Carcassonne. The journey seemed to have passed very quickly while Philip was telling his story.

"I said we would see Armand in the bar where I met up with him the other day," he said as they parked nearby.

When they entered *L'Homme Vert* the young Frenchman was already there. He rose to welcome Jackie with a kiss on both cheeks, but he almost ignored Jeanette.

"I am so glad you are back with us," he said. "Now our main task is over."

She smiled. "Such a lot has been going on while I was away. I'm sorry I've missed all the excitement."

"I saw Inspector Martin an hour ago," Armand announced, with Jackie translating for Philip. "He told me that they recovered the four dead bodies from the wrecked van last night and they are all in the hospital mortuary. I have to tell you that Gaston Lesmoines is not one of them. Nor was there any sign of him or the sixth man in a detailed search of all the properties in Castereau."

"I wonder what has happened to him."

"I don't know. You were there, and saw what happened when the van crashed."

"Yes."

"Did you see anybody get out of the vehicle?"

"No."

Armand shrugged. "Then it looks as though the other two weren't in the van when it went over the edge."

"Well, we didn't scramble down to the crashed vehicle before we set off in Candice's car to Couiza to report the accident to the police. So I suppose they might have got out after we left the scene."

"Martin doesn't seem to think anybody would have survived the fall down the hillside. The roof was crushed down almost on to the chassis and there was a big dent in the side. Apparently, it was quite a struggle to get the bodies out. They had to use special cutting equipment to open the van body up like a big tin can."

"It's a bit worrying," said Philip, "to think that Lesmoines and his mate might still be just round the corner."

"Well, Martin's circulated the description I gave him, to all police patrol vehicles with instructions to keep a special watch. They want to catch him as much as we do."

Philip had a sudden thought. "Is my car still there? They might have got away in that."

"I didn't ask. But I don't know how a vehicle like that would have got away from the village. The only road up to the place was blocked by the wreck of Lerenard's car and there are no ways out in any other direction except rough footpaths. Those tracks would test a big four-wheel drive vehicle. But I'll ask Martin about your car when I see him next."

"So what would be their alternative?"

Armand shrugged. "The only way would be to walk out. That's quite possible, of course. It's only about five kilometres to the nearest main road and that wouldn't be a problem, provided they weren't injured."

"Candice has also disappeared," said Jeanette.

"That's true," said Philip, "but somehow I don't see her working with Lesmoines. For a start, she was the one who made our escape possible."

He explained for Armand what had happened the previous afternoon, being careful not to mention the naked show that he and Jeanette had put on the moment the door was opened. He glanced at the girl and saw there was the ghost of a smile

231

crossing her features, but she seemed to have decided to keep quiet about their activities, now that Jackie had returned.

They talked around the subject for a while but nobody came up with an explanation for the disappearances. Then Philip changed the topic.

"I gather you actually saw Professor Ramise in Béziers yesterday."

"That's right." Armand explained, with Jackie again translating for Philip's sake, how he had seen Ramise go into the Central Post Office to collect his mail. "The interesting thing," he continued, "is that when he came out, he had a lady on his arm. She wasn't young – I suppose about the same age as him – but she was also a very stylish lady. I would say they were lovers."

He went on to explain how he had followed them back to a block of flats near the edge of the old city and seen them go into the building together. He had waited an hour but no-one had come out, so he had given up and come back to Carcassonne.

"Wait a minute," said Jackie. "That sounds just like the block where my flat is."

Armand gave them a few more details and she said she was almost sure it was the same place.

"I have taken some photos with my camera," he said, "but I have not yet had them developed."

"The description of the lady also sounds a bit like your Aunt Charlotte," agreed Philip. "I would definitely say she is stylish. It sounds as though we need to pay your aunt a visit to try and get an explanation."

"I will ring her and tell her we're going to join her for lunch."

"No. Let's just go there without warning her. We may catch your friend Hector there. I would also like a word with him."

There was a gleam in her eye as she agreed.

"And what about you, Armand? Are you going back to Paris today?"

He shook his head. "Probably tomorrow. I want another chat with Inspector Martin before we leave, and he won't be back on duty until ten tonight." He turned to grin at Jeanette. "You'll have to share *my* bed tonight, *ma cherie*."

So they said good bye and promised to ring the next morning.

# 45

They stopped for lunch on their way to Béziers, so it was nearly three o'clock when they arrived at Jackie's flat.

"I'd better not walk straight in," she said as she rang the bell from the entrance hall.

It was answered with a slightly hesitant, "*Bonjour.*"

"*Tante Charlotte! C'est moi! Jacqueline! Je suis revenue.*"

"*Oh, Jacqueline!*"

There followed a profusion of welcomes and other endearments between Jackie and her aunt, before the door was released and they took the lift to the third floor. As the doors opened, Charlotte was waiting for them, and Philip was included in the round of hugs and kisses on cheeks.

"Where have you been?" asked Charlotte as they followed her into the flat. "We were so worried about you."

"I'm sorry, Aunt. I am not allowed to tell you at the moment. However, I can say that it was a place where I was able to carry out some very valuable research. Hopefully, it will all be made clear in a few weeks."

"But what about Philip? He was in quite a state when he came here."

"I know. I've apologised. I left a note for him at the hotel, but somehow it didn't get passed on. I think he has forgiven me now." She turned her stunning smile on him. "I will do my best to make it up to him in the next week or two."

"It was such a relief to know she was safe," Philip admitted.

"And now you are back – what will you be doing? Will you be staying here with me? You know you would both be very welcome."

"We'd love to, Aunt, but we haven't got the time. The dig's starting up again at le Bézu and TV France will be breathing down my neck to get the cameras in. So we'll be staying at Quillan for a few more weeks."

"All right," was all that Charlotte said, but Philip thought he could detect a note of relief in her voice.

He decided to raise the question of Professor Ramise. "Are you alone here?"

"Yes, of course. Why should I not be alone?" But then she turned to face him as though expecting him to say more.

He smiled, hoping to relieve her of any unnecessary embarrassment. "I asked because I have been told Jackie's former professor, Hector Ramise, is actually an old friend of yours, and I believe he is in Béziers at the moment."

"Oh!" There was a long silence.

Philip asked, "Have I got it wrong?"

She shook her head. "No. You are correct. How did you find out we knew each other?"

"I went to Paris earlier in the week to try to see him, but he was away from the Sorbonne on a suddenly-arranged leave of absence. His secretary told me I would find him in Béziers."

"I see." She paused. "Why did you want to see him?"

"Well, at that time, I hoped he might be able to give me some clues as to Jackie's whereabouts, but there are also a couple of other coincidences which I hope he can clear up."

Jackie intervened. "He came to see me in Quillan when Philip was in England. In fact, he was the one who arranged for me to go on my – er – research visit." She moved forward and put a gentle hand on her aunt's arm. "He must have been involved in some way – probably quite a good way – with what has been happening in the last few weeks."

"Oh, yes. Yes, of course." Charlotte turned away and looked out of the window. "Yes, I have been seeing him recently from time to time."

"I'm not complaining about you meeting him," said Philip, "but why did you tell me you couldn't remember who he was when I first showed you his name on the list?"

"Yes, well -." She turned back. "I'm sorry, Philip, but suddenly seeing his name jerked that reaction out of me. I wanted to talk to Hector first, to find out how much I could tell you." She smiled briefly. "In fact, he seemed to welcome the fact that you might want to get in touch with him and, at that time, we thought he would be going back to Paris in the next few days."

"I certainly do want to talk to him. Do you know how to contact him?"

"Oh, yes. In fact, he is coming here at six o'clock to take me out for a meal. You and Jackie would be welcome to join us.

I'm sure he would like to see you both. But I can ring him and ask if he will come earlier so that he can talk to you here, if you wish."

They agreed that was a good idea, so they let Aunt Charlotte go into the other room to ring him.

"What do you think?" asked Philip.

"I don't know. I think she coped pretty well when you asked her out of the blue if she knew Hector. I don't think there's anything she knows which she wants to hide from us."

"I agree with that, but she has been a little bit coy about her friendship with the professor. Remember Armand said they were gazing at each other as if they were lovers."

Jackie shook her head. "We can't ask her straight out about their relationship. In any case, it's not strictly our business. I think we'll have to leave it to them to decide how much they want to tell us about that."

"OK. The questions I want to ask Hector have no connection with his friendship with Charlotte."

"Hush. Here she comes."

"Hector says he will come straight over to see you now," her aunt announced as she re-entered the room. "He will be here in about fifteen minutes."

"Does he live fairly close?"

"Just a short walk down the hill towards the river." She turned to Jackie. "Shall we have some tea while we are waiting?"

In fact, it was nearly half an hour before Professor Ramise turned up. When the bell rang Charlotte rushed to let him in and went to meet him at the lift. Jackie signed to Philip that he should let them be alone together for a few minutes.

When the professor entered the room, Philip recognised him immediately from the dark gimlet eyes and the goatee beard. They rose to welcome him, and he hastened to greet Jackie as an old friend, with a kiss on both cheeks. Then he turned to face Philip, who noticed once more his shortness of stature, being less tall than Jackie and about the same height as her aunt. He came forward and they shook hands.

"Will you have some tea, Hector?" Charlotte asked.

"Please."

"I'll go and make a fresh pot."

They sat down as she left the room. The professor turned to the younger man.

"Charlotte tells me you would like to ask me some questions."

"We both would. When I returned from a week in England, where I had to sort out various matters, I found that Jackie had disappeared. I now know that you had arranged for her to go to do some research, but nobody told me anything about what had happened. As far as I knew, she hadn't even left me a message. Of course, I was aware that she had been negotiating with men from the Ministry of Culture, to try to take control of the sorting and classification of the treasures we had found at le Bézu. Then I discovered that the treasure had also disappeared. Obviously, I was very worried about what had happened to Jackie as a result."

Ramise turned to her. "You have told him where you went?"

"Of course I have, Hector. He is my fiancé and deserves to know. But he is sworn to secrecy until the series comes out." She took a breath. "What we both want to know is whether you were the one who took the note I left with the concierge to give to Philip when he returned from England."

"Ah." He looked embarrassed. "Yes, I am afraid I did. You must realise, young man, that I knew nothing about you, except that Jackie had fallen head-over-heels in love with you. It was the first time she had really fallen for any man, and I didn't know what influence you might have had on her. I couldn't risk that the note might have exposed where she had gone and what she was doing. My – er – my principals were adamant that nobody else was to know about the offer they had made to her."

"Did you read the note?" asked Jackie. "If you had, you would have realised that I hadn't given away any secrets to Philip. I only told him that I would be away for a few days and that I was quite safe and asked him to wait for me to return."

"No I didn't," he admitted. "Having taken it, I knew that I would have problems with Philip if I told him about my part in the whole affair, so I decided to leave him in ignorance. I realise now that was a mistake."

Philip felt annoyed. "Why weren't you even prepared to put yourself out enough to tell me you knew where she was, but couldn't give me any details? You could have explained your part in the business and told me she would be back in a week or two."

The professor shook his head. "Would you have believed me? You knew no more about me and my character than I did about you. Wouldn't you have insisted that I at least got in touch with Jackie, and arranged for her to make some sort of contact with you to support my comments, otherwise you would make a big fuss? I didn't want to get involved in those sorts of complications, especially with the subsequent explanations I would have to make to the principals."

"To the Catholic Church, you mean?"

"Perhaps, but not only to them."

"Who else then?"

"I'm afraid I can't tell you that."

"Why not? It seems to me that you are trying to hide behind vague organisations who might or who might not exist."

Jackie could tell that Philip was starting to get angry and she intervened to calm the atmosphere.

"All right, darling." She put an arm round him. "But I *do* think you acted badly, Hector, and that you should have found a way to calm Philip's fears. As it is, you've caused him nearly three weeks of anguish, chasing all over France and interviewing dozens of people, and also putting himself in considerable danger."

From the expression on his face, it was obvious that the professor wasn't used to being lectured about his behaviour by his former pupils, even one as famous as Jacqueline Blontard. However, he took a deep breath and replied calmly.

"Yes, I apologise for any upset I caused you, Philip." He reached across and they shook hands. "If it is any comfort to you, I had decided I must contact you in the next couple of days, because Jackie was staying away much longer than I had originally expected."

At that moment, Charlotte returned with the fresh tray of tea and a few minutes were taken up with handing round cups.

Once they were all settled again, Philip said, "There is another matter I would like to discuss with you."

"What is that?"

"When I met your secretary at the university, she showed me a photograph of you receiving an award. I believe it was from the Austrian ambassador. She said it was for some research you had carried out into the history of the Habsbourg Royal Family."

The professor paused for a moment before replying. "That's correct. It was one of the proudest days of my academic life."

"I'm sure it was. Well, I noticed in the photograph that you had a magnificent badge on the breast pocket of your jacket. When I asked about it, Mademoiselle Palendrin told me it was the royal coat of arms of the Habsbourgs. She said you wore it because you had some sort of link with them."

Jackie was fascinated. "Is that correct, Hector?"

He nodded, a shade reluctantly. "Well, yes – but it's a very remote link."

"You've never mentioned it to me," said Charlotte.

"The reason I was interested," continued Philip, "is, that when I started searching for Jackie, I thought it likely that her disappearance had some link to the fact that the treasure had also disappeared. I was being helped to look for it by a woman who had used her wiles to find out from a young gendarme that the treasure had been moved under police escort to a warehouse in Carcassonne."

He was watching Hector carefully to check the man's reaction as he continued, "I – er – broke in to that warehouse, which I found was completely empty when I got there, except for a blazer hanging on the back of a door. The blazer had the same badge on the breast pocket. In fact, it looked identical to the one in the photograph on your office wall. Would that have been your jacket by any chance?"

There was a long silence. Despite his close attention to Hector's face, Philip couldn't tell whether the man had been expecting this disclosure or not.

"Was it yours, Hector?" asked Charlotte.

He nodded slowly. "I think it possibly was." He paused as he ruminated. "I often carry the blazer with me when I am travelling. I keep it to wear if I have any important meetings. I can't tell you how many times it has come in useful when I am talking to senior people."

He turned to Jackie. "After I had seen you off on your - er - your research project, I stayed in the hotel in Quillan for a night because I had other business to attend to in the area. I must have hung the jacket in the wardrobe." He shook his head. "When I came back to Béziers the next day I discovered, when I unpacked, that I no longer had it. I rang the hotel, and they checked the wardrobe in question, but they told me it was not there. I can only presume that somebody had taken it. I have no idea why it should have turned up in this place in Carcassonne."

"You didn't go to this warehouse yourself?"

"Certainly not. Where is it?"

"In the western industrial estate."

Hector shook his head. "So far as I can recall I have never been anywhere near there."

Philip found it impossible to decide whether the professor was telling the truth or had made up the story, so as not to have to explain why he was at the warehouse that night. If it was a lie, the man was certainly quick-witted.

"There is another strange side to the tale," he said. "I have seen the same coat of arms on the side of a bag which belonged to a man called Alain Hébert. Does that name mean anything to you?"

Jackie burst out, "What do you mean, Philip?"

But the effect on Ramise was even more dramatic. He fell back in his chair as though he had been struck.

"Where did you see that bag?" he gasped.

Philip was thinking quickly. "I don't think I can tell you that," he said. "The person who has the bag has especially asked to have his whereabouts kept secret."

The professor pointed a finger at Philip. "You *must* tell me where you saw the bag and who was in possession of it."

"Hector, you know yourself how important it is to respect a confidence. I will ask this person if I can disclose its location to you, but I can't do that without receiving their authority."

"It is vital that I have that bag in my possession as soon as possible."

Philip stared at the professor, uncertain about why he was suddenly so desperate to get the bag. "I will tell them that, but I'm sure they will want to know why it is so important to you?"

"I cannot tell you that. The only thing I can do, is give you a grave warning of the danger both you and the present holder of the bag are in, until you have returned it to me."

"Why do you want it so much?"

"I will pass it on to the rightful owners."

"And who are they?"

"That is also confidential. All I can do is tell you that it is absolutely essential that the bag is recovered by my principals. It is also extremely important that you have nothing to do directly with the bag or its contents. To dabble in this matter might put us all in extreme danger,"

# 46

On the journey back to Quillan, Jackie said, "Well, your information about that bag certainly brought our visit to Charlotte to a sudden end. I didn't have time to quiz her about her feelings for Hector."

"You said we should leave that to them."

"Yes, but I thought that, if I helped her with the washing-up after tea, I might have been able to drop a couple of hints which would have encouraged her to talk about him, and her feelings for him."

Philip grinned. "And wasn't Hector strange about that bag? I thought his warnings were a bit over the top."

"Be careful. He seemed to think the matter was very urgent – urgent enough to send us straight off to contact the man who has the bag. Who is this guy, by the way?"

Philip paused for a second before he told her, but he decided he must trust her, in the same way that she had been prepared to trust him. "Actually it isn't a man. It's César Renoir."

"The journalist woman? I thought she was in hospital."

"She was released from the prison hospital a couple of weeks ago. In fact, I helped her get away, because she was worried that *La Force Marseillaise* would be after her, now that it is led by this new bloke called *le comte*."

As briefly as he could, he told her the story of his rescue of César and taking her to the cottage rented by Alain Hébert near Rennes-les-Bains and of his contacts with her since. He also told her about the help he had received through her friend, Pierre, and of his visits to the cottage.

"Last time I was there, I noticed this bag with the Habsbourg badge on the side. It was just shoved under a side table in the entrance hall-way and it was only the badge that made me notice it."

"What did you do about it?"

"I pointed it out to César and explained to her why I was interested in it. I asked her if I might be allowed to see the contents, because I thought it might provide a link to Hector, who I had not been able to meet at that stage."

"And what *were* the contents?"

"I don't know." Philip shook his head. "César told me the bag had belonged to Alain Hébert and she thought she should look through what was in it before she showed it to me, just in case there were any reasons why she should keep any of them secret. She has promised to let me know if I can see the contents, when she has finished checking them out."

"So what are you going to do about it? Remember that Hector has warned you not to look at the contents of the bag."

Philip gazed at the road ahead. "Well, I'll have to tell César what the professor said. It's likely, that by the time I contact her, she will already have looked inside the bag so she can tell me what it contains." He grinned. "I don't feel inclined to just lie down and let your friend Hector walk all over me. It's obvious he has some urgent reason why he wants to get hold of the bag, but I fail to see how my finding out what is inside it will put any of us in danger. If I think it will, then I'll just have to keep quiet about it."

"Will you ask César to give you the bag so that you can pass it on to Hector?"

"In the first instance, that will be up to César. Unless the contents tell us something important, we don't know who the bag actually belongs to. At the moment, it is the property of the late Alain Hébert. Who are his heirs? How can we find out? What right has your professor to demand that it is given to him? Nothing is clear at present."

They continued to chew over the mystery on their way back to Quillan, but all they could decide was that he should ring César as soon as possible and see what she had found out – if anything. Philip said he would do that when he got up to their hotel room. But the little man who was waiting for them in reception changed all their plans.

As they entered the hotel, the girl at the desk called out, "Mademoiselle Blontard. There is a gentleman waiting to see you."

Jackie turned towards the seating area and a short, plump man wearing a dog-collar stood up to greet her. He had a round, friendly face and was clearly a priest.

"Mademoiselle Blontard," he said, as he shook her hand, "My name is Abbé Rivère. I have been asked to contact you by the bishopric in Narbonne. I believe you asked if you could explore certain parts of the church at Rennes-le-Chateau, to which access is denied to the general public, to see if you can find a way into the crypt beneath the church – if there is one. I have come to tell you that he has arranged for you to do that."

"Oh, my goodness!" Jackie clapped her hand to her mouth. "I wasn't sure they would give me the necessary permission."

"There are a number of conditions," said Father Rivère. "The first is that I must accompany you to ensure that none of the other conditions are broken."

"Of course. I don't mind that. Are you the parish priest?"

"No, and that leads to another condition. Although the priest of Rennes-le-Chateau will be told about your visit, he is to know nothing about which parts of the church we go into, or about what we might find there. For that reason, the visit is to be made at night when nobody will be there to see us arrive or depart. This is so that Abbé Bigard will not be able to tell his parishioners anything if they question him. I will have the keys in my possession which will give us access to the church and all the necessary rooms."

"Blimey," said Philip. "This is all cloak and dagger stuff, isn't it?"

The cleric shook his head. "I regret that anything to do with the church at Rennes-le-Chateau is very sensitive. There has been so much publicity about the place that we have to be very careful."

"A secret night visit is not a problem," said Jackie. She turned to Philip. "This is my fiancé – Philip Sinclair. Can he accompany us?"

"I will check. Meanwhile I must tell you about the other conditions. You are not to damage or move anything. You must not, for example, remove any capping stones from any sarcophagi which you may find. You are not to unblock any openings which may have been sealed up. You are not to remove anything from the church, and you are not to take any photographs. If you wish to take any further action as a result of anything you find, this must be the subject of a new application to the bishop of Narbonne and his permission must be obtained before you take any such action. You will be required to sign an agreement to this effect before I take you to the site."

"None of that presents a problem," said Jackie. "I would not expect anything less."

The priest reached inside his pocket and produced a sheet of paper. "This is the agreement which I have just described to you. Will you read it and sign it at the bottom, please?"

Philip waited, full of questions, while she read it through, signed it at the bottom and returned it to the Abbé Rivère. The man gave a little bow as he received it and put it back in his pocket.

"Thank you," he said. "When would you like to go to Rennes-le-Chateau?"

"Is tomorrow night too early for you?"

"No. I will collect you here at ten o'clock. Is that convenient for you?"

"Certainly."

With another little bow, the Abbé departed. As the front door closed behind him, Philip asked, "What on earth was that all about?"

Jackie turned to him, and the excitement was clear in her face. "Have you heard the story about the priest of Rennes-le-Chateau who became fabulously rich?"

"Er, yes, I think so, but I can't remember the details."

"Well, it was back in the 1890's – more than a century ago. The priest, whose name was Bérenger Saunière, was involved in renovating the parish church when he apparently stumbled upon a treasure or something valuable. Maybe he found some important documents, which were hidden in the church. Who knows? Anyway, as a result of his discoveries he became a very wealthy man. In the next twenty years or more he paid for a four-kilometre road to be built up to the village, which had previously only been accessible by mule-track. And he did all sorts of other good works in the area. He lived a very opulent life – far better than he could ever have done on a priest's meagre stipend. He often went to Paris and was supposed to have been friends with many famous and powerful people."

"Doesn't anyone know how he got all this money?"

"That's the mystery. For some reason, he would never disclose the source of his wealth and all sorts of possible scenarios have been suggested to explain why he kept it a secret. One of the most popular is that he came across some sort of important information that the Church or other authorities wished to suppress, and he was paid all this money to keep his mouth shut. But there may have been other reasons. There have been dozens of books written about the subject."

"So what has this to do with the crypt in the church?"

"That's just it. It was believed that Saunière found a way into the crypt which has since been hidden. So far, the church authorities haven't even admitted that there actually *is* a crypt below the church, and they have never allowed any member of the public even to try to enter it before now. I understand there was a man who was allowed in the 1950's to check for possible ways into the underground room, and he was said to have found three possible entrances, but it was never taken any further. I managed to persuade the people in the Vatican that somebody ought to at least be allowed to confirm or deny that there actually *is* a crypt and find out what it contains. They have agreed to let me go that far, as long as they have control over whatever information is released to the public."

"And you think you know how to get into this crypt?"

She smiled. "Well, I hope so. It can be seen that there is a quadrant-shaped room on the side of the church, which has no apparent door into it. The room is beside the Sacristy. That is the priest's robing room, which is not open to the public. Along one side of the Sacristy – the side against the secret room – I understand there is a row of full-height cupboards and wardrobes. It is speculated that the door into the secret room is hidden at the back of these cupboards. With the help of our little priest friend, we will see if we can find out."

"So tomorrow night is likely to be a night to remember."

Jackie had a smug smile on her face as she said, "My darling. Every night with you is memorable."

# 47

The gloomy weather which had settled over the city of Marseilles seemed to penetrate even into the luxury penthouse apartment of *le comte*. Gaston Lesmoines stood just inside the large, barely furnished room, looking out onto the grey Mediterranean Sea, and shifted nervously from one foot to the other. He had not been invited to sit by the nubile attendant who had been waiting for him when the lift doors opened and who had wordlessly showed him into this intimidating room.

The last few days had been a long and difficult journey for Lesmoines. His original intention had been to follow the van containing four of his men who were pursuing Lerenard and his colleagues down the mountain road, by making use of Sinclair's little sports car. But, when he witnessed the disastrous crash which had wiped out most of his force at a stroke, he had, of necessity, changed his plans. He knew the only way to avoid arrest was to get out of Castereau before the police turned up and started their investigation of the hiding place they had occupied for the last two weeks. So he and the last remaining man in his group, Albert, had been forced to make the five-kilometre walk on the rough tracks to get to the main road.

Once there, they had come upon a young couple picnicking in a lay-by. The display of a machine pistol had quickly persuaded them to abandon their lunch and hand over the car keys. With Albert in the back beside the wife, his gun prominently lying in his lap, and the young man in the front beside him, Gaston had driven to the outskirts of Toulouse. There he had dropped the couple off and taken the car into the no-go part of the city before they abandoned it.

However, Gaston had soon found that news of the disaster his group had suffered had somehow gone ahead of him, and suddenly nobody wanted to have anything to do with the man whose activities had led to the death of four of their number. Within a few hours he realised he was on his own and even Albert had disappeared. After a short period of thought, he decided his best option was to head for Marseilles where he still had some useful contacts.

When he reached the criminal capital of France, he nevertheless found that things had changed since his previous visit about four years ago. A new man was controlling the illegal activities in the area. It had taken him two days of asking questions and passing on privileged information before he was finally admitted to the presence of *le comte*. Now here he was, waiting to talk to the sinister crime boss.

"You've been asking to speak to me?"

The question, coming from just behind him, made him jump. He hadn't heard the man who had silently entered the room. Gaston spun round to confront the leader of *La Force Marseillaise* and immediately felt intimidated by his size, with his bald head and black beard.

Lesmoines hastily gathered his wits. "I have just come from Carcassonne."

"Ah. You have a message from Candice? I have heard nothing from her for more than a week."

"This Candice – is she your woman?"

A ghost of a smile flitted across the man's features. "One of them."

"There was some woman hanging around the area. What does Candice look like?"

*Le comte* described her. After a couple of questions Lesmoines said, "It sounds like a similar woman, but her hair was black."

"It could easily have been dyed."

"That's true." Lesmoines scowled. "That woman caused me a lot of trouble. I had the Englishman, Sinclair, and his helper, Lerenard, imprisoned. I was discussing with my guys how to get rid of them, when she suddenly turned up and let them out."

"That sounds like the sort of thing Candice would be able to do."

"She gave a gun to this man Lerenard. When we were chasing after them as they were escaping, he shot the driver of the van. It went off the road and four men were killed. So I have a bone to pick with your Candice."

*Le comte's* eyes were like steel. "Is that why you are here?"

"No. I no longer have enough men to handle the collection of the treasure. For that reason I have come to give you my information and help. I can lead your men to the hiding place in the Carcassonne area."

The leader of *La Force* was quiet for a while, apparently considering possible developments. Then he said, "Yes. I think you might be useful to me." His eyes narrowed. "But I warn you not to try to play with me."

Lesmoines had no intention of "playing" with the man, of whose violence and ruthlessness he had already heard. He said, "I only wish to receive a part of the treasure I have been searching for. The rest can be yours, monsieur. There will be enough for everybody."

"And where is this treasure?"

"It is stored in the cellars of a half-ruined castle called le Bézu, near Limoux. It will only be there for a few more days because I have been told it is going to be removed to a warehouse near Carcassonne before being taken to safe vaults in Paris. I have checked the warehouse and it is still empty at present, but I believe it will soon be in use. Time is important."

"So we will have to move quickly."

Now that he had *le comte's* interest, they began to discuss ways and means of collecting the treasure.

"First," said the boss, "I want to pick up Candice. No person walks out on me when I have given them a job to do. I want to know where she has been, who she has met and what she has done."

Gaston decided it was wise to co-operate. "I think I know where I can find her for you."

"Where is that?"

"I think I can pick up her trail in Quillan, which is a little town near Limoux. That is where the Englishman is staying, and I believe she was following him."

"That is good. We will take them both together. First, I will squeeze Candice until she squeaks. That will lead me to Pierre and, through the Englishman, to Mademoiselle Renoir."

"Who is Renoir?"

"César Renoir is a journalist who is also the daughter of the previous leader of *La Force*. She killed my lieutenant – a man called Montluçon. It is time she was removed from the scene."

Tough though he was, Gaston Lesmoines felt his blood run cold at the casual mention of Renoir's elimination. Truly, this was a man who was not to be messed around with.

"And when you have dealt with these two women – what is your next aim?"

"Recovery of the treasure, of course. It will make La Force the most powerful organisation in France. Montluçon was a hot-head. He allowed the goods to slip through his fingers. I do not intend to make the same mistake." He turned his steel-grey eyes on Lesmoines. "You will help me, and you will be rewarded."

"Does that mean you will come to Carcassonne yourself?"

"Of course. It seems I can no longer trust others to do the job for me. You will show me where to find these things."

Gaston hesitated. "Er – I am already known in that area."

"Fear not," said *le comte*. "You will not be seen by anyone who might report you."

Lesmoines nodded. He had more sense than to argue with this intimidating man.

# 48

Jackie and Philip reached César's remote cottage soon after ten the next morning. He was still driving the hire car that he had been keeping some distance from the hotel, and which he hoped had not yet been connected to him. He had carefully checked that he wasn't being followed, by taking false turns up side roads, and then returning to ensure that no vehicle was trailing them, somewhat to Jackie's amusement. But, as he told her, he had promised to make sure that he wasn't putting the journalist in danger.

A phone call to César from his bedroom the previous evening had received her agreement to him taking his fiancée, who was herself keen to talk to Mademoiselle Renoir. César also confirmed that she had looked at the contents of the bag with the badge of the double-headed eagle on the side. She said it mainly contained personal items which would be of no interest to him, but she had found a file containing papers which he could look at. Philip hadn't told César about the warning from Hector not to look in the bag. He reasoned it was too late now in any case.

He pulled in under the trees across the road from the cottage. They got out, and he led Jackie up the path to the front door. César, dressed in a high-necked white blouse and dark jeans, was obviously waiting for them, because she opened the door as they approached and took them straight into the front room where a tray of coffee was already standing on a low table. No introductions were necessary, although the two women had seen each other only once before - in the treasure room at le Bézu, where the dreadful climax to the search for the Templar treasure had occurred, and two men had been killed, one of them shot by César herself. Philip could tell they were remembering that experience from the careful way they spoke to each other.

He had also noticed, when they entered, that Alain Hébert's bag was no longer lying under the table in the hallway. He didn't know what had happened to it or to the file of papers César had referred to, and he had to endure a frustrating ten minutes while their hostess warmed up the cafetiere of coffee and then a further quarter of an hour while they sat drinking the stuff and trying to make small talk. At last, the journalist rose and left the room, to return a few minutes later with a blue cardboard folder. She seated herself, opened the file and took out a piece of paper.

"It is obvious from this," she said, "that Alain knew this man, Hector Ramise." She nodded at Jackie. "I believe you know him as well."

"He was my archaeology professor at university."

"Is that so?" She held up a piece of paper. "This is a letter from Monsieur Ramise, giving Alain directions on how to find the treasure at le Bézu – the treasure that Philip has told me is no longer there."

"We now know what has happened to that," said Philip.

"Indeed?" César raised her eyebrows. "Then you know more than anybody else. Where is it?"

Jackie shook her head. "We don't yet know exactly where it has been placed. All I can tell you is that it is safe and in the care of its rightful owners. I hope to be allowed to view it and catalogue it in due course."

"So what exactly does this letter say?" was Philip's frustrated question.

"As I said, it gives detailed instructions on where the treasure was located in the chateau of le Bézu. It also confirms that their agreement is still in existence."

"What does that mean?"

"It doesn't go into detail, but I think it suggests there was some sort of arrangement between them, perhaps to share the proceeds from revealing the location of the treasure to the government."

Jackie intervened. "What is the date on the letter?"

"I have checked that. It is only four days before the treasure was actually discovered. I think it means that Alain did not know exactly where to find the treasure when he first came to Rennes-les-Bains, but Monsieur Ramise had promised to provide the precise location when he was ready."

Philip rubbed his eyes as he thought about it. "So it seems that Hector knew about the treasure, but for some reason he was sharing the information with Monsieur Hébert who had got

*La Force Marseillaise* involved." He looked at Jackie. "I think Hector has some explaining to do."

"Yes," she agreed, "but why did he tell us that we would be in danger if we looked in the bag?"

"Perhaps it was not because of this," said César. "This letter is not the only piece of paper in the file."

"So what else is in there?"

The journalist shrugged. "Not a lot. It's mainly private letters, and there's a copy of Alain's agreement with *La Force Marseillaise*."

"Really? What does that say?"

"I haven't read it. I only looked at it briefly before you came."

"It might be worth reading through the agreement to see if it contains any unusual clauses."

"You have a more legal mind than I have." César handed the sheet of paper to Jackie. "*You* see if you think there's anything out of the ordinary."

She took it and scanned it quickly. She returned to check one of the clauses more carefully. When she looked up there was a gleam in her eye.

"Clause 7 says -." She read it carefully as she translated. "It says it is acknowledged that, for his personal protection, Monsieur Alain Hébert will lodge a letter with his lawyers, Amboisard Frères, which shall describe the – er – the parties to this agreement and their respective roles in carrying out the said agreement. It will also set out the aims of the parties jointly to carry out the objects of this agreement and this information shall be released to the authorities by his lawyers if the other members shall cause the death of Monsieur Alain Hébert."

"What on earth does all that mumbo jumbo mean?" asked Philip.

She read it once more to herself before replying. "As I understand it, this clause means that, if Monsieur Hébert is killed by the Force, all the information he holds – er – held, would be made public."

"It didn't do Alain much good," said César, "It didn't protect him from those murderers."

Philip chimed in. "You said the lawyers were Amboisard Frères. Do you think that means the Maitre Amboisard we know – the mayor of Quillan – is involved?"

"It certainly may," said Jackie. "We'll have to ask him."

"And at the same time, we can ask him why he hasn't made this information public. After all, he can't claim he doesn't know what happened to Hébert."

"Perhaps the Force has threatened him if he dares to release the information."

"Whatever the reason, we've got to ask the mayor what he knows about all this." Philip scratched his head. "The more we find out, the more mysteries we seem to uncover. In addition we need to ask Hector just how much *he* is involved in all of this." He turned to Jackie. "Don't you agree we must go back and talk to them both?"

"I suppose so. But first, we should go through all the papers in the file."

Philip thought that perhaps she was worried about whether they might upset Aunt Charlotte. However, he said nothing, and they spent the next fifteen minutes scanning the other papers, which nevertheless failed to uncover anything important. So they decided to leave César and return to Jackie's flat in Béziers.

"Before you go," interrupted César, "you asked me to help you with finding a chateau called Blanchefort."

"That's right." Philip's interest quickened. "Did you have any luck?"

"I noticed in that second piece of paper that there was a reference to a lady called Marie de Hautpoul de Blanchefort, and that set me thinking. So I looked at my notes about the various chateaux I was researching for the book I was asked to write, and I saw that this lady lived in a chateau, now partly ruined, in the little village of Rennes-le-Chateau."

"That's interesting . . ." Philip started.

Jackie laid a hand on his arm and jumped in to cut him off. "Rennes-le-Chateau. That's not far from here, is it?"

"About five kilometres across country, but twice that distance by narrow back-roads."

"Well, it would be interesting to look at the place when we have time." Jackie smiled as she got up. "We must leave now.

It's a long drive to Béziers and we don't want to miss Monsieur Ramise."

She led the way out, chatting about inconsequential things like the weather and the remoteness of the cottage. Philip trailed silently in her wake, aware that she didn't want to talk about César's disclosure. Jackie thanked César for her help and promised to let her know what they found out when they questioned Hector.

Settled in the car, she said to him, "You mustn't tell anybody about our permission to search for a way into the crypt at Rennes church."

"Sorry. I realised, as soon as I started to speak, that I was talking out of turn."

"Don't worry. No harm was done."

"However, I *do* think we should take a close look at the chateau when we are in Rennes."

"I agree. Maybe we'll have a chance tonight. Now we must go and talk to Hector."

However, when they arrived at Jackie's flat in Béziers, they were told by Aunt Charlotte that the professor wasn't there, and she didn't know when he would be back.

"Where has he gone?"

"He wouldn't tell me that. He just said he would be away for two or three days and that I was not to worry." She sighed. "Of course, that made me worry all the more."

"How odd that he should go off now," said Philip. "I had the impression that he urgently wanted us to bring him more information about the bag with the double-headed eagle on the side. Now he swans off as though he's forgotten all about it."

Jackie smiled. "Well, there's nothing more we can do until he gets back. No doubt he will be in touch with us as soon as he returns."

They spent the next hour drinking coffee and chatting idly to her aunt, trying to put the old lady's mind at rest.

# 49

In fact, at about that time, Hector Ramise was leaning on the parapet of the chateau in the Old City at Carcassonne. He had parked outside and made his way up through the narrow, cobbled streets lined with souvenir shops, until he reached the square in front of the highest point in the City. Then he had entered the chateau and climbed to the top of its walls, where he could enjoy the splendid views over the whole of the modern city of Carcassonne and the surrounding countryside. But actually, he was watching the crowds of sightseers milling round below to see if he could pick out the man who had said he would meet him here at two o'clock.

The previous afternoon he had made good use of his many contacts to find out a little about, and how to get in touch with, the man known as Marcus Heilberg and the secret organisation he represented. When he finally got through to the Grand Treasurer's office, the man's secretary had been unwilling to put him straight through to the great man. However, Hector had been able to provide her with enough information to excite Heilberg's interest.

"Please wait a minute, professor. I will check with the Grand Treasurer to find out if he is able to speak to you at present."

Sure enough, it was Heilberg himself who came on to the phone a short time later.

"What is your name, monsieur?"

"I am Hector Ramise. I am senior professor at the Sorbonne school of antiquities. I have acquired some information which I am confident will be of great interest to your organisation."

"Yes indeed. My secretary repeated to me what you told her. May I ask how you heard of us?"

Ramise was able to provide convincing evidence of the connections who had given him information about the Order, without compromising their own positions.

"I see." Heilberg ruminated briefly. "I do not wish to discuss this matter further with you on the telephone. If you are able to provide the necessary proof to support what you say to one of our agents, we may be willing to take this further."

"Who is this agent?"

"Where are you telephoning from?"

"I am at present in Béziers."

"In the Languedoc?"

"That is so."

"Give me your telephone number and one of our agents will contact you as soon as it can be arranged."

Hector did so and the call was immediately disconnected. Although feeling a little irritated at his rather summary treatment, he had the sense to remain in his flat and wait for contact to be made. In less than an hour the phone rang.

"My name is Armand Séjour, monsieur. Marcus Heilberg has asked me to contact you. I understand you have something which may be of interest to our organisation."

"I certainly hope so."

"We should meet so that you can show me the necessary evidence."

"Very good. Where are you?"

"I am in Carcassonne. Can you meet me here?"

Hector thought quickly. He favoured the idea of a meeting well away from his home. "Yes. I can be in Carcassonne in about two hours."

"Very well. Let us meet in the Old City at two o'clock tomorrow. I will be by the parapet in the north-east corner of the chateau. There will be many tourists around so we will not be noticed in the crowd."

"Quite right," agreed Ramise. "That is a good idea."

"I will be carrying a copy of tomorrow's edition of *Le Monde*. It would be suitable if you did the same."

"I will make sure of it."


So here he was, just a few minutes before two o'clock, neatly dressed and with his hair combed flat. The newspaper was tucked under his arm with the title showing. Photocopies of the first few pages of the list were folded inside his jacket pocket. He was surveying the crowds of tourists who were obediently following their various guides and giving rapt attention to the stories they were being told about events which had occurred in the Middle Ages.

Suddenly, he was startled by being tapped on the shoulder. He spun round to confront a surprisingly young man with a loose cardigan pulled over a T-shirt and slacks.

"Monsieur Ramise?"

"Yes. Er – you must be Séjour."

"Correct. It is a pleasure to see that you are so prompt."

Hector relaxed. "I thought it was important to be on time for our first meeting."

"Absolutely. It is important that we build a good business relationship with you." He smiled. "So what do you have for me?"

The professor reached inside his jacket and pulled out the three folded sheets of paper. "This is a photocopy of the first few pages of the original."

Armand separated the sheets of paper and scanned them briefly. It was clear to Hector that he didn't understand their true importance.

"Can you explain what these are, monsieur?"

"They are a part of a list of treasures deposited with the Order of the Knights Templar in the year 1244. Does that hold any significance for you?"

The young man shook his head.

"It was the same year that the Cathar Heresy was wiped out and apparently nobody was left to reclaim their treasures from the Templars."

"Aah." Realisation dawned on Séjour. "So how did you come to possess this list?"

"It is a long story." Ramise paused to assemble his thoughts. "For some years I have been senior professor of antiquities at the Sorbonne in Paris. It became known that I had links - admittedly tenuous links - with the Austrian Habsbourg family. A representative from the household approached me and asked me to produce a history of the family before all the information available was lost to the world. It was a major work which I was pleased to undertake. I thought it was important that the world should know the full story of their rise and their huge contribution to European stability. You may know that at one time they were rulers of the united kingdoms of Austria and

Hungary, together with huge areas of the Balkans and Northern Italy. They were also installed by the pope as the Holy Roman Emperors."

The young man nodded, now interested in the story.

"Well, to provide me with all the information I needed to write this history, I had to be given access to the family archives which were stored in a remote castle in the Austrian mountains." Hector decided not to reveal the name of the castle at this stage of the negotiations. "There was a colossal number of sheets of parchment, which was the main material used for writing in the thirteenth century. In fact I was never able to do more than try to organise it a little and roughly classify it. I am confident that much of the data in those archives has never seen the light of day. It could keep a team of people working for years, trying to sort through it. I also found certain records which had been buried in the archives and which had no direct relevance to the Habsbourgs. It included this dossier of which you see a copy of the first few sheets."

"So you decided to relieve the family of it?" Séjour understood this sort of motivation very well.

"Ahem," Ramise refused to let the young fellow's attitude annoy him "Along with this bundle of parchment was enough information for me to work out where the treasure was hidden." He gave a wintry smile. "I admit I saw an opportunity to gain some benefit from my researches without depriving the Habsbourgs of anything which rightfully belonged to them. So I took possession of the dossier and have since held it in my safe-keeping."

The two men were now completely immersed in the tale which Hector Ramise was telling. They were oblivious to the groups of guided tourists eddying round them.

"You mean you wanted to have a hand in the discovery of a fortune, some of which would end up in your pocket."

The professor was not amused. "Yes, if you wish to put it like that. After all, at that time, I thought this treasure no longer belonged to anybody. The Cathars were wiped out many centuries ago. Why should I not benefit from its discovery? I discussed what should be done with my cousin and life-long friend, Alain Hébert, and we decided we should go and search for it, In the event, because of my official duties, I had to leave

259

the search to Alain." He paused and looked down at the dusty masonry at his feet. "I realise now that it was an unwise thing to do. Poor Alain paid for the search with his life."

Séjour was gazing intently at the professor. This was getting very close to his own experience. "So, why do you now choose to get in touch with *us*?"

"For the simple reason that I believe your organisation has an interest in this matter. I have many useful contacts. From those contacts I have been able to deduce who has now taken ownership of the treasure." He smiled thinly. "Forgive me, but I suspect that your organisation would not wish to be involved in an expensive dispute about the ownership of a large number of these items. I believe that the publicity, which would be caused by publication of this list, would be something you would wish to avoid."

"I see." The young man's expression had hardened. "Do I understand that you wish to sell this list to the Order so that they can suppress it and avoid handing over the treasure or a part of it to the Ministry of Culture, or whichever person may be entitled to it?"

The professor bowed his head. "May I congratulate you on the speed with which you have arrived at an understanding of my position, even if I am somewhat embarrassed by the bluntness with which you have expressed it. Of course, what the Order decides to do with the dossier when it has possession of the documents would be up to them."

"So how much do you want us to pay you to hand over this list and any copies you may have taken?" Séjour pursed his lips. "I am sure you appreciate that we would require an undertaking from you that you would not retain any copies."

"Certainly. There is no dispute about that. I have taken only two copies, including this one, and I am confident I can recover the other copy."

"So – how much, Monsieur Ramise?"

The professor shook his head. "I have no idea what value your Order would put on the items in the list. I can only judge that the items would be worth a great deal in the present-day market."

"In other words, you wish us to make you an offer."

"That is the way I would see the situation developing."

"Hmm." Séjour turned away and gazed out across the modern city below the hill. "Are you negotiating with any other potential purchasers?"

"I certainly am *not*. The only organisation I wish to deal with is your Order."

"Unless you consider our offer is insufficiently generous."

Ramise merely nodded. There was a long pause.

At last Armand said, "Well, Monsieur Ramise, you must be aware that I am a mere agent of the Order. I make no decisions for them. My task is to obtain as much information as I can, to aid them in coming to a decision. First of all – how many pages are there in this list?"

"Nineteen."

"And have you counted the number of items described?"

"As far as I can make out, there are two hundred and eighty-six."

"Are you saying that this is a big part of the treasure found at le Bézu?"

The professor looked at him, surprised. "You know about le Bézu."

"I arrived on the scene just a few minutes after your cousin had been shot by the member of *La Force Marseillaise*, who had himself been killed by then." He frowned. "But you did not tell me what portion of the treasure was Cathar."

Ramise shrugged. "I do not know. I have never been to le Bézu. I did not see the treasure. I have no idea of its extent or what else was contained in the chests."

"Nevertheless, I presume you expect the Cathar part to be worth many millions of euros."

"Well – er – I suppose it is."

"And, if you are surrendering your detailed knowledge of this to the Order, you would expect to be paid a decent percentage of the value."

"Um, well, I will leave that entirely in your hands."

Séjour's face was expressionless as he said, "Not in my hands, Monsieur. However, I will try to convey my understanding of your offer to my superiors. I presume I may keep these photocopies to show to them."

"Of course."

He pocketed them. "Now I think we have no more to say to each other."

He turned his back on Ramise and walked towards the entrance to the Chateau.

# 50

It had already been dark for some time when Abbé Rivère called for them at their hotel in Quillan. Jackie and Philip were sitting in reception, taking coffee before their midnight visit to Rennes-le-Chateau. They were both dressed in dark jackets and trousers with trainers on their feet. They were discussing the night ahead in low tones when the plump little priest appeared at their table.

"Good evening." He gave a little bow. "I have been able to confirm that Monsieur Sinclair is allowed to accompany you to look at the church. Of course, the same conditions will apply to him as to yourself."

"We understand that," said Jackie. "Neither of us wishes to upset the Church. We are grateful for being allowed to visit the place." She sat up. "Would you like a cup of coffee before we go?"

"Thank you, no. I would prefer to start straight away. We are going to have a late night as it is."

"That's OK." Jackie stood up. "We're all ready. We've both got large torches." She waved hers at him.

The little man turned away without further comment, and they followed him outside.

"We will go in my car," he said. "I often call in to see the Abbé Bigard, so its presence will not be remarked on by anybody who might happen to see it there."

The drive to the village of Rennes-le-Chateau took them less than half an hour and little conversation was exchanged as they went. The priest seemed to be concentrating on his driving, along the dark, poorly-lit roads and Jackie's and Philip's minds were on the exploration ahead of them.

When they reached the village at the top of the hill, having ascended the winding road through the forest, Rivère drove straight to the middle and parked immediately outside the gates to the churchyard. There was no sign of anybody about. No lights were burning in house windows and no curtains were twitched aside to see who was abroad at this late time of night.

They got out of the car and closed the doors quietly. A silence settled over them. Nothing seemed to move. There were no animals or night birds about. Rivère locked the car and pulled a small torch out of his coat pocket with which he lit the way to the church door. The metal gate squeaked just a little as he opened it. They followed him up the path to the narrow little porch. Philip flashed his torch on the tympanum above the door and read the inscription – *"Terribilis est locus iste"* – and he shivered.

The Abbé unlocked the door and pushed it open. It gave scarcely a groan on its well-oiled hinges. As they entered, Jackie turned her torch on a figure to the left. She indicated it to Philip. There, painted in gory colours, was the near life-size figure of the devil carrying the shell-shaped holy water stoup on his bent shoulders.

"What an odd idea," muttered Philip.

"This church is full of strange decorations and statues. They were the ideas of the nineteenth century priest, Bérenger Saunière. He was the one I told you about, who became fabulously wealthy – no-one knows how he got his money or why he chose this strange way of demonstrating his Catholic faith." She spoke in English, perhaps to avoid upsetting the Abbé.

Philip pointed his torch at the wall opposite and slowly swung it round to reveal the walls of the church. As far as he could see there were no windows in the building, but there were paintings and gilded statues everywhere. He had never seen a church so heavily decorated. It almost seemed to be blasphemous, the plethora of gaudy colours and paintings. As a result, their surroundings seemed to press in on them, creating an almost over-powering atmosphere. It was extremely creepy.

Rivère stopped and turned towards them. He held out the bunch of keys which he had been carrying to Jackie. "I will go no further with you," he said. "I will wait outside in the car for your return. Please remember the conditions of your visit." And he scuttled out, pulling the door closed behind him.

"He was in a hurry to go," said Philip. "Do you think the old boy's frightened of the dark?"

She wrinkled her nose. "Well, it *is* a rather unusual place to spend part of the night, don't you agree? I'm not sure I'd like to sit here on my own in the dark with all these strange statues around me."

"I suppose you're right." He took a breath. "Now, what do we do?"

Jackie shone her torch up the nave towards the altar. It picked out the dazzling gold semi-circular wall at the far end. "Ah, yes. The door I want is the one hidden behind the large statue of Saint Antony of Padua." She pointed. "There – opposite that very grand pulpit."

"OK. You lead on."

When they reached the door she'd indicated, it took some time to find the correct key to open it. Philip shone his torch on the lock while she searched through the bunch. She tried several before she found the right one and it turned smoothly in the lock.

"We must remember this is the key to use when we come out," she said.

They opened the door and found themselves in a small room with a single chair and a small table on one side and a row of full-height cupboards all along the opposite wall.

"This is the sacristy," said Jackie. "It's the room where the priest puts on his vestments - his robes for the service. Now we will see whether the rumour is correct."

She started to open the cupboard doors. The first two were locked. When she found the key that opened them, they gave access to a cupboard full of shelves where various ornaments and cups and silver chalices were stored. She shut those doors and re-locked them.

"Those are the easily taken precious objects which belong to this church."

There were four other doors, and these proved to be unlocked. She opened the centre ones and Philip's nostrils were assailed with the mixed smells of camphor and incense. A collection of mainly black and white robes were hanging there, but he could also see more exotic gold, green and scarlet fabrics among them.

Jackie delved into the interior, pushing the garments to one side and pulling some out so that she could get behind them. She was pointing her torch all round the deep cupboards, with what seemed to Philip to be an almost frantic urgency. A couple of vestments came off their hangers and fell to the floor.

"Careful," he warned, but she took no notice, burrowing ever deeper into the cupboard.

Suddenly she burst out, "*Mon Dieu*! It *is* really here," and she went silent.

"What is it?"

She repeated, "Oh! *Mon Dieu!*"

"Jackie! What have you found?"

"It is the door to the secret room. It has been rumoured that this is the way into the crypt under the church, but nobody except the parish priest has ever seen it before, and I believe he was told he must go no further. The church authorities have paid me the extreme compliment of letting me enter the secret room. I may be the first to do so since Abbé Saunière more than a hundred years ago. Of course, the door is locked, but hopefully one of the keys will fit. Here – shine your torch for me to try to unlock it."

Philip obeyed her instructions and found himself looking at a very solid, mahogany-panelled, large door set in one end of a stone wall. It didn't seem to have a handle. The condition of the door and the brass lock was excellent. He guessed that was because they had hardly ever seen the light of day.

Jackie was sorting through the bunch of keys to find the one most suitable. She looked almost comic, wreathed about by long surplices and cassocks, and totally committed to her task of finding a way through the door. In fact, the very first key she selected slid straight into the keyhole, but she found it difficult to turn.

"It's so stiff because it has seldom been used," she complained. "Here, Philip, you have a go. Your fingers are probably stronger than mine."

He fought his way into the cupboard beside her, displacing several more robes as he did so. They slid to the floor behind him.

"Don't worry about those. We can tidy up when we come back," she said.

Philip waggled the key in the lock and pushed and pulled as he tried to get it to engage with the tumblers. Then suddenly it gave way and, with his final twist, revolved in an anticlockwise direction. Because there was no handle he just pushed at the door, and it swung slowly and stiffly open. He shone his torch into the blackness beyond and panned it round to see what was there.

"Careful," he warned. "There's a curved flight of stairs immediately inside the door and they're very steep."

Jackie pushed past him, almost roughly, in her anxiety to see what was below. "There's a handrail to hang on to," she announced. "Come on. I'll go first."

She set off down the precipitous stone steps which spiralled round to lead under the main church building. Philip was a little slower in following her. He extracted the bunch of keys from the lock. Observing there was no handle or lock on the outside of the door, he pulled one of the cassocks lying on the floor into the gap to make sure the door didn't accidentally close and maroon them outside the sacristy. Then he followed his fiancée.

He found himself at the top of a flight of stone steps which descended steeply into the semi-darkness, lit only by the remaining glow from Jackie's torch. She had disappeared through an arched doorway at the foot of the steps into another room. Following her, he discovered they were now in a very large, low room. Down the centre were two fat, moulded stone columns and a large block of masonry. These supported a fan-vaulted ceiling which spanned to matching half-columns on the surrounding walls. He guessed these formed the supports to the floor of the main nave of the church above.

Looking round the gloomy reaches of the crypt, he could see the stonework and paving were finely cut from flat ashlar stones with thin joints. There was very little detritus on the floor, which suggested no animals had been able to enter the room. The atmosphere of the place was one of silent reverence – perhaps even of awe. This was because the most striking features of the crypt were the six large sarcophagi which had been placed, one in each bay of the crypt, formed between the columns and the outside walls. They were simple masonry structures, standing on step-up plinths and with huge granite capping slabs projecting over the top of the stonework. The sides of the tombs had lettering deeply chiselled into them, and

Jackie was down on her knees beside the nearest one, inspecting the carvings by the light of her torch.

"What are these?" he asked.

"These inscriptions are in Latin." She pulled a small note-book and a pencil out of her inside pocket. "I hope, when I've translated them, that they will explain who has been interred here and give me some useful dates."

Philip's Latin was no better than his French so he left her to it and wandered off, using his torch to look round the crypt. It appeared to be roughly the same size as the nave of the church above, but was no more than ten feet high in the middle of the arches. To his right the central row of columns ended and there was a solid block of masonry reaching up to the vaulted ceiling which he thought was probably situated directly below the altar. Beyond that the room ended in a semi-circular wall similar to the main church.

He went to inspect the structure under the altar and discovered that it was formed of three thick walls with a hollow void in the middle of it. When he looked up into the roof of the space, he could see it was capped by a large stone slab. He shook his head. There was no way out up there. So he looked further round the crypt. On the opposite side of the room, he noticed a flight of steps disappearing into the wall. When he started to explore these, he found they were also blocked at the top by another great slab of masonry. He thought it was probably close to the location of the pulpit in the church above.

However, just beside the staircase was an opening in the wall which led into a narrow tunnel. Shining his torch before him, he followed it until it terminated in a small brick-lined room. Fixed to one wall were the half-rotted remains of a vertical wooden ladder leading up into a large, stone-lined box. He decided he must now be under the churchyard to the north of the main building, so it was likely that, from the outside, this would appear to be a tomb. But again, the void was capped by a big slab of stone. This also wouldn't provide them with an alternative exit. There was nothing else for him to see here. However, he thought he would measure how many paces it was outside the building so that he could come back to the churchyard in daylight and try to locate the actual tomb.

He retraced his way, trying to count measured paces to the opening from the crypt. But, when he was almost back in the big room, he suddenly noticed a blocked-up doorway on the left side of the tunnel. He stopped and studied it. It seemed it had once been a narrow opening, no more than three feet wide, with an arched top. Somebody had filled it up with rough, unmortared blocks but hadn't completely filled the arch at the top. As a result, it was quite easy for Philip to lift out a couple of the highest lumps of stone and place them on the ground to stand on, in order to look through the small opening he had created. He still couldn't see very much but, when he shone the torch into the darkness beyond, he was almost sure he could see some arched masonry sloping downwards away from his level.

He looked round. Jackie still seemed to be immersed in copying the inscriptions on the sarcophagi. She clearly wasn't interested in exploring alternative exits from the crypt at this stage. He reached up and pulled at one of the large stones at the top of the blocked-up opening. It came away quite easily and he had to jump back as it fell to the floor by his feet with a hollow thump. A couple more of the stones gave him enough height to have an unobstructed view through the enlarged opening into the corridor. He shone his torch down the tunnel again and was able to see a regular stone-lined passageway descending gently to the east in the general direction of the chateau. This was interesting.

However, aware of the condition that they were not allowed to unblock any openings, he decided he should put the fallen stones back in their position in the wall and then go back and see how his fiancée was getting on. So, after struggling to lift the lumps of stone back into place, he returned to the crypt.

Jackie was still scribbling away in her note-book, copying down the carvings. "I'm glad you've come," she said. "My torch is starting to fade. Can you use yours to light this last inscription? Then I'll have finished."

So he waited patiently while she made the last of her notes then she turned her dazzling smile on him. "This is most exciting."

"What is?"

"The information on these tombs is fantastic. I need to check up on my history and a few of the Latin words, but I'm more or less certain these are the tombs of the last of the Merovingians."

"The what?"

"They were the kings who ruled most of France - which was still called Gaul at the time - from the late fifth to the middle of the eighth centuries. It would be incredible if we could get permission to open the sarcophagi and record the contents and get DNA samples from the skeletons. It would hugely advance our knowledge of the early history of the nation. I wonder if I could get the church to agree to that?"

"I think that may be a problem." Philip found it difficult to get excited about some ancient royal family. "I don't somehow think the Roman Catholic Church will be enthusiastic about opening up tombs, especially if they may contain the remains of royalty."

Jackie refused to be down-hearted. "At least I have these inscriptions. Will they let me publish those, do you think?"

"You can only ask."

"Right." She made her decision. "We've seen all we need to, haven't we? Our torch batteries are starting to run down, so we'd better get back. I want to finish my translation of the carvings. Then I'll phone my contact in the Vatican first thing tomorrow."

"Hey. Don't you want to hear about what I've found?"

"Sorry, darling." She turned to face him. "What *have* you found?"

"Well, to start with, there are two other possible exits up into the church. One is under the altar and the other is a staircase below the pulpit."

"Oh, that's interesting. I wonder why nobody else has found those?"

"They've both been blocked off at the top by large stone slabs which would need heavy equipment to raise them from the church floor." He smiled. "However, I've also explored a tunnel, which I think ends under one of the tombs in the churchyard, and I've looked into another tunnel which has been partially blocked and seems to be leading in the direction of the chateau."

"You know we're not allowed to unblock any openings," she pointed out.

"Yes, but I've been able to see part of the tunnel through a gap in the top of the blocked-up wall."

"But the only way in and out of the crypt at present is through the back of the cupboard in the sacristy."

"I'm afraid so."

"OK. We'd better get out then, before our torches run out."

She tucked her note-book back in her jacket pocket and led the way to the stairs. Philip followed. At her instruction he closed the lower door and they climbed the steep steps to the wooden door leading into the back of the cupboards in the sacristy.

When they reached it, Jackie said, "Oh, heck. The door seems to have shut. I'd forgotten there's no handle on this side. How am I going to open it?"

"That's funny. I was sure I'd wedged some cassocks into the opening to stop it closing. They must have fallen out. Try pushing it. If the door isn't locked, it should open under pressure."

She had a go without success. Philip also tried. Then he peered into the crack between the door and the frame. What he saw made his blood run cold.

"I can see the latch is down. The door has been locked from the other side. It appears that we aren't the only ones who know about this way into the crypt, and whoever it is has decided that they don't want us to get out."

"Oh! *Mon Dieu*," she exclaimed. "What are we going to do now?"

Philip ran his hands over the door and the frame, but it was impressively solid. "I don't think I could break through this door without a set of special tools."

"And it won't be any good shouting," she pointed out. "Abbé Rivère will be shut in his car and won't hear us through two solid stone walls. We're just going to have to wait until he gets worried about how long we've been in the place and comes looking for us." She turned to look at him. "It's lucky we've got each other to share the wait."

# 51

It was a long time later that Jackie asked, "What's the time now, Philip?"

He switched on his torch briefly to consult his watch and immediately switched it off again to conserve the battery. "Nearly half past five."

They'd been sitting at the foot of the steps in the pitch dark for several hours. Conversation had now lagged.

"It'll be getting light in the next hour or so. What on earth has happened to Abbé Rivère?"

"I don't think you can count on him coming to let us out."

"What do you mean? Surely, he must be worried about us by now. He won't want to be found sitting in his car when the villagers wake up and start walking about. They'll ask him questions which he won't want to answer."

Philip snorted. "I'm prepared to bet that neither he nor his car are outside the church any longer. In fact, he probably cleared off soon after he gave you the keys and left the church."

"Why should he do that? The church will have been left unlocked. Anybody could just walk in."

"Precisely." He paused before he put his fears into words. "Let's face it, Jackie. Somebody must have followed us into the sacristy and removed the cassocks I had pulled into the gap for the precise purpose of stopping the door closing. Somebody wanted to make sure we were imprisoned down here." He shook his head. "We made a mistake in not locking the sacristy door behind us before we came down into the crypt."

"The Abbé wouldn´t want to leave us shut in here? He is supposed to be keeping his eye on us to make sure we kept to the terms of our agreement. We weren´t given permission to come down here to be entombed. Somebody else must have done it. But who?"

Philip shrugged. "I don't know the answer to that. It could have been Rivère, but it's more likely to have been some other character, who first scared him off or bought him off, before he came down and shut us in. All I *do* know is that our being shut

272

in down here is not accidental. I also noticed that Rivère scuttled off pretty quickly after he gave you the keys. Perhaps that should have made us suspicious."

Jackie was silent as she thought about it. Then she said, "So what are we going to do now? We've tried your mobile phone, and there's no signal down here, so we can't get hold of Jean-Luc or Armand."

"I've been thinking about it." He stood up. "I've decided that we've sat here long enough. We must see if we can find another way out of this place while we still have some light left in our torches."

"How can we do that?"

"There's only one possibility. The ways out into the nave and the tomb in the churchyard are out of the question as far as I can see. The capping stones over those exits must weigh several hundred-weight – sorry, two or three hundred kilos – in each case. So the first thing we must try is the side tunnel that I saw the start of. I think that's the best chance we have of getting out."

"You mean we will have to unblock the access to it." She reminded him, "We signed an agreement not to unblock any blocked-up openings."

"Yes, but that was before we were incarcerated here. I think it's much more important to get out, than to worry about some vague agreement. If we make it, we'll just have to say sorry if the bishop complains."

Jackie laid a hand on his arm. "Please don't talk like that, Philip. Surely somebody will come to let us out."

"Who knows we're here, other than the Abbé Rivère?"

"Well, the people in Narbonne."

Yes, but they're a hundred miles away and will assume Rivère is looking after us, until he tells them otherwise. That could be a number of days or even weeks. I don't fancy waiting that long."

"But that tunnel may not lead to an exit."

"Perhaps not. But at least we're making an effort." He started to cross the crypt. "Well, are you coming with me, or sitting here waiting to be rescued?"

"Of course I'm coming with you. Above all else, we must stick together. I'm not letting you out of my sight again, Philip Sinclair - not for a very long time."

"OK. Hold my hand. Leave your torch hanging round your neck on its lanyard. We'll just use mine for the moment. I'll give a quick flash from time to time to make sure we don't walk into anything."

When they had felt their way across the crypt, she continued to follow close behind him. She murmured, "I'm glad that at least I'm not on my own down here."

"Worried about the long dead spirits rising from their tombs?"

"No - just about being abandoned in the dark."

When they reached the blocked up entrance to the tunnel, Philip flashed his light at it, then handed the torch to Jackie.

"I think I can feel to remove most of the stones," he said. "Just turn on the light for a few seconds when I ask for it."

For the next quarter of an hour he worked, carefully removing the stones one by one, and tossing them out of the way up the other tunnel. He only needed Jackie to switch on the torch briefly on half a dozen occasions. He found it was surprisingly easy to make the wall low enough for him to get his foot up on top of it.

"Right. Give me the torch. I think I can climb over now." He turned the light on briefly to check where he should place his feet.

Then he carefully climbed over. When he was on the other side, with his feet firmly on the floor of the tunnel, he reached back for Jackie.

"OK. Hold my hand. Step carefully. Make sure you can take your weight on each step before you take the next one."

With a couple of minor stumbles, she made it and fell into his arms. They kissed briefly before he turned to inspect the tunnel. This time he let the light stay on for several seconds. He noticed the stone-lined corridor was running gently downhill and curved slightly to the right.

"Well, it looks clear enough," he said. "The masonry is in good condition and there is very little debris on the floor. If you hold on to my right arm we can set off. I'll keep my free hand touching the stonework on the left side of the tunnel and you do the same on the right. Take little shuffling steps and stop and tell me if you kick an obstruction. I'll flash the torch from time to time to make sure we're not going to bump into anything big. Is that OK?"

She sniggered as she grabbed hold of his arm. "Lead on, my hero."

The tunnel must have been the best part of a hundred yards long. Finally a flash of Philip's torch picked out a door ahead. He turned the torch on full to make sure that there were no obstacles in front of the door and it chose that moment to run out of battery.

He pushed it in his pocket. "Never mind. We've still got yours. Can you let me have it?"

She unhooked it from round her neck and handed it to him. "I don't think there's much battery left after using it to note down all those inscriptions. Use it very sparingly."

They shuffled right up to the door and he started to feel around for the handle.

"The door's roughly made, but it seems pretty strong," he reported. "I hope we haven't got to try and break it down."

His searching fingers located a rough iron lever handle and he pressed down on it. To his surprise the door started to open stiffly, and he could see there was a low level of light beyond it.

"Hallelujah!" he cried. "We've made it."

But the door would only move a few inches, before some obstacle behind it prevented it from opening further.

"Oh, God," complained Jackie. "We're still going to be stuck down here."

"We're not giving up that easily." Philip put his shoulder to the door and heaved at it. The timber gave way a couple of inches but would move no further.

"Here – give me a hand. When I say shove, push with all your might. Are you ready?"

At his signal they both gave a violent push. The door moved another inch and there was a grating noise behind it. But it remained stubbornly immovable after that.

He went down on his knees and reached round the door jamb. He felt about behind the door as far as he could, and his hand came into contact with a block of stone lying on the floor. As far as he could tell it was large.

"There's a bloody great chunk of masonry leaning against the door," he announced. "I would guess it must weigh the best part of half a ton. And there may be other stonework beyond that. I don't think we can move it any further."

"Can you get through the gap?"

"There's no chance. I can just about push my arm and shoulder through but the gap's not wide enough for my head."

She sniggered. "You shouldn't have such a large head."

"Ha! Ha! Do you realise we're trapped in here - defeated right at the last hurdle?"

"Let me try. I'm smaller than you."

"Your head may be, but what about the rest of your body?"

"Let me at least try. You may be able to bend the door a little further to give me more room."

He considered. "If I couldn't hold it back, you might get hurt."

"You'll just have to do your best to protect me, won't you? Neither of us wants to remain trapped down here for goodness knows how long."

"OK. I suppose we've got to try."

Jackie moved past him and started to squeeze sideways into the gap between the stone jamb and the edge of the door. She got her first arm and shoulder through easily and her head just made it, turned to the side. But her chest was too large to squeeze through.

"Careful, Jackie. You'll hurt yourself."

"I think I could force the top half of my body through if you could get another centimetre or two. Can you do that?"

"I'll try. I'll put my feet on the door either side of the handle. Can you spare a hand to support them?"

In that awkward position, with both feet against the door and both hands holding the door frame, he gave a violent push.

"That's done it," she called as she dragged her body through as far as the waist. "Phew, that's a relief."

"Don't get too relieved. You're trapped half in and half out. You've still got to get your hips and bum through."

"That's no problem. Undo the zip for me and I'll just slide out of my jeans."

"Are you sure?"

"Try it."

So he undid the zip and she kicked off her shoes. Then, with a violent wriggle, she forced her body through.

"Aah!"

"Are you all right?"

"Just grazed my hip a bit. It's amazing how flexible a body can be when necessary. Pass me through my clothes, please. It's cold."

When she had dressed and was standing up, he said, "Now we've got a problem. You're on one side of the door and I'm on the other. But first of all, what sort of a place are you in?"

She looked round. "Whatever it is, it's ruined. There are heaps of rubble everywhere. One is up against the door I got through. There are the remains of a couple of windows on one side of the room without any glass in them. The floor of the building above has collapsed on that side, and you can only see the bottom half a metre or so." She paused to assess the situation. "It must be near to dawn outside, because that is where the light is coming from."

"Can you move the rubble that's up against the door?"

"I think so, but it will take some time."

"Just clear enough for me to force the door open another three inches or so, and then I can join you."

"OK." She set to with a will, moving the rough stones with her bare hands. It took her about a quarter of an hour to clear enough for him to force the door open another couple of inches and get through to join her.

"Thank you, my darling."

"Oh, dear." She inspected her damaged hands. "Just look at my nails."

"We'll go into Carcassonne tomorrow, and you can have an hour or two with a beautician."

They hugged each other.

"However," he reminded her, "we're not out yet. Where do you think we are?"

"I guess we must be in the cellars of the old chateau. I noticed on a previous visit that it was partly ruined on the side just above the edge of the hill. I think our tunnel must have come out in the ruined part."

"How long has the chateau been like this?"

"I don't know. It could be centuries. I don't think the place has been lived in since before the Revolution and that was well over two hundred years ago."

"So – now, how to get out." Philip crossed to the windows, getting down on his knees below the sagging ceiling, in order to peer out. "You're right. We're on the edge of the hill here, with a grassy bank about twenty feet – er six metres – below at the foot of the wall. The bank falls down steeply to a path perhaps another five metres below that. Then it's all woodlands. I'd be happy to take a chance on jumping down there."

"I don't like the sound of that. I don't like heights."

"You mean you've come all this way from the crypt; forced your way through a narrow gap into this room; mucked up your hands clearing rubble to get me out; and you're not willing to jump twenty feet to escape?" He smiled sympathetically. "Well, there's a big bush just below the window to land in. I'm perfectly prepared to risk a drop like that."

"Well, I'm *not.* You could easily break a leg or something." Jackie looked round. "Surely there must be an easier way out – a door or something."

"If there is, I think it must have been covered with rubble from the collapsed building. Can you see anything?"

"Not at the moment."

"Exactly. If there had been an easy way into this room somebody would have found the tunnel and discovered this way into the crypt, and that would have knocked one mystery on the head."

"Yes," she agreed reluctantly. "I guess that's probably correct."

"I tell you what – I'm confident I can do the jump without seriously hurting myself. Then I can go and wake up some of the locals and get them to bring a ladder to help you down."

"Really? Is your French good enough for that?"

Philip snorted. "I can make myself understood when I need to. I'm not prepared to sit around until somebody we can shout to chooses to wander along the path. We could be here for days." He started to pull himself through the unframed opening onto the sill.

"Philip."

"Yes."

"Please be careful." She came and grabbed his arm.

"Of course I will."

He slid the rest of his body through the narrow opening and let his legs dangle while he held on to the stonework and looked down for a suitable landing spot. In fact, he reckoned the top of the bank was less than twenty feet below and, if he landed with bent knees, he would fall back away from the wall and land in a quite thick bush conveniently located just under his landing point.

"It's OK. Everything will be fine. Cheerio. See you in a little while." And he let go.

Surprisingly, it worked almost exactly as he had planned. The bush gave him an effective, if rather prickly, landing pad and it only took him a few minutes to struggle out of its clutches and totter down the bank to the path.

"Are you all right?" came floating down to him from above.

"Just fine. No problems. See you in a few minutes."

With a wave he set off along the path which he presumed would lead him up to the village.

# 52

In the event, it was nearly an hour later, when Philip got back to the point on the path below the window which he had jumped from. He had expected Jackie to be anxiously peering out to see what had happened to him, but there was no sign of her. Perhaps she had got fed up with waiting and fallen asleep.

When he had gone into the village, he had found it impossible to get any of the locals to open their front doors or even their windows to speak to him at this early hour. So, after trying about a dozen houses without success, he had hit upon the bright idea of contacting Jean-Luc Lerenard. When he phoned, he found the big man was already awake and worried about the fact that neither Philip nor Jackie had slept in the hotel last night.

"Where are you?" he demanded, as soon as Philip had explained their situation.

"I'm standing in the centre of Rennes-le-Chateau."

"Stay where you are. I will be there in fifteen minutes."

Philip only left the spot to walk the few yards to check whether the Abbé Rivère's car was outside the church. As he expected, the vehicle had gone. Furthermore, when he checked the church door, he discovered it was locked. So, whoever was involved in their incarceration, also clearly had a key to that door.

Jean-Luc arrived only about five minutes later than he had promised. He immediately led the way to the mayor's house. The man came down to the door in his night-shirt, in response to their determined knocking. Lerenard briefly explained the situation and impressed Philip with his knowledge of the place and his ability to galvanise the little man into action. In no time at all, the mayor had dressed and recruited two other locals to help. A considerable discussion took place about where to obtain the longest ladder, However, after several phone calls, a modern aluminium, three-part extending one was found. The little group then followed Philip back down the path to outside the window he had jumped from.

The first job was to extend the ladder to see if it would reach. It wasn't quite long enough. There was much tut-tutting about whether it would be too steep to provide a safe means of escape for Jackie. But Philip pointed out the bush he had fallen into.

"If you put the foot of the ladder in this bush it will have a shallower angle."

Lerenard was uncertain. "It will still be a very steep climb."

"I'm willing to try it. If I fall off, I'll land back in the bush for the second time. I'm prepared to risk that."

There was a profusion of chatter in French.

"Look," said Philip. "I'm the lightest one here. You four can hold the ladder steady. Then I'm sure I can make it."

It was obvious that no-one else was keen to do the climb, so the argument ended. During all this discussion there had been no sign of Jackie, which slightly concerned him. He was therefore anxious to get up the ladder and check what had happened to her. He hassled the others into setting it up just as he wanted and, getting a start from Lerenard's broad shoulders, he set off. The ladder was very steep. He had to cling to the main uprights and ease his way up step by step. As he went, he received much good advice from below, most of it in French, which he didn't understand and therefore ignored.

In this position, the ladder reached to within about two feet of the windowsill. When he got to the top, still with his head below the opening, he called out to let Jackie know he was close. He realised it would be difficult for her to start coming out of the window feet first, with her face looking into the room, while he guided her on to the top rung. He knew she wouldn't like the experience, but she was a sensible woman, so he was surprised when she didn't even look out at him.

"Jackie!" he called. "Are you there?"

There was no response.

"Come on. It will be a nasty sensation to start with, but you will be quite safe. There are four men holding on to the bottom of the ladder."

Still no reply.

"Jean-Luc is here. I rang him and he arranged it all. You know you can rely on him."

It seemed as though she couldn't even hear him.

"Jackie, will you please come to the window."

He waited a while longer, but it was clear there wasn't going to be any response. She obviously wasn't there. Where on earth was she?

He really had no alternative now, but to climb into the room to see what had happened to her. With a sick feeling, he started to ascend the last few rungs. There was a nasty moment when there were no more hand-holds on the ladder but he still couldn't quite reach the window. However, leaning tight against the wall, he managed to get his finger-tips onto the edge of the sill and ease himself up another rung until he could reach over and get a grip on the stonework. Then he pulled himself up one final rung, and he could see into the room. It was all just as it had been when he left, except that there was no sign of his fiancée.

"Jackie!" he called again. "What has happened to you?"

Since there was still no reply, he dragged himself half-way through the opening. He could feel his feet were now on the top rung of the ladder.

"Jackie! Are you there?"

He wondered where on earth she had disappeared to, as he pulled the rest of his body through the window, got into a crouch below the deeply sagging ceiling and moved into the centre of the room. She certainly wasn't here any longer.

He went to the door. It was still jammed nearly shut with the pile of rubble and large stones behind it. He doubted whether she would have gone back that way. He turned away and jumped with shock. She was standing just in front of him. Her face was flushed and her hair awry.

"I've got something fantastic to show you," she burst out. "Come on, follow me,"

She turned and made for the back of the room where she started to climb over the rough heaps of rubble. He noticed then that her shoes were covered in dust.

"When I was left here on my own, I decided to do a bit of exploring," she explained. "What I found is incredible."

She reached a place where the ceiling had almost completely come down. It rested at one end on a pile of stones. The next second, she had disappeared. Stumbling over the rubble behind her, Philip was suddenly able to see an open doorway in the back wall of the room.

"You've found a way out."

"No. This door leads into another room, but it's the only way in."

He reached the door and looked in.

"I think it's some sort of strong room," she told him. "It has survived the collapsed building all around it except for bursting the door open. There's loads of dust, but no significant damage to the contents."

Indeed there was a thick layer of dust and debris on the floor and a large chunk of masonry, which had smashed the door open, was lying in the opening. However, the ceiling and the walls were still intact. Jackie was standing in a small area of the floor just inside the door. The rest of the room appeared to be filled up with large old chests, stacked neatly two or three high, with walkways between them.

"Blimey," he gasped. "What's this? More treasure?"

She turned to him with her eyes glowing. "I think it's much more important than that. I was able to lever two of the chests open and they are full of parchments and other documents. I've looked at a few of the sheets and they are in a variety of languages, but most are in Latin. From the contents, it looks very much as though this could be a part of the long-lost archive of the Knights Templar. In fact, I believe there's a chance these could be some of the most important historical documents ever to have been found."

"Archives? That's old records, isn't it? Why are *they* so important?"

"Because the Templars were the international bankers of Medieval Europe. The Templar Preceptories received deposits from the nobility in their home towns when they were going on long journeys, such as the Crusades. When they got to their destinations, the nobles could draw on the funds they had left behind in the West whenever they needed money. Obviously all these transactions had to be recorded."

Philip shook his head. "I didn't realise the medieval world was so sophisticated."

"Oh, yes. The Templars also loaned huge sums to the various rulers of countries who wanted the money to pay for their wars and other large expenses. The charges the Templars made for this service brought the Order great wealth, and made many nations heavily in debt to them. The King of France, for example, was believed to owe them a large part of the total value of his kingdom at the start of the fourteenth century. That's the main reason why he arrested all the leaders of the Order in 1307 on various trumped-up charges which have since been proved to be false."

"Are you telling me these chests might contain the actual records of all those transactions?"

"That's right. It was always assumed that all the Templar archives were left in Cyprus after the Order was expelled from the Holy Land, and were destroyed when that island was overrun by the Ottomans in the sixteenth century. However, the relevant ones could have been kept in France. When Jacques de Molay and the other leaders returned the year before their arrest, the records would have been essential for the continuity of the Order." She took a breath. "The Templars were very strong in this part of France, and it was rumoured that many of them in this area escaped arrest in 1307. At least two of the Blancheforts were Templars and the archives could have been hidden here for safety."

"Wow. Another fantastic discovery to be trumpeted by the darling of French archaeology."

She looked at him sharply, aware of a hint of sarcasm. "No, Philip. This must be kept absolutely secret - for now, at least. If the word got out too soon that the archives had been discovered, it could cause a huge amount of trouble."

"Why, for God's sake?"

"For a start,, they could be worth untold sums of money. At auction a single document could be worth many thousands of pounds," She spread her arms. "And there may be hundreds, perhaps even thousands of those documents in these chests. Then there's the information they contain. For example, what exactly was the Cathar treasure that was deposited with them, and what happened to it? Did France repay the huge sums loaned to the nation by the Templars? What would the debt be worth now? Is it legally enforceable? It's probable there is a huge number of individuals and groups who would want to suppress the information contained in these chests, and who might go to considerable lengths to do that." She smiled. "You can see what a can of worms this discovery might open."

"So we have to keep this secret."

"Certainly, until we have a better idea of what exactly is here. Besides which, I may not be right. These chests may contain something completely different, and I might look a complete fool if we went public before I was sure of my facts. So, for now, please don't mention this to anyone."

"Not even to Jean-Luc?"

"Especially not to him. You know who his employer is."

"Yes." He grinned. "OK. My lips will be sealed."

"Thank you."

"One consideration though – who actually owns this pile of chests?"

"That's a teaser. I suppose that technically it belongs to the successor organisation to the Templars."

"Is there one?"

"It's rumoured there's a mysterious body in Paris which has kept the Order alive. But I don't know whether they can prove anything about ownership – or if they would want to."

"I presume the owners of this place could claim the right to anything found here. Who owns the chateau now?"

She shook her head. "I don't know for sure, but I expect it was confiscated at the time of the Revolution. It's probably in the ownership of the municipality now. Why do you ask?"

"Oh, no practical reason." He made his decision. "Well, I'd better rescue you before someone else decides to climb up the ladder to find out what has happened to us."

He led her out of the secret room and across to the window to start the difficult task of getting her down the ladder.

# 53

Candice Ambré was admitted to Marcus Heilberg's illustrious presence after waiting for nearly forty minutes in the secretary's office. She was not invited to sit down. Clearly her arrival in his office was unwelcome. The Grand Treasurer turned his baleful gaze on the smart young woman in front of him.

"I am not at all happy that you have come here personally," he informed her. "You know full well that our field operatives should not have direct contact with this office. In fact, I am surprised you even found out how to reach me."

Candice knew better than to admit she had enticed the information out of Armand Séjour. The Grand Treasurer would not be pleased to hear that any of his agents were discussing such things with each other.

"I am sorry, sir," she responded, "but I lost my indirect contact with you when Victor Solder was killed in the van crash at Coustereau village. I believed that what I needed from you was more urgent than waiting for another contact to be installed, and then for him to get in touch with me."

Heilberg was not an unreasonable man. He cleared his throat. "Yes, that was an unfortunate accident."

"You see, Monsieur, I have reached a difficult point in carrying out my instructions. I have successfully worked my way into the centre of *La Force Marseillaise* and am now sharing the bed of the leader – a man who calls himself *le comte*."

"Ha-hmm." Marcus did not wish to be made aware of details like that.

"This *le comte*," she continued, "has employed me to find and arrange the elimination of another leading member of *La Force*. She is a woman called César Renoir who is the daughter of the former leader, André Renoir. I presume, if she were to stand against him, she might be able to muster sufficient support to put his own position at risk."

She paused for a response, but none came.

"So far, I have been unable to track down Mademoiselle Renoir, because she is being helped by a young Englishman called Philip Sinclair, and he is assisted by an agent from the Vatican by the name of Jean-Luc Lerenard. That man is known to be an assassin who has often been used by big organisations to liquidate opponents, and I am afraid I might fall foul of such a dangerous man in carrying out my instructions."

At last a response was forced out of the Grand Treasurer. "Indeed?"

Candice was now in full flow. "As a result of this, I got in touch with your agent, Armand Séjour."

"You have been dealing with Séjour?" He did not sound pleased.

"It was essential that I did so," she explained, "because I became aware that he had been instructed by you to provide protection to the Englishman. My job now is to report to *le comte* that Sinclair is the man who knows where Renoir is. This will put him in a great deal of danger. If I don't tell him, I will destroy my credibility with *La Force Marseillaise*. I feel it is vitally important that I receive clear instructions as to what I should do in the future. Either I must eliminate the Englishman or cease to enjoy the confidence of *le comte*."

"Hmm." Despite his annoyance about her unasked presence in the office in Paris, Heilberg had to admit she had a point. The activities of young Sinclair were causing him a great deal of concern. In fact, they might also cost the Order an awful lot of money. It was time for a decision to be made about what to do with the Englishman, and that was a decision he did not wish to make by himself.

He looked up at the woman facing him across the table. "When did you arrive in Paris?"

"Less than an hour ago."

"You are confident you were not followed."

"Yes, Monsieur. I took steps to disguise my appearance."

"Very well. I want you to go to address number fourteen. My secretary will give you the details and an authority for you to be let in. You must wait there until I give you further instructions."

She bowed her head in acquiescence.

"I am aware of the urgency of this matter. I will get in touch with you as soon as I have reached a decision with the other members. Do you understand?"

"Yes, Monsieur."

He nodded in dismissal. As she left the room, he picked up the telephone. There was a lot to do in the next few hours.

# 54

It was Philip who had the bright idea. He and Jackie had gone to bed early on the Sunday evening, exhausted after their adventures and lack of sleep the previous night. He knew they had to be up early the following morning to help Jean-Luc Lerenard re-open the site at le Bézu, so he had set the alarm for seven o'clock. However, he was awake before it went off, full of enthusiasm and plans for the week ahead.

"I think we should buy the chateau at Rennes," he announced as he put down a cup of coffee he'd prepared for Jackie by her side of the bed.

"What!" She opened one eye and peered at him sleepily.

"We've been talking about getting a place round here. What could be better than that old chateau? Surely the place wouldn't be very expensive in its present run-down state, and between us we've got loads of money to do the restoration. If we bought the place, we'd automatically acquire all the contents of the building, including the Templar archives – if that's what they are. Then you could live above the stuff and research it at your leisure." He grinned. "What do you think of that idea?"

She was fully awake now and sat up. "Are you crazy? Even if we could find out who owns the place and persuade them to sell, it would take years to make it habitable."

"We could live in a caravan in the courtyard to start with. Then, while you are doing your researches, I could start the work. It wouldn't take long to repair a part of the roof and make at least one wing suitable for us to live in."

"But it would cost a fortune."

"Maybe." He looked into her eyes. "But now we've got a fortune, and what could be better than spending a part of it on restoring a half-ruined old building?"

"It's probably subject to all sorts of planning restrictions and other regulations."

"Jackie. You can't tell me the Ministry of Culture, or whatever other body is involved, wouldn't welcome the restoration of an old building which, otherwise, is likely to deteriorate gradually into a complete ruin."

She shook her head to clear it. "I suppose you're right, but I don't think you appreciate how much work would be involved. It could cost millions."

"Oh, I agree we'd have to look at the whole project very carefully before we decided to go ahead. We'd have to engage an architect to do plans and obtain detailed estimates for the work. But at least it would be worth looking into."

"Well," she temporised, "I suppose so, but it would take some time before we could start."

"Never mind. Those documents have probably been there for hundreds of years. Another year or two wouldn't ruin them. In fact, they would probably be better cared for by us, than if they were handed over to the government."

"All right. I agree we can start finding out about who owns the place." She smiled at his enthusiasm. "I can't resist you when you're in a mood like this."

"Is that an invitation?"

"No. It isn't." She jumped out of bed. "We've promised to meet Jean-Luc at eight and I need a shower and some breakfast to set me on my way. We haven't eaten much in the last couple of days." She patted his arm and gave him a peck on the cheek. "You'll have to keep your passion under control until this evening."

They met Lerenard half an hour later at breakfast. He was in his working clothes. He told them he had recruited a couple of young local lads to help him re-establish the site at le Bézu and had arranged to meet them in the town square at nine o'clock.

"I went up there on Saturday," he told them, "I think I can have the place looking like an archaeological site by the end of the week, so the cameras can come in next week."

"Goodness," said Jackie. "I must brush up on my script. I'll tell Alain to start getting things ready, but it'll probably be at least another fortnight before he can assemble all the equipment and the specialists together for a start on site."

Jean-Luc nodded. "When you're ready to start filming, I'll need to take on another half a dozen people and give them a short course in looking like archaeologists."

"But don't go to Toulouse for recruits," quipped Philip. "We don't want to pick up any of Gaston Lesmoines' guys."

"You will have to trust me," replied the big man, clearly having trouble with the English sense of humour.

Philip gave them a lift to Limoux, where they collected the two Land Cruisers and took them back to Quillan. One of the new men could drive, so Jackie wasn't needed after that. At Philip's urging, she agreed to return to Rennes-le-Chateau to start their search for the owners of the castle.

It took them some time to track down the local mayor who was only available for civic duties in the evenings. He was a local builder and they finally found him repairing the roof of a cottage a couple of kilometres away. However, when they persuaded him to descend the ladder to talk to them, he wasn't much help. He had no idea who owned the chateau. All he could tell them was, that if he ever had any problems in connection with the biggest building in his village, he referred the matter to his senior in Quillan to be sorted out.

"Do you mean Mayor Amboisard?" asked Jackie.

"That is so. He is the local lawyer."

"We know Monsieur Amboisard."

The man sniffed derisively. "Then you should talk to him."

He remounted his ladder to the roof.

Having returned to the hotel for a coffee, they made for the mayor's office. Amboisard welcomed them effusively. After an exchange of pleasantries, Jackie decided to approach the subject in a roundabout way.

"You know, Monsieur, that Philip and I are planning to be married in the near future?"

"I had heard." The old man leaned forward. "May I be the first to offer you my congratulations and best wishes?"

"Thank you." She paused to collect her thoughts. "We have also decided that we like this area very much and wish to purchase a house here and make it our home."

The solicitor smiled broadly. "What a splendid idea. If you would like any help in selecting a suitable place, I would be delighted to be of assistance."

Philip thought that he was no doubt imagining the fees he might charge for performing the conveyance.

"Well -." Jackie smiled disarmingly. "Over the weekend we went to Rennes-le-Chateau, among other places, and Philip had this idiotic idea of buying the chateau there and doing it up. Monsieur Castrier, the mayor, said that you dealt with matters concerning the place. We would like you to tell us who are the owners of the chateau so that we can approach them and find out if they are interested in selling."

"*Mon Dieu*!" Amboisard suddenly seemed short of breath. "Oh, dear. What a question to ask!"

"Why is it so strange?" asked Philip. "The place seems to be mouldering away and will soon be a complete ruin. It is of no use to anybody in its present condition."

The mayor turned his gaze on the young Englishman. "Do you know what you are talking about, Monsieur Sinclair? This is not England, where perhaps all the property changes hands frequently. The chateau you are interested in has probably remained in the same ownership for centuries."

"But they don't seem to be interested in restoring the place themselves," Philip pointed out. "It's no use to anyone in its present condition. Wouldn't it be to everybody's benefit if it was restored to its original condition?"

"And what is that, Monsieur? It would need much research and a lot of difficult work to restore it. The chateau will be listed by the nation as a place of historic interest. You must realise that it might take years to carry out the work fully in accordance with all the special regulations."

Somewhat to Philip's surprise, Jackie interrupted. "We are willing to put a lot of time and effort into restoring the place, Monsieur Amboisard. We believe we now have enough money between us to do the work and we would provide the necessary guarantees." She put her head on one side. "You are aware, of course, of my position and my qualifications?"

"Oh yes," he hastened to assure her. "There is no doubt about your suitability for a project of this type. But have you thought what you would do with the place when you have completed it? It will be a huge building – far too big for just the two of you."

"Surely that would be up to us. We intend to settle and have a family." Philip paused. "Perhaps we might consider using part of the building as a hotel."

The mayor shook his head. "I am not sure a hotel would be acceptable to the authorities in that location."

"Why not? After all, the village receives many tourists – a lot of them wealthy Americans. Those people would love to be able to actually stay in the place where the Abbé Saunière made his fantastic discoveries."

"But I'm not sure it would be regarded as suitable to turn the chateau into a hotel."

Philip was slightly offended by the man continuing to raise objections. "Monsieur Amboisard, we understand there are many questions to be answered and problems to be resolved, before we could decide how to use the place. The first question is whether the owners would be willing to sell and what would be an acceptable price. Can you please give us their name and address, so that we can at least approach them to see if they are interested in getting rid of the chateau?"

"Er -." The mayor paused before replying. It seemed clear to Philip that he was looking for a way to avoid putting them in touch with the owners. Why should he be doing that? At last he said, "Well, I think that first I should approach the people who own the chateau and give them an outline of your proposals. Then, if they are willing to talk to you, I will let you know."

"And, until you've spoken to them, you won't disclose who they are."

"They may wish to remain anonymous. They may prefer to deal with you through a third party."

"That seems very odd."

Jackie laid a restraining hand on his arm. "OK, Monsieur Amboisard. We will leave the matter with you. However, we would be grateful if you would come back to us as soon as possible, because we wish to make a decision about our future in the next week or two."

"I understand," said the old man. "I will contact you as soon as I have some information."

As they left, Philip suddenly remembered the letter César had shown them. He turned back. "We have heard, Monsieur, of a firm of lawyers in the area called Amboisard Frères. Is that you?"

The mayor looked at him sharply. "Where did you hear that?"

"I'm not sure." Philip turned to Jackie. "Would it have been your friendly professor - Hector?"

"I don't think so."

"Oh, I'll probably remember when we leave." He looked back at Amboisard. "*Is* it your firm?"

The old man had regained his equilibrium. "It probably is. I used to be in practice with my brother in Carcassonne. Of course, I resigned when I became mayor five years ago. However, my brother Anton has kept the old name. I can put you in touch with him if you need his help."

"I think that may be useful in the future. It is very likely we shall need the services of a lawyer we can rely on."

"I believe I have a card here." The mayor opened his desk drawer, ferreted around and emerged triumphant. "Here we are. It is one of my old cards, but the telephone number and address are still the same."

"Thank you very much. Philip took the card and had a quick glance at it. He noted the address was in Carcassonne, before he slipped it in his pocket. Then, with a further exchange of pleasantries, they left the mayor to make contact with the owners of the chateau.

"Why didn't you tell him you got the name of his firm from César?" asked Jackie as they walked back to the hotel.

"I think I need to keep her name out of things as far as possible."

She shrugged, but said nothing.

"And why do you think he was so negative about the chateau?" responded Philip. "After all, he'd stand to make some money if he acted for the existing owners in the sale of the place."

"Yes, he *was* very cagey," agreed Jackie. "Perhaps the owners are a very well-known group, and they don't want the locals to realise they own the place."

"But they could ask us to deal with them in confidence. They're not using the chateau, so it might be in their interest to get rid of it, to prevent any possible comments about the place becoming an eyesore. It's obvious that nobody has carried out

294

any maintenance on the place for decades – possibly centuries. If they had, they would surely not have left all those papers where they are."

She looked at him carefully. "You're right, of course. But perhaps the owners don't *want* anyone to start looking round the place."

"You're thinking about the condition put on our visit to the crypt, that we were not to unblock any blocked-up openings. That means you think it might be owned by the Catholic Church."

"But that doesn't make sense. If the Church wanted to stop people looking at the archives, it would be easier for them to remove the papers to the Vatican library or destroy them altogether."

Philip stopped and turned to her. "I agree. Perhaps we're looking at this from the wrong end. Perhaps we should think first about who shut us in the crypt. At least we know *they* weren't trying to stop us from discovering the archives."

"But who knew we would be there on Saturday night?"

"Well, obviously there's the priest. What's his name? Rivère. Who might *he* have told?"

"He said that the local priest knew nothing about the visit. So it's not likely to be anybody from Rennes-le-Chateau."

"He would probably have told the Catholic hierarchy in Narbonne when he got permission for me to join you. That means it was likely that Galbaccino knew."

"Perhaps he did," she agreed. "But why should he have us shut in the place when he'd put all the other conditions on our visit? And he wouldn't have done it himself. The obvious person for him to instruct would have been Lerenard."

"I agree with that. However, Jean-Luc was the guy who helped us get out of the place. He didn't give me any indication that he was reluctant to help. Besides, I don't think he was in daily contact with the Cardinal, and he's been a pretty reliable support to me over the past few weeks."

Jackie rubbed her forehead. "There's not really anybody else who would know about the visit. Of course, somebody who had been watching us could have followed when we were driven to Rennes."

"Candice, you mean."

"She's the most likely one."

"And she could have told *le comt*e or Gaston Lesmoines. But why would they be interested? Their method is usually to eliminate anyone who gets in their way."

"Don't remind me." She shuddered.

Philip shook his head. "I'm afraid it's a mystery we're not going to solve at present. So let's try something else. What about trying to track down your old professor, Hector Ramise? We need some answers from him."

"You're right. We'll go up to the bedroom and I'll ring Tante Charlotte and see if she has any news."

But Jackie didn't get a chance to do that.

# 55

When Philip and Jackie got back to the hotel reception, they found Hector Ramise was already waiting for them, seated in a chair facing the door, so that he wouldn't miss them. He rose to greet them, kissing Jackie briefly on both cheeks.

"Did you manage to get the bag?" was his immediate question.

Philip felt a little annoyed at the man's attitude.

"Look here, Professor," he responded. "The bag you're talking about belonged to Alain Hébert. He was in a relationship with César Renoir, the woman who now holds the bag. What right have you to demand it, as though it belongs to you?"

Ramise rounded on him, his chest puffed out like an enraged pigeon. He clearly didn't like being lectured to by an individual like Philip.

"In fact, young man, I am Alain's closest living relative."

"What!" Now some things were starting to become clear in Philip's mind.

"That's right. He and I were cousins. We enjoyed a close relationship for many years."

"I presume you can provide César with proof of that."

"I certainly can." The professor pursed his lips. "In fact, I have a copy of Alain's last will and testament at my house in Béziers. That names me as his heir, if anything should happen to him. He was in possession of a similar document signed by me."

"But since then, he has met César."

"That may be so, but I doubt the relationship had progressed sufficiently for him to have made a new will, naming her. The one I have was signed less than three months ago."

Philip thought quickly. "In that case, if you will be able to let me have a copy of the will which you hold, I will show it to César and ask if she is prepared to release the bag to you."

Ramise took a long, deep breath, as though he was about to deliver a reprimand to this objectionable young man, but then he seemed to realise he had no option but to agree.

"Very well. However, the matter is very important. If possible, I would like it to be settled today."

Philip shook his head. "Do you mean you're prepared to drive to Béziers and back this afternoon just to get a copy of the will?"

"Certainly, if necessary."

Philip thought that the professor must have decided the contents of the bag were very important, to go all that way on so minor a matter.

"Well, you can do that if you wish, but, as far as I am aware, the contents of the bag are nothing very special."

Hector looked at him sharply. "I thought I warned you not to look in the bag."

"I'm afraid that César had already looked in it when we got to her. She said it was mainly full of his clothes. The only item of any possible interest was a file containing a few papers."

"Did you see those papers?"

"A couple which she chose to show us."

"What were they?"

Jackie interrupted. "They didn't seem very important, Hector. They certainly weren't relevant to the things which Philip and I were interested in. I don't know why you're so bothered about it. I think you'll find the bag is unimportant, when you get it."

"I'm sorry, my dear, but I can't agree with you. It's absolutely vital that I get hold of it as soon as possible. If it seems so unimportant to this woman, I can't see why she should object to returning it to me."

"Look Professor," said Philip, trying to calm things down. "She doesn't know who you are. The contents may be of some sentimental value to her. Why should she just hand the bag over to somebody she doesn't even know?"

"I've told you why – because it is, in effect, my property."

"OK." He shrugged, "Then you'll have to prove it to her."

"Very well. I will leave for Béziers right now." Ramise squared his shoulders pompously. "Please arrange for her to see me when I return."

He departed without further discussion. Philip turned to Jackie.

"I'm astonished that he should consider it so important that he is prepared to drive two hundred kilometres to obtain the proof that César might need. He must be expecting to find something very important in that bag."

She shook her head. "I'm as surprised as you. I can't imagine what is so vital to him. I agree with you that there didn't seem to be anything important in the bag, unless the lady is keeping something secret from us, of course."

"Well, let's have some lunch and then I'll ring her. Surely she'll have to face up to it, if she's been telling us lies all along."

After a quick lunch, they went up to the bedroom for some privacy while he rang César. He briefly explained what the professor had told him and said that the man was on his way to get his copy of Alain Hébert's will.

"Professor Ramise seems to think that it is absolutely essential that he takes possession of his cousin's bag and its contents," he concluded. "He is adamant that they belong to him. Do you have any reason to refuse to let him have it?"

There was a long silence while César mulled over his question. At last she said, "No. The bag is not important to me. There is nothing in it which I wish to keep."

"Shall I bring the professor along to meet you and show you the will?"

"No. I do not wish to meet him, and I don't want him to know where I am living at present. In fact, I want you to tell him as little as possible about me. The fewer people who know I exist, the better."

Philip agreed this was reasonable. "OK. Shall I bring the copy of the will along with me when he gets back? It will probably be tomorrow morning before I can do that."

There was another pause while César considered this suggestion. Then she said, "Actually, Philip, I am not bothered about seeing the copy of the will. I will leave you to do that for me. But I *would* prefer you to come over this afternoon to collect the bag. I don't want to have any more to do with it."

"OK. If you want, I'll come over straight away. I presume you don't mind if I bring Jackie."

"Of course not."

But his fiancée declined to go. "I want a rest," she said. "I haven't had much sleep in the last few days."

So he set off on his own.

It was mid afternoon when he arrived at César's cottage. She let him in without hesitation and he accepted the offer of a cup of coffee. They didn't seem to know about tea in this part of the world.

"Come into the living room," she said. "The bag is all ready for you. However, I took one further look at it and I have discovered something rather strange."

"What's that?" He followed her in to the lounge.

"I took everything out of the bag this time instead of just riffling through it. And I discovered it has a false bottom. A flap lifts up and there is a secret section where he kept some other papers and his diary. I didn't know about that when you were here before."

Philip noticed the heap of clothes and other possessions in one of the armchairs.

She lifted up the now empty bag and handed it to him. "There you are."

He took it from her and inspected it. He noted a cardboard flap, fixed along one side, which was fabric-covered to match the rest of the interior of the bag. There was no longer anything left in the cavity below the flap.

"Did you say there were papers in here?"

"Yes. Here they are." She handed him about twenty sheets of photo-copied paper. "You can look through them while I get your coffee."

He took them and seated himself in one of the armchairs and started to look through the papers. At first glance they didn't mean a lot. They seemed to be copies of old lists written out in a clear calligraphic script. He found it difficult to make out any descriptions, not being familiar with the language, which he thought was probably Latin. This seemed to be confirmed when he found part of a number of descriptions contained the word *'aurum'* which he thought meant gold. He guessed it was a list of items which were possibly of some value.

He was still trying to fathom out the list when César returned with the coffee.

"Any luck?" she asked.

"I think it is written in Latin, but I don't know anything of the language. I think Jackie would be able to translate it."

"Well, please take them for her to look at. I´m not bothered about them."

"OK. Thank you." He smiled. "I wonder what they were doing in the secret compartment of Alain's bag."

She shrugged. "I have no idea."

She poured out the coffee and handed him a cup. She said, "There was also a diary which Alain was using. I would like to keep that, if you don't mind."

Philip nodded.

"It is in French, of course. He didn't fill it in every day. The last entry was about a week before he died. I remember he went into Carcassonne one day and that was probably the day when he made the entry. Do you want me to translate what he said?"

"If it won't upset you."

"No. It's all right." She opened the diary to a page. "Here it is. It's quite brief. It says: *took letter to Henri Amboisard – big man, bald, with a beard.* That's all."

"Amboisard. That's strange."

She looked at him. "You mean the mayor. But his Christian name is Gustav, and I wouldn't say he was particularly big."

"I wonder if it's a relative. We saw Monsieur Amboisard this morning. He told us he used to be in a law partnership with his brother, but I think he said the brother's name was Anton." Philip shrugged. "Perhaps they're a big family."

César closed the diary. "I don't think there is anything else you would be interested in."

She put it on the coffee table, picked up the things she had taken out of the bag and stuffed them back into it. Then she handed the bag to Philip. He placed the Latin list on the top, zipped it up and placed it on the floor beside him.

She shook herself. "Actually, I will be pleased to get rid of it."

Philip continued to drink his coffee and they had a desultory conversation. He wondered about César, and how she was coping with the loneliness she had experienced over the last few weeks. It was a relief to leave her and return to Jackie with the bag.

# 56

Philip parked the hire car along the street in Quillan, where he'd been leaving it for the last few days to avoid detection. He collected the bag from the boot and walked to the hotel. There was no sign of Hector in reception, so he presumed the Professor hadn't yet returned from Béziers. He went up to their bedroom, still carrying Alain Hébert's bag, to see whether Jackie was sufficiently rested.

When he tried the door, it was locked. He tapped on it a couple of times but there was no response. Leaving the bag outside the door, he went back down to reception and asked if Jackie had gone out. The receptionist said she hadn't actually seen her go out, but had found her room key lying on the counter. So the assumption was that she had left the hotel. The girl could give him no idea of where his fiancée had gone, and no message had been left. Taking the key, he returned to the bedroom to see if she had left him a note up there.

He let himself in and dumped the bag in a corner. He immediately spotted the piece of paper on his bedside table, weighted down by his alarm clock. He picked it up and read it:-

*There is a problem up at le Bézu. Have gone up there to sort it out. See you at dinner.*

Philip sat on the bed and considered his options. He didn't like the idea of Jackie being on her own, even though he knew Lerenard was already up at the site and would take good care of her. After all, it was only four days since she had returned to him. He sincerely hoped she wasn't going to disappear again.

Then he thought about transport. How had she got up to le Bézu? As far as he knew, both the Land Cruisers were up at the site. Lerenard's car was wrecked, unless he had hired another one. His own little sports car was still up at Castereau, and Jackie had no car of her own. He rang reception on the internal phone and, as far as his halting French could discern, the girl had not seen her leave in a car. The only other possibility was that Hector might have returned and chauffeured her up there, but Philip thought that was unlikely. It seemed the probable alternative was that one of the cars from le Bézu had come to collect her.

He was uncertain what to do next. He wanted to know what the problem was that needed her attention, so he got out his phone and rang her number. However, her mobile started ringing in her bedside drawer. She must have left in a hurry and obviously hadn't taken it with her. He tried Jean-Luc's phone but, after letting it ring for some time, he had to conclude he wasn't going to get a response. In desperation, he even tried Armand's number in Carcassonne. The young man answered immediately, and Philip realised he was lucky to find he was still there and hadn't gone back to Paris.

Jeanette was with Armand and, using her as an interpreter, he asked, "Has Jackie been in touch with him?"

"No, she hasn't."

"You see, I was out this afternoon and left Jackie in the room to rest. When I got back, she wasn't there."

"She has disappeared again?" Philip hoped he didn't detect any pleasure in the question.

"No. She hasn't disappeared. She left me a message saying she had to go up to le Bézu to sort something out, but I don't know how she would have got up there. She hasn't got her own car and I wondered if she might have asked Armand to drive her up."

"Just a minute, Philip."

He heard Jeanette translating his question and a short discussion ensued. After a couple of minutes, she came back on the phone.

"Armand says that Jackie has not been in touch with him but, if you wish, he will meet you in Couiza and you can go together to see if you can find her. Would you like him to do that?"

"Oh, that isn't necessary, Jeanette. I'll drive up to the site myself and I expect it will all be explained when I get there."

"Armand would be happy to go with you."

"That's all right. Thank Armand for his offer. I'll give him a ring when I've sorted it out." He rang off.

Philip left a message at the reception desk for Hector Ramise and then went out to his car and set off for le Bézu. He kept an eye on the light traffic coming the other way in case he might see Jackie or Jean-Luc returning to Quillan, but he didn't notice anybody he recognised. And when he left the main road there was hardly any traffic at all.

It took him nearly half an hour to get to the lay-by below the site. Sure enough, the two Land Cruisers were parked there. Sandwiched between them was another big four-wheel drive vehicle. Was this Hector's? Philip stopped behind them, with one pair of wheels on the grass verge to avoid completely blocking the narrow roadway. He jumped out and hurried up the track towards the castle, passing the display sign at the bottom. He noticed, that although it was still early evening, clouds had obscured the sun in the west, and it seemed to be getting dark when he was under the thick trees. As he climbed the rough path, he thought irrelevantly that the TV Company was going to have problems getting their heavy equipment up this steep slope to the remote site.

When he approached the top of the escarpment, he expected to hear the noises of human activity preparing the ground – stakes being driven in, shovels clearing areas, voices calling instructions – but all was silent. When he emerged from the tree cover and went through the eastern gateway, there was no sign of life. No preparations seemed to have been started yet.

He crossed to the site hut and tried the door. It was unlocked and opened easily to his pressure on the handle. Inside there were a few sheets of plans strewn around on the wide desk, but no other sign of activity. It was all most strange. Philip sensed something was wrong.

He stood outside the hut and looked round, uncertain where to go next. Where was everybody? All the cars were here. There ought to be at least five people somewhere on the site. It was two and a half weeks since he had last been here and nothing seemed to have changed since then. After a moment's thought, he decided the next most likely place for them to be, was in the treasure room. He would go and try that.

He set off down the slope towards the area that he and Armand had cleared a month ago. Soon he was following the narrow path they had cut through the waist-high undergrowth. There was still enough light for him to make his way easily, avoiding the rocks that stuck up out of the earth and pushing

305

aside the bramble tendrils which were starting to grow across the narrow strip. It didn't look as though anybody had come this way recently.

When he reached the bottom, he could see that nothing had changed down here either. He smiled grimly to himself as he noted that the rope, which was tied to the lower trunk of the hawthorn bush, was still dangling down the hole, giving access to the underground room. It was then that he realised that he hadn't brought a torch with him and he wouldn't be able to see anything if he did climb down.

Uncertain of what to do next, he knelt on the stone ledge above the shallow cave which had been revealed when he removed the stone wall several weeks ago. Looking down, he became aware that there was a glow somewhere in the darkness below him. It probably meant there was somebody with a light in the treasure room and some of it was filtering into the passageway behind the empty treasure chests. Catching hold of the rope he leaned further into the hole. Now he could hear voices – or, at least one voice. It was a man's voice and he seemed to be shouting. Was it Lerenard or Hector or somebody else? He wasn't sure about the other two guys that Jean-Luc had taken on.

Suddenly Philip felt the hairs standing up on the back of his neck – a sure portent of danger. What should he do? If Jackie was there, he must certainly do his best to give her help and protection, if she needed it. In any case he must find out what was going on. Without further hesitation he got to his feet, took a firm hold on the rope, and started to lower himself down the hole.

He went very slowly and carefully, trying to avoid making a noise. He was helped by the fact that he had come this way several times before and had already caused the loose stones and earth to fall down on his previous visits. He also knew about the irregular heap of rubble that he had landed on. So this time he was very careful about where he put his feet and how he transferred his weight on to them. The noise made by the man's shouting also masked any slight sounds Philip might make.

Letting go of the rope, he edged his way along the narrow passage behind the full-height treasure chests till he reached the gap which he remembered from his previous visits. Revealing as little of himself as possible, he peered into the room. He was unable to see the man who was talking but he did see, sideways on, the figure of Gaston Lesmoines. That made him realise for sure, that he was now in a dangerous situation.

The other man chose that moment to end his tirade. He made some final comment which seemed to suggest, as far as Philip's poor knowledge of French could make out, that he was giving the people he was talking to some kind of ultimatum. The man cleared his throat, spat on the floor and seemed to move away. Lesmoines turned as if to follow him and Philip saw another man cross his line of vision. It appeared that they were leaving the room and going down the corridor to the main door. Did that mean they were leaving? If they were, they had left the light on, which meant they intended to return.

After a while, Philip was fairly sure he heard a door open and, a few seconds later, close again. There was the sound of a lock being rattled. A bit later he heard the rumble of a man's voice talking in low tones. Was that Jean-Luc? There came a lighter response from a woman's voice. Philip was now certain it was Jackie.

He restrained himself from rushing into the room or shouting out to them in case Lesmoines might have left one of his henchmen behind as a guard. Carefully he eased his body through the gap between the chests, keeping a look-out for another man, but seeing no-one. When he reached the front of the chests, he could see that Jackie and Jean-Luc were seated back-to-back on the floor. Their upper bodies had been tied together and their legs stuck out across the stone flooring, bound at the ankles. Jackie was half-facing towards him and saw him instantly.

"Philip!" she called. "Thank God."

"Are you two the only ones here at the moment?"

"Yes. The others have left."

He ran over to them. "We must move quickly. When they get to the road, they will see my car. They may come straight back up here." He knelt beside Lerenard. "Have you still got those blades in your shoes?"

"Here you are. Catch hold of the sole and twist."

Philip fiddled to release the flat knife. "How many men are there?"

"There are four. The big one is *le comte*. He is the head of *La Force Marseillaise*. He seems to have teamed up with our old friend Gaston Lesmoines. Gaston still has one of the machine pistols we saw at Castereau, so he is dangerous. There are also two other toughs they have recruited."

"What about the two guys you took on?"

"They're no help. I think *le comte* sent them back to Quillan when he told Lesmoines to collect Jackie."

"That's right," she agreed. "One of them came up to my room and told me that Jean-Luc had a problem. He said he didn't know what the problem was. He had brought one of the Land Cruisers so that I could drive up to the site, but he also said he had finished for the day. So I drove up alone. Of course, Gaston was ducked down in the back seat of the car and didn't reveal himself until I had left Quillan."

"So we're on our own," said Lerenard. "You'd better hurry."

By now Philip had succeeded in getting the knife out of the big man's shoe. Remembering his instructions, he was careful in releasing the blade. But when he had done so, it was so sharp that it made short work of cutting through the ropes binding them together. After cutting through the cords on their ankles, he left it on the floor for Jean-Luc to pick up and pulled Jackie to her feet. She fell into his arms.

"Just look at you." He kissed her. "I leave you for a couple of hours and look what a mess you get yourself into."

"Oh, Philip. Next time I shall make sure I accompany you wherever you go." She hugged herself against him.

"We haven't got time for that," interrupted Lerenard. "Let's try and escape before they come back. How did you get in?"

"There's a rope down the hole behind those chests. Come on." Philip led the way and directed his fiancée to squeeze through the gap.

But at that second, they heard the rattling of the lock on the door. The men had returned.

# 57

Jackie slid easily through the slot between the tall treasure cupboards and disappeared. Jean-Luc was right behind him as Philip pushed himself into the narrow gap.

"Hurry up," instructed Lerenard. "If we're not careful they will catch us trapped in the room."

With a violent effort, Philip forced his body through into the passageway behind the cupboards. He turned to see Jean-Luc trying to squeeze his large body into the narrow gap. He reached out to help the big man, but it was clear that his body was too massive to get through.

"It's no good. I'm too big for this. You two get out. I can look after myself." He backed away and looked round the room.

At that moment Philip felt a small gust of cool air rush into the room. It could only mean that the outside door had been opened and the men were coming back along the corridor. In a few quick strides Jean-Luc crossed the room, opened the doors of one of the full-height, empty treasure chests, stepped inside and pulled the doors almost closed behind him. A brief silence settled as Philip watched through the narrow gap between the chests.

Only two men came into the room. First was Gaston Lesmoines, clutching his machine pistol and looking round in surprise. He made some excited comment which Philip couldn't translate. He guessed the large, bald man with the black beard who followed him was *le comte*. The man looked to where Lesmoines was pointing to the jumble of cut ropes in the middle of the floor and let out a roar.

They both looked round the room and *le comte* issued a terse, "*Cherchez les coffres*".

Lesmoines started to lift the lids of the low chests, peering into each to see if anyone was hiding in them. Philip wondered how long it would before they tried the upright chests and discovered Jean-Luc. Gun at the ready, the swarthy rogue threw back the lids of the lower chests around the centre of the room. Of course they all proved to be empty. Then he made for the tall cupboards, each with its narrow double doors. By chance, he started on the one beside where Lerenard was hiding. Philip wondered if he would go to the one next to it and discover his friend. However, *le comte* was standing more or less in front of that one, so he went the other way.

Chest by chest he worked his way round to the gap where Philip was peering out, and he quickly ducked back to make sure he wasn't seen. He needn't have worried. Lesmoines ignored the gap between the cupboards, presumably thinking it too narrow for anybody to be hiding there. Philip realised that only slim characters like himself and Jackie could squeeze through the narrow gap. In fact, they were actually fairly safe here, as long as the man didn't open fire with his machine pistol, shooting through the backs of the chests.

Next, Lesmoines opened the doors of the cupboard immediately in front of him. Philip's vision was almost completely cut off by one door as it swung across the gap. Now there was just a narrow slit created by the hinges for him to peer through. He eased himself into the gap so that he could see what was going on. As he did so, he saw the doors of Jean-Luc's hiding place open quietly. *Le comte*, with his back to the cupboard and concentrating on Lesmoines' search, didn't hear them. Next second, Lerenard had his knee in the man's kidneys and his arm round his neck. Although the two men were of a similar stature, Lerenard had the advantage of surprise and of being the fitter of the two. He brandished his sharp little knife in front of *le comte's* eyes.

The man let out a startled gasp which got Lesmoines' attention. He swung round to look at them, bringing the machine pistol up into the firing position as he did so. Lerenard let out a low growl, but it was his boss's squawk of terror which stopped Lesmoines firing. He obviously realised that if he fired at Jean-Luc he would be almost certain to hit *le comte* first.

A series of threatening comments took place between them which Philip didn't need any knowledge of French to comprehend. As they eyed each other, he suddenly had a bright idea. Lesmoines was standing right in front of the great chest beside him with its doors open. They were arguing. Presumably Lerenard was telling Lesmoines to leave the room, or his boss would get seriously damaged. What the response was, he couldn't make out as he slid back into the passageway behind the chests where Jackie was silently waiting.

Philip put his finger to his lips, grabbed Jackie by the hand and pushed her further down the narrowing corridor away from the cupboard. He motioned for her to stay there. Then he moved behind the big chest and leaned his weight against the back. It moved slightly but settled back on its base when the pressure was released. He realised these were colossal chests – at least seven feet high, four feet wide and two feet deep. They were constructed from inch-thick hardwood, and he guessed they must each weigh at least two hundred-weight. The question was, how could he move one? He thought that if he pushed it hard near the top, he might stand a chance of tipping it over.

He grabbed the rope hanging down the hole, pulled his body up and planted his feet against the back of the chest near the top. Then, with his shoulders against the rock wall, he shoved violently, straightening his body and his legs right out in front of him. Pushed at the top beyond its centre of gravity, the massive cupboard began to topple. He heard a gasp from Lesmoines as the man realised the danger he was in. His reaction was an ear-shattering burst of fire from the machine pistol. The next second, the chest crashed down on top of the crook and flattened him. The gun began to fire continuously inside his heavy wooden coffin until it ran out of ammunition. A few of the bullets burst through the thick timber, but most of them ricocheted at point-blank range into Lesmoines' own flattened body.

Philip stood on top of the fallen chest and looked at what he had caused to happen. The machine pistol had been pointing at *le comte* when the first burst had been fired, and there was a hole in his chest that Philip could have put his fist into. Even as he watched, the man fell to the floor and slumped to one side with a pool of blood spreading round his upper body.

Behind him, Jean-Luc was sitting back against the cupboard door with a surprised look on his face. He had dropped his knife and now his hands were clutching his body beneath his heart. Philip jumped off the cupboard, ran across and bent over him.

"Have you been hit?"

The big man took a gasping breath. "I think at least three slugs came through his body. Perhaps they've gone into my lung."

Philip straightened up and looked round. What should he do? Jackie was just climbing over the fallen treasure chest. He fumbled in his pocket for his mobile and pulled it out.

"Jean-Luc is hurt. Can you ring for an ambulance?"

"What about the other man?"

"He is beyond anybody's help."

"And Gaston?"

He's not going anywhere with a hundred kilos of treasure chest on top of him. That's if he's still alive, which I doubt."

She took his phone and tried to make the call. "There's no signal down here. I'll have to go outside to ring emergencies."

"Be careful. There are two other men somewhere out there. They probably heard the firing and will be coming this way. Stay just inside the door. You may get a signal there." He looked down at his friend, slumped near his feet. "Actually, there's nothing I can do for Jean-Luc at the moment. I'll come with you."

"There's no need," said a voice. "I speak Inspector Martin. He send helicopter. Will be here more quick than ambulance."

Philip spun round. "Armand! How did you get here?"

"I follow the two men. I see all that happens." He came over to Philip and gripped his hand. "We stop meeting this way," he quipped humourlessly.

He bent over Lerenard. "How is he?"

"Not good. He was standing right behind le comte when Gaston Lesmoines shot him. He says he thinks three bullets have hit him in his left lung."

Armand shook his head. "Not so bad, I think. There is no blood in his mouth."

"Christ! I hope you're right." Philip bent over Lerenard. "Do you think we should lie him down?"

"No. Do not move him. That may do more harm than good." Armand had lapsed back into French but Jackie translated.

"Tell him about the other two men," Philip told her.

The response was, "Do not fear. They have gone up to the site and Candice is following them. She will stop them with her little gun."

"What is Candice doing here?"

Jackie gradually extracted the story from him.

"I have discovered that Candice is working for the same organisation as me. She had been given the job of getting close to *le comte* to find out all about him. When we knew the head of *La Force Marseillaise* was coming to Carcassonne to go after the treasure, she was told to help me stop him."

"I thought she was trying to discover César's whereabouts so that *le comte* could eliminate her."

"Ah, Candice was telling *him* that was what she was doing, but all the time she was passing the information to our organisation without me knowing anything about it."

"The right hand didn't know what the left was doing."

"That's right." Armand took a quick look at the corpse by his feet, still oozing blood. "Also she found out who this mysterious man, *Le comte*, really is – er - was."

"So who was he?"

"He was the son of a Carcassonne lawyer named Anton Amboisard. He is also the nephew of our old friend Gustav Amboisard, the mayor of Quillan. He was working with his father and he was the man that Alain Hébert went to for legal advice. From the information Hébert gave him he was able to find out about the Templar treasure and to get himself into *La Force Marseillaise*. After the disaster, when Hébert and Montluçon were killed in this same room, he made himself the leader. The only thing that was wrong with his information was that he thought the treasure was still here. Our organisation had kept its removal very secret."

"But surely," said Philip, "Gaston Lesmoines knew it had been removed. He followed me to the warehouse in Carcassonne where he banged me on the head."

Armand shook his head. "I know nothing of that. Nobody tells me anything before Jeanette disappears." He pointed at Philip. "You tell about that."

"Meanwhile," said Jackie, "*le comte* thought I would know what had happened to the treasure so he sent the message by

Jean-Luc's assistant about there being a problem on site. That's what got me up here."

"So what do we do now?"

"We wait," said Armand, "for Inspector Martin to come in his helicopter. He will not be long, I think."

## 58

Inspector Martin had been as prompt as Armand had assured them he would be. He brought a doctor with him in the helicopter who carried out a careful inspection of Jean-Luc's injuries, which turned out to be less life-threatening than Philip had feared. He was able to state that two of the bullets had hit the big man's ribs and had been deflected into the cupboard behind him. These had broken one rib and caused extensive bruising, which was very painful, but not serious. The third bullet had entered the chest cavity between two of the ribs and a scan would be necessary before an operation was carried out to remove it. He did not think it had punctured the lung because of the lack of blood showing in his breath. Nevertheless, he wanted Lerenard to be removed by helicopter to Carcassonne Hospital as soon as possible.

The doctor took a brief look at *le comte* and confirmed the man was dead. The story was the same with Gaston Lesmoines when the heavy chest was lifted off his prostrate body. They counted at least fifteen bullet wounds to the head and upper body. Three of these had lodged in the brain, causing instant death. The bodies were left where they were, at the request of Inspector Martin, who didn't want them removed until his forensic team had completed their investigations. The doctor promised to send a vehicle to collect them later in the night, before he departed in the helicopter with the injured Lerenard.

Jackie and Philip were taken to one of the Land Cruisers for questioning. It didn't take long for them to give their brief story of the evening's events. They were then released, to drive back to Quillan in Philip's hire car, and told they would have to be available for further questioning during the next few days. The Land Cruisers were left at le Bézu overnight. As they left the site, the first of the police cars turned up, its blue lights flashing.

While driving back to Quillan, Philip and Jackie discussed their second violent evening in the treasure room.

"Armand turned up again like a guardian angel," she said. "I don't know how he contrives to do that."

"What happened to him after the police arrived?"

"I don't know. I think he went off to find Candice and help her with the other two men."

Philip grunted. "He seems to have some sort of special relationship with the police. They leave him free to go more or less where he wants. They didn't tell him he had to sit and wait to be questioned as they did with us. His 'organisation', as he refers to it, must carry a lot of clout."

"He already seemed to have developed a special relationship with Inspector Martin before tonight," she agreed.

"Well, I suppose we must be grateful that he seems to be on our side – especially now that we've lost Jean-Luc's assistance." He had a sudden thought. "What will you do about setting up the site now that the big man's going to be out of circulation for several weeks?"

"I'll hand that problem to Alain Gisours. He will have to find the men to do the work. Of course I'll have to supervise their activities to make sure everything looks right."

"Not on your own, you won't – not after your recent history. You're going to have an unpaid assistant supervisor."

That made her laugh. "How could I refuse an offer like that? OK, Assistant Supervisor, we'll get started first thing in the morning."

"What about those two fellows that Jean-Luc took on?"

"Let's see if they turn up again at the hotel tomorrow."

"In any case," said Philip, "we'd better abandon any idea of going up to the site tomorrow. I expect the police will still be swarming all over the place and they probably won't want us getting in the way."

She nodded in agreement.

"I'd also like to go and see the mayor to find out if he's had a reply from the owners of the chateau in Rennes. In addition I want to find out what he has to say about the actions of his nephew."

"*Mon Dieu*! What a surprise that was." She shook her head. "I thought old Amboisard was a lovely guy. I can't believe he knew anything about young Henri turning criminal."

"It seems unlikely, I agree. But I would still like to hear his comments."

Speculating about what had turned a respectable lawyer from being a well-known local businessman into the rogue leader of a criminal group, they arrived in Quillan and drew up in front of the hotel. Philip wasn't going to bother about disguising his use of the hire car any longer.

It was nearly ten o'clock by the time they got back to their bedroom. The chef had provided them with an impromptu meal, since dinner had been over for a couple of hours. So it was a tired but well-fed couple who wended their way upstairs arm-in-arm, planning an early night.

As they entered the room, Philip noticed the book lying on Jackie's bedside table. He bent down to look at it and saw the title *Une Histoire de Catharisme.*

He picked it up. "Oh, this is the book I bought in Paris."

Jackie looked across at what he was holding. "Yes, I went to the wardrobe for something, and I saw it lying on the top of your bag. Where did you say you got it?"

"I was just passing time, looking in a book-shop in the Champs Élysées, and I noticed it. I thought it might be interesting. So I bought it. Of course, I realised it was in French, but I was intending to start going through it with my dictionary, translating the chapter headings to start with." He grinned. "Then my lover returned, and I forgot all about it."

She smiled back. "When I started to look at it, I didn't intend to spend any time on it. I was too tired. But it sort of grabbed me. I've found out it's a very well-researched history, despite the fact that it was written more than fifty years ago. What really interested me was that there was a whole chapter on our old friends, the Blanchefort family."

"Really?"

"Yes – and it was very illuminating. Of course we already knew they were prominent Cathars. We also knew Bertrand was fourth Grand Master of the Templars. However, what we didn't know before was that, when the Albigensian Crusade was rolling south from Carcassonne, the family decided to seek the protection of the Templar brotherhood and made a gift of the ownership of all their properties to them"

"Did that include the castle at Rennes-le-Chateau?"

"Presumably. That's assuming it was still in their ownership."

"But the Templars were wiped out less than a century later. So who owns it now?"

"Who indeed? The ownership was also made more complicated by the actions of Simon de Montfort. Whenever he captured a castle, he generously handed it to one of his lieutenants to hold in the name of King Phillip. We don't know what his attitude was about properties owned by the Templars."

"Rafa Menton suggested it might have been Pierre de Voisins who took possession of the castle at Rennes."

"Well, if your friend Raphael is correct, I would guess he was only holding the place temporarily. I don't think there was ever any record of *his* being a Templar." She took a breath. "In any case we don't know who was awarded the castle after the demise of the Templars."

"Hopefully Mayor Amboisard will be able to tell us something about that tomorrow morning."

"Otherwise," said Jackie, "you may have to go back to Rafa to see whether he can find out more about it."

Philip nodded. "We seem to be going round in circles on this one. Well, I'm tired. Let's have some sleep and we can have another go at it in the morning."

They had scarcely cuddled up in bed and were just dozing off, when he was suddenly wide awake. In the rush of other events, he had forgotten all about Hector Ramise. What on earth had happened to the man? He should have returned with his copy of the will several hours ago. He had made such a fuss about it being urgent this afternoon. So where was the professor now?

Philip made himself lie still so as not to disturb Jackie. But his mind was turning over all the mysteries which still existed in their life. Meanwhile, her breathing steadied and she slumbered beside him. It was well over an hour before he also finally fell asleep.

# 59

They were at breakfast next morning when they were surprised by the sudden arrival of Gustav Amboisard. He looked round, saw them and raised a hand. Then he made straight for their table.

"Goodness," said Jackie, "it looks as though the mountain has come to find Mohammed."

The mayor stopped at their table, breathing heavily. Philip noticed there was a strained look about his features.

"I apologise for disturbing you at breakfast," he said.

"That's all right, Monsieur. Will you sit down and join us?"

"Thank you." He pulled out a chair and sat down. "I would just like a coffee."

Philip waved to the waiter and asked him to fetch a fresh jug. When it came, he noticed that Amboisard preferred it black. The way he drank it almost straight down and refilled his cup made it appear that he needed a stimulant.

"As I say," he continued, "I'm sorry to trouble you so early, but I have to leave for Carcassonne as soon as possible and I wished to talk to you before I went."

"To Carcassonne?" asked Philip. "Are you still a partner in the law firm with your brother?"

"Indeed I am – although a sleeping partner at present. So - following the disclosures, if I may call them that, about my nephew - my brother and I will doubtless be facing close questioning by the police and the legal licensing authorities." He sighed. "It could mean we have to close the business, and that would create many problems for our clients."

"Did Henri work for the firm?"

"Indeed he did – at least until recently. He told my brother that he wanted to have a six-month sabbatical to take a special course of study in European law." He shook his head. "But of course, we know now why he did it."

"Did neither you nor your brother have any clue about what he was doing?"

"*I* certainly had none." Amboisard pursed his lips. "Personally, I had seen little of the young man in the last few years. But, when he was a boy, I always found him rather strange and withdrawn. Of course I couldn't discuss that with my brother, but I wondered whether it came from his mother. She was a white West Indian from Martinique. I believe her family used to own extensive sugar plantations out there, but had fallen on hard times following the eruption of Mount Pelée in 1932. I understand the family came to France to escape their problems in Martinique. She was born some time after the war and, in due course, met and married my brother. But to me she seemed to have different values from us French. In addition," he sighed, "she died when Henri was only ten years old."

Jackie and Philip were silent as they digested his comments.

Amboisard continued, "I have resigned my position as examining magistrate. I think Paris will appoint someone from high up in the Justice Ministry to take over from me."

"Why is that necessary?"

"Oh, this has become a big investigation now – one of the biggest in the whole of France. Altogether, eight people have been killed and two others seriously injured. The criminal fraternities in Marseilles and Toulouse are involved. The publicity will be more than I can cope with, especially with my personal links to one of the criminals involved."

"But *you* didn't know Henri was involved with *La Force Marseillaise*."

"That may be so. However, I have been here all the time. The question will be, how did I allow such a big scandal to develop? The primary blame is bound to be laid at my door." He shrugged. "Oh, I am not worried for myself. I have had a good innings. It is probably the right time for me to retire. There will be wide ramifications locally, and the authorities will want some heads to roll."

Philip was only just starting to appreciate how significant an event had taken place. Would it have an impact on Jackie's new television series?

He asked the mayor, "How is it likely to affect us?"

"Well, until the new man arrives you will have to take your instructions from Inspector Martin of the Carcassonne police department. He will be in charge and will be spending a lot of his time here, unless the *Sureté* decide they want to send their own man down to take over." He nodded at Jackie. "Also, your

TV company will be breathing down everybody's necks, because they will want to get their series tied up while the publicity is at its height."

"Really?" Philip could see that it was also starting to dawn on Jackie that she was likely to be even more in the public eye.

"Oh, yes. TV France wields a big sword in the modern French nation." The lawyer smiled bleakly. "I am not likely to be their favourite person – anybody's favourite person."

There was a long silence while they all thought about how they were likely to be affected. At last Philip said, "What I don't understand is why *le comte* – er – Henri Amboisard thought the treasure was still at le Bézu?"

"Presumably Gaston Lesmoines told him that was where it had been found. After all, he had gone back to Toulouse and got a gang together to break into the treasure room. I suppose they holed up in the deserted village of Castereau while they prepared to move in." The mayor gazed out of the window at the houses across the valley. "However, with the help of Candice, you foiled their attempt. I suppose after that he must have taken the information to *le comte* and the two joined forces."

"Indeed it looks like that." Philip massaged his forehead. "Blimey! It's all so complicated. It'll be a relief to get this over with and settle down to the mundane everyday life of buying a house and settling down in the Languedoc." He paused for a moment. "With that in mind, Monsieur Amboisard, have you spoken yet to the owners of the chateau at Rennes?"

"I have. In fact, that was the primary reason why I came to see you before I left Quillan."

"So what is their reply?"

"Their reply is that they wish to talk to you themselves about a number of things, including the sale of the chateau."

"A number of things? What does that mean?"

"Ah, unfortunately they were not willing to give me that information. Instead they asked where they could contact you, and I told them that both you and Mademoiselle Blontard were likely to be in this hotel for the next few days." He smiled. "I am sure you will hear from them in the very near future."

"And meanwhile we just have to sit here and wait."

"I'm afraid you do."

Jackie joined in. "But, Monsieur Amboisard, just who *are* these people?"

"Alas, that is all I have been authorised to say to you. I understand they will tell you everything they wish you to know when they contact you." He finished his coffee and rose to his feet. "Well, I must be on my way. If you need any information about what is going on in Quillan or at le Bézu, I have instructed Sergeant Leblanc to give you all the help he can. I believe Inspector Martin will be calling here later this morning to interview you. I apologise for not being able to tell you any more than that."

Jackie rose to her feet and took his hand. "Thank you very much for your help, monsieur. I hope all goes well for you in Carcassonne and that we shall see you again soon."

Despite his frustration at not being given the information that he believed they were due, Philip felt he had to do the same. The old man shook both their hands warmly then raised his in farewell. He turned away, strode across the room and out of the door. If anything, he now gave the appearance of a man from whose shoulders a huge weight had been lifted. Philip and Jackie resumed their seats.

"Well," he asked her, "What do you make of that?"

"Actually," she smiled at him, "I feel as though we've made some progress. The owners of the chateau at least seem to be taking us seriously. Hopefully, we'll know a bit more in the next few days."

"Meanwhile we just have to sit and wait for something to happen."

"I can't imagine that there could be anyone I would rather sit and wait with." She smiled again. "We haven't had the opportunity to rest and relax much together, have we?"

"You can say that again." He jumped to his feet. "I don't want any more to eat or drink. Let's go up to the room and start a bit of relaxing before we go for a stroll round the town and have a coffee."

They left the dining room hand in hand.

# 60

After breakfast next morning, Philip decided to ring Raphael Menton.

"I've got his number," he told Jackie. "He was very helpful to me last week, and I'm sure he wouldn't mind me ringing him to see if he can give us any help in finding out who owns the chateau at Rennes."

"OK. I agree it would be a good idea to know who we are talking to when they contact us." She smiled. "You ring him and see what he's got to say. I'm going to the bathroom."

Philip dug out his mobile and keyed in Raphael's number. To his surprise the call was answered almost straight away.

"Is that Rafa?"

"*Oui* – er – yes."

"It's Philip Sinclair. Do you remember me?"

"Of course I do. How are you, Philip?"

"I'm fine. The good news is that my fiancée, Jackie, turned up on Thursday. She'd been doing some secret research at the Vatican."

"The Vatican? Do you mean in Rome?"

"That's right." Philip chuckled humourlessly. "Because she had to keep it secret, she couldn't tell me where she had gone. Nevertheless, she left me a note which apparently told me not to worry, and that she would be back in a few days. However, her professor, who had arranged the trip, thought that even her brief note was too much information, and he destroyed it."

"*Mon Dieu*! What did you think of that?"

"Not a lot. He claimed he was going to tell me not to worry, but he never got round to it." Philip took a breath. "In any case, her promise to be back in a few days extended in the end to more than two weeks, so I think I'd have been very anxious about her absence by the time she finally turned up."

"I should think so too." Rafa paused. "So your theory that she might have been in a Chateau de Blanchefort was wrong?"

"Yes. I'm sorry if you think I wasted your time on what we English call 'a wild goose chase'."

323

"A wild goose chase – I like that." Rafa chuckled. "But do not worry, Philip. I was very interested in looking up information that might have helped you. That is the sort of thing I like to do."

"In any case, it might not be completely wasted time." Philip paused, assembling his thoughts. "Jackie and I have become interested in one of the chateaux that you dug up information about. That is why I am ringing you. If we give you the details of the place, would you be able to find out who owns it now?"

"Er – what is this place?"

"It is a half-ruined chateau in a little village in the Languedoc called Rennes-le-Chateau. Jackie and I have made enquiries in the area but, either nobody knows who owns it, or else they will not tell us."

"That shouldn't be too difficult. Does it have a name, this chateau?"

"I don't think it does, but it is the only building in the village which could be called a chateau. And the village is very small. It has fewer than a hundred inhabitants. We think the place might once have been owned by the Blancheforts - that is, back in the thirteenth century, at the time of the Cathars. So it may have been called the Chateau de Blanchefort at that time."

"But you don't think the same family still owns it? Some of these aristocratic families have held on to ruined property for many generations."

"Well, the one thing we have been able to find out, is that the Blancheforts were prominent Cathars. When the Albigensian Crusade was sweeping south towards them they apparently went to the Templars for protection and, as a result, they gave all their lands to the Knights Templar."

"When did that happen?"

"Oh, a long time ago – in the early part of the thirteenth century. It was probably between 1210 and 1215. Of course, the Templars were wiped out themselves less than a century later, and we want to know what happened to the place after that."

"I see." Rafa paused. "I have found out a little about that sort of thing in the past. Whatever could be clearly identified as

Templar property was confiscated and taken into the ownership of the French crown. But the Templars were very crafty about hiding the ownership of many of their holdings and Philip le Bel, the French king at the time, had great difficulty in tracking that stuff down."

"Is that going to make it difficult for you?"

"It will depend on each property and how it is identified in the national property register." He took a breath. "But that doesn't matter, Philip. I have the location of the property and some history for it. I will see what I can find out."

"Thank you very much, Rafa. Your help is most appreciated." He smiled to himself. "Do you have any idea how long it might take you?"

"It will not take long if it is listed in the register – which it should be. In fact, I may be able to come back to you later today. However, I warn you that the answer may be negative. That would be even quicker."

"That's fantastic, Rafa. I will be in your debt."

"Don't thank me. It is my job and I enjoy doing it."

"Nevertheless I *am* grateful. And, if things turn out right, I may have a way to repay you."

"Oh-oh. That sounds interesting. OK, Philip, I will come back to you later today."

"Thanks again. Cheerio." The line went dead.

Jackie had come back from the bathroom and heard the end of the conversation. "So, your friend Rafa is going to find out what he can."

"Yes. He's a very good lad."

"While I was listening, I noticed you have brought the bag back for Hector. When I looked at it, I found these on top." She brandished the papers. "What are they?"

"Oh, those." He gave her a conciliatory smile. "César discovered there was a secret compartment in the bottom of the bag which contained those papers and Alain Hébert's personal diary. She allowed me to have a quick look at the diary. But she insisted she wanted to keep it for sentimental reasons."

"Was there anything of interest in it?"

"Not a lot. The only recent entry was few days before he was killed by Montluçon. It recorded that he went to meet Amboisard in Carcassonne and gave a letter to the lawyer to be released to the authorities if anything happened to him. At first, I thought it must be our friend the mayor. But I now realise that he was referring to Henri Amboisard – *le comte* - who of course made sure the letter was either forgotten or destroyed."

"In other words, that man was also indirectly responsible for Alain Hébert's death in addition to all his other crimes."

"That's right. He was certainly a nasty piece of work." Philip pointed to the papers in her hand. "The only other stuff in the secret compartment were those papers. They don't mean anything to me. I believe they are written in Latin."

"They certainly are and, from what I've seen so far, they could be very important."

"What do you mean?"

"Well, the first sheet starts off with," she translated slowly, "a list of the goods deposited by the retainers of a man called Pierre-Roger de Mirepoix. Do you know who he was?"

"I haven't a clue."

"I've heard of him. He was the leader of the remaining Cathars who were besieged in the castle at Montségur. That means it is quite possibly a record of the items of Cathar treasure which were spirited away from the castle and deposited with the Templars some weeks before they surrendered to the besiegers. It occurs to me that it could be the same stuff that you found the receipt for."

"Good God! So what is on the list?"

"I haven't been through it yet. There are about twenty sheets of paper here." She fanned the pages out and glanced quickly at each sheet. "Oh, there must be the best part of three hundred items here."

"What sort of things are we talking about?"

"Well, the first item is a solid gold – I think it translates as a lectern. You know, the sort of thing that supports a book like the bible while it is being read to the congregation. Of course, the book would have been the Cathar equivalent. That item alone would probably fetch the best part of a million euros if it was auctioned."

She thumbed through the pages. "Here's another item I can translate. It's a pair of solid gold candlesticks five cubits high. Depending on the decoration, they would be worth an absolute fortune." She turned to him, the truth dawning on her face. "Do you know, I believe this could be a list of a large part of the treasure we found at le Bézu. I remember the photographs which you took through the back of the damaged chest showed gold objects. I believe, if we check your photos, we may be able to identify items like that."

Philip stared at her. "I wonder how on earth that guy, Alain Hébert, got hold of this list?"

"I don't know."

"Do you think he got it from your professor?"

"What – Hector Ramise?"

"That's right. Do you think that's why the Professor was so anxious to get the bag back?"

"Surely not."

"Well, he claimed the bag was his by right. It has to be because there's something in it which he desperately wants."

Jackie shook her head slowly. "I really don't know. We'll have to ask him. Where on earth is he, by the way? I wasn't surprised he didn't come back yesterday. That was probably because he realised, when he got to Béziers, that it was a long return drive, and he might have found everybody was in bed when he got here. But I would have thought he would have made sure he was here early this morning, so that he could catch up with us before we went out."

"Have you got his phone number?"

"No. But I'm sure Tante Charlotte will have it."

"You'd better give her a ring then. You can use this one." He handed her his mobile.

"Thanks." She went round to her bedside cupboard to get the number from her pocket diary while he went to the bathroom.

When he came back a few minutes later, she handed the phone back to him. "Charlotte hasn't seen Hector for four days. She thought he was in Carcassonne."

"So he didn't call in to see her when he got back to Béziers?"

"Obviously not."

"Did she give you his number?"

"Yes. I've rung that as well. There's no reply."

"In that case I expect he's on his way back here right now."

"Let's hope so."

Philip smiled. "Well, I don't know about you, but I don't feel like resting any more. Let's go across the square for a coffee."

Tucking the papers away in her bedside cupboard, they locked the bedroom door behind them and went downstairs.

# 61

Just as they reached reception Inspector Martin came in through the front door. He was looking dishevelled, and Philip guessed he had been up all night.

"Monsieur, Mademoiselle." He hastened across the lobby to meet them.

"Oh, God," muttered Jackie. "More questions." But that assumption was wrong.

The policeman halted in front of them. "I was just coming to see you. I am afraid that Monsieur Lerenard's injuries are worse than the doctor thought. The bullet which entered the chest cavity has damaged the lung and it has collapsed. They are assembling a team at the hospital to perform a major operation."

"Oh, my God." Philip felt dreadful. Had his actions led to the possible death of the man he had come to regard as his friend?

Jackie was less emotional in her response. "I am sorry to hear about that, inspector. Will you see him before he has the operation in order to give him our best wishes?"

"It is more important than that, Mademoiselle. He has asked to see you before he receives the anaesthetic. Apparently, there are some important things he wishes to tell you."

"*Mon Dieu*! Does that mean we have to go to the hospital now?"

"Indeed yes." He turned to Philip. "If you will take your car, I have come to escort you. I will go in front to clear the way through the traffic so that no time will be lost."

Philip looked at her. "Is there anything you want to get from the bedroom?"

"No."

"Let's go then." He led the way outside.

They had never driven from Quillan to Carcassonne so quickly. With the flashing blue light in front of them, cars pulled in to the side of the road to let them through. Speed restrictions were ignored, they were given right of way at junctions, and they were at the hospital in less than half an hour. They were told to park the car in a corner of the ambulance bay and a hospital security attendant was set to stand guard over it.

They hurried through the hospital to the preparation room outside the operating theatre, where they found Jean-Luc in a light blue gown, connected up to a bewildering variety of tubes and sensors which were linked to a number of bottles and monitor screens. He looked pale and tired and was breathing with difficulty. He was not in the least like the big, powerful man that Philip had become used to. Nearby was a surgeon in his green scrubs watching one of the monitors. He turned at their arrival. He raised his hand with fingers and thumb extended.

"*Cinque minutes.*" He turned away and left through one of the double doors.

Philip gently took the hand which was lying loosely on the coverlet. "I'm sorry about this, Jean-Luc."

"Do not worry." The big man's voice was scarcely more than a whisper. "I have called you here because I received a confidential communication from the cardinal earlier this morning."

"From Galbaccino?"

"That's right."

"Doesn't he know you're about to have a serious operation."

"I presume he wasn't given that information. Do not worry - this will not take long. Monsignor has two messages for you. The first is that Abbé Rivère has been questioned about the events the other night in Rennes-le-Chateau church and has confessed to abandoning you. It seems that a man, who I presume was Lesmoines, approached him in his car and threatened the priest if he didn't drive away immediately. Rivère went to see the bishop yesterday to make sure you would not be permanently entombed in the crypt."

Jackie had been listening by Philip's side. "Gaston must have been following us and seen a way to get rid of us before he and *le comte* went for the treasure."

"Yes." Lerenard's response was more of a gasp.

Philip was worried about him. "Don't bother to talk now, Jean-Luc. It can't be that important. It can wait until after the operation."

"No. The other message is more important." He took a shallow breath. "I must tell you this, just in case."

"All right then. But be brief."

"I will be." He turned to Jackie. "The cardinal apologises that he cannot be here to discuss with you the question of the sarcophagi you found in the crypt of the church in Rennes-le-Chateau. He asked me to tell you that he has nevertheless considered your request to be allowed to open the tombs."

"What's this?" asked Philip.

She laid a hand on his arm. "I'm sorry, darling. I haven't had an opportunity to talk to you about it." She paused. "You remember I made a note of the engravings on the sides of the tombs in the crypt? The fact is that I started to translate my notes while you were visiting César Renoir, and I am more or less certain that these are the tombs of six of the Merovingian kings."

"Who the heck are the Merovingians?"

"They were the Royal family who ruled the three kingdoms which made up France before the nation was united under Charlemagne. They were rumoured to be in the direct line of descent from the daughter of Christ." She smiled. "They may well have been your distant cousins." She turned back to Lerenard. "What does the cardinal say?"

"He says he cannot give his consent at this stage. Apparently the Church recognises that it has a responsibility to the descendants of the bodies in the tombs and must obtain their consent before giving you permission."

"My goodness!" she exclaimed. "How on earth do we find out who are their surviving relatives?"

There was an interval while Jean-Luc struggled to get enough breath to continue. "Also the Church is aware of its responsibility to the government of France. They cannot allow you to proceed without the approval of the Ministry of Culture. They are willing to meet the government representatives to discuss the matter, but he is not hopeful about a satisfactory outcome."

"I may know how to achieve that," she said.

Another break followed while Lerenard got enough oxygen into his one remaining lung to continue. He smiled faintly. "Yes. He said he thought you might be able to bring more influence on them than he can exert. So, in a way, the matter is in your hands."

"OK," said Philip. "Is there anything else we need to know?"

"No."

"Then I think we should give you a chance to rest before the operation."

And at that moment the surgeon returned. In French he told them that their time was up and they must leave.

"It is important," he said, "that my patient is allowed to rest and relax. I am going to give him an injection to make him sleep."

He was followed by a nurse carrying a deep metal tray with a syringe and a bottle of some sort of fluid.

Jean-Luc smiled weakly. "In any case I have no more to tell you. You must make contact with Galbaccino in the Vatican if you want to discuss further details."

"We will leave him alone now." Jackie laid her hand on Philip's arm.

"OK, Jean-Luc. We will be praying that the operation is a success. Hopefully we will hear later today." He raised his hand and Lerenard responded with a weak wave.

Jackie took his arm and shepherded him out of the room. When they got back to the car, a hospital orderly approached them and asked them politely to move the car as soon as possible. So they got in and started back on the return drive to Quillan, now without the police escort.

"What's all this about the Merovingians? Why are they important?" Philip asked as they pulled out on to the main road outside the hospital.

Jackie took a breath. "I hadn't told you this before, but I understand there is an architectural feature round the church at Rennes-le-Chateau that is called a funerary band. It is very exceptional and usually only occurs where the bodies of members of a Royal bloodline have been laid to rest in the place. It is something I have been trying to get more information about for some time."

"Why on earth should royalty be buried in a little village church? I would have thought they would choose a cathedral in the capital."

"What you have to remember is that Rennes is all that remains of the much larger Visigothic city called Rhedae. It is said that about fifteen hundred years ago it had a population of more than twenty thousand inhabitants – more than Paris at that time or any other city in Europe, with the possible exceptions of Rome and Constantinople. The Visigoths made it the southern capital of their empire."

Philip shook his head. "That's too long ago to interest me."

"No. This is important." She turned to face him. "The first Merovingian king, the founder of the dynasty, was Clovis the first. He reigned over the whole of Gaul, as it then still was, from about 480 AD for thirty years or so. He was the first king of the Franks – the beginning of France as an independent country. He was an important figure in the history of our nation." She paused for dramatic effect. "It is just possible I have found the location of his earthly remains."

"And you think the government would consider that to be important?"

"Of course I do. Clovis is a man as important to French history as Charlemagne, Louis XIV or Napoleon. It could be a great discovery for the country."

"So you shouldn't have a problem persuading the government to bring pressure on Galbaccino to give you permission to open the tombs?"

"Hmm." She gazed back at the road ahead. "I'll have to think about exactly how to approach them. I think it would be a good idea in the first instance to talk to my boss at TV France – Alain Gisours. He could be very helpful here. He knows a lot of the right people. We don't want to rush into this without careful thought."

"OK. I'll leave all that to you. It looks as though you're going to have plenty of time to sort it out. I don't think much is going to happen in the next few days."

How wrong he was.

# 62

When they got back to Quillan they found Tante Charlotte and Hector Ramise waiting for them. Philip noticed they were dressed in travelling clothes and appeared to have recently arrived from Béziers.

"Aunt," Jackie exclaimed and rushed across to kiss her on both cheeks. "I see you've found Hector, but what are you both doing here?"

Charlotte had risen to greet her niece, but now she sat down again. "I got in touch with Hector after you rang this morning, and we had a long and serious talk. I pointed out to him that it was important for us to come here and talk to you both."

"A serious talk? What is this about?"

"Oh, let Hector explain. He will be better at it than I am." She sat back and looked expectantly at her partner.

The professor appeared hesitant about starting his explanation. So Philip said to him, "I have persuaded César Renoir – she is the woman who had Alain Hébert's bag – to let me have it to give to you. The only thing she wanted to retain was his personal diary. She let me look through it so that I could see for myself that there was nothing important in it. It seemed to me that there was only one entry which was of any interest to us, and that didn't refer to you."

"What was that?"

"It was a note, four days before your cousin's death, that he had met a lawyer in Carcassonne and given him a letter. It was to be made public if anything happened to him." Philip took a breath. "It interested me because the lawyer was named as Amboisard, who I first thought might have been a person we knew. He is the mayor of Quillan. However we now know that the man in question was his nephew, otherwise calling himself *le comte*, who was the leader of a criminal gang known as *La Force Marseillaise*. Of course, because of that, the letter was never made public."

"Ah," said Ramise. "That explains why it was several days before I was alerted to the death of my cousin."

"César found the diary in a secret compartment in the bottom of the bag. The only other stuff in there was a sheaf of papers. They are photocopies of some sort of list that is written in Latin. I have shown them to Jackie, and she has started to translate them. She thinks they may be a schedule of precious objects."

The professor smiled bleakly. "It was that list which I wanted. Unfortunately, it is no longer of any importance."

"Why not?" demanded Jackie.

He shook his head. "I cannot tell you that."

"Now look, Hector," she responded. "A couple of days ago, you said it was vitally important that you recovered this bag. In fact, you tried to tell us we would be putting ourselves in danger if we so much as looked at the contents."

"I admit I may have been exaggerating a little."

"Exaggerating!" She shook her head. "And then, yesterday afternoon, you were prepared to drive all the way back to Béziers to fetch your copy of Alain Hébert's will to prove you were entitled to be given the bag. Furthermore, you insisted that Philip went to see the possessor of the bag to persuade her to part with it. And now you tell us it's no longer important." She paused for breath. "I think you owe us an explanation."

Charlotte leaned forward and laid a hand on the professor's arm. "Jackie's right, Hector. You must tell them what you told me yesterday evening."

Ramise looked down at the floor, his expression a mixture of hesitation and embarrassment. At last, he made up his mind. "Very well. The bag and most of its contents were unimportant to me. The only thing that mattered was the list you have referred to."

"And why was that so important?"

"I thought it could be worth a lot of money to me. I have the original list, hand-written on vellum, which I discovered by chance when I was researching the history of the Habsbourg Royal family. Although the list had nothing to do with them, it had somehow got caught up with various documents in the Habsbourg archives. I think at one time those might have been held at their place in Rennes-le-Chateau which is only a few kilometres from here."

335

Philip opened his mouth to respond, but Jackie raised a hand to silence him.

"Yes," she said, "we have been to Rennes. But why do you think the Habsbourg archives would have been lodged in a little village in the Languedoc, so far from Austria?"

"I know that one of the daughters of the Habsbourgs married into the Hautpoul de Blanchefort family in the eighteenth century. The family seat at that time was at Rennes-le-Chateau."

"But why would she have taken the archives with her when she was married?"

Ramise shook his head. "That I don't know. I can only assume that they contained some kind of documents which it was vital to prevent from becoming public in Hungary. Maybe they thought the information would be safer if it was moved to France. Remember that Budapest was the capital of the Holy Roman Empire at the time."

"So what is this information?"

"I don't know that, and I didn't come across anything scandalous when I went through the archives. All I can tell you is that important documents were hidden away in Rennes-le-Chateau at the time of the French Revolution and were later discovered and returned to Budapest. Although I have no proof of this, I presume it was the village priest, Berenger Saunière, who found them in the 1880's. That was possibly the reason why he became so wealthy, from payments made to him by the Habsbourgs to keep his discoveries confidential."

"My goodness!" Jackie sat down with a bump. "What an extraordinary story." She turned to Philip. "I think I need a drink, darling."

"How about coffee and brandy?"

"That sounds a good idea."

In fact, they all decided they liked the thought of an early evening pick-up, so Philip went to the Reception desk and placed their order. When he came back, he found that Jackie had continued to question the Professor.

"So what is this list about, Hector, if it has nothing to do with the Habsbourgs?"

Philip knew she already had her own ideas about it.

"I think the list has something to do with the Cathars," Ramise replied. "I believe it may be a list of the treasures they put in the hands of the Templars when they were close to surrendering. Remember the Blancheforts were prominent members of both groups."

"Is there any evidence to support that theory?"

"I believe so. The language and style are much older than the way Latin was written in the eighteenth century. I haven't had the opportunity yet of researching the list in depth, but I believe many of the items listed carry indications of French origin – not Austrian."

"That sounds a bit speculative."

Jackie's questioning of his authority led Ramise to burst out with, "And furthermore, I have received clinching proof of that in the last twenty-four hours."

"Which is?" she asked coolly.

"The organisation with which I was hoping to negotiate a price have confirmed my theory is correct."

The discussion was brought to a halt by the arrival of the coffee and brandy and there was a pause while it was poured out and handed round. When the girl departed, Philip was the first to take up the questioning again.

"What I don't understand is why you needed the copy in Alain Hébert's bag when you already had the original."

Jackie turned a pitying gaze on him. "Don't you see, darling. He was offering the list to them so that they could suppress it. Presumably there is information in it which this organisation doesn't want to become public. In order to do that he had to give them the copies he had taken as well as the original."

"So why has this copy now become unimportant?"

"Because," said Ramise, "my clients have decided there is now no prospect of preventing the information becoming generally known in the academic world."

"Why is that?"

"The reason is that somebody else has discovered the location of the Templar archives from which this list became detached." He raised his head and looked accusingly from one to the other of them. "I'm told it is *you two* who have scuppered my chances of making a fortune. *You* discovered the archives in the basement of the chateau in Rennes and the Order has realised that it cannot prevent somebody as famous as my former pupil, Jacqueline Blontard, from making the discovery public." He paused briefly. "So they have decided they no longer have any reason to buy the list from me."

Philip and Jackie looked at each other in astonishment.

"How did they know we had found the archives?" she asked. "I have told nobody about our discovery."

"And I certainly haven't," Philip hastened to assure her. "And it can't be Jean-Luc, because he only climbed the ladder to below the window when I rescued you."

"And nobody else had any reason to look round the place. Everybody thought it was a ruin."

The Professor shook his head. "I don't know how they found out, but they did. As a consequence, I am left with a worthless set of papers."

"I think you're being unnecessarily depressed about it," said Jackie. "Presumably the whole story will come out in the next couple of years about what is in those archives. There will be a lot of publicity. The possessor of the original list, inscribed on vellum, as you say, will be able to realise a very good price for it if it is put up for auction."

Ramise visibly brightened when he heard this, but it was Charlotte who spoke next.

"Personally I am very pleased it turned out like this," she said, "because Hector has now decided to give up his professorship at the Sorbonne and retire back to Béziers." Her eyes sparkled. "Who knows what may happen as a result?"

It was a relaxed Hector and Charlotte who decided to stay the night at the Castle Hotel and share a cheerful dinner with Philip and Jackie.

# 63

At dinner that evening, Charlotte leaned forward and rested her hand on the professor's arm. "There is one further thing you have to tell Philip, Hector."

"What is that?"

"You know very well what it is." She shook her head gently. "You must tell him what happened at the warehouse so that the air will be completely cleared between you. Then he will know everything."

There was a long pause before Ramise attempted a shrug. "Very well." He turned to face Philip. "I owe you an apology, young man."

"Me?"

"Yes. You see, I *was* at the warehouse in Carcassonne on the night when you were struck on the head. I didn't do it, but I *was* there, and I didn't try to stop it."

"I don't understand."

"I will explain. After I heard about my cousin's death, I went to Carcassonne to try to find out exactly what had happened to him and, I might as well admit it, what had also happened to the treasure." He paused. "I knew from previous experience that the best source of information in a situation like this would come from the criminal underworld. So I visited a number of back street bars and let it be known that I would pay for any verifiable evidence about what had happened at le Bézu."

"Mon Dieu!" exclaimed Jackie. "I didn't know you went in for that sort of thing, Hector."

"I'm sure you didn't." He smiled weakly. "Well, the fact was that my visits to the bars had an almost immediate result. That evening I was approached at my hotel by a man who identified himself as Gaston Lesmoines." He nodded at Jackie. "He told me he had worked for you at le Bézu but that you had given him the sack. He didn't know why. He said he needed money to go back to his home in Toulouse."

"The liar," she burst out. "He knew just why I hadn't got a job for him any longer, and he also had plenty of money. All the workers received a generous pay-off."

Ramise shrugged. "I must admit I didn't ask too many questions about that. Nor did I let on to him that I knew you. I just wanted to know what had happened up there." He took a breath. "Anyway, Lesmoines admitted that he didn't know very much about the killing of my cousin. He seemed to think it had been an accident and that Alain had got in the way of a stray bullet."

"That's rubbish, for a start," said Philip.

"Perhaps it is. Perhaps that is the news which had spread through the criminal fraternity." He raised a finger. "But the more important thing for me was this. He said he had been told that the treasure had been moved to a warehouse in Carcassonne for a couple of nights before it was to be sent to a secure place in Paris. He offered to take me to the warehouse and get me into the place. In return for that information, he wanted to be paid ten thousand euros."

"Ten thousand?"

He nodded, a guilty grin on his face. "I knew it was ridiculously cheap. If I found the treasure and only took a few small items, they would be worth many times that. I reasoned that nobody was likely to miss them, because I doubted if anybody had had the chance, in the short time since it had been discovered, to prepare an inventory of the stuff." He gulped. "So – I don't know what came over me – but I agreed. I suppose I thought it was my chance to retire as a wealthy man."

There was a long silence while Philip wondered what to say. Here was this proud professor, from the most prestigious university in France, admitting to flirting with the idea of stealing national treasures. He wondered whether it was this flaw in Ramise's character which had led to his falling out with Jackie's uncle.

But the man was continuing. "So, late that evening, we drove to a place near the warehouse in my car and parked it out of sight. As we made our way to the building, I noticed there was absolutely nobody around except for a little sports car parked across the road which appeared to be empty.

Philip interjected, "That was mine."

"Was it? I suppose that should have made me suspicious. However, we went round to the back of the warehouse and Lesmoines had no difficulty at all in opening the door with one of his skeleton keys." He paused for a second. "Of course, when we got inside, we found the place was empty. It was a warm night, and I was feeling stifled, so I took off my jacket and hung it behind the door in the small room. Then we went all round the place with our torches, searching to see if there was any evidence that the treasure had been there. Lesmoines was cursing his head off, but all I wanted to do was to get out of the place as soon as possible. Then, suddenly we heard the noise of somebody moving up on the roof and there came an awful screaming sort of noise which frightened me half to death."

"That was probably me drilling holes in the roof metal," admitted Philip.

"I think it worried Lesmoines too. He said we must get out before we were discovered. So we went back out through the door, which he locked behind us with his skeleton key. Then we started to make our way back to the car as quietly as we could. We were afraid there might be several men outside. We were nearly there when I realised I had left my coat behind. At first Lesmoines said we would have to forget it, but I pointed out to him that it had my wallet in the pocket and inside the wallet was the cheque for ten thousand euros made out to him, which I had written in front of him and promised to give him when we found the treasure. Of course, that made him see that it could be used as evidence that we had been there, so he agreed we must go back for it."

He took a breath and continued. "We returned to the warehouse, and he quietly eased open the steel door at the back. I stayed outside but I saw there was a light on inside. I could see that you were in the room and had just got hold of my jacket. Lesmoines reached round the frame and switched the light off. You must have heard a sound as he approached, because you turned round. Then he switched on his torch and shone it in your face. I hadn't realised until then, but he must have been carrying some sort of cosh in his pocket which he took out. I saw him hit you. It seemed to be very hard, and you immediately collapsed in a heap. Lesmoines just grabbed the jacket and came to the door. He was obviously intending to leave you there. But I was worried that you were seriously hurt, so we went back in and checked." He smiled weakly at Philip. "We turned you over and laid you on your back. Lesmoines said you were only stunned and would soon recover. It was then that he recognised you. 'This is the man who has seduced Jacqueline Blontard,' he told me. 'Leave him. He will be all right.'"

The professor shook his head. "So we left you to come round on your own. But when we got outside, he said to me, 'That man will not have come alone. I will find out who has come with him.' So I waited while he went round to the front of the warehouse. Nothing happened for a time, and I wondered how long I was going to have to wait. I didn't fancy hanging around any longer than necessary. Then I heard the sound of a car engine starting not far away. I went round to the front of the building, keeping well out of sight in the shadows. When I got there, I couldn't see anybody – no cars, no sign of Lesmoines, nothing. Then I saw another man coming along by the fence the other side of the warehouse. It wasn't Lesmoines. This man was much too big. Lesmoines was a small man. I didn't fancy meeting this fellow, so I decided it was time for me to get away. Very carefully, I made my way back to my car and drove back to the hotel. The next morning, I returned to Béziers after breakfast." He turned to Philip. "I have to say I am sorry you were knocked out. I hope you soon recovered."

The young man grinned. "There was no permanent damage. I think the one who suffered most was Jeanette, Armand's girl-friend. She was waiting in my car and Lesmoines took her to a remote village where he kept her imprisoned for a week until Jean-Luc and I turned up and helped her get away." He had a sudden thought. "In fact, my car is still there. I must find out from the police if I can go and get it back."

That comment led to the others asking him to tell them all about the events in Castereau a few days before, culminating in their dramatic escape from Lesmoines' gang.

"My goodness! What a night of stories," said Jackie, when he had finished.

Her aunt took a deep breath. "I hope, Philip, that we have now cleared the air. Hector has promised me faithfully that he will never get involved in such nefarious adventures again."

Before anyone could reply. the receptionist suddenly appeared at their table.

She spoke to Philip. "There is a telephone call for you, monsieur."

"Oh! That may be news about Jean-Luc's operation," he said to the others. "I won't be long."

He got up and followed the girl into reception and picked up the phone where she indicated it, lying on the counter. "Hello."

"Philip? This is Rafa. I have some information for you."

"Hello Rafa. You're working late."

"That is because I have found out some information which I think you will find very interesting."

"What? About the owners of the chateau?"

"That's right. I have found that it is actually owned by a rather boring property company called Northern Properties – that is an approximate translation."

"Oh. How do we get in touch with them?"

"Wait a minute, Philip. I decided to look further into the ownership of the company." He paused for dramatic effect. "What I have discovered is that Northern Properties are themselves owned by an organisation called – wait for it – they are called *Vendredi Treize*."

"*Vendredi Treize*?"

"That's right. Is your French good enough to translate it?"

"I think so. It means Friday the thirteenth."

"And what organisation was destroyed on Friday the thirteenth?"

The truth dawned on Philip. "Of course. That is the day when the French king seized the Templar wealth and imprisoned their leaders. But that happened hundreds of years ago."

"Approximately seven hundred. But this makes it seem likely that a secret organisation was set up soon after the demise of the official Knights Templar Order to control all the property and other assets which they were able to hide from the royal authorities. I have been searching records and contacting people I know, to find out what I can about this group." There was another dramatic pause at the other end of the line. "As far as I can make out, *Vendredi Treize* has become a fabulously rich and hugely influential organisation – not only in France, but throughout the whole of Europe. They have somehow been able to do this while still remaining virtually unknown to the media and the general public." He paused again. "I think you are up against an organisation you cannot beat, my friend."

"Why is that?"

"Because they are so powerful. They have their fingers in every pie, as you English say. Many of the top people in the French nation are members of the Order. Who knows - maybe even the President. And my informants tell me they have their tentacles in the upper echelons of every country in Western Europe." He paused again. "I think you will not be able to get much from *Vendredi Treize*."

Philip took a deep breath. "Blimey. I'll have to tell Jackie and see what her response is to that. Presumably you can tell us how to get in touch with them – if we dare."

"But of course. Do you have a pen and paper?"

"Just a minute."

Philip pulled a pen out of his pocket and waved at the receptionist. She handed him a piece of paper when he indicated he wanted to write something down. Carefully, Raphael spelled out an address and phone number and added a contact name. When he had finished, Philip thanked him.

"I am sorry to be the bearer of such bad news," said the young Frenchman. "But I think we have reached the end of the line, my friend."

"That may be so," agreed Philip, "but thank you very much for what you've done, Rafa. I'm sure we'll be in touch again soon."

"I hope so, but I think there is nothing more I can do for you on this one. Goodbye."

The phone went dead.

# 64

After breakfast next morning, Hector and Charlotte left to return to Béziers. The other two settled down to have a coffee in reception.

"I've been thinking about what Hector told us last night and there's one thing I don't understand," said Philip.

Jackie rested her warm hand on his. "What is that, my darling?"

"If Lesmoines thought the treasure had been moved to Paris, why did he take *le comte* back to the treasure room at le Bézu?"

"Goodness knows." She thought about it for a moment. "We can only presume that, wherever he got the information from that the treasure had been taken to Paris, he suspected he'd been told a load of lies to persuade him to give up his hunt for it."

Philip shook his head. "I suppose so. Of course, we'll never know now."

Further discussion was brought to an end when they saw a big, dark blue Citroen pull up outside. Inspector Martin was driving, and Armand was sitting beside him. In the back was Candice, now once again with long, silver-blonde hair and dressed to kill.

"Oh, *Mon Dieu*! More questions," complained Jackie.

Philip went out to greet them. "I thought you didn't dare to come to Quillan," he joked to Armand.

"Now that Monsieur Amboisard has gone, he is safe," interpreted Candice.

"So what are you two doing here with the police?"

"There are a lot of things we need to tell you," she said. "But first you must talk to the inspector."

Coffees were ordered all round and the next hour was spent giving Martin a more detailed picture of what had happened two nights earlier up at le Bézu. Philip had been worried about the fact that it was his action, in pushing over the chest on top of Lesmoines which had led directly to the deaths of the two criminals and the serious injuries to Jean-Luc. However, the policeman seemed unworried about it.

"I will give my report to the examining magistrate in a few days and I'm sure he will agree that your actions were reasonable in the circumstances," he said. "After all, the only innocent person who suffered was the man Lerenard and he seems to be recovering satisfactorily."

"Do you have news of him?"

"I called in to the hospital on the way here, and they told me the operation to re-inflate his lung had been satisfactory and he is now resting in recovery. He should be fully fit again in about two weeks."

"Oh, thank God. I have been worried about him."

"Do not worry. How do you English say it – all is well that ends well."

"I hope you are right."

Once again Philip was grateful for the more practical way in which the French seem to investigate a crime.

Jackie asked, "So who is the new examining magistrate?"

It was Candice who answered her. "He should be here very soon." Looking out of the window, she said, "In fact, I think this is him arriving now."

A sleek, silver Mercedes limousine was just pulling up behind the police car in front of the hotel. A uniformed chauffeur got out from the driver's seat and opened the rear door to allow a short, rather anonymous-looking man to emerge. But Philip noticed that, despite his lack of stature, he seemed to have a presence and a self-confidence about him that made one notice him immediately.

The man paused for a moment, looking round the square and up at the hotel building. Then he shrugged his jacket up on his shoulders and made for the entrance to the hotel. As he came up the steps and pushed open the front door, Armand got to his feet. He crossed to meet the man and said something to him in French. They shook hands and the new arrival patted the young Frenchman on the shoulder in a paternal way.

Candice had also risen. "This is our boss," she told them. "This is Monsieur Marcus Heilberg. He is a well-known lawyer in Paris, and he has been appointed as the new examining

346

magistrate, looking into the events over the last few weeks in and around le Bézu castle."

Looking round, Philip noted that everyone had risen to meet the important newcomer, including himself.

"This is Mademoiselle Jacqueline Blontard, our most famous lady archaeologist," introduced Candice.

"I know of you, of course, from your television series." Heilberg's voice was deep and a little hoarse. Philip noticed that he had chosen to speak in excellent English.

The lawyer advanced across the room, took her hand in his, and shook it warmly. Meanwhile Candice continued the introductions, but the lawyer took little note of the others, merely giving nods to each one.

He turned back to Jackie. "You will not have heard of me before," he said, "but I am also Grand Treasurer of an Order called *Vendredi Treize*, and it is mainly in that role that I have come to speak to you."

Slightly nettled, Philip intervened. "So you're the chap we have to negotiate with about the purchase of the chateau in Rennes-le-Château." The repetition of the word "chateau" made him feel slightly awkward.

The Grand Treasurer seemed to become aware of him for the first time. He let go of Jackie's hand and offered to shake Philip's. The proffered hand was hard and cold, and Philip released it quickly.

"That is so. I am authorised by my Council to reach an agreement with you." He turned back to Jackie. "The Council is also aware that your primary motivation in seeking the ownership of the chateau is to look at the Western Archive of the Order of the Knights Templar which you discovered there."

Her mouth dropped open. "How do you know about that?"

The Grand Treasurer turned to Armand with a smile. In French he said, "You had better confess now, my boy."

"Er -." The young Frenchman turned a bit pink but he started to explain, the girl interpreting for him. "Well, Candice and I have been following you ever since you returned from Rome. We, er –." He nodded to Heilberg. "We have a good relationship with the Holy See, so it was not difficult for me to find a place to watch you, without being seen by you." He took a breath. "I was waiting near the church in Rennes-le-Chateau

347

when you and Philip turned up in the car of the Abbé Rivère. The only thing I was not ready for was to see Gaston Lesmoines appear just after you had arrived. As a result, I had to stay in hiding while you went into the church. I saw the priest come out again after opening the church for you. Later I saw Lesmoines go to Rivère's car. Soon after that the little priest drove away. Later, after Lesmoines had gone into the church and come out again and I was certain he had gone, I tried to follow the route you had taken."

He smiled. "Unfortunately I was unable to get a key to the sacristy until the village priest went to open up at nine o'clock. You did not know that I could have let you out of the crypt by the route you had taken to get in there, but you had already found another way out. This man," he indicated Philip to the others, "doesn't let anything defeat him."

He turned back. "So I carefully followed the route you had taken. I got to the chateau, only to find that you had already rescued Jackie through a window. After that I took a look round and that was when I discovered the chests of papers. Of course, I did not know they were important at the time."

"We had known of the existence of the Western Archive," said Heilberg, "but we had no idea where it was hidden. You must realise that we have hundreds of similar properties spread around France and the rest of Europe. Many of them are in a ruinous condition like le Bézu. We cannot search or excavate them all or, indeed, any more than a few of them."

Philip shook his head at the massive size of this organisation. "So what is your reaction to our request to purchase the place now that you know about the archives?" he asked.

"Ah, yes." The Grand Treasurer ruminated for a while. "I must tell you that the full Council of the Preceptories met yesterday in Paris and discussed what our response should be to your request. Should we, for example, remove the contents before we sold it to you? Would that be dangerous if Mademoiselle Blontard discovered they had been removed and decided to make a fuss about it? We had a number of important things to consider." He paused momentously. "In the end the Council decided, almost unanimously, to leave the final decision to the President of the Order."

"Almost unanimously?" questioned Jackie.

"Yes. The President himself was not able to be present due to his illness, so his opinion could not be given. You must realise that he was a very old man – now well into his nineties. He had been bedridden for several weeks and was not expected to live much longer."

"So were you able to get his decision?"

Heilberg nodded slowly. "Armed with the Council's resolution, I and two other senior members went to see the President at his home. Although he was physically very weak, his brain was still functioning well, and we were all confident that he understood our decision and accepted the responsibility the decision placed upon him. However, he knew he was by now very close to death. In fact he drew his last breath while we were with him and his doctor, who was by his side during our visit, pronounced to us that he was dead."

"Oh no!" exclaimed Philip. "What on earth happens now?"

"Ah! Do not fear. He was able to give us his decision before he died."

"And what was his decision?" asked Jackie anxiously.

"Well, it is not quite as simple as that." The Grand Treasurer gave a brief smile. "Because he was close to death, he told us that it was right that the new President who replaces him should be the one to make the decision."

"Oh, *Mon Dieu!*" she complained. "So now we have to wait for your Council to elect a new President."

"That is true, but he gave it as his dying wish that his nomination for the new President should be accepted by the Council. Although it is an unusual selection, I have no doubt that they will do so."

"OK," said Philip. "Do we know who this new President is going to be?"

"Indeed you do."

"Then for God's sake tell us who it is."

"Of course I will," said Heilberg. "But, before I do that, I should reveal to you that our recently-deceased President was the Chevalier Héremond Fragonard who I believe, Mademoiselle, was your maternal grandfather. Is that correct?"

"Oh, Grand-Papa!" She sat down heavily and burst into tears.

"May I be the first to offer you my sincerest condolences, Mademoiselle. Your grand-father was a great person."

"I knew he was an old man," she sobbed, as Philip tried to comfort her. "But nobody told me he was ill." She shook her head. "I've been so busy recently that I've seen very little of him – just a couple of brief visits in the last six months. Oh, I feel dreadful. I think I am his nearest living relative, and I should have been there with him when he died."

"Please do not distress yourself, Mademoiselle. He was strong and fit for his age until the last few weeks. He would not let anybody but me know of his sudden deterioration. I believe that he had simply decided that he had had enough of this world and was ready to go to meet his maker."

There was silence, punctuated only by Jackie's sobs, before he continued. "I must also tell you, that he had carefully watched your own spectacular career, as you rose to the top of your profession and became a much-loved icon of the French nation. He was very proud of you, and of the name to which you brought so much honour."

"Thank you for telling me that," Jackie sniffed. "I only wish I could have had the chance to say goodbye to him."

"Unfortunately, that could not be. But he *was* able to leave you a final message which he vouchsafed to me in the presence of the other people in the room." The Grand Treasurer paused. "So I have to tell you that it was his dying wish that it should be you who should take over the presidency of the *Vendredi Treize Order* and lead it into the twenty-first century."

A stunned silence greeted his announcement.

"Bloody hell!" Philip was the first to recover. "What will your Grand Council say about that?"

"I am confident they will comply with the President's dying wish."

"I don't know about that," said Philip. "But I warn you that, if I am any judge of Mademoiselle Blontard, she will not allow *Vendredi Treize* to skulk any longer in the shadows. She will insist that everything is brought out into the open. She will want your records and accounts to be published. Your archives will have to be researched and the results reported to the nation. Your treasures will need to be put on show to the public. Your properties will have to be registered in your own name. Will the Council be willing to have all this dirty washing hung out for public inspection?"

The Grand Treasurer shuddered, but he faced the young Englishman resolutely. "I think they will have to. The Order must face the transition to becoming a part of modern public life. Perhaps it should register as a charity so that all may benefit from its wealth and the richness of its history." He turned to Jackie, now with her self-control re-established as she dabbed her eyes with Philip's handkerchief. "Are you ready to give me your decision, mademoiselle?"

She took a deep breath and stood up. "What do you think, darling?"

"I think you should accept," said Philip. "I can't think of anybody better-qualified to modernise this part of French society and drag it out of its dark secrecy into the open, modern world."

"You realise it would involve us going to Paris from time to time. Presumably Marcus would oversee most of the day-to-day affairs of the Order, but I wouldn't be prepared to be a mere figurehead, just presiding over meetings and being their mouth-piece."

"I'm sure you wouldn't. Visits to Paris wouldn't be a problem for me. I would like to explore the city and sample all it has to offer."

She gave Philip a sharp look, but didn't respond. Instead, she turned back to the Grand Treasurer. "I am prepared to accept the position subject to the Council agreeing to eschew its secrecy and open up its activities to the view of the world. I therefore wish you to arrange a general meeting of the Council for me to give my views to them. If they vote to accept me on that basis, then I will take on the Presidency."

"That can be done very quickly, Mademoiselle. Just give me today and tomorrow to set up the office of the examining magistrate down here and I will return to Paris to call the meeting of the full Council. I can probably arrange it for Saturday morning, if that would suit you. It is a good day to get the members away from their other duties."

"That would be suitable for me," she said. "Meanwhile, I wish to make my first executive decision."

Heilberg blinked. "What is that, Mademoiselle?"

"My first priority is to complete the television series about the Albigensian Crusade, which I am contracted to finish this summer. To do that I need to have the site at le Bézu set up again for the cameras. Jean-Luc Lerenard was going to do it for me, but he will be in hospital for at least the next two weeks. I need a man to manage the works for me and I have decided to appoint an employee of the Order to do the job." She pointed at Armand. "I wish to transfer Monsieur Séjour to the payroll of TV France until filming on site has been completed and the site restored to the condition it was in before excavations began."

Candice translated this for Armand and gave his response. "He asks if you are sure he is suitably qualified for the job?"

"Tell him not to fear. I will be watching him and telling him what to do. Tell him I was very impressed with his work when he was excavating the part of the site above the treasure room." She grinned. "And I will allocate Philip to assist him in this new role. It will be an opportunity for them both to learn more of each other's language."

"Thank you very much." Philip wasn't sure whether to be pleased or sorry about her decision to organise his life for him. He was certain of one thing – sharing the future with Jacqueline Blontard was going to be interesting.

The meeting broke up after that. Marcus Heilberg and Inspector Martin went to the town hall to formally set up the investigation. Armand and Candice were booked into rooms in the hotel.

In a quiet moment, Philip took Armand aside and asked him in his rather pigeon French, "I have a question for you, Armand. Was it just chance that led Jeanette to find me in that pavement cafe in Paris a couple of weeks ago?"

The Frenchman looked into his eyes and gripped his elbow. "My friend, you left a trail a kilometre wide behind you in your search for your fiancée. We needed to take care of you for the sake of everybody's protection."

Philip nodded. "Thank you. I have been wondering about that."

THE END

If you enjoyed this book you might like to know this is the second book in **The Languedoc Trilogy** and the activities of these characters are continued in **The Treasure of the Visigoths**.

**A message from the author**

I hope you enjoyed this book. If you did, you can help me by giving it a review. Reviews are my most powerful marketing device in getting my books noticed. I am unknown to the great majority of readers. I can´t afford to pay for advertisements. But I have something more powerful, and that is a loyal group of readers.

Honest reviews of my books will help to bring them to the attention of other readers. So I would be grateful if you would spend five minutes giving **The Legacy of the Templars** a review.

Thank you very much – Michael Hillier.

This is the fifth in the **Adventure, Mystery, Romance Series** of novels created by **Michael Hillier.** The others are:-

**The Eighth Child (AMR No 1)** – Alan Brading witnesses the shooting of his French-born wife in a London street. The police seem to think it is a mistaken terrorist attack. When he recovers from the mental problems caused by the shock, he travels to her home-town in the Loire Valley to try to find the murderer, whom he has seen there. However the local people in Chalons are hostile to his enquiries. Only his wife´s younger sister, Jeanette, is willing to help him uncover what happened forty years ago. Together they risk their lives in their pursuit of the truth.

**The Mafia Emblem – The Wolf of Hades (AMR No 2)** – When Ben Cartwright discovers the decapitated body of his Italian business partner, he finds out that he is in danger of losing his carefully built-up wine importing business. He flies to Naples to try to recover the company, but becomes caught up in the ancient vendetta between two of the oldest families in Southern Italy. His partner´s sister, Francesca, doesn´t like him. However she joins him in their fight for their lives in the erupting volcanic area of the *Campi Flegraei.*

**Dancing with Spies (AMR No 3)** – Caroline Daley is travelling down the Adriatic on a ferry which breaks down and has to limp into the port of Dubrovnik. However the Yugoslav Civil War is in progress and the beautiful city is under siege from the Serb-led JNA. She becomes caught up in the seething web of violence and espionage among the ancient buildings. Her only hope of escape seems to be to put her trust the arrogant journalist, Ralph Henderson. And are they all in danger? Surely the JNA won´t open fire on the World Heritage Site, will they?

**The Secret of the Cathars (AMR No 4)** – Philip Sinclair is bequeathed the unusual legacy of the journal of a long-dead Cathar *parfait* by his grandmother, together with the request to go to the chateau of Le Bézu in the French Pyrenees to search for the mysterious treasure of the Cathars. There he meets famous French archaeologist Jacqueline Blontard who is carrying out research for her next TV series. Together they start looking, unaware that they are being followed by representatives from the Catholic Church, a mysterious powerful body in Paris and a group of criminals from Marseilles. Nothing can prepare them for what their search will unearth.

**The Discovery of Franco´s Bankroll (AMR No 6)** – Middle-aged former playboy Sebastian Bishop finds himself marooned on the Costa Blanca without any means of earning a living. His solution is to offer his services as an escort to rich single ladies. Of course he doesn´t realise this is going to lead him into deep, deep trouble. After spending the night with a Spanish Contessa, he discovers her strangled body in the morning. He is sure to be charged with her murder. His desperate attempts to prove his innocence involve him with several groups of people trying to find the Nazi stolen hoard shipped to Spain in the last days of the war and threaten his life.

**Bank-cor-Rupt (AMR No 7)** - Andrew Denbury is summoned to his bank one morning and told they are calling in the overdraft on which his business runs, and they will appoint a receiver. What can he do? His wealthy father-in-law hates him and won´t help. His wife is only interested in leading an enjoyable social life with her upper-class friends. His suppliers are furious because the bank has bounced their cheques. The only person who believes in him is his secretary, Samantha. Somehow Andrew must try to find a way to confound the destroyers of his business. He conceives a plan which may save him, with Samantha´s help. But will it work when he puts it into practice?

**Network Virus (AMR No 8)** - Charlotte Faraday is searching for a twelve-year-old girl who has gone missing. Is she the victim of a paedophile gang led by a rich, dissolute local gentleman? To complicate matters, the girl's mother has been raped a few nights earlier in the car park behind the Red Garter Nightclub by a soldier who has escaped back to his regiment which is currently training in Germany. Meanwhile Stafford Paulson, is convinced that the death of Joanne de Billiere is suspicious. They are not helped in their enquiries by creeping corruption in the Devon and Cornwall police force.

**The Treasure of the Visigoths (AMR No 9)** – The third novel in the **Languedoc Trilogy** follows Philip when he inadvertently finds himself on the trail of the treasure of the Temple in Jerusalem, which was captured by the Visigoths when they sacked Rome in the fifth century. It is complicated by Jackie´s concentration on launching her television series about the Cathars and by the other two women who are anxious for their own reasons to replace her.

**The Tangled Web (AMR No 10)** – How does it come about that Martin Ferris suddenly find himself on a remote Cornish island, cut off by the tide and with no means of getting back to the mainland? Somebody wants to blame him for passing military secrets to the Russians. Who is it and how have they managed to arrange his life for him? And where has the beautiful Tina come from? – (to be published in 2022.)


**Other novels** by **Michael Hillier:-**

**The Property People**

**The Gigabyte Detective**


Go to his website (http://mikehillier.com) for further details on all his writing.

**About the author**

**Michael Hillier** gets the inspiration for many of his books from family holidays to various beautiful locations in the world. Exploring historic towns and buildings has brought to light a host of untold stories which get his creative juices flowing.

He has completed twelve novels to date and there are several others which are partly written. Eight of the novels have been published and are for sale on various sites, including Amazon, Apple, Barnes and Noble (Nook), and Kobo. The most popular novel to date is **The Secret of the Cathars** which has sold substantially more than ten thousand copies.

He has split his novels into three groups – detective novels, a three-volume historical saga, and the **Adventure/Mystery/ Romance** series which has been explained on his website mikehillier.com.

Printed in Great Britain
by Amazon

12618373R00205